THE HIGHFIELD MOLE

BOOK ONE

THE HIGHFIELD MOLE

BOOK ONE
THE CIRCLE IN THE SPIRAL

by
RODERICK GORDON and BRIAN WILLIAMS

With illustrations by
BRIAN WILLIAMS

MATHEW & SON

First published in 2005
by Mathew & Son Limited
www.mathewandson.com
Email: info@mathewandson.com

A catalogue record for this book is available from
the British Library

ISBN 0-9548399-0-0

Edited by Andrew Swanston
Design by Ned Hoste/2H
Printed by WS Bookwell

IN MEMORIAM

Elizabeth Oke Gordon
1837 –1919

"Everything unknown
is doubted."

Anon.

PART ONE
BREAKING GROUND

CHAPTER ONE

SCHLAAK! The pickaxe hit the wall of earth and, sparking on an unseen shard of flint, sank deep into the clay, coming to a sudden halt with a dull thud.

"This could be it, Will!"

Dr Burrows crawled forwards in the cramped tunnel. Sweating and breathing heavily in the confined space, he began feverishly clawing at the dirt, his breath clouding in the damp air. Each greedy handful revealed more of the old wooden planking beneath, exposing its tar-coated grain and splintery surface, which was thrown into stark relief by the combined glare of their helmet lamps.

"Pass me the crowbar."

Will rummaged in a satchel, found the stubby blue crowbar and handed it to his father, whose gaze was fixed on the wall of wood before him. Forcing the flat edge of the tool into a tiny gap between two of the planks, Dr Burrows grunted as he put all his weight behind it to gain some purchase. He then began levering from side to side. The planks creaked and moaned against their rusted fixings until, finally, they bellied out, breaking free with a resounding crack. Will recoiled slightly as a clammy breeze bled from the ominous gap Dr Burrows had created.

Urgently, they pulled two more of the planks out of place, leaving a shoulder-width hole, and paused for a moment in silence. Father and son turned and looked at each other, sharing a brief conspiratorial smile. Their faces, illuminated in each other's light beams, were smeared with a war paint of dirt. They turned back to the hole and stared in wonder at the dust motes floating like tiny diamonds, forming and reforming unknown constellations against the nightblack opening.

Dr Burrows warily leant into the hole, Will squeezing in beside him to look over his shoulder. Their helmet lamps cut into the abyss and, to their left, they illuminated a curved, tiled wall. Their beams, sinking deeper, swept over old posters whose edges were peeling away from the wall and waving slowly, like tendrils of seaweed caught in the drift of powerful currents at the bottom of the ocean. Will raised his head a degree, scanning even further along until he caught the edge of an enamelled sign. Dr Burrows followed his son's gaze until both of their lamps fixed on the name.

"*Highfield & Crossly North*! This is it, Will, this is it! We found it!" Dr Burrows' excited voice echoed about the dank confines of the disused train station. They felt a slight breeze on the backs of their necks and something blew along the platform and down onto the rails, as if sent into an animated panic by this rude intrusion, after so many years, into its sealed and forgotten catacomb.

Will kicked wildly at the timbers around the opening, throwing up a spray of rotten shards, until, suddenly, the ground below him slid away and spilled into the cavern. He scrambled through the opening, grabbing his spade as he went. His father was immediately behind him as they crunched a few paces on the firm surface of the platform, their footsteps echoing and their helmet lamps cutting swathes into the surrounding gloom.

Cobwebs hung in skeins from the roof, and Dr Burrows blew as one draped itself across his face. As he looked around, his light caught his son, a strange sight with a shock of white hair sticking out like bleached straw from under his battle-scarred miner's helmet, his alarmingly pale blue eyes flashing with enthusiasm as he blinked into the dark. It was difficult to describe Will's clothes, other than that they appeared to be of the same red-brown hue and texture as the clay he had been working in. Such was the pasting, it covered him right up to his neck, making him appear like an artist's sculpture that had been miraculously infused with life.

As for Dr Burrows himself, he was a wiry man of average height – one wouldn't have described him as tall or, for that matter, short, just somewhere in the middle. He had a round face with piercing brown eyes that appeared all the more intense due to his gold-rimmed pebble glasses.

"Look up there, Will, look at that!" he said, as his light picked out a sign above the gap through which they had just emerged, that read "Way Out" in large black letters. Then they turned on their handheld torches, whose beams combined with those of their weaker helmet lamps, ricocheting through the darkness to reveal the full extent of the platform. Roots hung from the roof and the walls were caked with efflorescence and streaked with chalky limescale where fissures had seeped moisture. They could hear the sound of running water somewhere in the distance.

"How's this for a find, Will?" Dr Burrows said with a self-congratulatory air. "Just think, nobody has set foot down here since the new Highfield line was built in 1895." They had emerged onto the platform at one end, and Dr Burrows now shone his torch into the opening of the train tunnel to their side. It was blocked by a collapse of rubble and earth. "It'll be just the same down the other end – they would've sealed both ends," he said.

As they picked their way along the platform, gazing at the walls, it was just possible to make out blocks of crazily cracked cream tiles with dark green edging. Gas lamps sprouted every 10 feet or so – a number still had glass shades on them.

"Dad, Dad, over here!" Will called, "Have you seen these posters? You can still read them. I think they're adverts for land or something? Here's a good one … *Wilkinson's Circus … to be held on the Common … 10th day of February 1895*. There's a picture," he said breathlessly as his father joined him. The poster had been spared any water damage, and they could make out the crude colours of the red big top, with a blue man in a top hat standing in front of it. "And look at this one," Will said. "*Too Fat – Doctor Gordon's Elegant Pills!*" The heavy line drawing showed an old, bespectacled man with a beard proffering up a container.

They walked further along, stepping around a mountain of rubble that spilled onto the platform from an opening. "That would've led through to the other platform," Dr Burrows said.

They paused to look at an ornate cast iron bench. "This'll go nicely in the garden. All it needs is a rub-down and a few coats of gloss," Dr Burrows was muttering as Will's torch beam alighted on a dark wooden door hidden in the shadows.

"Dad, wasn't there an office or something on the plan?" Will asked, staring at the door.

"An office? Yes, I think you're right," his father said, fumbling through his pockets and then finding the piece of paper he was looking for. Will didn't wait to hear his father's pronouncement, but pushed on the door, which refused to move. Dr Burrows stuffed the paper away and together they tried to shoulder it open. The door was badly warped in the frame, but on the third attempt it groaned loudly at the disturbance and swung open, a fine shower of silt falling on their heads. Coughing, and rubbing the dust from their eyes, they went into the room, pushing through a shroud of cobwebs.

"Wow!" Will exclaimed quietly. There, in the middle of the small room, they could make out a desk and a chair, furred with dust. Will moved cautiously behind the chair and, with his gloved hand, brushed away the layer of cobwebs on the wall to reveal a large, faded map of the railway system.

"Could've been the stationmaster's office," Dr Burrows said as he swept dust off the top of the desk with his arm to reveal a blotter upon which rested a grimy teacup and saucer. Next to them, a small object haemorrhaged green onto the surface of the desk. "How fascinating! A railway telegraph, exquisitely made; brass, I would say."

Two of the walls were lined with shelves, stacked with decaying cardboard boxes. Will pulled one of them down and, as it threatened to fall apart in his hands, carried it quickly over to the desk. He lifted off the misshapen lid and looked in wonder at the bundles of old tickets. He picked one of these out, but the perished rubber band crumbled, shooting a confetti of tickets over the desktop.

"They're blanks – they were never printed up. They'll just have the station name on them," Dr Burrows said as he knelt down and tugged at a heavy object on a lower shelf, wrapped in a rotten cloth that dissolved at his touch. "and here ..." Will turned to look at the machine, which resembled an old typewriter with a large pull handle on its side, "... is an example of an early ticket-printing machine. Bit corroded but we can probably get the worst off."

"What, for the museum?"

"No, for *my* collection," Dr Burrows replied. He hesitated and his face took on a serious expression. "Look, Will, we're not going to breathe a word about this, any of this, to anyone. Understand?"

They stood in the office, each lighting the other's face with his miner's light as dust eddies swirled around their heads with every breath, like miniature tornadoes.

"Remember what happened the time with the Roman villa? That bigwig professor turned up, hijacked the dig and grabbed all the glory. I discovered that site, and what did I get? A tiny acknowledgment buried in his pedestrian paper."

"Yeah, I remember, Dad," Will said, recalling his father's fury at the time.

"Want that to happen again?"

"No, s'pose not."

"Well, I'm not going to be a footnote on this one. I'd rather no one knew about it. They're not going to nick this from me, not again. Agreed?"

"Agreed. Never again," Will said, nodding in assent and sending his light bouncing up and down the wall.

Dr Burrows glanced at his watch. "We really ought to be getting back, you know."

"Okay," Will replied grudgingly.

His father caught the tone. "There's no hurry, is there, Will? We can take our time to explore the rest tomorrow."

"All right," Will said half-heartedly, moving towards the door.

Dr Burrows patted his son affectionately on his hard hat as they were leaving the office

"Sterling work, Will, I must say. All those months of digging really paid off, didn't they?"

They retraced their steps to the opening and, after a last look at the platform, clambered back into the tunnel. Twenty or so feet in, the tunnel blossomed out so they could walk side by side. If Dr Burrows stooped slightly, it was just high enough for him to stand.

"We need to double up on the braces and props, Will," Dr Burrows pronounced, examining the expanse of timbers above their heads. "You're about one every seven feet rather than the one in four we decided."

"Sure. No problem, Dad."

"And we need to shift this lot out," Dr Burrows said, nudging a mound of clay on the tunnel floor with his boot. "Don't want to get too constricted down here, do we?"

"Nah," Will replied vaguely, not intending to do anything

about it. Although his father often used the word "we" when describing certain actions, he didn't himself offer to participate in any of the hard labour. He saw himself more as the mastermind of their so-called "joint projects", only making an appearance when the proceedings became interesting.

Dr Burrows whistled abstractly through his teeth as he bent to inspect a tower of neatly stacked buckets and a heap of planking. As they made their way along, the tunnel climbed, and he stopped every so often to test the wooden props on either side. He smacked them with the palm of his hand, his obscure whistling rising to an impossible squeak as he did so.

The passage levelled out and widened into a larger chamber where there was a trestle table and a pair of sorry-looking armchairs. They dumped some of their equipment on the table, then climbed the last stretch of tunnel to the entrance.

Just as the town clock finished striking seven, a length of corrugated iron sheeting lifted an inch in a corner of the Temperance Square car park. It was early autumn, and the sun was just tipping over the horizon as father and son, satisfied the coast was clear, pushed the sheeting back to reveal the large timber framed hole in the ground. They poked their heads out, pausing for a last check that there was nobody else in the car park. They needn't have worried, as the immediate area was predominantly industrial and all but deserted at weekends. Once the sheeting was back in place, Will kicked dirt over it to disguise the entrance.

A breeze rattled the hoardings around the car park as a discarded newspaper rolled along the ground like a tumbleweed, scattering its pages as it gained momentum. Some of these lifted into the air for short-lived flights, as if trying to escape, and others, doomed to remain on the ground, flapped in rain-filled puddles like beleaguered birds. As the dying sun silhouetted the warehouses and reflected off the burgundy-tiled façade of a nearby Peabody Estate tenement block, the two Burrows, ambling out of the car park, looked every part a pair of prospectors leaving their claim in the foothills to return to town.

CHAPTER TWO

On the other side of Highfield, Terry Watkins, "Tipper Tel" to his mates at work, was dressed in his pyjama bottoms and cleaning his teeth in front of his bathroom mirror. He was tired and hoping for a good night's sleep but his mind was still somersaulting because of what he'd seen that afternoon.

It had been an awfully long and arduous day. They were demolishing the ancient white leadworks to make way for a new office block for some government department or other. He wanted more than anything to go home, but he had promised his guv'nor that he would take out a few courses of brickwork in the basement of the old building to explore what lay behind before he left. That would allow him to plan what the team would be doing the next morning as they began the attack on the foundations. The significant risk, as ever with these brownfield sites, was that there were metal contaminants, in which case the ground would need to be capped with a layer of concrete. He was hoping that this wouldn't be the case.

As the portable floodlight glared behind him, he swung his sledgehammer, cracking open the handmade bricks which revealed their bright-red innards like eviscerated animals. He swung again, fragments spinning off onto the soot-covered floor of the basement, and swore under his breath because the whole place was just *too damned well built*.

After further blows, he waited until the mire of brick dust settled. To his surprise, he found the patch of wall was only one brick thick. There was a sheet of old pig iron where the second and third layers of brick should have been. He belted it a couple of times and it resounded with a substantial clang on each blow. It wasn't going to give up easily. He breathed heavily as he pulverised the bricks around the edges of the metal surface to discover, in fact, that it had hinges and even, to his amazement, a handle recessed into its surface.

It was a *door*.

He paused, panting for a moment while he tried to work out why anyone would want access to what rightfully should be part of the foundations.

Then he made the biggest mistake of his life.

He used his screwdriver to lever the handle out, a wrought iron ring which turned with surprisingly little effort. The door swung inwards with help from one of his work boots and it clanged flat against the wall, the noise echoing for what seemed for ever. He took out his torch and played it into the pitch black of the room. He could see it was at least 20 feet across and was, in fact, circular. He walked out onto a stone surface just inside the door, tottering back when he discovered that he wasn't standing on the floor but on a ledge, with an ominous darkness the other side. There was no floor – it appeared to be bottomless. He had walked into a huge brick well. As he looked up, he couldn't see the top of the well – the brick walls curved dramatically up into the darkness, past the limits of his little pocket torch. A strong breeze seemed to be coming from above, making the sweat clammy on the back of his neck. Playing the beam around, he noticed what steps, maybe a foot wide, led down around the edge of the wall, starting just below the stone ledge. He stamped his feet on the first step and, as it felt sound, he began to descend cautiously so as not to slip on the fine layer of dust and bits of straw and twigs that littered them. Hugging the diameter of the well, he climbed down, deeper and deeper, until the floodlit door was just a postage stamp way above him.

The steps finished and he found himself on a solid stone floor. Using his torch, he could see many small pipes of a dull gunmetal colour lacing up the walls, like a drunken church organ. He traced the route of one of them as it meandered upwards and saw that it opened into a funnel, as if it were a vent of some kind. But what attracted his attention more than anything was a door with a small glass porthole. Light was unmistakably shining through it, and the thought flashed into his mind that he had blundered into the Underground. A low humming sound of machinery reinforced this thought.

He slowly approached the window, a circle of old glass as thick and uneven as several bottle bottoms, mottled and scored with time, and peered through. Through its undulations, there was a scene resembling a scratchy old black-and-white film. He couldn't believe his eyes. There appeared to be buildings and streets. And beneath the light of glowing spheres of slow-moving fire, people were milling around. Fearsome-looking people. Anaemic phantoms dressed in old-fashioned clothes.

He wasn't a particularly religious man, attending church sporadically for weddings and the odd funeral, but he wondered for a moment if he had stumbled upon an annexe of hell, or at least some sort of purgatorial theme park. He recoiled from the window and crossed himself, mumbling woefully inaccurate *Hail Marys* and scuttled up the stairs in a blind panic, barricading the door lest any of the demons escape. He ran through the deserted building site and padlocked the main gates behind him.

As he drove home in a daze, he wondered what he would tell the guv'nor the next morning. Although he had seen it with his own eyes, he couldn't help but replay the vision over and over again in his mind. By the time he had reached home, he didn't know what to believe.

He couldn't resist bringing it up with his family; he had to talk to somebody. His wife, Aggy, and their two teenage sons assumed he'd been drinking and so he got short shrift from them over supper. They held up imaginary bottles and, between peals of cruel laughter, glugged them until he fell silent. But he just couldn't drop the subject, and eventually Aggy told him to put a sock in it and stop babbling about infernal white-haired monsters and glowing balls of fire as she watched '*Stenders* on the TV.

So here he was in the bathroom, scrubbing away at his molars and wondering if hell really did exist, when he heard the start of a scream – his wife's scream, the one usually reserved for mice or errant spiders in the bath. But it was cut short before she could follow through into the full-bodied wail.

His instinctive alarm bells rang, his nerves jittering like short circuits as he spun about, only to have the lights go out and the world turn upside down, quite literally, as he was hung by his feet by something so much stronger than him, something possessed of such superhuman strength that he could find no way to fight back. Then, as his arms and legs were pinned down, thick material was wound around him, binding his whole body, until he became a human roll of carpet, and was carried off sideways just like one. Shouting was out of the question as his mouth was obstructed, and it was only with the greatest effort that he managed to breathe. At one point, he thought he heard one of his son's voices, but it was so brief and muffled, he couldn't be sure. He had never been so terrified for his family, and himself, in his whole life. And so thoroughly helpless.

CHAPTER THREE

The Highfield museum was a glory hole – a repository for redundant belongings that had been spared the town dump. The building itself was the former town hall, which had been converted simply by the haphazard arrangement of old glass cases and careworn vitrines, themselves as arcane as the objects they housed.

In a grim turn-of-the-century dentist's chair, Dr Burrows settled down to his sandwiches using, as he habitually did, a display case of early-20th-century toothbrushes as a makeshift table. He flicked open his copy of *The Times* and gnawed on a limp salami and mayonnaise sandwich, seemingly oblivious to the dirt-encrusted dental implements below, which local people had bequeathed to the museum as an alternative to shying them.

In the cabinets around the main hall where Dr Burrows now sat, there were many similar arrangements of spared-from-the-dustmen articles. The "Granny's Kitchen" corner was of particular interest, as the assortment of stained and rusty egg whisks, apple corers and tea strainers was extensive. A pair of rusty Victorian mangles stood proudly by a long since defunct 1950s Old Faithful *Electric* washing machine that now shed rust flakes as voraciously as it once had consumed the soap variety. The "Clock Wall" was just as fascinating for its mediocrity. True, there was one item that caught the eye – a Victorian picture clock with a scene painted on a glass panel of a farmer with a horse pulling a plough – but, unfortunately, the glass had been broken and a vital chunk was missing where the horse's head had once been. Around it was a carefully arranged display of 1940s and 1950s wind-up and electric wall clocks in dull plastic pastel hues – none of these were working, as Dr Burrows hadn't quite got around to seeing to them yet.

Highfield, one of the smaller London boroughs, had a rich past, starting as it did in Roman times as a small settlement, and, in more recent history, swelling under the full impact of the industrial revolution. However, not much of this rich past had found its way into the little museum, and the borough had become what it was now: a desert of bedsits, two ups and two downs, and nondescript shops that couldn't afford more central locations.

Dr Burrows, the curator of the museum, was also its sole attendant, except on Saturdays, when a rota of old-age pensioners manned the fort. And always at his side was his brown leather briefcase, which contained a number of periodicals, half-read textbooks and historical novels. For this is how Dr Burrows occupied his days, punctuated by the odd nap and very occasional clandestine pipe-smoking in "The Stacks", a large storage room chock-full of foxed postcards and abandoned family portraits that would never be put out on display due to the lack of space, or inclination.

Tucked in amongst the dusty exhibits and old mahogany showcases, he would put his feet up and read voraciously all day with Radio 4 playing in the background on a "tranny" that had been left to the museum by a well-meaning local. Other than the rare school party that desperately needed a local outing during wet weather, very few visitors came to the museum and, once having seen it, they were unlikely ever to return.

Dr Burrows, like so many others, was doing a job which originally had been a stopgap. With a young child at home and no available posts in any of the London universities, he had taken the curatorship with the notion that he would seek out a more fulfilling job afterwards. And, as with so many other people, the certainty of a regular pay cheque and the security that came with the job had meant that 12 years had passed in a flash and with it any thoughts of looking for an alternative. It wasn't as if he didn't have the requisite qualifications. He had an impressive academic record: a degree in archaeology, followed up with a further qualification and then, for good measure, a doctorate. But as he accumulated the letters after his name and grew older in the process, the positions available to him had grown fewer in number and more sought-after. So, in the end, it was looking like a career in teaching or nothing – except that he had happened to spot the museum job in *The Highfield Bugle* and sent in his details, thinking he had better find *something* and *quick*.

So, here he was, with a doctorate in Greek antiquities, his dark tweed jacket replete with professorial patches on the elbows, watching the dust settle on the rather tired and ordinary exhibits, unaware that the dust was also settling on himself.

Finishing off his sandwich, Dr Burrows crumpled the greaseproof wrapper into a ball and playfully launched it at a 1960s orange plastic wastepaper basket on display in the "Kitchen" section. It missed, bouncing off the rim and coming to rest on the parquet floor. He let out a small sigh of disappointment and reached into his briefcase, rummaging around until he retrieved a bar of chocolate. It was a treat he tried to save until mid-afternoon to give the day some shape. But he felt particularly forlorn today and willingly gave in to his sweet tooth, ripping the paper off in an instant and ravaging the whole bar in just two mouthfuls.

Just then, the bell on the entrance door rattled and Oscar Embers tapped in with his twin walking sticks; the 80-year-old former stage actor had formed a passion for the museum and signed up for the occasional Saturday afternoon vigil after donating some of his autographed "Spotlight" portraits to the archives.

Dr Burrows, seeing the old man bearing down on him, tried to finish his crammed mouthful of chocolate, but found that he had rather overstepped his capacity. Chewing manically, he realised that the pensioner, still very much in possession of his wits, was closing in far too quickly. Dr Burrows thought of fleeing to his office but, realising it was too late, sat still, his cheeks puffed out like a hamster as he attempted to manoeuvre a smile into place.

"Good afternoon to you, Roger," Oscar said cheerfully, while fumbling in his coat pocket, "Now where did that thing go?"

Dr Burrows managed a tight-lipped "Hmmm" and nodded enthusiastically, hoping this would buy him some time. He was given a respite when Oscar began to wrestle with one coat pocket and then another. Dr Burrows got a couple of crafty chews in, but then the old man looked up, still grappling with his coat as if it was fighting back.

Oscar stopped trawling his pockets for a second and peered myopically around the glass cases and walls. "Can't see any of that lace I brought in the other week. Are you going to put it on display? I know it was a little threadbare in places, but good stuff all the same, you know." As Dr Burrows did not answer, he added, "It's not out, then?"

Dr Burrows tried to indicate the storeroom with a flick of his head. Never having known Dr Burrows to be so silent for so long, Oscar gave him a quizzical look, but then his eyes lit up as he found his quarry. He produced it slowly from his pocket and held it in front of Dr Burrows, cupped in one hand.

"I was given this by old Mrs Tantrumi, you know, the Italian lady who lives just off the end of the High Street – in Gladstone Street. It was found in her cellar when the gas people were doing some repairs. Stuck in the dirt, it was. One of them kicked it with his foot. I think we should include it in the collection. It's a fine example of a ..."

Dr Burrows, cheeks puffed, braced himself for yet another not-quite-antique egg timer or battered tin of used pen nibs. He was taken off guard when, with a magician's flourish, Oscar held up a small glowing globe, slightly larger than a golf ball, encased in a dull-gold metal cage.

" ... a light ... thing of some ..." Oscar tailed off. "Matter of fact, I don't know *what* to make of it!"

Dr Burrows took the item and was so fascinated, he quite forgot that Oscar was watching him intently as he chewed his mouthful.

"Teeth giving you gyp, my boy?" Oscar asked. "I used to grind them like that too, when they got bad. Just awful – know exactly how you feel. All I can say is that I'm glad now that I took the plunge and had them all out in one go. It isn't so uncomfortable, you know, once you get used to one of these." Dr Burrows quickly tried to head off the apparition of Oscar's dentures as the old man reached into his mouth.

"Oh no, my teeth are fine," he managed to say, holding up his hand in Oscar's face. He swallowed the last piece of chocolate in his mouth with a large gulp. "Just a bit dry today," Dr Burrows rubbed his throat. "Need some water."

"Ohhh, better keep an eye on that, y'know. Might be a sign that you've got that diabetes malarkey. When I was a lad, Roger – " Oscar's eyes seemed to glaze over as he remembered " – some doctors used to test for diabetes by tasting your ..." he lowered his voice to a whisper and looked down in the direction of the floor "... waters, if you know what I mean, to see if there was too much sugar in them."

"Yes, I know," Dr Burrows replied automatically – he was far too intrigued by the gently glowing globe to pay any attention to Oscar's medical curiosities. "Very strange. I would venture to say, offhand, that this dates from, possibly, the 19th-century, looking at the metalwork and ... the glass I would say is early, definitely hand blown ... but I have no idea what's inside. Maybe it's just a luminous chemical of some type – have you had it out in the daylight for long this morning, Mr Embers?"

"No, kept it safe in my coat since Mrs Tantrumi gave it to me yesterday. Just after breakfast, it was. I was on my constitutional – it helps with the old bowel ..."

"I wonder if it could be radioactive," Dr Burrows interrupted sharply, to stop Oscar from talking further. "I've read that some of the Victorian rock and mineral collections in other museums have been tested for radioactivity. Some pretty fierce specimens were uncovered in a batch up in Scotland –

powerful uranium crystals that they had to shut away in a lead-lined casket in the archives. Too hazardous to keep out on display."

"Oh, I hope it's not dangerous," Oscar said, taking a hasty step away from Dr Burrow. "Been walking around with it next to me new hips – just imagine if it's melted the ..."

"No, I don't expect it's that potent – it probably hasn't done you any real harm, not in 24 hours." Dr Burrows gazed into the sphere. "How very peculiar, you can see the liquid moving inside ... looks like it's swirling ... like a storm ..." he lapsed into silence and then shook his head in disbelief. "No, must be the heat from my hand that's making it behave like that ... you know ... thermoreactive."

"Well, I'm pleased you think it's interesting. I'll let Mrs Tantrumi know you want to keep it," Oscar said, taking another step back.

"Definitely," Dr Burrows replied. "I'd better do some research to make sure it's safe before I put it out. But, in the meantime, I'll drop Mrs Tantrumi a line to thank her, on behalf of the museum." He hunted in his jacket pocket for a pen, but couldn't find one. "Hold on a tick, Mr Embers, while I fetch something to write with."

He walked out of the main hall and into the corridor, managing to stumble over an ancient and gnarled length of timber, dug out of the marshes the previous year by some over-zealous locals who swore blindly that it was a prehistoric canoe, but which he hadn't found a place for yet. Dr Burrows opened the door with "Curator" painted on the frosted glass. The office was dark, as the only window was blocked by crates stacked high in front of it. He groped for the light on his desk but before he found it, he happened to glance at the sphere in his hand.

The light it was giving off appeared to have turned from the gentle glow he saw in the main hall to a much more intense light-green fluorescence. As he watched it, he could have sworn that the light was growing even brighter and the liquid inside moving even more vigorously.

"What substance becomes more radiant the darker the surroundings?" he muttered to himself. "No, I must be mistaken, it can't be! It must be that the luminosity is just more noticeable in here."

But it *had* grown brighter, and he didn't need his desk light to locate his pen; the globe was giving off a sublime green light, almost like daylight. As he returned with his donations ledger to the old man waiting for him in the main hall, he held the globe in front of him. Sure enough, when he emerged into the daylight, the globe dimmed again.

Oscar opened his mouth and was about to say something, but Dr Burrows beetled straight past him, through the museum door, and out into the open. He heard Oscar shouting "I say! I say!" as the museum door slammed shut, but Dr Burrows was so intent on the sphere, he completely ignored him. As he held it up, he saw that the glow had all but extinguished and that the liquid had darkened to a dull greyish colour in the glass sphere. The longer it was exposed to daylight, the darker it became, until it was almost black, like oil. Still dangling the globe in front of him, he returned inside, watching as the liquid began to whip up into a miniature storm and shimmer eerily again. Oscar was waiting for him, with concern on his face.

"Fascinating … fascinating, " Dr Burrows said.

"I say, thought you were having the vapours, old chap. I wondered if maybe you needed some air, rushing out like that? Not feeling faint, are you?"

"No, I'm fine, really I am, Mr Embers. Just wanted to test something. Now, Mrs Tantrumi's address, if you'd be so kind."

"So glad you're pleased with it," Oscar said. "While we're about it, I'll let you have my dentist's number, so you can get those teeth seen to, pronto."

CHAPTER FOUR

Will was resting on the handlebars of his bicycle at the entrance to a stretch of wasteland encircled by trees and wild bushes. He glanced at his watch and decided he would wait no more than five minutes for his long overdue friend, Chester.

The land was one of those forgotten lots you find on the outskirts of any town. This one hadn't yet been consumed by the municipal waste station next to it; nor had it succumbed to the amoebic spread of new housing, probably due to its proximity to the rubbish mountains that rose and fell with depressing regularity. Known locally as "The Forty Pits", due to the numerous craters that pitted its surface, some almost reaching 10 feet in depth, it was the arena for sporadic battles over imaginary territorial zones between two opposing teenage gangs, the Clan and the Click, their numbers drawn from Highfield's rougher housing estates.

It was also the favoured spot for kids on their track bikes and, increasingly, stolen mopeds. These were run into the ground and then torched, their carbon-black machine skeletons littering the far edges of the Pits, where weeds threaded up through their wheels and around their rusting engine blocks. Less frequently, it was also the scene for sinister adolescent amusements such as bird or frog hunting; all too often, they were slowly tortured to death and their sorry little carcasses impaled on sticks in sadistic youthful glee.

As Chester turned the corner towards the Pits, a bright

metallic glint caught his eye. It was the polished face of Will's shovel, which he wore slung across his back, like a samurai navvy.

Chester smiled and picked up his pace, waving to Will, who lazily waved back. As Chester jogged along, clutching a rather ordinary, dull garden spade to his chest, he could make out Will's startlingly pale complexion under his baseball cap and sunglasses. Will's clothes were an eclectic affair: an oversized cardigan with leather elbow pads and ridiculously thick piping around the ends of the sleeves, and dirt-encrusted trousers – a pair of old cords of indeterminate colour, due to the fine patina of dried mud and clay that covered, to varying degrees, most of what Will referred to as his "digging kit". In fact, the only things he kept really clean were his beloved shovel and the exposed metal toecaps of his work boots.

"What happened to you then?" Will asked with a note of annoyance as Chester finally reached him.

"Sorry, got a puncture," Chester puffed. "Had to drop the bike back home and run over here – bit hot in this weather."

Will glanced up uneasily at the sun, which shifted between the clouds, and he frowned. It was an enemy to him – Will's lack of pigmentation meant that even the sun's meagre power on an overcast day could burn his skin. The albinism gave him the almost pure white hair that spilt out from under his hat, and his pale blue eyes, which now darted impatiently towards the interior of the Pits.

"Come on then, let's get straight to it. Wasted too much time already," Will said curtly as he pushed off on his bicycle with barely a glance at Chester. "This way, keep up," he shouted, as Chester failed to match his speed.

Chester, still trying to catch his breath, called after Will, "I thought we were there!"

Chester Rawls, almost as wide as he was tall, and strong as an ox, known variously as Cuboid or Chester Drawers at school, was the same age as Will but had evidently benefited from either better nutrition or the physical inheritance of a weightlifter's body. One of the more inspired pieces of graffiti in the school lavatories had proclaimed that his father was a wardrobe and his mother was a bow-fronted desk.

Although the growing friendship between Will and Chester seemed unlikely, the one aspect that had singled them out at school had also been responsible for bringing them together: their *skin*. For Chester, it was severe bouts of eczema, which resulted in flaky and itchy patches of raw skin. This was due, he was told unhelpfully, to either an unidentifiable allergy or nervous tension. Whatever the cause, he had endured the teasing and barbed jibes from his fellow pupils, the worst for him being " 'orrible scaly creature", until he could take no more and had fought back, using his physical advantage to quash the taunters with great effect.

Likewise, Will's milky-pink pallor separated him from the norm, and for a while he had borne the brunt of chants of "Chalky" and "Frosty the Snowman". More impetuous than Chester, his temper had snapped one winter's evening when the detractors had ambushed him on the way to a dig. Unfortunately for them, Will had used his spade to great effect, and a bloody and one-sided battle had ensued in which teeth were lost and a nose was badly broken.

Understandably, both Will and Chester were left alone for a while and treated with the begrudging respect given to mad dogs. However, both boys remained wary of the other pupils, aware that if they let their guards down, renewed outbreaks of persecution were more than likely. So, other than Chester's inclusion in a number of school teams due to his size and strength, both were inclined to remain outsiders, loners at the edge of the playground. Secure in their shared isolation, they talked to no one and no one talked to them.

Will rode between the alternating grassy mounds, craters and heaps of rubbish left by fly-tippers, careering to a halt as he reached the far side. He dismounted and hid his bicycle in a small dugout beneath the shell of an abandoned car, its make unrecognisable due to the rust and salvaging it had endured.

"Here we are," he announced, as Chester caught up.

"Is this where we're going to dig?" Chester panted, looking

around at the ground by their feet.

"Nope. Back up," Will said. Chester took a couple of paces away from Will, regarding him with bemusement.

"Are we going to start a new one?"

Will didn't answer, but instead knelt down and appeared to be feeling for something in a thicket of grass. He found what he was looking for – a knotted length of rope – and, standing up, took up the slack and pulled. To Chester's surprise, a line cracked open in the earth and a thick panel of marine ply rose up, soil tumbling from it to reveal the dark entrance beneath.

"Can't have those scumbags messing around in my excavation, can I?" he said possessively as Chester peered into the void.

"We're not supposed to be going down there, are we?"

But Will had already begun to lower himself into the opening, which, after a drop of five feet or so, continued to sink deeper at an angle.

"I've got a spare hat for you," Will said from inside the opening as he donned a yellow hard hat and switched on the miner's light mounted on its front. It shone up at Chester, who was hovering indecisively above him.

"Well, are you coming or not?" Will said testily. "Take it from me, it's completely safe."

"Are you sure?"

"Of course," Will said, thumping a support to his side and smiling confidently to give his friend some encouragement. He continued to smile fixedly as, in the shadows behind him and out of view from Chester, a small shower of soil fell against his back. "Safe as houses. Honest."

"Well …"

Once inside, Chester was almost too surprised to speak. A tunnel, five feet or so wide and the same in height, ran at a slight incline into the darkness, the sides shored up with old timber props at frequent intervals. It looked, Chester thought, exactly like the mines in those old cowboy films shown on the telly on Sunday afternoons.

"This is cool! You didn't do all this by yourself, Will, you can't have!"

Will grinned smugly. "Certainly did. I've been at it since last year – and you haven't seen the half of it yet. Step this way."

He replaced the ply, sealing the tunnel mouth. Chester watched with mixed emotions as the last chink of blue sky disappeared. They set off along the passage, past stores of planks and shoring timbers stacked untidily against the sides. All of a sudden, the passage widened to an area the size of a reasonably sized room – two tunnels could be seen branching off each end of it. In the middle were a small mountain of yellow buckets, a trestle table and two old armchairs. The timber planking of the roof was supported by rows of Stilson props, adjustable iron columns scabbed with rust.

"Home again," Will said.

"This is just … wild," Chester said in disbelief, then frowned. "But is it really okay to be down here?"

"Course it is. My Dad showed me how to batten and prop – you know this isn't my first …" Will hesitated, wondering whether to tell Chester about the train station he had unearthed with his father, and then thought better of it. He didn't know him that well. "And it's perfectly secure. It's better not to tunnel under buildings – that requires stronger tunnel props and a lot more planning. Also, it's not a good idea where there's water or underground streams – they can cause the whole thing to slip in."

"There's isn't any water around here, is there?" Chester asked quickly.

"Just this." Will reached into a cardboard box on the table and handed his friend a plastic bottle of water. "Let's just chill out for a while, Chester."

They both sat in the old armchairs, sipping from the bottles while Chester looked up at the roof and craned his neck in the direction of the two branch tunnels.

"It's so peaceful, isn't it?" Will sighed.

"Yes," Chester replied. "Very … er … quiet."

"It's more than that, it's so warm and *calm* down here. And the smell … sort of comforting, isn't it? Dad says it's where we all came from, a long time ago – cavemen and all that – and where we all end up eventually. So it feels sort of natural to us, home from home."

"Suppose so," Chester agreed dubiously.

"You know, when I was young, I always thought that when you bought a house, you owned everything under it."

"What do you mean?"

"Well, your house is built on a plot of land, right?" Will said, thumping his foot on the floor of the cavern for effect. "And anything below that plot, going right down to the Earth's core, is yours as well. Of course, as you get nearer the centre of the planet, the "segment", if you want to call it that, gets smaller and smaller until you hit the very centre of our planet."

Chester nodded slowly, at a loss to know what to say.

"So I always imagined digging down – down into your slice of world and all those thousands of miles that are going to waste, while you just sit in a building perched on the very crust of the Earth," Will said, dreamily.

"Yes, I see," Chester said, catching on to the idea. "So if you were to dig down, you could have like a skyscraper, but facing the wrong way. Like an ingrown hair or something." He involuntarily scratched the eczema on his forearm.

"Yes, that's exactly right. Didn't think of it like that, good way of putting it. But Dad says you don't actually own all the ground under you – the government has the right to build Tube lines and things if they want to."

"Oh," Chester said, wondering if that was the case, why they had been talking about it in the first place.

Will jumped up. "Right, grab yourself a pick, four buckets and a wheelbarrow, and follow me down here." He pointed out one of the dark tunnels. "There's a bit of a rock problem."

⋯◆⋯

Meanwhile, back up at ground level, Dr Burrows strode purposefully as he made his way home – he enjoyed the chance to think while he walked the mile and a half or so, and, besides, it meant he could save on the bus fare. He stopped outside the newsagents, abruptly halting in mid pace, teetered slightly, rotated 90 degrees and entered.

"Dr Burrows, we thought we'd lost you," the man behind the counter said as he looked up from a newspaper spread open before him. "Thought you might've gone on a round-the-world cruise or something?"

"Ah, no, alas," Dr Burrows replied, trying to keep his eyes off the Snickers, Mars bars and Walnut Whips that were displayed enticingly in front of him.

"We've kept your backlog safe," the shopkeeper said as he bent below the counter and produced a stack of magazines. "Here they are. *Excavation Today, The Archaeological Journal* and *Curators' Month.* All present and correct, I hope?"

"Tickety-boo," Dr Burrows said, hunting for his wallet. "Wouldn't want you to let them go to anyone else!"

The shopkeeper raised his eyebrows. "Believe me, there isn't exactly an excessive demand for these titles round here," he said as he took a £20 note from Dr Burrows. "I say, looks like you've been working on something," the shopkeeper said, spotting Dr Burrows' fingernails. "Been down a coal mine?"

"Hmm," Dr Burrows replied, looking at the black lines of encrusted dirt, conspicuous against the pale skin of his hands. "Spot of DIY in my cellar. Good thing I don't bite them, isn't it?"

Dr Burrows left the shop with his new reading matter, trying to tuck it securely into the side pocket of his briefcase as he pushed the door open. Still grappling with the magazines, he backed blindly out onto the pavement, straight into somebody moving at great speed. As a result of the collision, Dr Burrows dropped his briefcase and magazines, gasping as he rebounded off the short but very heavy-set man, who had felt as solid as a locomotive. Dr Burrows, stuttering and flustered, tried to apologise but the man strode on purposefully, adjusting his sunglasses and inclining his head a degree to give Dr Burrows an unfriendly sneer.

Dr Burrows was flabbergasted. It was a *man-in-a-hat.* Dr Burrows always wished he suited hats; in his youth, he had aspired to a trilby or a jaunty fedora, but something about the shape of his head or perhaps his face meant that they just didn't suit him.

Of late, he had begun to notice, amongst the run-of-the-mill that sought refuge in the hinterland of Highfield, a type of person that seemed, well, different, without sticking out too much. Being an inveterate people-watcher, and having analysed the situation, as Dr Burrows was wont to do, he assumed that these people had to be related to each other in some way. What surprised him most was that nobody else in the Highfield area seemed to have registered the rather peculiarly slope-faced men wearing flat caps, black coats and very thick dark glasses, at all.

As Dr Burrows had barged into the man, slightly dislodging his jet-black glasses, he'd had a chance to scrutinise a "specimen" at close quarters for the first time. Apart from his oddly shaped face and wispy hair, he had very light blue, almost white eyes against a pasty, translucent skin. But there was something else: a peculiar smell about the man, a *mustiness*. It reminded Dr Burrows of the battered suitcases of mildewed clothes that from time to time were dumped on the museum steps by anonymous benefactors.

He watched the man move smoothly, almost glide, down the High Street, and then a passer-by crossed the road, blocking his line of sight. In that instant, the man-in-a-hat was gone. Dr Burrows blinked, squinting through his spectacles as he looked up and down the High Street, but, although the pavements were not busy, he couldn't for the life of him locate the man again.

It occurred to Dr Burrows that he could have tailed the man-in-a-hat to see where he was going, but, mild-mannered as he was, Dr Burrows disliked any form of confrontation and quickly decided this was not advisable given the man's hostile demeanour. So, any thought of detective work was quickly abandoned. Besides, he could find out on another day where the man, and perhaps the whole family of hatted lookalikes, lived. When he was feeling a little more intrepid.

Underground, Will and Chester took turns at working the rockface, which Will had identified as a type of sandstone. He was glad that he'd recruited Chester to help with the excavation, as he really seemed to have a knack for the work. He watched with quiet admiration as Chester swung the pickaxe with immense force, and once a fissure opened up in the face, seemed to know exactly when to pry out the loose material, which Will quickly shovelled into buckets.

"Need a break?" he suggested, seeing that Chester was beginning to tire. "Come and have a breather." Will meant this literally, because with the entrance blocked, it all too soon became very airless and stuffy where they were, 20 feet or so from the main chamber.

"If I take this tunnel much further," he said to Chester as they both pushed loaded wheelbarrows, "I'll have to sink a vertical shaft for ventilation. It's just that they are so ... so very *dull* when I could be making more headway."

They reached the main chamber and sat in the armchairs, drinking the water appreciatively.

"So what do we do with all this?" Chester said, indicating the filled buckets in the wheelbarrows.

"Lug it to the surface and tip it in the gully at the side."

"Is it all right to do that?"

"If anyone asks, I just say I'm digging a trench for a game of war," Will replied. Taking a swig from his bottle, he swallowed noisily. "They don't care. After all, to them we're just a bunch of daft kids with buckets and spades," he added dismissively.

"They would bloody care if they saw this – this is not what ordinary kids do," Chester said, his eyes flicking around the chamber. "Why *do* you do it, Will?"

"Have a look at these."

Will leant over and lifted up a plastic crate from the side of his chair from which he took out a series of objects, placing them on the table. Amongst them were Codswallop bottles – Victorian soft drink bottles with strangely designed necks that contained a glass marble – and a whole host of medicine bottles of different sizes and colours, all with a beautiful frosty bloom from their sojourn in the soil.

"And these," Will said reverentially, as he picked out an entire range of Victorian pâté jars of differing sizes with decorative lids and names in swirling old writing that Chester had never seen before.

"I haven't found any fossils yet, but you never know your luck," Will said wistfully, looking in the direction of the branch tunnels.

CHAPTER FIVE

Dr Burrows whistled as he swung his briefcase in step with his brisk pace. He rounded the corner at 6.30 pm precisely, as he always did, and his house came into view. It was one of many crammed into Broadlands Avenue – regimented brick boxes with just enough room for a family of four. The only saving grace was that this side of the road backed onto the Common, so at least the house had views of a big open space, even if one was forced to see them from rooms barely large enough to swing a hamster.

As he let himself in and stood in the hall, sorting the old books and magazines from his briefcase, Will rode into Broadlands Avenue, his spade glinting under the first red glow of the newly lit street lights. At breakneck speed, he slalomed in between the white lines in the middle of the road and banked wildly as he shot through the open gate, his brakes reaching a squealing crescendo as he pulled up under the carport. He dismounted, locked up his bicycle and entered the house.

Will was the sort of child who, even if he did not swing any of his pets, needed ample space. As a result, he was rarely to be found in the house except at mealtimes and to sleep, treating it like a hotel, as many kids his age did. The only problem with this yearning to be outside was that he couldn't be exposed to sunlight for any length of time, so was happy to go underground at any opportunity he could take.

"Hi Dad," he said to his father, who was now poised awkwardly just inside the sitting room, still holding his open briefcase in one hand as he watched something on television that had caught his eye en route to the kitchen.

Dr Burrows was unarguably the biggest influence in Will's life – a casual comment or snippet of information he happened to drop could inspire his son to embark on the wildest and most extreme "investigations". Despite this shared interest in the buried past, father and son spoke little, leading very separate lives, although Dr Burrows always managed to be in at the kill on any of his son's digs if he suspected that there was going to be something of true archaeological value. Dr Burrows didn't much like life at home, preferring to bury his nose in the books he kept down in the cellar, *his* cellar. Here, he could escape, losing himself in dreams of echoing Greek temples and Roman colosseums.

"Oh yes, hello Will," he answered absent-mindedly after a long pause, still distracted by the television. Will looked past his father into the sitting room, where his mother was sitting, equally mesmerised by the programme.

"Hi Mum," Will said and then left, not expecting a response.

Mrs Burrows' eyes were glued to an unexpected development in the casualty ward.

"Hello," she eventually replied several minutes later, although Will had long gone.

Dr Burrows had met Will's mother, Celia, when they were both at university. She'd been a zany media student and Dr Burrows had been attracted to her enthusiasm for a career as a news reporter or a job in film or television.

Unfortunately, it was indeed television that had filled her life for the last decade. She sat in front of it through morning, afternoon and evening, juggling her schedules with a pair of video recorders when favourites, of which there were many, clashed.

If one has a mental snapshot of a person, an image that is first recalled when one thinks of them, then Mrs Burrows' would be of her lying sideways in her favourite armchair, a row of remotes neatly lined up on the arm and her feet resting on a footstool topped with television pages ripped from the newspapers. These were her "Telly Maps", numerous television schedules fastidiously annotated with a yellow highlighter pen and little red arrows to ensure she didn't miss anything vital.

Surrounded by a haphazard slag pile of videotapes, there she sat, day after day, frozen in the flickering light of the screen, occasionally twitching a leg just to remind everyone that she was alive. Her television life was not to be interrupted by anyone or anything. The sitting room, her domain, was furnished with tired, inherited furniture: odd wooden chairs painted shades of purple and turquoise, a couple of mismatched armchairs with faded loose dark blue covers and a sofa with threadbare arms. Mrs Burrows had requisitioned a 1960s circular plastic table which Dr Burrows had picked up from a second hand shop and this was littered with her old magazines, mostly the *Radio Times* and copies of *Hello!*. The carpet was an oppressive floral affair, with horrible giant orange and yellow sunflowers and, at the end of the room, fighting with the carpets, mustard and purple curtains hung either side of the French doors – these had been *in situ* when they bought the house, and they had never got around to replacing them.

"Hi Sis," Will said as he entered the kitchen, immediately going to the fridge and opening it. "What's for dinner? I'm starving."

"Hello mole boy," Rebecca replied, pushing the fridge door

shut as she handed her brother an empty packet. "Here, have a look at the picture. It's sweet and sour chicken, rice and some vegetable thingy. They were doing a two-for-one at the supermarket, so I thought I'd give them a try. How's the latest dig going, by the way?"

"Bit of a struggle – we've hit a layer of sandstone."

"We?" Rebecca looked at him quizzically. "I'm sure you said *we*, Will. You don't mean Dad's working on it with you, do you? Not during museum hours?"

"No, Chester from school gave me a hand."

Rebecca nearly slammed her fingers in the microwave. "You mean you actually asked somebody else to help you?" she said in amazement. "Well, that's a first. Thought you didn't trust anyone with your projects?"

"No, I don't usually, but Chester's okay. Really," Will replied, a bit taken aback at his sister's reaction.

"Can't say I know him well enough, except that he's called ..."

"I know what they call him," Will cut her off sharply.

Rebecca was several years younger than Will, and couldn't have been more different from him; she was slim and dainty for her age, in comparison with her brother's rather stocky physique. And with her dark hair and sallow complexion, she wasn't bothered by the sun, even at the height of summer, while Will's skin would redden and burn in a matter of minutes.

Being so dissimilar, they had always got on well. Their interests were diametrically opposed, and this lack of overlap meant they rarely squabbled or fought with each other. Having said this, they both showed a passing interest in each other's pursuits – Will in Rebecca's domestic efficiency, principally because of the regular meals and clean clothes, and Rebecca in Will's eccentric hobby because of its sheer absurdity, in her eyes at any rate.

The pity was that they never spent much time together. There weren't the family outings that you would ordinarily expect, because Dr and Mrs Burrows had such completely divergent tastes. Even family holidays were unusual, to say the least. Will would go off with his father on expeditions around the country. They might even sleep in the car to save money when they went to Lyme Regis on fossil hunting expeditions, to search for recent landfalls on the coast or to find disused quarries further inland. Rebecca, on the other hand, accompanied her mother to central London, where they would go shopping or see the latest films – activities chosen entirely by Mrs Burrows.

Tonight, the Burrows were sitting with their meals on their laps watching an endlessly repeated 1970s comedy that Dr Burrows seemed to be enjoying. No one spoke during the meal except Mrs Burrows, who at one point mumbled, "Good ... this is good." It may have been in praise of the microwave food, or possibly the finale of the dated sitcom, but nobody bothered to enquire. Having finished his meal, Will left the room without a word, putting his tray by the kitchen sink and then thundering upstairs with a canvas bag of recently found items clutched in his hands.

Dr Burrows was the next out, walking into the kitchen where he deposited his tray on the table. Although she hadn't finished her food yet, Rebecca followed him.

"Dad, there's some cheques on the table for you to sign ... to pay a couple of bills."

"Have we got enough in the account?" he asked as he tossed his signature off on the bottom of the cheques, not even bothering to read the amounts.

"I told you last week, we have quite a cushion, particularly after I got a better deal on the house insurance. Saved us a few pennies on the premium."

"Right ... very good. Thanks," he said, picking up his tray and heading towards the dishwasher.

"Just leave it on the side," Rebecca said quickly, remembering how he'd broken both the dishwasher and the washing machine in the past. Once she'd caught him attempting to programme the former by pressing the buttons in random sequences, as if he was trying to crack some secret code. Rebecca had no alternative but to banish him from the kitchen. She insisted he kept well out of the way and was more than happy that he found other diversions in the cellar to keep himself occupied.

Rebecca shoved the cheques in envelopes ready to be sent in the morning and then sat down to complete the shopping list for the next day. She was, strangely enough, the engine, the powerhouse behind the Burrows' house. Unfortunately for one so young, it befell upon her not just to do the shopping, but also to organise the meals, the cleaning lady and just about everything else that normal parents would, in any ordinary household, take responsibility for. She was meticulous in her organisation; a notice board in the kitchen listed all the provisions she required at least a fortnight in advance. She kept carefully labelled wallet files of the family's bills and financial situation in one of the kitchen cupboards – neither of her parents even knew they were there.

Back in the sitting room, Mrs Burrows flicked a remote to commence her nightly marathon of soaps and chat shows saved on video while poor Rebecca cleared up in the kitchen. As she stacked the dishwasher, loaded the washing machine and took out the rubbish, she pictured herself as a modern-day Cinderella with two-and-a-half ugly sisters, Will being the fraction as he was considerably less effort than the others.

By nine o'clock, Rebecca had finished her chores and then her homework on the half of the kitchen table that wasn't taken up by the empty coffee jars Dr Burrows kept promising he'd do something with. She then went upstairs to go to bed. Passing the bathroom, she glanced in and saw Will admiring his finds on the bathroom mat.

"Just look at this!" he said proudly as he held up a small bag made of rotten leather and very carefully lifted up the fragile flap. He gently took out a series of clay pipes. "You usually only find bits that the farm labourers chucked away as they snapped or just dropped them, but none of these are broken. Bet they're 18th-century."

"Lovely," Rebecca said vaguely, and then gasped. "Look what you've done to the bath! Will, you've got to clear that up. What a mess!" Will had left a thick mud sludge in the bottom.

"Don't worry, Becky, the cleaning lady'll do it," he said

dismissively as he gathered up his treasures in the bath mat and went into his bedroom. Here he thoughtfully placed the items next to his many other treasures on the shelves that completely covered one wall of the room – his museum, as he called it.

Rebecca rolled up her sleeves and set about cleaning the bath, muttering "I don't know what I've done to deserve this" and "Where did I go wrong with that boy?" – things which Mrs Burrows was always too preoccupied to say.

Will and Rebecca were self-regulating as regards their bed times. As there weren't the usual parental rulings about it being too late, they had nothing to rebel against, and were actually rather sensible about the hours they kept. Their bedrooms were diminutive – hers at the front of the house and his at the back. He always slept with the window wide open, and it must have been about two o'clock in the morning when he was woken by a sound. It emanated from the garden and he immediately recognised it.

"A wheelbarrow?" he said as his eyes flicked open. "A *loaded* wheelbarrow?" He got out of bed and went to the window. There, in the light of the half moon, he could just about make out his father pushing a barrow down the path and through a gap in the hedge at the end of the garden. Dr Burrows then moved out onto the Common, where Will lost sight of him behind some trees. Dr Burrows had always kept strange hours because of his catnaps in the museum, but this level of activity was unusually lively for him.

"What is he up to?" Will said to himself. Earlier that year, Will had helped him to excavate and lower the floor of the cellar by a couple of feet, and then lay a new concrete floor so increasing the headroom. Then, a month or so later, they dug an exit from the cellar up to the garden and installed a new door, as his father had wanted another entrance.

As far as Will knew, the job had finished there. Will felt a pang of resentment – *what was his father doing that was so secretive, and why hadn't he asked him to help?* Still groggy with sleep and preoccupied with dreams of his own underground projects, Will put it from his mind and returned to his bed.

CHAPTER SIX

The next day, after school, Will and Chester resumed their work at the excavation. Will was just returning from dumping the spoils, his wheelbarrow stacked high with empty yellow buckets as he trundled to the end of the tunnel where Chester was hacking away at the stone layer.

"How's it going?" he asked Chester.

"It's not getting any easier, that's for sure," Chester replied, wiping the sweat from his forehead with a dirty sleeve and smearing dirt across it in the process.

"You take a break. Let me have a look."

"Okay."

Will shone his helmet lamp over the rock surface, the subtle browns and yellows of the strata gouged randomly by the tip of the pickaxe, and sighed loudly. "I think we'd better call a halt to evaluate the situation. No point banging our heads on a sandstone wall! Let's have a drink."

"Yeah, good idea," Chester said gratefully.

They walked back to the main chamber, where Will handed him a bottle of water.

"Glad you wanted to come back again. It's pretty addictive, isn't it?" he said to Chester who was staring into mid-distance.

Chester looked at him. "Well, yes and no, really. I want to help you get through the rock, but I'm not so sure after that. My back and arms really ached last night, you know."

"Oh, you'll get used to it and, besides, you're a *natural*."

"You think so? Really?" Chester beamed, delighted with the accolade.

"No doubt about it. You could be nearly as good as me one day!"

Chester punched him playfully on the arm and they laughed, but their laughter petered out as Will's expression turned serious.

"What is it?" Chester asked.

"We're going to have to rethink our approach here – the sandstone vein might just be too much. We've no way of knowing how thick it is." Will knitted his fingers together and rested his hands on his head, an affectation he had picked up from his father. "What do you think about ... about going under it?"

"Under it? Won't that take us too deep?"

"Nah, I've gone deeper before."

"When?"

"A couple of my tunnels went much further down than this," Will said evasively. "You see, if we dig under it, the sandstone, being a solid layer, will act as a roof for the new tunnel. It's perfectly safe."

"What if it isn't? What if it collapses with us underneath?" Chester looked distinctly unhappy.

"You fret too much. Come on, let's get on with it!" Will had already made up his mind, and was starting off down the tunnel when Chester called after him.

"Will, what are we actually digging for? I mean, is there anything on any of the maps? Is there any point to this at all?"

Will was quite taken aback by the question and it was some seconds before he replied. "No, there's nothing marked on the Ordnance Surveys or Dad's archive maps. That's why I thought it might be interesting to have a look. It's interesting because it's a challenge and you never know what you might discover along the way – perhaps some fossils or an ancient rubbish dump where you can get bucketfuls of fantastic finds."

"So, if we aren't heading for anything in particular, I was just wondering, why not work on the other tunnel?"

"A hunch," Will said simply and was off down the tunnel before Chester could utter another word. He shrugged and picked up his pickaxe.

"I must be bloody mad. What on earth am I doing here?" he mumbled to himself. "Could be at home … on the PlayStation right now … warm and dry." He held out his arms and looked down at his mud-sodden clothes. "Bloody mad!" he repeated several times.

—◄◉►—

Dr Burrows' day had been the usual. He was reclining luxuriously in the dentist's chair with a newspaper folded in his lap, on the brink of slipping into his post-teatime nap, when the door of the museum burst open. Former Major Joe Carruthers of the Queen's Own strode purposefully in and, with a thud of his heels, came to a sudden stop in front of the reception desk. He scanned the room until he located Dr Burrows, whose head was lolling drowsily in the dentist's chair.

"Look sharp, Burrows!" he bellowed, almost taking pleasure in Dr Burrows' reaction as his head jerked up. Joe Carruthers, a veteran of the Second World War, had never lost his military bearing or his brusqueness. Dr Burrows had given him the rather unkind nickname "Pineapple Joe" because of his striking red and bulbous nose – possibly the result of a war injury or, as Dr Burrows speculated, more likely from the excessive consumption of gin. He was surprisingly sprightly for a man in his seventies, and tended to bark loudly. He was the last person Dr Burrows wanted to see right now.

"Saddle up, Burrows, need you to recce something for me, if you can spare a mo? Course you can, see you're not busy here, are you?"

"Ah, no, sorry, Mr Carruthers, I can't leave the museum unattended. I'm on duty, after all," Dr Burrows said sluggishly as he reluctantly left the last vestiges of his sleep behind.

Joe Carruthers continued to holler at him from across the museum hall. "Come on, man, this is a *special* duty, y'know. Want your opinion on something. Me daughter and her new hubby bought a house just off the High Street. Been modernising the kitchen and they found something … something funny."

"Funny how?" Dr Burrows asked, still irked by the intrusion.

"Funny hole in the floor."

"Why don't you call the builders, then?"

"Not that sort of thing, old man. Not that sort of thing at all."

"Why?" Dr Burrows asked, his curiosity roused.

"Better if you come and have a gander for yourself, old chap. I mean, you know all about the history hereabouts. Thought of you immediately. Best man for the job I told my Penny. This chappie really knows his stuff, I said to her."

Dr Burrows rather relished the idea that he was regarded as the local historical expert, so he got to his feet and self-importantly put his jacket on. Having locked the museum, he fell into step beside Pineapple Joe's forced march along the High Street and they soon turned into Jekyll Street. Pineapple Joe only spoke once as they turned another corner, into Martineau Square.

"Those damn dogs – people shouldn't let them run loose like that," he grumbled as he squinted at some papers blowing across the road in front of them. "Should be on a lead." Then they arrived at the house.

Number 23 was one of the terraced properties that lined each side of the square, built of brick with typical early Georgian features. Although they were narrow, three-floored houses with thin slivers of garden at the rear, Dr Burrows had admired them on many occasions when he'd been in the area. He loathed the modern box he lived in, and had always dreamt of being able to buy a property of similar age to these. He was actually quite glad that Pineapple Joe had butted into the museum – he welcomed the chance to have a look inside one.

Using his fist, Pineapple Joe knocked on the original four-panelled Georgian door with enough force to cave it in, Dr Burrows wincing with each blow. A young woman answered the door, her face lighting up with recognition at the sight of her father.

"Hello Dad. You got him to come, then." She turned to Dr Burrows with a self-conscious smile, and then opened the door fully, standing aside to allow them to enter.

"Do come down to the kitchen. Bit of a mess, but I'll put the kettle on," she said, closing the door behind them.

Dr Burrows followed Pineapple Joe as he stomped over the dustsheets in the unlit corridor, where the wallpaper had been half-stripped from the walls.

Once in the kitchen, Pineapple Joe's daughter turned to Dr Burrows. "Sorry, how rude, I didn't introduce myself. My name's Penny *Hanson* – I think we've met before." She emphasised her new surname proudly. For an awkward moment, Dr Burrows looked so totally mystified at this suggestion that she flushed with embarrassment and quickly mumbled something about making some tea, while Dr Burrows, indifferent to her discomfort, began to inspect the room. It had been gutted and the plaster stripped back to the bare brick, and there was a newly installed sink with half-finished cupboard units along one side.

"We thought it was a good idea to take out the chimney breast, to give us the space for a breakfast bar over there," Penny said, pointing at the wall opposite the one with the new units. "Our architect said it would be okay with a brace up there in the ceiling." She indicated a gaping hole where Dr Burrows could see that a new metal joist had been bedded in. "But when the builders knocked out the old brickwork, the back wall fell down and they found this. I've rung our architect, but he hasn't called me back yet."

At the rear of the fireplace, a heap of soot-stained bricks indicated where the hearth wall had been and then, directly behind, there was a space like a priest's hole with a vent in the floor, about two feet by four in size. Crouching down, Dr Burrows stepped between the loose bricks and, at the edge of the opening, peered down into it.

"Ah ... have you got a torch?" he asked. Penny left – returning shortly with one. He shone it down into the opening. "Brick lining, early 19th-century, I would venture. Seems to have been built at the same time as the house," he muttered to himself as Pineapple Joe and his daughter watched him intently. "But what the blazes is it for?" he added. The strangest thing was that as he leant over and peered down into it, he couldn't see where it ended – it seemed to go on for ever.

"Have you tested how deep it is?" he asked Penny, straightening up.

"What with?" she replied simply.

"Can I have this?" Dr Burrows picked up a jagged half-brick from the pile of rubble by the collapsed hearth. She nodded and he turned back to the hole and stood poised to drop it in.

"Now listen," he said to them as he released it over the vent. They heard it knock against the sides as it fell, the impacts growing quieter until only faint echoes reached Dr Burrows, who was now kneeling over the opening.

"Is it …?" Penny began.

"Shhh!" Dr Burrows hissed impolitely, making her start as he held his hand up. After a moment, he raised his head and frowned at Pineapple Joe and Penny. "Didn't hear it land, but maybe there's something soft at the bottom," he suggested. "Seemed to bounce off the sides for ages, but how … how can it be *that* deep?" Then, seemingly oblivious to the grime, he lay down on the floor and stuck his head and shoulders into the hole as far as he could, probing the darkness below him with the torch in his outstretched arm. He suddenly froze and started to sniff loudly.

"Can't be!"

"What's that, Burrows?" Pineapple Joe asked. "Something to report?"

"I might be mistaken, but I swear there's a bit of an updraft," Dr Burrows said, pulling his head out of the gap. "Why that should be, I just don't know – unless the whole terrace was built with some form of ventilation system between each house. But I can't for the life of me imagine why. The strangest thing is that the duct ..." he swivelled around onto his back and shone his torch upwards above the hole, " ... appears to carry on up, just behind the normal chimney. I presume it also vents as part of the chimney stack, on the roof?"

What Dr Burrows did not tell them, did not dare tell them, because it would have appeared too outlandish, is that he had smelt that peculiar mustiness again – the same smell he had noticed on his collision with the man-in-a-hat the day before in the High Street.

—◦—

In the underground tunnel, Will and Chester were finally making progress. They were digging out the soil below the sandstone when Will's pickaxe hit something solid.

"Damn! Don't tell me the bloody rock carries on down here as well!" he yelled, exasperated. Chester immediately dropped his barrow and came running in from the main chamber.

"What's the matter, Will?" he asked, surprised at the outburst.

"Damn and blast it!" Will said in a growl, violently attacking the obstacle with his pickaxe.

"What? What is it?" Chester shouted at his friend, who was definitely acting out of character. He was shocked. He had never seen Will loose his cool like this before. Will was like a boy possessed.

Will increased his attack with the pickaxe, working at fever pitch as he struck wildly at the rockface. Chester was forced to take a step back to avoid his swings and the torrents of soil and stone he was throwing out behind him.

Suddenly, Will stopped and fell silent for a moment. Then he chucked down his pickaxe and sank to his knees to scrape frantically in front of him.

"Well, just look at that, will you?"

"Look at what?"

"See for yourself," Will said breathlessly.

Chester crawled in and saw what had excited his friend so much. Where Will had cleared the soil away, there were unmistakably several courses of a brick wall visible under the sandstone layer, and he'd already loosened some of the first bricks.

"But what if it's a sewer or railway tunnel, or something else like that? Are you sure we should be doing this?" Chester said anxiously. "It might be something to do with the water supply. I don't like this!"

"Calm down, Chester, there's nothing on the maps around here. We're on the edge of the old town, right?"

"Right," Chester said hesitantly, unsure what his friend was getting at.

"Won't be anything built in the last 100 to 150 years – so it's unlikely to be a train tunnel, even a forgotten one way out here. I went through all the old maps with Dad. I suppose it might be a sewer, but if you look at the curvature of the brick as it meets the sandstone, then we're probably near the top of it. It could just be the cellar wall of an old house – or maybe some foundations, but I wonder why it was built under the sandstone? Very odd."

Chester took a couple of steps backwards and said nothing, so Will resumed his efforts for a few minutes and then stopped, aware that Chester was still hovering nervously behind him. Will turned and let out a resigned sigh.

"Look, Chester, if it makes you happy, we'll stop for today and I'll check with my Dad tonight – to see what he thinks. Okay?"

"Rather you did, Will. You know ... in case."

———◦———

Dr Burrows said goodbye to Pineapple Joe and his daughter, promising to find out what he could about the house and its architecture from the local archives. He glanced at his watch and grimaced. He knew it was not acceptable to leave the museum closed for so long, but he wanted to look at something first.

Several times he walked around the square, examining the terraced houses on the four sides. The whole square had been built at the same time, and each house was identical. But what interested him was the idea that they might all have the mysterious ducts running through them. He crossed the road and went through the gate into the middle of the square, which had at its centre a paved area surrounded by uncared-for strips of grass and a few neglected rose bushes. Here he had a better view of the roofs, and he pointed with his finger as he tried to count exactly how many chimney pots there were on each one.

"Just doesn't add up," he frowned. "Very peculiar indeed."

He turned, left the square and, making his way back to the museum, arrived just in time to close up for the day.

CHAPTER SEVEN

The next day, Dr Burrows was in the museum, sorting out the button cabinet under the window. He was leaning over the showcase, adding some newly acquired verdigrised brass army buttons from assorted regiments to the erratic lines of plastic, mother-of-pearl and enamel buttons in the display. He was becoming rather impatient because the loops on the backs of the army buttons meant that they just wouldn't lie flat on the baize-covered backing board however hard he pressed down on them. He exhaled with sheer frustration and, hearing a car horn sounding in the road outside, happened to glance up.

Out of the corner of his eye, he caught sight of a man on the opposite side of the road walking towards the High Street. He wore a flat cap, a long coat and, although the day was distinctly overcast with only intermittent glimpses of the sun, a pair of dark glasses. It might easily have been the man he had bumped into outside the newsagents, but he couldn't be sure as they all looked so similar.

"Right," he decided, "as good a time as any."

He put down the box of buttons and hurried through the museum to the main door, which he locked behind him. As he stepped outside onto the street, he located the man up ahead, walking with, the strange gliding gait that he was now so familiar with and, at a respectable distance, followed him into the High Street, where the man's pace did not abate.

As Dr Burrows followed some way behind, the man turned

left down Disraeli Street, then crossed the road and took the first right into Gladstone Street past the old convent. Dr Burrows was about 50 feet behind him when, before he knew it, the man drew to a sudden halt and turned to look directly at him. Dr Burrows felt a tremor of fear as he saw the sky reflecting off the man's glasses and, sure the game was up, averted his gaze for an instant in an attempt to portray a picture of nonchalance. When he looked back again, the man had vanished.

His eyes frantically scanning up and down the street, Dr Burrows began to walk briskly, then broke into a run as he neared the spot where he had last seen his quarry. As he reached it, he noticed a narrow entrance between two of the small almshouses. It had an arched opening and ran like a narrow tunnel until it reached the back of the houses where the alleyway continued, uncovered. As Dr Burrows peered in, the lack of daylight in the passage made it difficult to see just what was there. Beyond that, he could make out something at the far end. It was a wall. The back of a building, in fact, cutting off the alleyway altogether. A dead end.

Checking the street one last time, he shook his head in disbelief. There was definitely no sign of the man in the alleyway, so he took a deep breath and started down it. He cautiously picked his way, wary that the man might be lying in wait in an unseen doorway. As his eyes adjusted to the shadows, he could make out soggy cardboard boxes and milk bottles, mostly broken, scattered across the cobblestones.

He was relieved when he emerged back into the light again and paused to survey the scene. The alleyway was formed by garden walls to the left and right, and at its far end was a three-storey building, an old factory which, from its architecture, Dr Burrows guessed dated from the 1950s. The floor of the alleyway was an obstacle course of empty dustbins, the innards of a tumble drier that someone had evidently tried to dismantle, and a couple of old televisions.

He threaded his way through all this until he reached the factory wall, which, having no windows until its uppermost storey, couldn't have provided the man with any means of escape.

"So where in the blazes did he go?" thought Dr Burrows as he turned and looked down the length of the alleyway, through the covered portion to the street, where a car flashed by. To his right, the garden wall had a three-foot trellis running along it, which would have made it almost impossible for the man to climb over. The other wall had no such encumbrance, so Dr Burrows walked up to it and peered over. It was a garden of sorts, neglected and barren, with a few tawdry shrubs and a stretch of muddy ground where the lawn should have been – this was peppered with faded plastic dishes containing dark green water.

Dr Burrows gazed helplessly into the private wasteland and, for a moment, looked as if he was about to turn away and forget the whole thing when, quite unexpectedly, he lobbed his briefcase over the wall and rather awkwardly clambered after it. The drop was greater than he expected and he landed badly, in a sitting position on the mud. He tried to get up, but his shoes lost their purchase and he sat back down again, his outstretched hand managing to flip one of the dishes of algae-water up his arm and neck. He swore silently and brushed as much of it off as he could and then rose to his feet again, stumbling and flailing like a drunken man until he regained his balance.

"Damn, damn and damn!" he said through clenched teeth as he heard a door open behind him.

"Hello? Who's that? What's going on?" came an apprehensive voice.

Dr Burrows wheeled around to face an old lady who was standing not five feet away, with three cats around her feet watching him with feline indifference. The old lady's sight was apparently not good from the way she was moving her head from side to side. She had wispy white hair and wore a floral housecoat. Dr Burrows took her to be at least in her eighties.

"Er ... Roger Burrows, pleased to meet you," Dr Burrows said, not able to think of anything more inventive at such short notice to explain his unorthodox means of entry. The expression of concern on the old lady's face was all at once transformed.

"Oh, Dr Burrows, how very kind of you to drop by. What a nice surprise."

Dr Burrows was surprised, and not a little confused. "Yes, er ... well ... I happened to be passing this way."

"So very courteous of you. Something you don't see much of these days. It's very nice of you to call."

"Oh, not at all," he replied hesitantly. "My pleasure entirely."

"Gets a bit lonely with just my pussycats for company. Would you care for some tea? The kettle's on the boil."

Dr Burrows was floundering – he'd anticipated having to make a quick getaway over the wall when he first saw her. This reception of such hospitality and warmth was the last thing he expected. Lost for words, he simply nodded and, stepping forward, his shoe caught the rim of another food dish, which flipped its contents up his leg. He stooped to wipe a slimy gob of algae from his sock.

"Do be careful, Dr Burrows," the old lady said. "I put those out for the birds." She turned, her entourage of cats darting before her into the kitchen. "Milk and sugar?"

"Please," Dr Burrows said, standing outside the kitchen door as she bustled around inside, getting a teapot down from a shelf.

"This is very kind of you," Dr Burrows said, in an attempt to fill the silence.

"Not at all, it's you, who is very kind. I should be thanking you."

"Yes?" he stuttered, still frantically trying to work out exactly who the old lady was.

"Yes, for your very nice letter. Can't see as well as I used to, but Mr Embers read it to me."

Suddenly it all fell into place and Dr Burrows sighed with relief, the fog of confusion blown away by the cool breeze of realisation.

"The sphere! It *was* an intriguing object, Mrs Tantrumi."

"Oh good, dear."

"Mr Embers probably told you I need to get it checked."

"Yes," she said, "Don't want everyone to become radio-controlled, do we?"

"No," said Dr Burrows, trying not to smile, "wouldn't do at all. Mrs Tantrumi, the reason I dropped in ..."

"Yes?" she said, stirring the teapot.

"Well, I was rather hoping you could show me where you found it," he said.

"Oh no, dear, wasn't me – it was the gas men. Shortbread or a custard cream?" she said, holding up an old tin.

"Er ... shortbread, please. You said the gas men found it?"

"Yes, just inside the basement."

"Through here?" Dr Burrows asked, looking at an open door at the bottom of a short flight of steps. "Mind if I take a look?" he said, pocketing the shortbread as he began to negotiate the mossy brick steps to the basement.

Once inside the doorway, he could see that the basement was divided into two rooms. The first was empty, save for plastic dishes of extremely dark and desiccated cat food, and loose rubble strewn across the floor. He crunched through to the second room, which lay beneath the front of the house. It was much the same as the first, except that it was darker and had an upright piano in one corner, which looked as if it was falling apart from the damp, and, in a shadowy recess, an old wardrobe with a broken mirror. He opened one of its doors and was immediately struck by the same musty odour he had smelt on the man in the street and latterly in the duct at Penny Hanson's house. Inside were several overcoats – black, as far as he could make out – and an assortment of flat caps and other headwear stacked in a compartment on one side.

Remarkably, the interior of the wardrobe didn't feel gritty to the touch, unlike everything else in the vicinity, which was covered with a fine layer of dust. In addition, when he rocked it away from the wall to check if there was anything behind it, the wardrobe itself appeared to be in surprisingly good shape. Finding nothing there, he turned his attention once again to its interior. Beneath the hat compartment, he found a small drawer which he slid open. Inside, there were five or six pairs of glasses. Taking one of these and pulling an overcoat from its hanger, he made his way back out into the light.

"Mrs Tantrumi," he called from the bottom of the steps. She waddled to the kitchen door. "Did you know there's quite a few things in a wardrobe down here?"

"Are there?"

"Yes, some old coats and sunglasses. Are they yours?"

"No, hardly ever go down there myself. The ground's too uneven. Do bring them closer so I can see."

He went to the kitchen door, and she reached out and ran her fingers over the material of the overcoat as if she was stroking the head of an unfamiliar cat. Heavy and waxy to the touch, the coat felt strange to her. The cut was old-fashioned, with a shoulder cape of heavier material.

"I can't say I've ever seen it before. My husband, God rest his soul, may have left it down there," she said dismissively and returned into the kitchen.

Dr Burrows inspected the dark glasses. They consisted of two pieces of thick and absolutely flat, almost opaque glass, similar to welders' goggles, with curious spring mechanisms on the arms either side – evidently to keep them snug against the wearer's head. He was puzzled. Why would the strange people keep their belongings in a forgotten wardrobe in an empty basement?

"Does anyone else come here, Mrs Tantrumi?" he said to Mrs Tantrumi as she stirred the teapot.

"I don't know what you mean," she said, looking confused.

"Just that I've seen some rather odd characters around this part of town – always wearing big coats and sunglasses, like these." Dr Burrows tailed off, as the old lady was looking so worried.

"Oh, I hope they aren't those criminal types one hears about. I don't feel safe here any more – Oscar is so very kind, though. He visits me most afternoons, as I don't have anyone close by, any family. My son went to America, you see. The firm he works for moved him and his wife ..."

"So you haven't seen any people in these sort of coats – men with white hair?"

"No, dear, can't say I know what you're talking about." She looked enquiringly at him and then began to pour the tea. "Do come in and sit down."

"I'll just put these back," Dr Burrows said, returning to the basement. Before he left, he couldn't resist a quick inspection of the piano, lifting the cover and pressing a few keys that either gave dull clunks or completely detuned twangs. He tried to pull it away from the wall, but it creaked and threatened to fall apart, so he stopped. Then he walked around both basement rooms and, hoping to find a trapdoor, clumped his feet over the ground. He did the same in the small garden, stamping around the lawn whilst trying to avoid the plastic dishes, all the time watched curiously by Mrs Tantrumi's cats.

───◄●►───

On the other side of town, Chester and Will were once again back in the Forty Pits tunnel.

"So what did he say?" Chester asked as Will used a mallet and coal chisel to loosen the mortar between the bricks in the unidentified structure.

"We looked at the maps again and there's nothing on them," Will lied, as his father had not emerged from the cellar all night. "No water mains, sewers or anything on this plot. This brickwork is pretty tough, you know – this thing was built to last."

Will had already removed two layers of bricks, but hadn't broken through yet.

"Look, if it is water or sewage on the other side, under pressure, just make sure you get to the far side of the main chamber, and the flow should carry you up to the entrance," Will said, renewing his efforts on the brickwork.

"What?" Chester asked quickly. "A flow ... carry me up? I don't like the sound of that. I'm off." He turned and began to walk away with an anxious expression on his face as Will determinedly set about chiselling around another brick, chipping away at the wedge of mortar at its edge. Without warning, part of the mortar exploded with a high pneumatic hiss, and a chunk of it shot straight past Will's gloved hands like a stone bullet and struck the tunnel wall behind him. He dropped his tools and fell back on the ground in astonishment. Shaking his head, he pulled himself together and set about the task of removing the brick, which accomplished in seconds.

"Oh Chester!" Will called.

"What?" Chester shouted from the cavern. "What is it?"

"There's no water!" Will shouted back, his voice echoing oddly. "Come and see."

Chester returned unenthusiastically to find Will had indeed penetrated the wall, and was holding his face up to the small breach he'd made and sniffing at the air.

"It's definitely not a sewage pipe, but it *was* under pressure," Will said.

"Could it be a gas pipe?"

"Nope, doesn't smell like it and, anyway, they weren't made of brick. Judging by the echo, it's quite a large space." His eyes flashed with anticipation. "Just knew we were onto something. Fetch me a candle and the iron rod from the main chamber, will you?"

After Chester had returned with the items, Will lit the candle a good distance back from the breach and then carried it slowly before him, nearer and nearer the opening, watching the flame intently with every step he took.

"What does that do?" Chester asked as he looked on in fascination.

"If there are any gases you'd notice a difference in the way it burns," Will answered matter-of-factly. "They did this when they cracked open the pyramids." There was no change in the flickering flame as he brought it closer, then held it directly in front of the opening. "Looks like we're clear," he said as he blew the flame out and immediately reached for the iron rod

Chester had leant against the tunnel wall. He lined it up carefully with the breach and then rammed the 10 foot pole through, pushing it all the way in until only a foot protruded from between the bricks.

"It hasn't hit anything – it's pretty big …" he said excitedly as he let the pole pivot down through the gap to check the depth. "… but I think I can feel the floor. Right, let's widen this a bit more."

They worked together and, within moments, had removed enough bricks for Will to slither through headfirst. He landed with a muffled groan.

"You okay?" Chester called.

"Yes. Just a bit of a drop," Will replied. "Come in feet first and I'll guide you down."

Chester made it through after a tremendous struggle – his shoulders being broader than Will's. Once he was in, they both began to look around.

It was an octagonal chamber, with each of its eight walls arching up to a central point about 20 feet above their heads. At its apex was what appeared to be a carved stone rose. They shone their torches in a hushed reverence, taking in the Gothic beading set into the perfectly laid brickwork. The floor was also constructed from bricks laid end on end.

"Awesome!" Chester whispered. "Who'd have ever expected to find anything like this?"

"It's like the crypt of a church, isn't it, but," Will said, "the strangest thing …"

"Yes?" Chester shone his torch at Will.

"It's absolutely bone dry. And the air's sort of sharp, too. I'm not sure …"

"Have you seen this, Will?" Chester interrupted, now flicking his torch around the floor and then over the wall nearest him. "There's something written on the bricks."

Will immediately studied the wall closest to him. "You're right. They're names: James Hobart, Andrew Kellogg, William Smith, John Ditwell … " Will said quietly, reading the elaborate Gothic script carved into the face of every brick.

"Simon Gray, Daniel Lethbridge, Silas Samuels, Abe Winterbotham, Caryll Pickering … there must be thousands in here," Chester said.

Will pulled his mallet from his belt and began to knock on the walls, taking soundings to see if there was any sign of a hollow or adjoining passage. After he had methodically tapped away at two of the eight walls, he suddenly stopped and clapped his hand to his forehead, swallowing hard.

"Do you feel that?" he asked Chester.

"Yeah, my ears popped. It's like pressure," Chester agreed, sticking a gloved finger roughly into one of them. "Like when you take off in a plane."

They were both silent, as if waiting for something to happen. Then they felt a tremor, an inaudible tone, somewhat akin to a low note played on an organ – a throb was building, seemingly in their skulls themselves.

"I think we should get out." Chester looked at his friend blankly, swallowing now not because of his ears, but due to the waves of nausea welling up inside him.

For once, Will did not disagree. "Okay," he said, blinking as spots appeared before his eyes.

They both clambered through the gap in double-quick time, then made their way to the armchairs in the cavern and slumped in them. Although they had said nothing of it to each other at the time, the strange sensations had ceased almost immediately they were outside the chamber.

"What *was* that in there?" Chester asked.

"I don't know," Will replied. "I'll get my Dad to come and see it – he might have an explanation. Must be a pressure build-up or something."

"But do you think it's a crypt, from where a church once stood … with all those names?"

"Maybe," Will replied, lost in thought. "But somebody, craftsmen, built this very carefully – not even leaving any off-cuts or rubbish behind as they went, and then just as carefully sealed it up. Why on earth would they go to all that trouble?"

"I didn't think of that. You're right."

"And no doors. There wasn't even a sign of any connecting passages. A self-contained chamber with names, like some sort of memorial?" Will pondered, completely foxed. "What are we on to here?"

CHAPTER EIGHT

Having learnt that Rebecca could be very unforgiving, and that it was really not worth incurring her wrath, not before mealtimes, at any rate, Will stamped the worst of the mud from his clothes before bursting in through the front door. Slinging his rucksack to the floor, the tools still clattering against each other, he froze with astonishment.

A very odd scene greeted him. The door to the sitting room was *closed* and, crouched down beside it, Rebecca had her ear pressed to the keyhole. She frowned the moment she saw him.

"What …?" Will's question was cut short as she rose swiftly, shushing him with a forefinger to her lips. She seized her bemused brother by the arm and pulled him forcibly into the kitchen.

"What's going on?" Will asked in an indignant whisper, turning his head to look at the sitting room door again. The remarkable fact that the door was closed seemed to trouble him more than having caught his sister in the act of snooping. "That door has been wedged open for as long as I can remember," he said. "You know how she hates …"

"They're arguing!" Rebecca said momentously.

"They're *what*? About *what*?"

"I'm not sure. The first thing I heard was Mum shouting at him to shut the door, and I was just trying to hear more when you barged in."

"You must have heard something."

"They've been arguing in low voices and, I mean, it must be important – she's missing *Neighbours*."

"How do you know she's not videoing it?" Will asked mischievously.

"There's nothing funny about this, Will, this is serious," Rebecca said.

He opened the fridge and idly inspected a yogurt before putting it back. "So what could it be about then ... any idea? I don't remember them ever doing this before."

"Well, there was one time," Rebecca corrected him. "When Dad forgot to call into the TV rental shop and Mum missed ..."

"But that was ages ago," Will said. "Anyway, I'm starving – is it ready yet?" he said, looking at the oven.

Just then the sitting room door was slung open, making both Will and Rebecca jump, and Dr Burrows stormed out, his face bright red and his eyes thunderous as he made a beeline straight for the cellar door opposite in the hall. Fumbling with his key and muttering incomprehensibly under his breath, he unlocked it and then slammed it after him.

Will and Rebecca were still looking around the corner of the kitchen door when they heard their mother shouting.

"YOU'RE GOOD FOR NOTHING, YOU BLOODY FOSSIL! YOU CAN STAY DOWN THERE AND ROT FOR ALL I CARE, YOU STUPID OLD RELIC!" she shrieked as she slammed the sitting room door with an almighty crash.

"That can't be good for the paintwork," Will said distantly.

"Stop it, Will," Rebecca said anxiously. "Something's terribly wrong. Take it from me, I know these things. Mum and Dad don't do this." She pulled herself away from the view of the sitting room door to check the oven.

"It's all a bit of a bore, really. I need to talk to him about the excavation – we found something today," Will said.

"You can forget that! You won't see either of them tonight, and my advice is just stay out of the way until things blow over," Rebecca said, shaking her head in disapproval. "If you want some fodder, help yourself – it's in the cooker. Help yourself to the lot. I've lost my appetite." Will's face lit up for the first time that evening. "You know, you're as bad as your Dad, no feelings!" she snapped, and abruptly walked out of the kitchen, leaving her brother looking from the empty doorway where she'd been to the oven, then back to the doorway again.

He wolfed down two and a half of the oven-ready meals and made his way up the stairs in the now uncannily quiet house. There weren't even the strains of the television coming from the sitting room below as he carefully polished his spade with a cloth until it gleamed, reflecting abstract forms on the ceiling above him. Then he laid it on the floor beside his bed and, switching off the light on his bedside table, slipped under the duvet.

CHAPTER NINE

Will woke with a lazy yawn, smacking his lips together noisily. He looked blearily around the room and, noticing the light creeping around the edges of the curtains and the surprising lack of the usual morning hubbub in the house, sat up sharply as it dawned on him that something was not quite right. He glanced at his alarm clock. He had overslept. The events of last night had completely thrown him and he had forgotten to set it. He found some relatively clean articles of his school uniform in the bottom of his wardrobe and, quickly dressing, went across to the bathroom for a perfunctory round of toothbrushing. He followed this with some half-hearted haircombing, to dislodge the traces of mud and clay that stubbornly adhered to his white fringe.

Emerging from the bathroom, he saw that the door to Rebecca's room was open and paused outside to listen for a moment. He had learnt not to blunder straight in; this was her inner sanctum, and she had berated him for entering unannounced several times before. As there were no signs of life, he cautiously ventured in. It was as spotless as ever – her bed immaculately made and her casual clothes laid out in readiness for her return from school – everything clean and shipshape and in its place. He spotted her little matt black alarm clock on her bedside table. "Why didn't she get me up?" he thought to himself.

He then saw that his parents' door was ajar, and couldn't resist putting his head around the corner. The bed hadn't been slept in. This was not right at all. His father always left the house just before him in the mornings, but his mother never got up until everyone else had gone.

Where were they? Will reflected on the previous evening's argument between his parents, the gravity of which now began to sink in. Contrary to what his sister thought, Will did have a sensitive side. It wasn't that he didn't care, he just found it difficult to show his emotions. He simply preferred to hide his feelings and self-doubt either behind a show of flippant bravado, where his family were concerned, or a mask of total indifference, where other people were involved. It was a defence mechanism he'd developed over the years to cope with the sporadic outbreaks of taunting about his appearance. *Never show your feelings, never react to their mindless jabbering, never give them the pleasure.*

To an outsider, it would have appeared that the Burrows household was unusual, to say the least. To most people, it would have seemed chaotic. All four occupants were quite different, like four strangers thoughtlessly thrown together by circumstances beyond their control but, somehow, it had always worked well; each knew their place and the end result, if not entirely happy, was at least harmonious. After all, it was the only way of life that Will and his sister had ever known, so they didn't think to question it. But now the mechanism was whirring madly, a flywheel had become egocentric, and the whole thing was in danger of destroying itself, of coming crashing down. At least that's how it felt to Will that morning.

As he tiptoed downstairs, he had the oddest feeling of being an intruder in his own home. He glanced at the sitting room door. It was still closed. Mum must have slept in there, he thought as he went into the kitchen. On the table was a single bowl and, from the few remaining Rice Krispies clinging to the spoon and sides, he could tell that his sister had already had her breakfast and left for school. The fact that she hadn't cleared up after herself, and the absence of his father's cornflake bowl and teacup on the table or in the sink, rang vague alarm bells in his head. This frozen snapshot of everyday activity had become the clue to a mystery, like the little pieces of evidence at a crime scene that, if read in the right way, would give him the answer to what exactly was going on. By the simple absence of his family, the mundane had been transformed into something far more sinister, into an eerie, silent tableau that he now studied as he tried to make sense of the situation.

But it was no good. There were no answers here, and he realised he should be on his way.

"This is like a bad dream," he muttered to himself as he hastily poured his Weetos into a bowl. "Total cave-in," he added, crunching on the cereal.

CHAPTER TEN

An hour had gone by, and the thrill of being alone in the cavern had paled. As Chester lolled in one of the two broken-down armchairs in the Forty Pits tunnel, he formed yet another little marble of clay between his fingertips, adding it to the growing pile on the table next to him. He then began to aim them half-heartedly, one after another, at the neck of an empty Volvic bottle that he had balanced precariously on the rim of a nearby wheelbarrow.

Will was long overdue and, as Chester threw the little projectiles, he wondered what could have possibly got in the way of his friend's arrival. This alone wasn't of great concern, but he was anxious to tell Will what he'd discovered when he had first entered the excavation.

When Will finally appeared, he walked at a snail's pace down the incline of the entrance tunnel, his shovel resting on his shoulder and his head hung low.

"Hi Will," Chester said brightly, as he lobbed a whole handful of the clay balls at the defiant bottle. All of them, predictably, failed to hit the mark. There was a moment of disappointment before Chester turned to Will for a response. But Will merely grunted and, when he did look up, Chester was disturbed by the marked lack of sparkle in his friend's eyes. All that infectious enthusiasm was gone and in its place was an uncharacteristic emptiness. Chester had noticed something wasn't right over the past couple of days at school – Will seemed to be avoiding him, and when Chester had caught up with him, his friend had been withdrawn and non-communicative.

An uneasy silence grew between them in the chamber until Chester, unable to stand it any longer, blurted out, "There's a block …"

"My Dad's gone," Will interrupted sharply.

"What?"

"He locked himself in the cellar, but now we think he's gone."

Suddenly it became clear to Chester why his friend's behaviour had been odder than usual. He opened his mouth and then shut it again. He had no idea how to respond.

"Becky says we shouldn't worry, that he's just in a strop and will come back," Will said as he slunk down, as if exhausted, into the closest armchair. "But it's not like him. He wouldn't do that, not without saying *something*."

"When did this happen?" Chester asked awkwardly.

"Couple of days ago – he had some sort of row with Mum."

"What does she think?"

"Hah, nothing! She hasn't said a word to us for days," Will said.

Chester glanced at the tunnel branching off the chamber and then at Will, who was contemplatively rubbing a smear of dried mud from the shaft of his spade. Chester took a deep breath and spoke hesitantly. "I'm sorry, but ... there's something else you should know."

"What's that?" Will said quietly.

"The tunnel's blocked."

"What?" Will said, his eyes instantly filling with fiery enthusiasm once more as he leapt out of the armchair and dashed into the mouth of the tunnel. Sure enough, the entrance into the peculiar brick room was impassable – in fact, only half of the 20 foot passage still remained.

"I don't believe it." Will stared helplessly at the tightly packed barrier of soil and stone, which reached right up to the roof of the tunnel, making it completely impassable. He tested the props and stays immediately in front of it, tugging at them with both hands and kicking their bases with the steel toecap of his work boot. "Nothing wrong with those," he said, squatting down to test several areas of the spoil from the pile with his palms. He cupped his hand, scooped up some of the earth and examined it as

Chester watched with admiration for the way his friend was investigating the scene.

"Weird."

"What is?" Chester asked.

Will held the earth up to his nose and sniffed it deeply. Then, discarding the rest of the soil, he rolled a pinch of it between his fingers.

"What's up, Will?"

"The props further into the tunnel were completely secure – I gave them a once-over before we left last time. There hasn't been any rain recently, has there?"

"No, I don't think so," Chester replied.

"No, and this earth doesn't feel nearly damp enough to cause the roof to slip in – there's no more moisture than you'd expect. But the weirdest thing is all this." He reached down, plucked out a chunk of stone from the pile and tossed it over to Chester, who caught and examined it with a bewildered expression.

"I'm sorry, I don't understand. What's important about this?"

"It's limestone. This infill has limestone chips in it. Feel the surface of the rock. It's chalky – totally the wrong texture for sandstone. That's particulate."

"Particulate?" Chester asked.

"Yes, more grainy. Hang on, let me check to make sure I'm right," Will said as he produced his penknife and, with the largest blade, picked at the clean face of another piece of the rock, all the while talking. "You see, they're both sedimentary rocks, and look pretty much the same. Sometimes it's quite hard to tell the difference. The tests you can use are to drop acid on it (which makes limestone fizz) or look at it with a magnifying glass to see the coarser quartz grains you only get in sandstones, but this is the best method, by far."

"Here we go," Will said as he took a minute flake of the stone he'd prised from the sample and, to Chester's amazement, slipped it off the blade and into his mouth. Then he began to nibble it between his front teeth.

"What *are* you doing, Will?"

"Mmmm," Will replied contemplatively, still biting it, "Yes, I'm pretty sure this is limestone … it breaks down into a smooth paste … if it was sandstone, it'd be crunchier and squeak as I bit down on it."

Chester winced slightly as he heard the sounds coming from his friend's mouth. "Are you serious? Doesn't that knacker your teeth?"

"Hasn't yet," Will grinned. He reached between his teeth to reposition the flake and chewed on it for a little longer. "Definitely limestone," he finally decided, spitting out the flake of rock. "Want to try?"

"No, that's okay," Chester replied quickly.

Will waved his hand in the direction of the roof above the cave-in, "I don't believe there'd be a deposit, a pocket of it above here – I know the geology of this area pretty well."

"So what are you saying?" Chester asked. "Someone came down here and blocked up the tunnel with this stuff?"

"I don't know," Will said, kicking the edge of the huge heap in frustration.

"You don't think it might've been some of the Clan?" Chester asked, then added, "Or even the Click?"

"No, that's not likely. There'd be other signs. No one's been through the entrance with enough material to do this, especially not them. And why would they just block up this tunnel? They would've wrecked the whole excavation. No, it doesn't make sense," he said, bemused.

"No," Chester echoed.

"Someone really didn't want us to go back into there, did they?" Will said.

⟡

Rebecca was in the kitchen doing her homework when Will returned home. He was just slotting his spade in the umbrella stand and hanging his yellow hard hat on the end of it, when she called to him from around the corner.

"You're back early."

"Yeah, we had some trouble in one of the tunnels and I couldn't be bothered to do any digging," he said as he sat down at the table next to her.

"No digging?" Rebecca said, looking alarmed. "Don't you go to pieces on me as well."

"I can't figure out what happened. It couldn't be seepage, and the really odd thing was that the infill ..." he tailed off as Rebecca rose from the table and busied herself at the kitchen sink, clearly not listening to him any more. "You don't think he's in trouble down there, do you?" he asked, as the thought occurred to him.

"Who?" Rebecca said distantly, washing a saucepan.

"Dad. Because it's been so quiet, we've all assumed he's gone somewhere, but he could still be in the cellar. What if he's ill or something? If he hasn't eaten for two days, he might have collapsed." Will rose from his chair. "I'm going to take a look," he said decisively to Rebecca's back.

"Can't do that. No way," she said as she spun around to face him. "You know he doesn't like us to go down there without him."

"I'm going to get the spare key." With that, he left the room, leaving Rebecca standing by the sink, clenching her fists in her yellow Marigolds.

He reappeared in the doorway seconds later. "Well, are you coming or not?"

As Rebecca stood hesitantly in front of the sink and failed to answer, a flash of anger suffused Will's face. "Okay, okay," she eventually replied with a resigned tone, snapping off her gloves.

They went to the cellar door and, so their mother wouldn't hear, unlocked it very quietly. They needn't have worried, because the sound of a barrage of gunfire was coming thick and fast from behind her door.

Will turned on the light and they descended the varnished oak stairs that he had helped his father fix into place. As they stood on the grey painted concrete floor, they both looked around the room in silence. There was no sign of Dr Burrows. The room was crammed with his belongings, just as Will and Rebecca remembered it. His extensive library covered two walls, and on another were shelves housing his "personal" finds, including a railwayman's lamp, the ticket machine from the disused railway station and a careful arrangement of primitive little clay heads with clumsy features. Against the fourth wall stood his workbench, on which his computer sat, with a half-finished Curly Wurly in front of it.

As they surveyed the scene, the only thing that seemed out of place was a wheelbarrow filled with earth and small rocks by the door to the garden.

"What's that doing here?" Rebecca asked.

"I saw him taking a load out to the Common one night."

"When was that?"

"Couple of weeks back," Will replied. "I suppose he might have brought this in for analysis or something." He reached into the wheelbarrow, rubbed the soil between his fingers and smelt it. "High clay content," he observed, and shoved both hands deep into the soil, grabbing two large handfuls. He turned to Rebecca with a quizzical expression.

"What?" she said impatiently.

"I was just wondering where this could have come from," he said, letting it fall through his fingers back into the wheelbarrow.

"What are you going on about? He's obviously not here, and none of this is going to help us find him," Rebecca said, with such finality that Will was left speechless. "I'm going back upstairs." She flounced up the wooden stairs and shut the door behind her.

Lost in thought, he rubbed his hands together to get the soil off, then stood motionless in the centre of the room until his inquisitiveness got the better of him. He went over and sat at the bench, flicking casually through the papers on top of it. There were photocopied articles about Highfield, faded sepia tones of old houses and tatty sections of maps. One of these caught his eye – comments had been scribbled on it in pencil. He recognised his father's spidery handwriting.

"*Martineau Square – the key? Ventilation for what?*" he read, frowning as he traced the network of lines drawn around each side of the four terraces. "What's he up to?"

Looking under the bench, he found his father's briefcase and emptied out its contents, mostly magazines and newspapers, onto the bench top. In a side pocket of the briefcase, he found some loose change in a small brown paper bag and a clutch of empty sweet wrappers that brought an affectionate smile to his face. Then he crouched down under the bench and started to thumb through the archive boxes that were stored there.

His search was cut short by his sister calling quietly from the top of the cellar stairs that supper was ready. Before making his way upstairs, he made a short detour over to the back door to check the coats hanging there.

Back up in the hall, he passed a cacophony of applause and laughter from behind the closed door and went into the kitchen.

"Good thing we don't want to watch TV, isn't it?" he said to Rebecca, who had put their food out on the kitchen table.

"Don't be so bloody heartless," she replied curtly. "Poor old Mum, she's really going through it. I'm sure I heard her crying when I got home."

The two of them ate in silence until Will looked up at her. She had a fork in one hand and a pencil in the other as she did her maths homework.

"Becky, have you seen Dad's hard hat or overalls?"

"No, he keeps them in the cellar. Why?"

"You haven't seen them anywhere else, have you? In the wardrobe upstairs?"

"No, he never puts them there," she said categorically, and although she hadn't finished yet, took her plate over to the sink and scraped the uneaten food into the bin. "They're bound to be down in the cellar somewhere."

"There's no sign of them," Will said pensively.

"Well ... shouldn't we tell Mum they're gone?" she said, then suddenly added, "Will, you don't think he was working on a dig somewhere, and got ..."

"I know what you're thinking. No – he would've mentioned something to me. Besides, when would he have had a chance to go off on another excavation? He was always here or at the museum – he never went anywhere else, did he? Not without me knowing." Will tailed off as Rebecca watched him intently.

"I know that look. You've thought of something, haven't you?" she said suspiciously.

"No, it's nothing," he replied. "Really."

CHAPTER ELEVEN

The next day, Will awoke early and, having donned his work clothes, bounded energetically downstairs, thinking he would grab a quick breakfast and maybe link up with Chester to see if he was willing to excavate the blocked tunnel at the Forty Pits site. Rebecca was already lurking in the kitchen; it was obvious she had been waiting for him to appear and collared him the moment he turned the corner.

"It's up to us to do something about Dad, you know," she said, as Will looked at her with a slightly startled expression. "Mum's not going to do anything – she's given up."

Will just wanted to get out of the house; he was desperately trying to pretend to himself that everything was normal. Since the night of the argument between his parents, he and Rebecca had been getting themselves to school as usual. The only break from the norm was that they had been taking their meals in the kitchen without their mother. She had been stealing out to help herself to whatever was on offer in the fridge and had been eating it, predictably enough, in front of the television. Rebecca knew what she'd been up to because pies and chunks of cheese had gone missing along with whole loaves of bread and tubs of margarine.

They had seen her on a couple of occasions in the hallway as she shambled to the lavatory in her nightie and her slippers with the backs trodden down. Although she acknowledged them on these chance encounters with a slight nod, they had both been too wary of her to say anything.

"So what do you think then? Do I call the police or not?" Rebecca stood in front of the dishwasher, her arms crossed aggressively as she pressed her brother for a decision.

"I don't know. Anyway, where do you think he could have gone?" Will asked.

"Your guess is as good as mine," she answered sharply.

"I went by the museum yesterday and it was all shut up." It hadn't opened for days now – not that anyone had rung the house to complain.

"So maybe he's left Highfield?" Rebecca suggested.

"But why?"

"Adults do this. My friend Ella had it happen to her. Her parents argued because Ella's mum had a kiss on the cheek from her dad's best friend. That was it. Just a kiss, Ella said, and now her parents have gone their own ways."

"Because of a kiss?" Will said with a smirk. "It must have been a bit more than that."

"Whatever," Rebecca shrugged her slim shoulders. "But *we're* going to have to take the matter in hand now." She had often heard her father use the expression, and fell silent to give it full effect. "And we have to let Mum know what we're going to do."

"All right," Will concurred, looking longingly at his spade as they entered the hallway. He just wanted to get away from the house.

Rebecca knocked on the sitting room door and they both entered. Mrs Burrows did not avert her gaze from the inane interview with another manicured pop child on the television. They both stood there, unsure what to do next, until Rebecca went over to her mother's chair, took the remote from where it rested on the arm and turned the television off. Mrs Burrows' eyes did not move from the blank screen.

"Mum," Will said nervously. "Mum, we can't find Dad anywhere and ... it's four days now."

"We think we should call the police ..." Rebecca said, quickly adding, "...unless you know where he is?"

Their mother's eyes lowered from the screen to the VCRs below it, but they could both see that she wasn't focusing on anything, and that her expression was terribly sad. She suddenly looked very helpless; Will just wanted to ask her what was wrong, what had happened, but couldn't bring himself to. As they stood there, their hearts pounding, Will glanced at Rebecca, who looked as if she was about to burst into tears.

"Yes," Mrs Burrows replied softly. "If you want to." And that was it. She fell silent, her eyes still downcast, and so they both filed out of the room.

Rebecca had called the local police station and they arrived several hours later, a man and a woman, both in uniform. Will let them in.

"Rebecca Burrows?" the policeman asked, looking past Will into the house as he removed his hat and then took out a small notebook from his breast pocket and flipped it open. Just then, the radio on his lapel issued a burp of unintelligible speech and he slid the switch on its side to silence it. "Sorry 'bout that," he said.

The female PC spoke to Rebecca. "You made the call?"

Rebecca nodded in response, and the female PC gave her a comforting smile. "You mentioned your mother was here. Can we talk to her, please?"

"She's in here," Rebecca said, leading the way to the sitting room door and knocking lightly on it. "Mum," she said softly, opening the door for the two PCs and then standing to one side. Will started to follow them in, but the policeman turned to him.

"Tell you what, son, I could murder a cup of coffee."

As the policeman shut the door behind him, Will turned to Rebecca with an expectant look.

"Oh, all right," she said, stomping into the kitchen.

As they waited in the kitchen, they could hear the low drone of adult conversation coming from behind the door, until, several cups of coffee and what felt like an eternity later, the policeman emerged alone. He walked into the kitchen and placed his cup and saucer on the table next to them.

"I'm just going to have a dekko over the place," he said. "For clues," he added with a wink, and had left the kitchen and gone upstairs before either of them could react. They sat there, looking at the ceiling as they listened to his muffled footsteps moving from room to room on the floor above.

"What does he think he's going to find, exactly?" Will said. They heard him come down the stairs and walk around the ground floor and then he appeared back in the kitchen doorway. He fixed Will with a quizzical look.

"There's a basement, isn't there, son?"

Will escorted the policeman down into the cellar and stood at the bottom of the oak steps while he cast his eye over the room. He seemed particularly interested in Dr Burrows' exhibits.

"Unusual things your dad has. I suppose you've got receipts for all these?" he said, picking up one of the dusty clay heads. Noticing Will's startled expression, he continued, "Only joking. I understand he works in the local museum, doesn't he?"

Will nodded.

"I went there once on a school trip … oh, a long time ago." He noticed the earth in the wheelbarrow. "So what's that here for?"

"I don't know. Could be from a dig that Dad's been doing. We usually do them together."

"Digs?" he asked and Will nodded in reply.

"I think we'd better take a look outside now," the policeman said, looking at Will intently, his demeanour taking on a sternness that Will hadn't seen before.

In the garden, Will watched as he systematically searched the borders. Then he turned his attention to the lawn, crouching down every so often to examine the bald patches where one of their neighbour's cats was accustomed to relieve itself, so killing off the grass. Coming back into the house, he put his hand on Will's shoulder.

"Tell me, son, no one's been digging out there recently, have they?"

Will shook his head and they moved into the hall, where the policeman's eyes alighted on Will's gleaming spade in the umbrella stand.

Noticing his interest in his spade, Will tried to manoeuvre

himself between it and the policeman, to obstruct his view.

"Are you sure you haven't been digging in the garden?" the policeman asked again, staring at Will suspiciously.

"No, not for years," Will replied. "I dug a few pits on the Common when I was younger, but Dad put a stop to that – said someone might fall in."

"On the Common, eh? Big holes, were they?"

"Quite big. Didn't find anything much there, though."

The policeman looked at Will strangely and wrote in his notebook. "Much like what?" he asked with narrowed eyes.

"Oh, bottles and some old junk."

At that point, the policewoman came out of the sitting room and joined her colleague by the front door.

"All right?" he said to her, tucking his notebook back into his breast pocket with a last penetrating look at Will, which wasn't lost on Rebecca who had walked out of the kitchen.

"I got everything down," the policewoman replied, and then turned to face Will and his sister. "Look, I'm sure there's nothing to worry about but, as a matter of form, we'll make some enquiries about your father. If you hear anything or need to talk to us, about anything at all, you can contact us on this number." She handed Rebecca a printed card. "In many of these cases, the person just comes back – they just need to get away, some time to think things over." She gave them a reassuring smile and then added. "Or calm down."

"Calm down about what?" Rebecca ventured. "Why would Dad need to calm down?"

The policeman and woman both looked a little surprised, glancing at each other and then back at Rebecca.

"Well, after the disagreement with your mother," the policewoman said. Will and Rebecca were waiting for her to say more, to explain what the argument had been about, but she turned to the other officer. "Right, we'd better be off."

"Bloody adults! I told you they're all the same – live in a world of their own," Rebecca said in an exasperated tone, after she had shut the door behind them.

CHAPTER TWELVE

"Will? Is that you?" Chester said, shielding the sun from his eyes as his friend emerged from the kitchen door into the rather cramped back garden behind the Rawls' house. He had been whiling away the time that Sunday morning by swatting bluebottles and wasps with an old badminton racket, easy targets as they grew lazy in the noonday heat. He cut a comical figure, his oversize frame accentuated by baggy shorts, flip flops and a beanie hat, and his bare shoulders reddened by the sun.

Will stood with his hands in the back pockets of his jeans, looking a little preoccupied. "I need a hand with something," he said, checking behind him that Chester's parents weren't in earshot.

"Sure, what with?" Chester replied, flicking off the mutilated remains of a large fly stuck on the frayed strings of his racket.

"I want to take a look around the museum tonight," Will replied. "At my Dad's things."

"What, you mean break in?" Chester said quietly. "I'm not …"

"I have the keys," Will cut him short. "I just want to have a quick look and need somebody to watch my back."

Lowering his racket by his side, Chester thought for a moment as he gazed at the house and then back at Will. "Okay," he said, "but we'd better not get caught."

After it had grown dark, they stole up the museum steps. Will unlocked the door and they slipped quickly through. The interior was just visible in the zigzag shadows thrown by the interlacing bands of weak moonlight and the yellow neon of streetlamps outside.

"Follow me," Will whispered to Chester as, crouching low, they crossed through the main hall towards the corridor, dodging between the glass cabinets and grimacing as their trainers squeaked on the parquet flooring.

"Watch the ..."

"Ouch!" Chester cried, as he tripped over the marsh timber lying on the floor just inside the corridor and was sent sprawling. "What the hell's that doing there?" he said angrily as he rubbed his shin.

"Come on," Will whispered urgently.

Near the end of the corridor, they found Dr Burrows' office.

"We can use the torches in here, but keep your beam down low."

"What are we looking for?" Chester whispered.

"Don't know yet. Let's check his desk first," Will said in a hushed voice.

As Chester held his torch for him, Will sifted through the piles of papers and documents. It wasn't an easy task as Dr Burrows was clearly as disorganised at work as he was at home and there was a great deal of correspondence, receipts and other documents in four sizeable towers on the desk. The computer screen was all but obscured by a proliferation of curling yellow Post-it notes stuck around it. As they searched, Will focused his efforts on anything that was written on loose-leaf pages in his father's barely legible scrawl.

Finishing the last of the piles of papers, they found nothing of note, so they each took one side of the desk and set about the drawers.

"Wow, look at this." Chester produced what appeared to be a stuffed dog's paw fixed to an ebony stick from amongst a load of empty tobacco tins. Will simply looked at him and frowned briefly before resuming his search.

"Here's something!" Chester said excitedly as he was investigating the middle drawer. Will didn't bother to look up from the papers in his hand, thinking it was another obscure object.

"No, look, it's got a label with writing on it." He handed it to Will. It was a little book with covers of red-brown marbling and a sticker on the front that read *ex-libris* in ornate and swirling copperplate-like letters with a picture of an owl wearing massively round glasses.

"*Journal*?" Will said, "That's definitely my Dad's writing." He opened the cover. "Bingo! It looks like a diary of some sort." He fanned through the pages. "He's written something on quite a few of these." Pushing it into his bag, he asked, "Are there any others?"

They quickly searched the remainder of the drawers and finding nothing, decided it was time to leave. They made their way towards the Forty Pits, as it was close by and they knew they wouldn't be interrupted there. As they slunk through the streets, ducking behind cars when anyone appeared, they felt alive with the thrill of the forbidden mission at the museum, and couldn't wait to review the information they'd unearthed. They both hoped it might provide some clues as to Dr Burrows' whereabouts. Reaching the Pits, they descended into the main chamber, where they arranged the inspection lights and made themselves comfortable in the armchairs. Will began to pore over the pages.

"The first entry is not long after we discovered the lost train station," he said, looking up at Chester.

"What train station?"

But Will was too engrossed in the journal to explain. He recited slowly in broken sentences as he struggled to decipher his father's writing. "*I have recently become aware of a small and ... in ... incongruous grouping of interlopers coming and going amongst the general populace of Highfield. A group of people who have a physical appearance that sets them apart. Where they come from or what their purpose is I have yet to ascertain but, from my limited observation of them, I believe that all is not what it seems. Given their apparent numbers (5+?) ... homogeneity of their (racial?) appearance ... I suspect they may cohabit or at the very least ...*" He tailed off as he scanned the rest of the page. "I can't quite make out the rest," he said, looking up at Chester. "Here's something," he said, flicking the page over. "This is clearer."

"Today a rather intriguing and baffling artefact came into my possession by way of a Mr Embers. It may well be linked to these people, although I have yet to … substantiate this. The object is a small globe held in a cage of some type of metal, which, as at the time of writing, I have not been able to identify. The globe emits light of varying intensity depending on the degree of background illumination – what confounds me is that the relationship is directly inverse – the darker the surroundings, the brighter the light it emits. It defies any laws of physics or chemistry with which I am familiar."

Will held up the page so that Chester could see the rough sketch his father had made.

"Have you actually seen it?" Chester enquired. "This light thing?"

"No, he's kept all this to himself," Will replied. Turning the page, he began to read again. *"Today I had the opportunity to … scrutinise, albeit for a brief moment, one of the pallid men at close quarters."*

"Pallid? Like in pale?" Chester said.

"Don't ask me," Will answered, and then read out his father's description of the mysterious man. He went on to the episode with Pineapple Joe and the inexplicable duct in the house, and his father's thoughts and observations on the whole of Martineau Square. There followed a large number of pages debating the likely structure within the terraced houses that lined the square. Will leafed through these until he came to a photocopied extract from a book stapled into the journal.

"It says *Highfield's History* at the top of the page and it seems to be about someone called Sir Gabriel Martineau," Will said. *"Born in 1673, he was the son and heir of a successful dyer in Highfield. In 1699, he inherited the business, Martineau, Long & Co. from his father, and expanded it considerably, adding a further two factories to the original premises in Heath Street. He was known to be a keen inventor, and was widely recognised for his expertise in the fields of chemistry, physics and engineering. Indeed, although Hooke (1635-1703) is generally credited with being the architect behind what is essentially the modern air pump, there are a number of historians who believe that he built his first prototype using Martineau's drawings.*

In 1710, during a period of widespread unemployment, Martineau, a deeply religious man who was renowned for his philanthropism and paternal attitude towards his workforce, began to employ a substantial number of labourers to build dwellings for his factory workers, and personally designed and oversaw the construction of Martineau Square, which still stands today, and Grayston Villas, which was destroyed in the Blitz. Martineau soon became the largest employer in the Highfield district and it was rumoured that Martineau's Men (as they became known) were engaged in digging a substantial underground network of tunnels, although no evidence of these remain today.

In 1718, Martineau's wife contracted tuberculosis and died aged 32. Thereafter, Martineau sought solace by joining an obscure religious sect, and was rarely seen in public for the remaining years of his life. His home, Martineau House, which formerly stood on the edge of Highfield old town, was destroyed by a fire in 1733, in which Martineau and his two daughters were said to have perished."

Will looked up. "Did you know any of this?" Chester shook his head. "There's some more stuff on the next pages about these *pallid* men and then some pages have been torn out. The last entry," he said, flipping forward in the notebook, "is from Wednesday – the day of the argument."

"It is my intention to go through this very night – it is the next step and one I have to take. I hope I am able to complete this journal on my return." Will looked at Chester with a confused expression. "It ends there. What the blazes does that mean? What does he mean return? From where?"

Chester looked blank.

"You know, Chester, two things have been bugging me. First is, I saw him working on something at home very early one morning – 'bout a fortnight before he disappeared. I reckon he was digging on the Common ... but that doesn't stack up."

"Why?"

"Well, when I saw him, I'm sure he was pushing a barrow load of spoil *to* the Common, not *away* from it. Second thing is, I can't find his overalls or hard hat anywhere."

CHAPTER THIRTEEN

"Oi, snowflake, hear your old man has done a runner," a voice shouted at Will as soon as he entered the classroom. There was an immediate hush in the room as everyone turned to look at Will, who, gritting his teeth, sat down at his desk and started to take his books out of his bag.

Speed, a vicious, skinny kid with greasy black hair, was the self-appointed leader of a gang of similarly unpleasant characters. They were habitually to be found clumped together like a swarm of blackfly behind the bike sheds, where they would sneak off for cigarettes when the duty teacher's back was turned. They were known as "The Greys" due to the dirty clouds of smoke wafting around their heads like temporary shrouds as they huddled together, coughing nastily and trying to get through their cigarettes before they were caught in the act.

They all dressed in uniforms in a similar state of disorder with unfeasibly large tie knots, threadbare sweaters and crumpled shirts, half-tucked into baggy trousers. They had the appearance of a group of malnourished waifs that had been pulled out of the canal and then left in the wind to dry. And they were mouthy and obnoxious to anyone in the school unfortunate enough to cross their paths.

One of their more disagreeable turns was to surround an unsuspecting pupil and, like a pack of malevolent hyenas, frog-march him to the centre of the playground, where they would taunt and tease him until he broke down. Will had had the misfortune to witness one of these events, a terrified first former who, surrounded by Speed and his gang, had been forced to sing *Baa Baa Black Sheep* at the top of his voice, over and over again. This took place in front of a crowd of pupils transfixed by the spectacle with the same ghoulish fascination that compels a passer-by to look at the hapless victim of a bad car crash. As the petrified boy stumbled over the words until he was mouthing them soundlessly, Speed prodded him mercilessly in the ribs to make him resume again. A crowd of onlookers self-consciously sniggered and nudged each other in half-concealed relief that they'd been spared the same fate. Will had never forgotten the poor child choking over the words as he sobbed with fear. Now it was Will who was the target of Speed's unwanted attention.

"Can't blame him, can you? Probably got pissed off having a freak for a son," Speed sneered, his voice full of derision.

Hunched doggedly over his desk, Will pretended to search for a page in his textbook. His pulse raced and his face felt hot; he knew it would be betraying his anger. He just hoped that he wouldn't have to end up fighting Speed.

"Oi, Mr Whippy, I'm speaking to you! Are you or are you not fatherless? Are you or are you not a …"

The fury welled up inside Will and he suddenly stood up, his chair scraping on the wooden floor as it shot back and then toppled over. Will glared at Speed, who also rose from his desk, his face contorted with spiteful relish as he realised he'd hit home with his jibes. Simultaneously, three of the Greys behind Speed leapt excitedly out of their chairs with predatory glee.

"Has the Milky Bar Kid had enough?" Speed sneered, moving with a swagger between the desks towards Will, his snickering entourage in tow.

Clenching his fists by his side, Speed stood in front of Will. Although Will wanted to take a step back, he knew he had to stand his ground. He could smell the other boy's stale breath and see a fleck of spittle on his top lip nestling amongst the few black curls of bum fluff and adolescent acne.

Speed pushed his face even closer, so that it was inches away from Will's, and arched his back like a second-rate boxer.

"Well … have … you?" he said, emphasising each word with a finger jab at Will's chest.

"We've all had enough of you." Chester's ample bulk suddenly moved into view as he positioned himself behind Will. Speed glanced uneasily at him and then back at Will.

"I reckon the odds are a bit more even now, aren't they?" Chester continued. He examined his fingertips, looking self-composed and relaxed while Speed began to fume, his eyes watery with fury and frustration.

Knowing the whole class was watching him, and that the ball was in his court to make some sort of response, Speed could only think of hissing dismissively through his teeth. It was a lame attempt to save his pride and everyone knew it. Chester looked at him pityingly and then drew himself up, puffing his chest out like a sergeant major. With that, two of Speed's entourage deserted him, skulking back to their desks and leaving only the smallest Grey in attendance. Although he was a small, wiry boy who looked as though he should still be in short trousers, he was clearly up for a fight.

"Well, what are you going to do now with just a midget as back-up?" Chester smiled coldly at Speed.

Fortuitously, at that very moment the teacher entered, and realising what was afoot, cleared his throat loudly. It did nothing to deflate the stand-off between Will, Chester and Speed, so he walked over and ordered them to sit down in no uncertain terms.

Will and Chester took their places, leaving Speed still standing with his diminutive henchman hovering behind him. The teacher glowered at them and, after a few seconds, they skulked back to their desks. Will leant back in his chair and looked at Chester, nodding his thanks.

Returning from school later that day, Will crept into the house, taking pains not to alert his sister that he was home. Before he opened the cellar door, he paused in the hallway to listen. He heard the strains of "*You Are My Sunshine*"; Rebecca was doing the housework upstairs. He quickly descended into the cellar and unbolted the garden door where Chester was waiting patiently.

"Are you sure it's okay for me to be here?" he asked. "Doesn't feel right."

"Don't be daft, course it is," Will insisted. "Now, let's see if we can find anything down here."

They investigated the shelves, then went through the archive boxes. There efforts were unfruitful, so they stood looking around the room.

"That was a waste of time," Will said disconsolately.

"So where'd you think that came from?" Chester asked, pointing at the wheelbarrow.

"Haven't figured that out yet. I suppose we could have a shufty around the Common. See if he was up to something there."

"Big area," Chester said, unconvinced. "Anyway, why would he bring it down here?"

Will shrugged and looked over the bookshelves for one last time, noticing something at the side of one of the units.

"Hang on a minute, that's odd," he said as Chester ambled over.

"What is?"

"Well, there's a plug in a socket down here and I can't quite see where the cable goes. Hang on," he said as he switched the socket on and they both looked around the room; it didn't appear to have had any effect.

"What's it for, then?" Chester said.

"It's definitely not an outside light."

"Why's that?" Chester asked.

"Because we haven't got any," Will replied as he went to the other end of the shelves, peering into the dark corner between the two units, then stepping back and looking at the shelves thoughfully. "It doesn't seem to come out again on this side."

Taking the stepladder from beside the garden door, he set it up in front of the bookshelves and climbed up to inspect the top of the unit.

"No sign of it here, either," he said. "This just doesn't make sense." He was about to climb down when he stopped and ran his hand over the top of the shelves.

"Anything?" Chester asked.

"Load of brick dust," Will replied as he jumped down from the ladder and immediately tried to pull the end of the shelf unit away from the wall.

"There's definitely a bit of give. Come on, give me a hand," he said.

"Maybe it's just badly fixed on," Chester suggested.

"Badly fixed on?" Will said indignantly. "I helped put these up."

Then they both pulled together and, although a thin sliver opened up at the rear of the unit, the shelves appeared to be firmly secured at the top.

"Let me check something," Will said as he mounted the stepladder again. "There seems to be a loose nail lodged in this bracket." Will yanked it out and let it fall onto the concrete floor by Chester's feet. "We used screws to fix this onto the wall," he said, looking down at Chester with a bewildered expression.

Will jumped down from the ladder and they both pulled on the unit again. This time, shuddering and creaking, it swung out from the wall to reveal that it was hinged at one end.

"What has he been up to?" Will said, as both of them stared at the rough-hewn opening in the bottom half of the wall. The bricks had been removed to form a hole some three feet square. Inside, a passage was visible, illuminated by a motley array of old neon strip lights burning along its length.

"So that's where the cable goes."

"Wow!" Chester gasped, his face a picture of surprise.

Will smiled at Chester. "Well, looks like a hands-and-knees job." Before Chester had time to say anything, Will ducked into the passage and was crawling along it at a fair lick. "It seems to turn a corner here," came his muffled voice.

As Chester watched through the hole in the wall, he saw Will twist around and then sit down, his face disconsolate under the glow of the lights. "Oh no!" he heard Will say, followed by a sigh.

"What is it?" The blood drained from Chester's face. His first thought was that Will had discovered the body of his father there.

"The tunnel's blocked here. Cave-in," Will said.

"Oh," Chester said, visibly relieved.

Will scrambled back out of the passage and then through the hole in the wall and into the cellar again. He stood up and was taking his school blazer off when he noticed his friend's grim expression.

"What is it?"

"You don't think he's under all that, do you?" Chester said almost in a whisper, the horrific image rearing up in his mind. "He might have been … crushed," he added ominously.

Will looked away from his friend and thought for a moment. "Well, there's only one way to find out."

"Shouldn't we get the police?" Chester stammered, taken aback by his friend's detachment. But Will wasn't listening. His eyes had narrowed with the look of preoccupation that meant his mind was churning away, formulating a plan of action.

"You know, the infill is exactly the same as in the Pits tunnel – it's all wrong. There are lumps of limestone again," he said, rolling up his sleeves. "This is too much of a coincidence." He leant into the mouth of the passage. "And did you notice the props?" he said, running his hand over the ones just inside the opening. "This was no accident. This lot has been hacked at and pulled in on purpose."

Chester leant into the hole to look at the props, which had deep notches sliced in them and, in places, were almost cut right through, as if someone had been wielding an axe.

"God, you're right," he said.

Will rolled his sleeves up. "Better make a start, then. There's no time like the present." He ducked into the passage, dragging a bucket behind him that he'd found just inside the opening.

Chester looked down at his school uniform and opened his mouth to say something, but then thought better of it as he removed his blazer and hung it on the back of a chair.

CHAPTER FOURTEEN

"**G**o!" said Will in an urgent whisper, as he crouched low within the shadows of the hedgerow bordering the Common at the bottom of the garden.

Chester growled with the effort as he heaved the overloaded wheelbarrow into motion, and then weaved precariously between the trees and shrubs. Reaching the open ground, he lurched off to the right towards the gullies they were using to dump the spoil.

From the mounds of fresh earth and small cairns of rock already deposited there, it was evident to Will that his father had used these gullies for the very same purpose. On occasion, when fatigue was setting in and they couldn't face the 200 yard dash to the gullies, they would instead spread the contents of the wheelbarrow over the grassy inclines of the Common closer to home, kicking the soil around until it was sufficiently dispersed.

Will was keeping a watchful eye for any passers-by whilst Chester swiftly emptied out the barrow into the gully. As he deftly spun it about for the return journey, Will kicked in any large pieces of rock and clumps of soil and clay.

As they retraced their route back to the garden, the wheel on the old barrow began to squeal piercingly, as if complaining at the countless trips it had made. The noise cut through the peaceful calm of the balmy summer evening.

Both boys froze abruptly in their tracks, looking around to check whether the sudden squealing had attracted any attention from the nearby houses.

Chester leant forward, trying to catch his breath, his hands resting on his knees as Will squatted down to examine the offending wheel.

"We'll have to oil that bloody thing again."

"Duh, do you think so?" Chester said.

"I think you'd better carry it back," Will replied coldly as he straightened up.

A crestfallen look descended over Chester's face and his jaw dropped in utter disbelief. "You what?" he said loudly.

"Shh! Keep it down, will you? Come on then, I'll give you a hand," Will said as he took hold of the front of the barrow.

They lugged it the remaining distance, grunting and cursing beneath their breaths, and treading lightly as they crossed the back garden, then negotiated the small ramp down into the cellar.

"My turn at the face, I suppose," Will said as they both slumped down in exhaustion on the concrete floor, their backs against the wall.

Chester glanced at his watch. "Actually, I think I ought to be getting home, Will."

"Yeah, I suppose you're right," Will nodded, as Chester slowly got to his feet and began to gather his things, "See you tomorrow."

"Yep," Chester replied faintly, without even a look at Will as he shuffled out of the cellar by the garden door.

They went through this same ritual every evening after school. Will would very carefully open the garden door, without making a sound, to let Chester in. They would get changed and immediately begin working for two or three hours at a stretch. The excavation was particularly slow and torturous, not only because of the limited space in the tunnel and the fact that they had to keep the sound to a minimum, but because they could only tip the excavated material onto the Common under cover of nightfall. At the end of every evening after Chester had gone, Will made sure that the shelf unit was pushed back into place, the floor was swept and the garden door was locked.

This time he had an additional task; as he saturated the axle of the noisy wheel with oil, he wondered how much further it was to the end of the tunnel and, not for the first time, if there would be anything there. He was concerned that they were running out of supplies; without his father's help with materials, he had been forced to salvage as much timber as he could from the Forty Pits, so that as the tunnel beneath the house progressed, the other one became more and more precarious.

Later, as he sat at the kitchen table, eating yet another supper that had gone cold, Rebecca appeared at the door and leant against the door jamb.

"So, what are you up to?"

"What do you mean?" he replied, with his mouth full.

"What's going on down there? I knocked on the door and you didn't answer. Why do you always keep it locked?"

"No reason," he said dismissively, examining a dry slice of curling beef on the end of his fork.

"Just look at the state of you! Your clothes are a disgrace – suppose you expect me to wash them all again?" she said, folding her arms aggressively.

"No, not really," Will replied, avoiding her eyes.

"Don't think I haven't spotted that stupid oaf hanging around the back door every night after school. You're digging something, aren't you? How can you even think of digging another one of your useless holes at a time like this?"

"There's no need to be like that. I miss Dad too, you know," he said as he took a bite out of a cold roast potato, "but it's not going to help if we just mope around the house, feeling sorry for ourselves … like Mum."

"Well, at least she cares," Rebecca hissed, her eyes shining with anger as she stormed off.

Will finished the congealed meal, slowly chewing each mouthful and ruminating on the events of the last month as he stared into the middle distance.

Afterwards, up in his bedroom, Will took out a geological map of Highfield, marking the spots where he thought his house stood and the direction he calculated his father's tunnel in the cellar was taking, Martineau Square and Mrs Tantrumi's house. He looked at the map for a long time, as if it was a puzzle he could solve, before he finally slipped into an uneasy and fitful slumber, in which he dreamt of the sinister people his father had described in his journal.

In the dream he was dressed in his school uniform but somehow it had become covered in mud and was tattered and torn at the elbows and knees. He had lost his satchel and, worse still, as he wasn't wearing his shoes and socks, he was walking barefoot down a long, deserted terraced street. The street felt familiar and at the same time strange and foreign to him. He wasn't really sure where he was as everything was vague and blurred under a dull half light. He couldn't tell whether it was twilight or early dawn as he glanced up at the low sky, which was yellowy-grey and formless. Anxiety welled up inside him and he fidgeted with the ragged material of his sleeves. He didn't know if he was late for school or for supper, but he was certain he was meant to be somewhere or doing something; something vitally important.

He kept to the centre of the street. The only sounds were those of his breathing and the slap of his naked feet on the damp cobblestones, which echoed off the houses on both sides. They stood ominous and dark; no light shone from behind their blind windows, nor did any smoke rise from their precariously tall and twisted black chimney stacks.

He was feeling so very cold and alone when, in the distance, he caught a glimpse of a figure crossing the street. He squinted through the weak light and knew instantly that it was his father. His heart leapt with joy and he began to wave, but then stopped as he sensed the buildings were watching him. He didn't know how he knew, but he was certain these dormant exteriors harboured something threatening; a force, like a tightly coiled spring, holding its breath and lying in wait for him behind the dusty grey net curtains.

Will shivered. It was something calculating and malevolent that wanted nothing more than to hurt him. His fear grew to an unbearable pitch and he broke into a trot towards his father and shouted to him, but his voice was hollow and reedy, as though the air itself was swallowing his words the instant they left his lips.

He ran faster, speeding down the street as he tried to catch up with his father, but he did not seem to be getting any closer to him. And the faster he ran, the narrower the street became so that the houses on either side were closing in on him with every stride. He could now clearly see their blank windows, smeared with dirt and greasy fingerprints, and that within their dark doorways, shadowy figures skulked threateningly and began to spill out onto the street as he passed them. He faced directly ahead, not daring to look at them as they crowded at the edges of his vision.

As he ran faster and faster, almost tripping on the slick cobblestones, they amassed behind him in such numbers that they were indiscernible from each other, coalescing into a sweeping blanket of darkness. Their fingers extended like wisps of animated black smoke, clutching at his sides and his back as he desperately sought the figure of his father ahead. But his legs were seizing up; the more he tried to accelerate, the slower he became. It was as though he was running through molasses and the shadowy figures, weighing him down with their inky tendrils, were sapping the energy from his body and turning his feet into leaden dead weights until he was forced to come to a complete standstill. The shadows enveloped him and he caught a last brief glimpse of the tiny figure of his father as the view was cut off and he was finally engulfed in a jet-black blanket. It folded over him and suddenly he was weightless and falling into a pit. He hit the bottom with such an impact that it knocked the air from his lungs and, gasping for breath, he rolled onto his back and saw for the first time the stern, heavy, disapproving faces of his pursuers as they peered down at him.

Still trying to catch his breath, he opened his mouth, but before he knew what was happening, it was filled with earth – he could taste it as it smothered his tongue, pressing it down with its weight – and stones dashed and scratched against his teeth. The dry, acrid earth in his throat made him choke. Flailing his arms and clawing at his face, he tried to push it away, but they continued to rain it down on him.

Gagging and retching, Will awoke, his mouth dry and his body swimming in a cold sweat as he sat up. In a panic, he fumbled for the switch to his bedside light. With a click, its comforting yellow glow bathed the room in reassuring normality as he glanced at his alarm clock. It was still the middle of the night. He fell back onto his pillow, staring at the ceiling and breathing heavily, his body still trembling. The memory of the soil clogging his throat was as fresh and vivid in his mind as if it had really happened. And he lay there, staring up at the ceiling and catching his breath, and trying to avoid falling asleep again, until the sun came up.

CHAPTER FIFTEEN

The weeks passed until finally a police inspector called to speak to Mrs Burrows about her husband's disappearance. He wore a dark blue raincoat over a light grey suit and was well spoken, if a little brusque, as he introduced himself to Will and Rebecca and asked to see their mother. They showed him into the sitting room where she sat waiting.

As they followed behind the policeman, they gasped, thinking that, somehow, they must have entered the wrong room. The eternal flame that burnt in the corner, the television, was silent and dark, and, just as remarkable, the room was incredibly neat and tidy. During the weeks when the room had been strictly off limits to them, they had both imagined it must have degenerated into chaos and pictured it littered with half-consumed food, empty packets and dirty plates and cups. It now looked spotless, but, what was more astounding, was their mother herself. Instead of her drab couch-potato garb of dressing gown and slippers, she had changed into one of her best summer dresses, done her hair and even put on some make-up.

Will stared at her with astonishment as he spluttered, "Mum, this is … this is …"

"Detective Chief Inspector Beatty," his sister helped him out.

"Please do come in," Mrs Burrows said, rising from her armchair and smiling.

"Thank you, Mrs Burrows … I know this is a difficult time."

"No, not at all," Mrs Burrows beamed. "Rebecca, would you please put the kettle on and make us all a nice cup of tea?"

"That's very kind, thank you, ma'am," DCI Beatty said, hovering awkwardly in the centre of the room.

"Please," Mrs Burrows motioned towards the sofa. "Please, do sit down."

"Come on, Will, you can give me a hand," Rebecca said, grabbing her brother by the arm as she tried to pull him towards the door. He didn't move, still rooted to the spot by the sight of his mother who, it seemed, was back to the woman she hadn't been for years.

"Er … yeah … oh yes …" he managed.

"Do you take sugar?" Rebecca asked the DCI, still tugging at her brother's arm.

"No, white and no sugar, please," the DCI replied.

"Right, milk no sugar and, Mum, just the two sweeteners?"

Her mother smiled and nodded at her and then at Will, as if she was amused by his bewilderment. "And maybe some custard creams, Will?"

Will snapped out of his trance, turned and accompanied Rebecca into the kitchen, where the pair of them looked at each other in wide-mouthed disbelief, shaking their heads.

While Will and Rebecca were out of the room, the DCI spoke to Mrs Burrows in a low, serious voice. He said that they had been doing everything they could to locate Dr Burrows, but since there was no news at all of his whereabouts they had decided to step up the investigation. This would entail the photograph of Dr Burrows being more widely circulated and, as the DCI put it, they wanted to conduct a "detailed interview" with her down at the station. They also wanted to speak to her children, and anyone else that had had contact with Dr Burrows just prior to his disappearance.

"I'd like to ask you a few questions now, if that's all right. Let's start with your husband's job," the DCI said, looking at the door and wondering when his tea was going to arrive. "Did he mention anyone in particular at the museum?"

"No," Mrs Burrows replied.

"I mean, is there someone there he might have confided in …"

"About where he's gone?" Mrs Burrows finished the sentence for him and then laughed slightly coldly. "You won't have any joy on that line of investigation, I'm afraid. That's a dead end."

The DCI sat up in his chair, a little startled at Mrs Burrows' response.

She continued; "He runs the place single-handed; there aren't any other staff. You might consider interviewing the old codgers who help him out at weekends, but don't be surprised if their memories aren't what they used to be."

"No?" the DCI said, a small smile showing at the edges of his mouth as he wrote in his notebook.

"No, most of them are in their eighties. And why, can I ask, do you want to interview me and my children? I have already told the uniformed police everything I know. Shouldn't you be putting out an APB?"

"An APB?" the DCI smiled broadly, "We don't use that term over here. We put emergencies out on the radio …"

"And my husband isn't an emergency, is he? Like house burglaries – you don't even bother to investigate those now, do you? Unless someone gets killed, like that incident with that poor farmer who was only defending himself." Mrs Burrows' voice was loud and aggressive. "And you stitched him up good and proper, didn't you? A five-year sentence!"

At that very moment, Will and Rebecca appeared with the tea and the room went quiet as Rebecca put the tray on the coffee table and handed one of the mugs to the DCI. She took the other over to her mother, whose eyes never left the DCI. Will, clutching a plate of biscuits, had also entered the room and, as the DCI didn't seem to object to them being there, they both sat themselves down.

The silence grew uneasily, Mrs Burrows' eyes still narrowed with hostility as she glared at the policeman, who was looking into his tea.

"I think we may be getting ahead of ourselves here, Mrs Burrows. Can we just focus on your husband again?" he said.

"I think you will find that we are all very focused on him. It's you I'm worried about," Mrs Burrows said tersely.

"Mrs Burrows, you 'ave to realise that some people don't …" the DCI began, and Will noticed that his accent had a definite Cockney twang to it, as if it had suddenly lost some of its veneer, "… don't want to be found. They want to slip off because, maybe, life and its pressures 'ave become too much for them to 'andle."

"Too much to handle?" Mrs Burrows echoed.

"Yes, we 'ave to take that possibility into consideration."

"My husband couldn't take pressure? What pressure, exactly? The problem was that he never had any bloody pressure at all, or drive for that matter."

"Mrs Burrows …" the DCI tried to get a word in, glancing helplessly at Will and Rebecca, who were both watching him and their mother intently.

"Don't think I don't know that most murders are committed by family members. That's why you want to question us at the station, isn't it? To find out whether we *dunnit*."

"Mrs Burrows," the DCI began again quietly, "nobody's suggesting that a murder has been committed 'ere. Can I suggest that we start again and see if we can get off on the right foot, this time?" he suggested, trying to get command of the situation.

"Sorry – I know you're only trying to do your job," Mrs Burrows said in a calmer voice, and then sipped her tea.

The DCI nodded and took a deep breath as he glanced down at his notebook. "I know it's a difficult thing to think about," he said, "but did your husband have any enemies? Maybe from business dealings?"

At this, much to Will and Rebecca's surprise, Mrs Burrows put her head back and laughed out loud. The DCI muttered something about taking that as a "no" as he scribbled in his little black notebook. He seemed to have regained some of his composure.

"I have to ask these questions," the DCI said, looking

straight at Mrs Burrows, "Did you ever know him to drink excessively or take drugs?" Again Mrs Burrows unleashed a loud guffaw.

"So what did he get up to in his spare time? Did he have any hobbies?"

Rebecca immediately shot a glance at Will.

"He used to do excavations … archaeological digs," Mrs Burrows answered.

"Oh yes." The DCI turned to Will. "I understand you helped him out, didn't you, son?" Will nodded at him. "And where did you do all this digging?" the DCI asked.

Will cleared his throat and looked at his mother and then at the DCI, who was waiting, pen held expectantly in hand, for an answer.

"Well, all over, really," Will said. "Round the edge of town, on rubbish tips and places like that."

"Oh, I thought they were proper affairs," the DCI said.

"They *were* proper digs," Will said firmly. "We found the site of a Roman villa once, but mostly it was 18th and 19th century items we were after."

"Just how extensive … I mean how *deep* were the holes you dug?"

"Oh, just pits, really," Will said evasively, willing him not to pursue the line of questioning.

"And were you engaged in any such activities around the time of his disappearance?"

"No, we weren't," Will said, very aware of Rebecca's eyes burning into him.

"You're sure he wasn't working on anything, maybe without your knowledge?"

"No, I don't think so."

"Okay," the DCI said, putting away his notebook. "That's enough for now."

Chester and Will didn't hang around for long outside the school the next day. They'd spotted Speed and one of his faithful followers, Blogsy, loitering a little distance beyond the gates. Speed was leaning against the railings with his hands in his pockets, staring at them, whilst Blogsy, a nasty little specimen with ginger frizzy hair that gave his head the appearance of a burst cushion, was taking great delight in throwing small stones, which he fished out of the pockets of his parka, at any girls who happened to pass within range. This would elicit squeals and indignant curses, which made Blogsy cackle with a demonic relish.

"I think he's looking for a return match," Will said, glancing over at Speed, who glared straight back at him until Chester caught his eye. At this point, Speed contemptuously turned his back on them, muttering something under his breath to Blogsy, who simply sneered at them and gave a harsh, derisory laugh.

"Screw 'em," Chester growled, as he and Will began the journey home, deciding to take a short cut back.

Their school was a modern yellow-brick and glass job tacked onto the edge of a 1970s estate. Known locally as Roach City, for obvious reasons, the infested blocks that comprised the estate were in a constant state of disrepair due to the endemic indifference that most London councils showed to their property and tenants. It was said that rubbish collections were only necessary every other week, as any organic material left out was very conveniently devoured by the ubiquitous rats and cockroaches. It wasn't by any means a scenic route, but compared with the longer haul around the perimeter of the estate, it cut a good 15 minutes off the boys' journey home. The risk with it was that it took them through the home turf of the Click, who made Speed and his gang look like girl guides.

As they walked side by side through the estate, the weak rays of the sun glinting off broken glass on the tarmac and in the gutters, Will slackened his pace almost imperceptibly, but enough that Chester noticed.

"What's up?"

"I don't know," said Will, looking up and down the road and glancing apprehensively down a side street as they passed it. "It's just a feeling, it's nothing."

"Speed's got you all paranoid, hasn't he?" Chester replied with a smile, but nevertheless he began looking around a little more vigilantly himself.

As they left the estate behind them, they resumed a more normal pace. Soon the end of the High Street loomed into view and they passed by the museum. As Will did every night, he glanced at it in the vain hope that the lights would be burning, the doors open and his father back in attendance. Will just wanted everything to be normal again – whatever that was – but once again it was closed, its windows dark and unfriendly. The council had evidently taken the decision that for now it was cheaper to simply close it rather than look for a temporary stand-in for Dr Burrows.

Will looked up at the sky; heavy clouds were beginning to pull across and blank out the sun.

"Should go well tonight," he said, his mood lifting. "As it's getting dark earlier, we won't have to wait to start tipping."

Chester had started talking about how much faster it would be if they could use power tools, and also how much easier the proceedings would be if they could do away with the need for the cloak-and-dagger subterfuge, when Will mumbled something under his breath.

"Didn't catch that, Will."

"I said: don't look now, but I think there's somebody following us."

"You what?" Chester replied and, not being able to stop himself, immediately turned to look behind.

"Chester, you idiot!" Will said.

Sure enough, 30 feet or so behind them was a short, stocky man in a trilby, black glasses and a dark, tent-like overcoat that reached almost to his ankles. His head was facing in their direction, although it was impossible to be certain if he was really looking at them.

"Shit!" Chester whispered. "I think you're right. He's just

like the ones in your dad's journal. But he's not after us, is he?"

"Let's slow down a bit and see what he does," Will suggested.

As they reduced their speed, the mysterious man did likewise. "Okay," Will said, "how about if we cross the road?"

Again the man mirrored their actions, appearing to float uncannily behind them, like a disembodied shadow. And when they increased their pace again, he sped up to maintain the distance between them.

"He's definitely following us," Chester said, the panic audible in his voice for the first time. "Why though? What does he want? I don't like this – I think we should take the next right and leg it."

"I don't know," Will said, deep in thought. "I reckon we should confront him."

"You've got to be *joking*! Your dad has disappeared off the face of the earth not long after seeing these people and, for all we know, this man could've been responsible. He might be part of the gang or something. I say we get out of here and call the police. Or get help from someone."

They were silent for a moment as they looked around.

"No, I've got a better idea. What if we turn the tables on him? Trap him," Will said. "If we split up, he can only follow one of us, and when he does, the other can come up behind him and …"

"And what?"

"Like a pincer movement – sneak up behind and knobble him," Will was getting well into his stride now as the plan of action firmed up in his mind.

"He could be dangerous, totally *hat stand* for all we know. And what are we going to knobble him with? Our schoolbags?"

"Come on, there's two of us and only one of him," Will said as they glimpsed the shops in the High Street ahead. "I'll distract him while you rugby tackle him – you can do that, can't you?"

"Oh great, thanks," Chester said, shaking his head. "He's bloody huge – he'll make mincemeat of me!" Will looked into Chester's eyes and smiled mischievously.

"Oh God, all right," Chester sighed. "The things I do," he said as he looked quickly back and then made to cross the road.

"Whoa! Scrub that," Will said. "I think they've got the jump on us!"

"They?" Chester gasped as he rejoined his friend. "What do you mean *they*?" he said as he followed Will's gaze to a point further up the street.

There in front of them, some 20 paces ahead, was another of the men. He was almost identical to the first one, except that he sported a flat cap pushed down low over his forehead so that his dark glasses were only just visible under its peak. He also wore a voluminous coat that was flapping gently in the wind as he stood in the middle of the pavement.

There was now no question in their minds that these two men were after them.

As Will and Chester drew level with the first of the shops in the High Street, they both stopped and looked around. On the opposite pavement, two old ladies were chatting to each other as they bundled along with their wicker trolleys creaking on their wheels. One was dragging a recalcitrant Scottish terrier decked out in a tartan dog coat behind her. Apart from that, there were only a few people in the distance.

Their minds were racing with thoughts of shouting for help or flagging down a car if one happened to pass by, when the man in front started towards them. They both realised they were running out of options as the two men closed in.

"This is too weird, we're well and truly snookered ... I mean we're really screwed. Who are these guys?" Chester said, his words running into one another as he stared back over his shoulder at the man in the trilby. As he advanced towards them, the heavy thud of his boots on the pavement sounded like a pile driver. "Any bright ideas?" Chester asked desperately.

"Right, listen, we leg it across the road straight towards the one in the flat cap, feint right, then cut left and into Clarke's. Got it?" Will said breathlessly, as the spectacle of the flat-capped man in front loomed closer and closer.

"Clarke Brothers" was the main grocery shop in the High Street, with a brightly striped awning and immaculately arranged stalls of fruit and vegetables either side of its entrance. Now the light was beginning to dwindle, the glare seeping out from the shop windows beckoned to them invitingly, like a beacon. As it spilled out onto the side of the street, it illuminated the man in the flat cap, his wide, muscular form almost blocking the entire width of the pavement.

"Now!" Will shouted as they darted across the road. The two men appeared to glide in to intercept them as they hared across the tarmac, their school bags bouncing wildly on their backs. The men were moving much faster than either Will or Chester had anticipated and the plan quickly went to hell, turning into a chaotic game of tag as the two boys dodged and weaved between the lumbering men, who tried to grab them with huge outstretched hands.

All of a sudden, Will squawked as one of the men caught hold of him by the scruff of his neck. Then, more by accident than by design, Chester collided with the man's back. The impact knocked off the man's dark glasses to reveal his bright pupils, shining devilishly like two pearls under the brim of his hat. As he turned in surprise, Will took the opportunity to push away from him, with both arms pressed against the man's chest. The collar of Will's school blazer ripped off with a rending tear as he leapt away. The man's head spun back to Will and, with a growl, he slung the detached collar down and lunged in a renewed effort to grab him again.

In a blind dash of panic, Chester, his head down and his shoulders bunched up, and Will, half-falling and half-whirling like an uncoordinated Dervish, somehow made it to the door of Clarke's as, lurching forward, the man wearing the trilby took a last swipe at them, and missed.

Will and Chester's momentum carried them straight through the door, squashed together between the jambs as the bell above the door rang like a demented Morris dancer. They ended up in an unruly heap on the floor of the shop and

Chester, coming to his senses, immediately twisted around and slammed the door shut, holding it closed with both feet.

"Boys, boys, boys!" said Mr Clarke Junior, teetering perilously atop a stunted stepladder as he arranged a display of corn dollies on a shelf. "What's all the pandemonium? A sudden desperate yearning for my exotic fruits?"

"Er, not exactly," Will said, trying to catch his breath as he picked himself up from the floor and made an attempt to act naturally, despite the fact that Chester was now standing somewhat awkwardly with his shoulder braced against the door behind him.

At this point, Mr Clarke Middling rose from behind the counter like a human periscope.

"What was that terrible racket?" he asked, clutching papers and receipts in both hands.

"Nothing for you to worry about, dear," Mr Clarke Junior smiled at him. "Don't let us distract you from your paperwork. It's just a couple of tearaways in search of some rather special fruit, I'll wager."

"Well, I hope they don't want kumquats, we are all out of kumquats at the moment," Mr Clarke Middling said in a dour voice, as he slowly retracted below the counter again.

"Then kumquat may," laughed Mr Clarke Junior in a singsong voice, at which Mr Clarke Middling groaned from behind the counter.

"Don't you mind Middling; he always gets in such a tizzy when he's doing the books. Paper, paper everywhere, and not a drop to ink," Mr Clarke Junior pontificated, adopting a theatrical pose in front of an imagined audience.

The Clarke brothers were a local institution. They had inherited the business from their father, as he had from his father before him. For all anybody knew, there had probably been a Clarke's in business when the Romans invaded, selling turnips or whatever vegetables were in vogue at the time. Mr Clarke Junior was in his forties, a flamboyant character with a penchant for hideously garish blazers, which he had run up for him by a local tailor. Dazzling lemon-yellow, puce-pink and powder-blue stripes danced between the tables of sensibly red tomatoes and the downright sober greens of the cabbages. Part-grocer, part-vaudevillian performer, with his infectious high spirits and inexhaustible armoury of quips and puns, he was a great favourite amongst the ladies of the borough, both young and old, yet oddly enough he had remained a confirmed bachelor.

On the other hand, Mr Clarke Middling, the older brother, couldn't have been more different. A staunch traditionalist, he frowned upon his brother's exuberance, both in appearance and in manner, insisting on the sober, age-old uniform, the old shop coat his forefathers had sported. He was painfully clean and neat; his clothes could have been ironed whilst he was wearing them, such was the crispness of his mushroom-brown coat, white shirt and black tie. His shoes were so beautifully polished and his hair, cut in the short back and sides of a new conscript, was oiled flat with such a glistening sheen, that from behind one would have had a hard time telling which way up he was.

So the two brothers, within the green-hued confines of the shop, were not unlike a caterpillar and a butterfly trapped in a pod. With their constant antagonistic bickering, the flippant joker and his foil resembled a variety act in constant rehearsal for a performance that would never take place.

"Expecting a rush on my lovely gooseberries, is it?" Mr Clarke Junior said in a mock Welsh accent and smiled cheekily at Chester who, still propped against the door, made no effort at a response, as if struck dumb by the whole situation. "Ah, the strong, silent type," Mr Clarke Junior lisped as he danced down the steps of his stepladder and whirled in a flourish to come face to face with Will.

"It's young Master Burrows, is it not?" he said, his expression suddenly becoming serious. "I am so sorry to hear about your dear father. You've been in our thoughts and in our prayers," he said, placing his right hand softly on his heart. "How is your mother bearing up? And that delightful sister of yours ..."

"Fine, fine, both fine," Will said distractedly.

"She's a regular here, you know, a valued customer."

"Yes," Will blurted a little too quickly, as he tried to pay attention to Mr Clark Junior at the same time as keeping an eye on the door against which Chester remained buttressed, as if his life depended on it.

"A highly valued customer," Mr Clarke Middling said from behind the counter, accompanied by the rustle of papers.

Mr Clarke Junior nodded and smiled. "Indeedy, indeedy. Now you just park your lovely selves there while I get a little something for you to take home to your mother and sister." Before Will could utter a word, he had spun gracefully on his heels and practically tap danced into the stockroom at the back of the shop. Will took the opportunity to go over to the window to check the whereabouts of their two pursuers, and recoiled with surprise.

"They're still there!" he said.

The two men were standing on the pavement, one directly in front of each window, staring in over the display tables of fruit and vegetables. It had now turned quite dark outside and their faces floated like ghostly white balloons under the illumination from the shop's interior. They were both still wearing their impenetrable glasses, and Will could make out their bizarre hats and the waxy shine of their angular coats with the unusual shoulder mantles. Their craggy, slanting faces and their clenched mouths looked uncompromising and brutal.

Chester spoke in a low voice: "Get them to call the police." He gestured with his head at the counter, where they could hear the frantic rustling of papers. Just then, Mr Clarke Junior fluttered back into the shop with a basket piled high with an impressive array of fruits, a large pink bow tied to the handle. He handed it to Will with both hands outstretched as if he was about to break into an aria.

"For your mother and sister and, of course, you, old chap. A little something from me and the old codger as a token of our sympathy for your predicament."

"Better a codger than an upstart," came the muffled voice of Mr Clark Middling.

Pointing at the windows, Will opened his mouth to explain about the mysterious men.

"All clear," Chester said loudly.

"What's that, dear boy?" Mr Clarke Junior asked, looking past Will at Chester, who was now standing in front of one of the windows and peering up and down the street.

"What's all clear?" Mr Clarke Middling sprung up from behind the counter like a deranged jack-in-the-box.

"Papers!" Mr Clarke Junior ordered like an angry schoolmistress, but his brother remained above the counter.

"Er … just some kids," Will lied. "We were being chased."

"Boys will be boys," Mr Clarke Junior giggled. "Now please do remember me to your dear sister, Miss Rebecca. You know, she really has such a good eye for quality produce. A gifted young lady."

"I will," Will nodded and forced a smile, "and thanks for this. Ever so kind, Mr Clarke."

"Oh, think nothing of it," he said.

"We do hope that your father returns home soon," Mr Clarke Middling said dolefully. "You shouldn't worry; these things happen from time to time."

"Well … it's like that Gregson boy … terrible thing that," Mr Clarke Junior said with a knowing look and a sigh. "Then there was the Watkins family last year." Will and Chester watched him as he seemed to focus somewhere between the ranks of the courgettes and the cucumbers. "Such nice people, too. No one's seen hide nor hair of them since they …"

"It's not the same thing, not the same at all," Mr Clarke Middling interrupted his brother sharply, then coughed uneasily. "I don't think this is the time or place to bring that up, Junior. A little unsympathetic, do you not think, given the situation?"

But Junior wasn't listening; he was in full flow now and not to be stopped. Crossing his arms and with his head tilted to one side, he took on the aura of one of the old dears he habitually gossiped with.

"Like the flippin' Marie Celeste it was when the police got there. Empty beds and the boys' uniforms all laid out for school the next day, but they were nowhere to be found, none of them. Mrs W had half a pound of our green beans that day, if I recall, and a couple of watermelons. Anyway, no sign of any of them anywhere."

"What … the watermelons?" Mr Clarke Middling asked in a deadpan voice.

"No, the family, you silly sausage," Mr Clarke Junior said, rolling his eyes.

In the silence that ensued, Will looked from Mr Clarke Junior to Mr Clarke Middling, who was staring daggers at his wistful sibling. He was beginning to feel as though he'd stepped through the looking glass.

"Ho hum, better get on," said Mr Clarke Junior, with a last look of sympathy at Will. Trying to straighten the collar of

Will's blazer and then realising that it had been torn off, he shrugged and patted him affectionately on the arm before he pranced delicately up his stepladder again, singing: "Beetroot to me, mon *petit chou* …"

Mr Clarke Middling had sunk out of sight once again and the rustling of papers resumed, accompanied by the whirr of an old fashioned adding machine. Will and Chester cautiously opened the shop door halfway and peered nervously into the street. Will moved out onto the pavement in front of the shop.

"Anything?" Chester asked.

"Nothing," Will replied. "No sign of them."

"We should've got the police."

"And tell them what?" Will said. "That we were chased by two weirdos in sunglasses and silly hats. And that they just disappeared?"

"Yes, exactly that," Chester said, irritated with the cavalier way in which Will was regarding the whole episode. "Who knows what they were after?"

"Forget it. Do you really want to go through all that rubbish when we've got work to do?" Will said, scanning up and down the High Street and feeling more relaxed because of the greater number of people that had appeared on the street. At least they would be able to call for help if the two men turned up again. "The police would probably think we're just a couple of kids horsing around. Anyway, it's not as if we've got any witnesses."

"Maybe," Chester agreed grudgingly, as they started towards the Burrows' house. "There's no shortage of fruitcakes around here," he said, looking back at the Clarkes' shop, "that's for sure."

Will had begun to pick at the garish basket and the pink ribbon, now undone, flapped in the breeze behind him. He was devouring the grapes as he poked around the rest of the basket, wondering what he was going to have next.

"Come on, hand me that 'nana, then," Chester said.

CHAPTER SIXTEEN

"All this evidence points to a deliberate dismantling," Will said, squatting next to Chester on a pile of rubble in the cramped confines of the workface.

They had now reclaimed about 30 feet of the tunnel, which had begun to dip down in a sharp incline, and found they were running critically short of timber. Will had hoped they would be able to salvage some of the original props and planking from the tunnel itself. What confounded them both was that very little of it was still there, and that much of the timber they did find was damaged beyond use. They had already reclaimed all they could from the Forty Pits without causing the whole thing to collapse in on itself.

"So what are you saying? Your dad pulled all this down?" Chester asked as he looked round.

"What, backfilled it? No, that's hardly likely, and even if he did, we'd have found more struts. It doesn't make sense," Will said. Leaning forward, he picked up some of the gravel. "You know, I reckon most of this is virgin infill. It's all been lugged here from somewhere else – precisely the same thing that happened at the Pits."

"But why go to the trouble of filling it in when you could simply collapse the whole thing?" Chester asked, still mystified.

"Because you'd have trenches opening up under people's houses or across their gardens," Will replied despairingly to his friend.

They were both exhausted. The last section had been particularly hard going, made up mostly of sizeable chunks of rock, some of which even Chester found it difficult to manhandle into the wheelbarrow by himself.

"I hope we're nearly through," Chester sighed. "It's really beginning to get to me."

"Tell me about it." Will rested his head in his hands, staring vacantly at the tunnel wall opposite. "You do realise, don't you, there might be nothing at all at the end of this? A dead end?"

Chester looked at him, but was too tired to say anything. So they sat there in silence, deep in their own thoughts, and after a while Will spoke. "What was Dad thinking of, doing all this and not telling us what he was up to? *Me* especially," he said, with a look of sheer exasperation. "Why would he do that?"

"He must have had a good reason," Chester offered.

"But all the secrecy; keeping a secret journal. I don't understand it. We were never a family that kept things from each other like that."

"Well, you had the Pits tunnel," Chester interjected.

"Dad knew about that. But you're right I never told Mum,

because she's just not interested. I mean, we weren't exactly a …" Will hesitated, searching for the right word, "… *model* family, but we all got on and everyone sort of knew what everyone else was up to. Now everything's so messed up."

Chester rubbed some soil out of his ear with his forefinger and finished it off with his thumb. He looked at Will thoughtfully. "My Mum thinks you shouldn't keep secrets from each other. She says they always have a knack of coming out and causing nothing but trouble. She says a secret's just the same as a lie. That's what she tells my Dad, anyway."

"And now I'm doing exactly that to Mum and Becky," Will said, bowing his head.

When Chester had gone and Will finally emerged from the cellar, he headed for the kitchen, as he always did. Rebecca was sitting at the kitchen table, opening the post.

"Anything interesting to eat?" he said to his sister as he was passing her on the way to the fridge. "What's this?" He stopped to pick up a package neatly wrapped in brown paper that was lying on the side, and examined it. "It's addressed to Dad. I think we should open it," he said, as he reached for a dirty butter knife left on a plate next to the sink. Cutting into the brown paper, he excitedly tore open the cardboard box inside and then ripped away a cocoon of bubble wrap to reveal the luminous sphere, glowing from its time in the darkness.

He held it up before him, his eyes sparkling both with excitement and the waning light emanating from the sphere. It was the object he had read about in his father's journal.

Rebecca had stopped reading the telephone bill and was looking at it intently.

"There's a letter in here as well," Will said, reaching into the cardboard box.

"Here, let me see it," Rebecca said, her hand snaking across the table. Will took a step back, holding the sphere in one hand while he shook open the letter with the other. Rebecca withdrew her hand and, disgruntled, sat back in her chair, watching her brother's face as he leant on the counter by the sink and began to read the letter aloud. It was from University

College's Physics Department.

Dear Roger,

It was wonderful to hear from you again after all these years – it brought back warm memories of our time together at university. It was also good to catch up on your news – Steph and I would love to visit when convenient.

As regards the item, I apologise for taking so long to respond, but I wanted to be sure I had collated the results from all concerned. The upshot is that we are well and truly stumped.

As you specified, we did not breach or penetrate the glass casing of the sphere, so all our tests were non-invasive in nature.

On the matter of the radioactivity, no harmful emissions registered when it was tested – so at least I can put your mind at rest on that one.

A metallurgist carried out an MS on a microscopic shaving from the base of the metal cage – he agreed with your view that it's Georgian. He thinks the cage is made out of pinchbeck, which is an alloy of copper and zinc invented by Christopher Pinchbeck (1670-1732). It was used as a substitute for gold and only produced for a short while. Apparently, the formula for this alloy was lost when the inventor's son, Edward, died. He also told me that genuine examples of this material are scarce and it's hard to find an expert who can give an unequivocal identification. Unfortunately, I haven't yet been able to get the cage carbon dated to confirm its age – maybe next time?

What is particularly interesting is that an x-ray revealed a small, free-floating particle in the centre of the sphere itself that does not alter its position even after rigorous physical agitation – this is puzzling, to say the least. Moreover, from a physical inspection, we agree with you that the sphere appears to be filled with two distinct liquid factions of differing densities. The turbulence you noted in these factions does not correspond to temperature variations, internal or external, but is unquestionably photoreactive.

Here's the rub – the boys over in the Chemistry Department have never seen anything like it before. I had a fight on my hands to get it back from them – they were dying to crack the thing open in controlled conditions and run a full analysis. They tried spectroscopy when the sphere was in full fluorescence (at maximum excitation its emissions are in the visible spectrum – in layman's terms, not far off daylight, with a level of UV within acceptable safety levels), and the "liquids" appeared to be predominantly helium and silver based. We can't make any more headway on this until you allow us to open it.

One hypothesis is that the solid particle at the centre may be acting as a catalyst for a reaction that is triggered by the absence of light? We can't think how at this juncture, or come up with any comparable reactions that would occur over such a long period of time, assuming the sphere really does date from the Georgian era.

Remember, helium was not discovered until 1895 – this is at odds with our estimate for the date of the metal casing.

In short, what we have here is a real conundrum. We would all very much welcome a visit from you for a multi-faculty meeting so we can schedule a programme for further analysis of the item. It may even be useful for some of our team to drop into Highfield for a quick investigation into the background.

I look forward to hearing from you.

With kindest regards,

Tom
Professor Thomas Dee

Will put the letter on the table and met Rebecca's stare. He examined the sphere for a moment, then went over to the switch and, shutting the door to the kitchen, flicked off the lights. They both watched as the sphere grew in brilliance from a dim greenish luminescence to something approaching daylight, all in a matter of seconds.

"Wow," he said in wonder. "And they're right, it doesn't even feel hot."

"You knew about this, didn't you? I can read you as easily as a comic book," Rebecca said, staring fixedly at her brother's face, lit by the strange glow.

Will didn't respond as he turned the lights on but left the door shut – they watched as the sphere dulled again. "You know you said no one was doing anything about finding Dad," he said eventually.

"So?"

"Chester and I found something of his in the museum and have also been ... um, making our own enquiries."

"I knew it," she said loudly. "What have you found out?"

"Shh," Will hissed, glancing at the closed door of the sitting room. "Keep it down. I'm *certainly* not going to worry Mum with any of this. Last thing I want to do is get her hopes up. Agreed?"

"Agreed," Rebecca confirmed.

"We found a book Dad was keeping notes in – a sort of journal," Will said slowly.

"Yes and ..."

As they both sat at the kitchen table, Will recounted what he had read in the journal and also their encounter with the strange pallid men outside the Clarkes' shop. He stopped short of telling her about the tunnel under the house as, to him, it was just a *little* secret.

CHAPTER SEVENTEEN

I t was a week later when Will and Chester finally made the breakthrough. Dehydrated from the heat at the workface and with muscles that were cramped and fatigued by the relentless cycle of digging and tipping, they were on the verge of calling it a day when Will's pick struck a large block of stone and it tipped backwards. A pitch-black opening yawned before them.

Their eyes locked onto the fissure, which exhaled a damp and musty breeze into their tired and dirty faces. Chester's instincts screamed at him to back away, as if he was about to be sucked into the opening. Neither of them said a word; there were no great cheers or exultations as they gazed into the impenetrable darkness, with the dead calm of the earth all around them. It was Chester who broke the spell.

"I suppose I'd better be off for my tea, then."

Will turned and looked at him with incredulity and then erupted into hysterical laughter as he picked up a clod of earth and slung it at his grinning friend who ducked to avoid the projectile, a low chuckle coming from beneath his yellow hard hat.

"You …" Will said, searching for an appropriate epithet.

"Yeah, what?" Chester beamed. "Come on, then, let's have a look see," he said, leaning into the gap next to Will.

Will shone his torch through the opening. "It's a cavern … can't make out much in there … must be quite big. I think I can see some stalactites and stalagmites." Then he stopped. "Listen!"

"What is it?" whispered Chester.

"Water, I think. I can hear water dripping." He turned to Chester.

"You're joking," Chester said, his face clouding with concern.

"No, I'm not. Could be a Neolithic stream – the earth is riven with them, you know."

"Here, let me see," said Chester, taking the torch from Will.

Tantalising as it was, they decided against any further excavation there and then. They would resume the following day when they were fresh and better prepared. Chester went off; he was tired but quietly elated that their work had borne fruit. It was true that they were both badly in need of sleep and Will was even, unusually, considering taking a bath as he swung the shelves back into position. He did the usual sweep up and made his way lethargically to his room.

As he passed Rebecca's door, she called out to him. Will grimaced and held as still as a statue.

"Will, I *know* you're out there."

Will sighed and pushed open her door. Rebecca was lying on her bed, where she'd been reading a book.

"What's up?" asked Will, glancing around her room. He was constantly astounded at how infuriatingly clean and tidy it always was.

"Mum said she needs to discuss something with us."

"When?"

"She said as soon as you came in."

"God, what now?"

Mrs Burrows was in her usual position as they entered. Slumped to one side in her armchair like a deflated mannequin, she raised her head dozily as Rebecca coughed to get her attention.

"Ah good," she said, pushing herself into a more normal sitting position and, in the process, knocking a couple of remote controls onto the floor. "Oh bum!" she exclaimed.

Will and Rebecca sat themselves down on the sofa while she rummaged feverishly through the pile of tapes at the base of her chair. Eventually coming up with both remotes, her hair hanging forward in straggles and her face flushed from the effort, she positioned them very precisely on the arm of her chair again.

"I think it's time we faced the possibility that your father isn't coming back, which means we have to make some rather crucial decisions." She paused and glanced at the television. A model in a spangled evening dress was revealing a large letter "V" on the Catchphrase wall, with several other letters already on show. Mrs Burrows muttered "The Invisible Man" under her breath as she turned back to Will and Rebecca. "Your father's salary was stopped three weeks ago and, as Rebecca knows, we are already running on empty."

Will turned to Rebecca, who simply nodded in agreement, and their mother continued. "All the savings have gone and what with the mortgage and everything else to consider, we are going to have to cut our cloth …"

"Cut our cloth?" asked Rebecca, a little startled, as the penny was beginning to drop.

"'Fraid so," their mother said a little distantly, "and I'm not going to be around for a short while. I've been advised to spend a little time in a … well … sort of hospital; somewhere I can rest and get myself back on form."

At this, Will raised his eyebrows, wondering just what form his mother could be referring to. She had been set in her current form for as long as he could remember.

His mother continued. "So, while I'm gone, you two will have to go and stay with your Auntie Jean."

Will and Rebecca looked at each other with identical expressions of dread, as an avalanche of images fell through Will's mind. Auntie Jean's tower block, with the public spaces crammed with rubbish bags and disposable nappies, and the graffitied lifts reeking of urine. The streets filled with the burnt out cars and the endlessly screaming scooters of the gangs and small-time drug dealers, and the sorry groups of drunks that sat on the benches, squabbling ineffectually amongst themselves as they downed their purple cans of "Trampagne". These images were replaced by the picture of his mother sitting in a dressing gown in some impersonal common room with brown carpets and nicotine-stained ceilings, watching television with other glassy eyed women as attendants brought cups of tea around to them … in fact, much like home for Mrs Burrows.

"No way!" he suddenly blurted out, as if waking from a nightmare and making Rebecca jump and his mother sit bolt upright, once again knocking the remotes off the arm of her chair.

"Oh drat and blast!" she said, craning her neck to see where they had fallen.

"I'm not going to live there. I couldn't bear it, not for a second. What about school, what about my friends?"

"What friends?" Mrs Burrows replied spitefully.

"That's not fair," Rebecca piped up. "And you can't really expect us to go there, Mum. It's awful, it smells, the place is a pigsty."

"And Auntie Jean smells," Will added.

"Well, there's nothing I can do about that. I have to get some rest; the doctor said I'm very stressed, so there's no debate. We've got to sell the house and you're just going to have to stay with Jean until …"

"Until what? You get a job or something?" Will cut in sharply.

Mrs Burrows glared at him. "This is not good for me. The doctor said I should avoid confrontations. This conversation is over. *Goodbye,*" she snapped suddenly, in her best Anne Robinson, and turned on her side again.

Out in the hall, Will sat on the bottom step of the stairs while Rebecca stood with her arms folded, leaning against the wall. Both of them were numbed by what they had just heard.

"Well, that's the end of us," she said mournfully, the implications all too clear for the two of them.

After a moment, Will stood up decisively. "I know what I'm going to do."

"What?"

"Have a bath."

"You need one," Rebecca said as she watched him wearily climb the stairs.

CHAPTER EIGHTEEN

"Matches."

"Check."

"Candles."

"Check."

"Swiss army knife."

"Check."

"Spare torch."

"Check."

"Balls of string."

"Check."

"Chalk and rope."

"Yep."

"Compass."

"Er ... Yep."

"Extra cells for the helmet lights."

"Check."

"Camera and notebook."

"Check, check."

"Pencils."

"Check."

"Water and sandwiches."

"Ch ... planning a long stay, are we?" Chester asked as he looked at the absurdly large packet wrapped in silver foil. They were carrying out a last-minute equipment check down in the cellar, marking off items against a list Will had made at school earlier that day during his Domestic Sciences class. After ticking them off, they placed each item in the rucksacks. When they were finished, Will closed the flap on his rucksack and shrugged it onto his back.

"Okay, let's go," he said, with a look of deadly intent on his face as he reached for his trusty spade.

They drew back the shelves and, once inside, pulled them to behind themselves, jamming them shut by means of a makeshift latch Will had rigged up. On all fours, Will led the way, moving ahead swiftly.

"Hey, wait for me," Chester called after him, taken aback by his friend's impetuous enthusiasm.

At the face, they dislodged the remaining blocks of stone, which fell away into the darkness and landed with dull splashes. Chester was about to speak when Will pre-empted him.

"I know, I know, you think we're about to be swept away in a flood of raw sewage or something," Will peered through the enlarged opening. "I can see where the rocks fell – they're sticking up out of the water. It can only be about ankle deep."

With that, he turned and started to climb through the breach. He stopped for a moment on the brink, winked at Chester and dropped out of sight, leaving his friend dumbfounded for an instant until he heard Will's feet land in the water with a loud splash.

There was a drop of about six or seven feet. "Hey, pretty cool," Will said, as Chester scrambled through after him. Will's voice echoed eerily about the cavern, which was around 15 feet in height and 30 feet long, and, as far as they could make out, crescent-shaped. They had entered near one of the extremes and so were only able to see as far as the curvature allowed. The sides and roof were made up of rough rock, and stalactites speared down as their counterparts reached up. The floor was flooded with murky water, out of which, much to their surprise, the remains of a machine of some description projected. Large red-brown rusting cogwheels held within a buckled cast iron frame stood proud of the inky water. It was as if a locomotive had been mercilessly disembowelled and then left to die.

A silt bank ran along the far edges of the cavern. At first, Will thought that it was streaked with minerals or something similar, but on closer inspection, he saw that it was littered with bolts with chunky hexagonal heads, spindles and countless pieces of jagged cast iron shrapnel. The rust from these intermingled with shadowy patches in the silt that, from their appearance, Will assumed to be oil spills. He screwed up his nose. The whole chamber smelt dank and stale. As they stood there in a stunned silence and surveyed this worthless treasure trove, they became aware of a faint scratching sound.

"What's that?" Chester whispered as they trained their miner's lights in the direction of the sound. Will moved further into the cavern, treading carefully on the uneven floor, invisible beneath the water.

"What is it?" gasped Chester.

"Shh!" As they were looking at the water, a sudden movement followed by a small splash made them both jump.

A sleek white object leapt out of the water, streaked along one of the metal members and stopped still on the apex of a huge gearwheel protruding from the water. It was a large rat with a perfect white coat and large, bright-pink ears. It was facing them, standing up on its back legs, its translucent whiskers twitching and vibrating in the torchlight as it sniffed the air.

"Look! It doesn't have any eyes," Will hissed excitedly.

Chester shuddered in response. Sure enough, where there should have been eyes, there was not even the tiniest break in the sleek, snowy fur.

"Yuck, that's disgusting," Chester exclaimed in dismay as he took a step back.

"Adaptive evolution," Will replied.

"I don't care what it is!"

The animal twitched and arched its head in the direction of Chester's voice. The next instant it was gone, diving into the water and swimming to the opposite bank, where it scurried away.

"Great! He's probably gone to get his mates," Chester said. "This place will probably be swarming with them in a minute."

Will laughed. "It's only a bloody rat."

"That was no normal rat – who's ever heard of eyeless rats?"

"Come on, will you, you big girl. Don't you remember the three blind mice?" Will said with a grin as they began to move around the crescent bank, playing their torches into the nooks and crannies in the walls and up onto the roof of the cavern above them. Chester was stepping apprehensively about the rocks and iron debris, constantly peering behind him for an imagined army of sightless rats. "Oh God, I hate this," he grumbled.

As they approached the shadows at the far end of the chamber, Will increased his pace and Chester did likewise, determined not to be left behind.

"Whoa!" Will stopped in his tracks, Chester bumping into him. "Look at that!"

Set into the roughly hewn rock of the wall was a door. Will's torch flicked over its dull, scarred surface – it looked ancient but substantial, with rivet heads like half golf balls spaced around its frame and three massive handles down one side. Will stepped forward and touched its surface – it was shiny, black and uneven, like burnt treacle. He tapped lightly on it with his knuckles. "It's metal." Then he reached up and grasped the uppermost handle and tried to yank down on it, but it refused to move. He handed Chester his torch and then, using both hands, he tried again, pulling down with all his weight, but nothing happened.

"Try the other way," suggested Chester.

Will tried again, this time pushing upwards – it creaked a little and, to his surprise, it then swivelled smoothly and clunked into an open position. He did the same with the other two handles and stood back. Retrieving his torch from Chester, he placed one hand against the centre of the door, ready to push it open.

"Well, here goes," he said to Chester, who for once did not raise any objection.

PART TWO
THE COLONY

CHAPTER NINETEEN

The door swung open with a subdued metallic groan. They paused for a moment, adrenaline coursing through their veins as they directed their lights into the dark space beyond. They were both ready to turn and flee in an instant, but hearing and seeing nothing, they stepped carefully over the metal lip at the base of the doorframe, holding their breaths while their hearts pounded in their ears.

Their torch beams licked unsteadily about the interior. They were standing in an almost cylindrical chamber, no more than 10 feet long, with pronounced corrugations along its length. In front was another door, identical to the one they had just come through, except for a small panel of misty glass held within a riveted frame, like a diminutive porthole.

"Looks like some sort of airlock," Will said breathlessly as he moved further into the chamber, his boots thudding on the grooved iron flooring. "Get a move on," he said unnecessarily to Chester, who had followed him in and, without being asked, was closing the door behind them, turning the handles so all three were engaged again.

"Better leave everything as we find it," Chester said, "just in case."

Having tried to see through the opaque porthole with no success, Will cranked open the three handles on the second door and pushed it outward. There was a small hiss, as if air was leaking from a tyre valve. Chester threw Will a questioning look, which he ignored as he ventured into the short adjoining room. About 10 feet square, it had walls like the keel of an old boat, a patchwork quilt of rusting metal plates held together

132

with crude welds.

"There's a number on here," Chester observed as he locked down the handles on the second door. Peeling and yellowing with age, there was a large "5" painted on the door beneath the murky porthole.

As they moved cautiously forwards, their lights picked out the first details of something in front of them. It was a trellis of interwoven metal bars, running from floor to ceiling and completely blocking the way. Will's light projected jerky shadows against the surfaces beyond as he pushed on the trellis with his hand. It was solid and unyielding. He tucked his torch away and, gripping the damp metal, pulled himself as close as he could.

"I can see the ceiling and walls, but …" he said, twisting his head around, "but the floor is …"

"A long way down," Chester interjected, the brim of his hard hat scraping against the trellis as he tried to get a better view.

"I can tell you there's sod all like this on the maps."

"Hang on, Will! Look at the cables!" Chester said loudly as he spotted the chunky matt lines through the trellis. "It's a lift shaft," he added enthusiastically, his spirits suddenly buoyed by the thought that far from being something inexplicable and menacing, what they had encountered was recognisable and familiar. *It was a lift shaft.* For the first time since they had left the relative normality of the Burrows' cellar, he felt safe, imagining that the shaft must descend to a railway tunnel or something equally mundane. He even dared to let himself think that this could herald the end to their half-cocked expedition. He looked down to his right, located a handle and, yanking on it, slid the panel across. It grated horribly on its runners.

Will took a step back in surprise. In his haste, he'd failed to notice that the barrier was, in fact, a sliding gate and now watched as it opened before them. Once Chester had pushed it all the way back, they had an unobstructed view of the dark shaft. Their headlights played on the heavy greased cables running down the middle of the shaft into the darkness below, into the abyss.

"It's one hell of a drop," Chester shivered, gripping the edge of the trellis gate tightly as his gaze was swallowed up by the vertiginous depths. Will turned his attention from the shaft and began to look around the iron chamber behind them. Sure enough, attached to the wall at his side, he found a small box made of dark wood with a tarnished brass button protruding from its centre.

"Yes!" he cried triumphantly, and without a word to Chester, pressed the button, which felt greasy beneath his fingertip.

Nothing happened.

He tried again.

And once more, *nothing*.

"Chester, close the gate, close it!" he shouted, unable to contain his excitement.

Chester rammed it across and Will jabbed at the button again. There was a distant vibration and a reverberating clank from deep inside the shaft. And then the cables jerked into life and began to move, the shaft filling with a loud, whining groan from the winching equipment, which must have been housed not far above them. They listened to the clanging echoes of the approaching lift.

"Bet it's the way down to an underground station." Chester turned to Will, a big grin of anticipation on his face.

Will frowned with annoyance. "No way. I *told* you there's nothing here. This is something else altogether."

Chester's optimism evaporated, his expectant smile wiped from his face as they both approached the trellis grating again, pushing their heads against it so their helmet lamps flicked into the black shaft.

"Well, if we don't know what this is …" Chester said, "… there's still time to go back."

"Not now. Come on, we can't give up now."

They both stood listening to the approaching lift for a

couple of minutes until Chester spoke. "What if there's someone in it?" he said, backing away from the grating as he once again began to work himself up into a panic.

But Will couldn't tear himself away. "Hang on, I can't quite … it's still too dark … Wait! I can see it, I can see it! It's like a miners' cage-lift!" Staring hard at the lift as it inched ponderously towards them, Will found he was able to see through the grill that formed its roof. He turned to Chester. "Relax will you, there's nobody in it."

"I didn't really think there was," Chester retorted defensively.

"Yeah, right, you big wuss."

Satisfying himself it was empty, Chester shook his head and sighed with relief as the lift arrived at their level. It shuddered to a clangorous halt and Will lost no time in pulling back the gate and taking a few steps in. Then he turned to Chester who was hovering on the brink, looking decidedly uncomfortable.

"I don't know, Will, it looks well shonky," he said, his gaze shifting around the lift's interior. "Might not have been serviced for ages." With cage walls and a scratched steel plate floor, the whole thing was covered with what looked like years of oily grime and dust.

Without a moment's hesitation, Will jumped up and down a couple of times, his boots clanging on the metal flooring. Chester looked on, terrified, as the lift rattled within the trellis frame.

"Safe as houses." Will grinned impishly and, placing his hand on the brass lever inside the lift, he looked Chester in the eye. "Are you coming … or are you going back to fight the rat?"

That was enough for Chester, who immediately moved into the lift. Will slid the gate shut behind him, and pushing and holding the lever down, the lift once again shuddered into motion and began the descent. Through the caging, interrupted every so often by the dark mouths of other levels, they saw the rock face slowly sweeping by in muted shades of browns and blacks and greys, ochres and yellows.

A damp breeze blew about them and at one point Chester

shone his light through the grill above them, up into the shaft and onto the cables, which appeared like a pair of dirty laser beams fading into deep space.

"How far down do you think it goes?" Chester asked.

"How should I know?" Will replied gruffly.

In fact, it was almost five minutes before the lift finally came to a halt with an abrupt and bone-shaking bump that made them fall against the sides of the cage.

"Maybe I should have let go of the lever a bit earlier," Will said sheepishly.

Chester threw his friend a blank look, as if nothing really mattered any more, and then they both stood there, their lights throwing giant diamond silhouettes from the lift cage onto the walls beyond.

"Here we go again," Chester sighed as he slid back the gate and Will pushed impatiently past him into another metalplate room, rushing through it to get to the door at the far end.

"This is just like the one above," Will noted as he busied himself with the three handles on the side of the door, which had a large "0" painted on it.

They took a few tentative steps into the cylindrical room, their boots ringing out against the undulating sheet-metal flooring and their torch beams illuminating yet another door in front of them.

"Seems we only have one way to go," Will said, striding towards it.

"These things look like something out of a submarine," Chester muttered under his breath.

Standing on tiptoes, Will looked through the small glass porthole, but couldn't make out anything on the other side. And when he tried to shine his torch through it, the grease and the scratches on the ancient porthole only refracted the beam so that the glass became more opaque than ever.

"Damn it," he said to himself, and with that he passed his torch to Chester and rotated the three handles. He pushed against the door. "It's stuck!" he grunted. He tried again, without success. "Give me a hand, will you?"

Chester joined in and, with their shoulders braced against the door, they pushed and shoved with all their might. Suddenly, it burst open with a loud hiss and a massive rush of air, and they stumbled through into the unknown.

Their boots now ground on cobblestones as they regained their footing and straightened up. Before them was a scene that they both knew, for as long as they lived, they would never forget.

It was a street.

They found themselves in a huge space almost as wide as a motorway, which curved off into the distance to their left and right. And looking across to the opposite side, they saw it was lit by a row of tall street lamps.

But what stood beyond these lights, on the far side of the cavern, really took their breath away. Stretching as far as they could see in both directions, were *houses*.

As if held in a trance, Will and Chester moved towards this apparition. As they did so, the door slammed shut behind them with such force they both wheeled around.

"A breeze?" Chester asked his friend, with a baffled expression.

Will shrugged in response – he could definitely feel a faint draught on his face. He put his head back and sniffed, catching the stale mustiness in the air. He shone his beam around the door and played it on the wall above, illuminating the huge blocks of stone that formed it. He raised the circle of light, higher and higher, and their eyes were compelled to follow the wall up into the shadows above, where it met the opposing wall in a gentle arch, like the vaulted roof of a huge cathedral.

"What is all this, Will? What is this place?" Chester asked, grabbing him by the arm.

"I don't know – I've never heard about anything like this before," Will replied, staring wide-eyed about the huge street. "It's truly awesome."

"What do we do now?"

"I think we … we should have a look around, don't you? This is just incredible," Will marvelled. Consumed with the irresistible urge to explore, to learn more, and light-headed with the first heady flush of discovery, he struggled to order his thoughts. "Must record it," he muttered as he hoisted his camera out and began to take photographs.

"Will, the flash!"

"Oops, sorry." He slung the camera around his neck. "Got a little carried away there." Without another word to Chester, he suddenly strode across the cobblestones towards the houses. Chester followed behind his fellow explorer, half crouched and grumbling under his breath as he scanned up and down the road for any sign of life.

The buildings appeared to be carved out of the very walls themselves, like half-excavated architectural fossils. Their roofs were fused with the gently arching walls behind and where one might have expected chimneys, there was an intricate network of brick ducts sprouting from the tops of the roofs, which ran up the walls and disappeared above, like petrified smoke plumes. As they reached the pavement, the only sound apart from their footfalls was a very low humming, which seemed to be emanating from the very ground itself. They paused briefly to inspect one of the streetlights.

"It's like the …"

"Yes," Will interrupted, unconsciously touching his pocket where his father's luminescent orb was carefully wrapped in a handkerchief. The glass sphere of the streetlight was a much larger version of this, almost the size of a football and held in place by a four-pronged claw atop a cast iron post. A pair of snow-white moths circled erratically about it like epileptic moons, their dry wings fluttering against the surface of the glass.

Will stiffened abruptly and, lifting his head back, sniffed – looking not unlike the eyeless rat on the cogwheel.

"What is it?" Chester asked with trepidation. "Not more trouble?"

"No, just thought … I caught something. It was like … ammonia … something sharp. Didn't you notice it?"

"No." Chester sniffed several times. "I hope it's not

poisonous?"

"No, no. Anyway it's gone now, whatever it was. And we're okay, aren't we?"

"Suppose so. But do you think anyone really lives here?" Chester replied as he looked up at the windows of the buildings. They turned their attention to the nearest house, silent and ominous, as if it was daring them to approach.

"I don't know."

"Well, what's it all doing here, then?"

"One way to find out," Will said as they gingerly approached the house. It was simple and elegant, constructed of sandstone masonry, almost Georgian in style. They could just make out heavily embroidered curtains behind the 12-paned windows either side of the front door, which was coated in a green treacle gloss and had a doorknocker and bell push of deeply burnished brass.

"167," Will said in wonder as he spotted the digits above the knocker.

"What *is* this place?" Chester was whispering as Will caught a faint flicker of light in a chink between the curtains. It shimmered, as if it came from a fire.

"Shhh!" Will said as he crept over and crouched down below the window. He slowly rose above the sill and peered with one eye through the small gap. His mouth gaped open in silent awe. Through this impromptu spy hole, he could see a fire burning in a hearth. Above this was a dark mantelpiece on which there were various glass ornaments. And, as the light from the fire danced around the room, he could just make out some chairs and a sofa and the walls, covered in a multitude of framed pictures of varying sizes.

"Come on, what's there?" Chester said nervously, continually looking back at the empty street, as Will squashed his face against the dirty pane of glass. "You won't believe this!" Will replied, moving aside to let his friend see for himself, his cheek smudged with grime from the window. Chester eagerly pressed his nose against it.

"Wow! It's a proper room!" he said, turning to look at Will, only to find he was already on the move, working his way along the front of the house. He stopped as he reached the corner of the building.

"Oi! Wait for me," Chester hissed, terrified that he was going to be left behind.

Beside the building and the next one in the row, a short alley ran straight back to the tunnel wall. Will poked his head around the corner and, once he was satisfied that it was clear, beckoned to Chester that they should move on to the next house.

"This one's 166," Will said as he examined the front door, almost identical to the one on the first house. He tiptoed to the window, but was unable to see anything at all through the dark windows.

"Anything in there?" Chester asked.

Will held a finger to his lips and then made his way back to the front door. Looking at it closely, a thought occurred to him and his eyes narrowed. Recognising the look, Chester reached out to try to stop him, spluttering, "Will, no!"

But it was too late. Will had barely touched the door when it swung inward. They exchanged glances and then moved silently inside, twinges of excitement and anxiety simultaneously surging through them. The hallway was spacious and warm, and they both became aware of a pot-pourri of smells – cooking, fire smoke – and of human habitation. It was laid out just like any normal house; wide stairs started halfway down the corridor, with brass carpet rails at the base of each riser. Waxed wood panelling ran up to a handrail, above which was wallpaper of light and dark green stripes. Portraits in ornate, dull gold-coloured frames hung on the wall depicting sturdy looking people with huge shoulders and pale faces. Chester was peering at one of these when a terrible thought struck him.

"They're just like the men that chased us," he said. "Oh great, we're in a house that belongs to one of those nutters, aren't we?" he added as the awful realisation hit him. "This is bleedin' nutty town!"

"Shhh!" Will cut him short. Chester stood riveted to the spot as Will cocked an ear in the direction of the stairs, but there was nothing, only an oppressive silence.

"I thought I heard … no …" he said and moved towards the open doorway to their left, then looked cautiously around the corner. "This is just fantastic!"

They couldn't help themselves – they had to enter the room. A cheery fire crackled in the hearth. Around the walls were small pictures and silhouettes in brass and gilt frames. One in particular caught Will's eye: "The Martineau House", he read on the inscription below. It was a small oil painting of what appeared to be a stately home surrounded by rolling grasslands.

By the fireplace were chairs upholstered in a dark red material with a dull sheen. There was a dining table in one corner and in another a musical instrument that Will presumed was a harpsichord. The room was lit by two tennis ball-sized spheres suspended from the ceiling in ornate pinchbeck cages.

The room brought to Will's mind a museum his father had taken him to with a display called "How we used to live". As he looked around, he reflected that this wouldn't have been out of place.

Chester sidled up to the dining table where two plain white bone china cups sat in their saucers.

"There's something in these," he said with an expression of sheer surprise. "Looks like tea!"

He hesitantly touched the side of one of the cups and looked up at Will, even more startled.

"It's still warm. What's going on here? Where are all the people?"

"Don't know," Will replied. "It's like … like …"

They looked at each other with dumbfounded expressions.

"I honestly don't know what it's like," Will admitted.

"Let's just get out of here," Chester said and they both bolted for the door. As they reached the pavement again, Chester collided with Will as he stopped dead.

"What are we running for?" Will asked.

"Er … the … well …" Chester blathered in confusion as he struggled to put his concerns into words. For a moment they lingered indecisively under the sublime radiance of a street light.

Then Chester noticed with some dismay that Will was staring intently at the road as it curved into the distance with the tunnel. "Come on, Will. Let's just go." Chester shivered as he glanced back at the house and up at the windows, certain that there was someone there. "This place gives me the creeps."

"No," Will replied, not even looking at his friend. "Let's follow the road along for a bit. See where it goes. Then we can leave. Okay?" he said, already striding off.

Chester stood his ground for a moment, looking longingly across the road at the metal doorway through which they had first entered. With a groan of resignation, he grudgingly followed Will along the line of houses. Many had lights in their windows but, as far as they could tell, there were no signs of any occupants.

As they came to the last house in the row, where the road curved off to the left, they paused for a moment, deliberating whether to go on or call it a day. His voice squeaking with desperation, Chester was pleading that they turn back when they became aware of a sound behind them. It began like the rustling of leaves, but quickly grew in intensity to a dry, rippling cacophony.

"What the …" Will exclaimed.

Shooting down from the roof, a flock of birds the size of sparrows dived towards them, like living tracer bullets. They both instinctively ducked, raising their arms defensively in front of their faces as the pure white birds whirled around them in synchronised agitation.

Will began to laugh. "Birds! It's only birds!" he said, swatting out at the mischievous flock but never making contact. Chester lowered his arms a little and began to laugh too, albeit a little nervously, as the birds darted between them. Then, as quickly as they'd appeared, the birds swept upwards and vanished round the bend in the tunnel. Will straightened up and staggered a few steps after them, but then froze.

"Shops!" he said in a startled voice.

"Huh?" Chester replied.

Sure enough, down one side of the street stretched a parade of bow-fronted shops. Without speaking, they both began to walk towards them.

"This is unreal," Chester muttered as they reached the first shop with windows of hand-blown glass that distorted the wares inside like badly made lenses.

"Jacobson Cloths," Chester read from the shop sign and then peered at the rolls of material laid out in the eerie, green-lit interior.

"A grocery shop," Will said as they moved on.

"And this one's some sort of hardware shop," Chester observed.

Will gazed up at the arching roof of the cavern above them. "You know, by now we must be nearly under the High Street."

Soaking up the strangeness of the ancient shops and peering into the windows, they kept walking, driven by their careless curiosity, until they came to a place where the tunnel split into three. The centre fork appeared to descend into the earth at a marked angle.

"Right, that's it," Chester said resolutely. "We're leaving now. I'm *not* going to get lost down here." All his instincts were screaming out that they should turn back.

"Okay," Will replied, "but ..."

He was just stepping off the pavement onto the cobbled road when there was an ear-splitting crash of steel on stone. In a blinding flash, sparks spraying from their hooves, four white horses, breathing heavily and pulling behind them a sinister black coach, bore down on him. Will didn't have time to react as, at that very instant, they were both yanked off their feet and hoisted into the air by the scruffs of their necks.

Two huge gnarled hands of a single man held them dangling helplessly.

"Interlopers!" the man shouted, his voice fierce and gravelly, lifting the pair up to his face and inspecting them with a look

of repugnance. Will tried to bring his spade up to beat the man off, but it was wrested from his grip.

He was wearing a dark blue uniform of coarse material that rasped as he moved. By the side of a row of dull buttons, Will caught sight of a five-pointed star of light yellow material stitched into the coat. Perched precariously on his impossibly wide head, he wore a helmet that was ridiculously small, like a novelty hat from a fair. But, far from giving him a comical appearance, it served to emphasise the huge, menacing bulk of their captor, clearly some sort of policeman.

"Help," Chester mouthed silently at his friend, his voice deserting him as they were buffeted about in the man's grip.

"We've been expecting you," the man rumbled.

"What?" Will stared at him blankly.

"Your father said you'd be joining us before long."

"My father? Where's my father? What have you done with him? Put me down!" Will tried to swivel around, kicking his feet out in an attempt to strike the man.

"No use wriggling." The man hoisted the struggling boy even higher in the air and sniffed at him. "Topsoilers.

Disgusting!"

Will sniffed back.

"Don't smell too good yourself."

The man gave Will a look of withering scorn that stilled him. Then the man held Chester up and sniffed at him too. In sheer desperation, Chester tried to headbutt the man, who jerked his head back, but not before Chester, with a wild swing of his arm, had swiped his helmet. It spun from his head, exposing his pale scalp, which was covered with short tufts of wispy white hair.

The man shook Chester violently by the collar and then, with a horrible growl, knocked the boys' heads together. Although their hard hats protected them from any injury as they crashed noisily against each other, they were so shocked by his ferocity that they immediately abandoned any further thoughts of resisting him.

"Enough!" the man shouted, as the stunned boys heard a chorus of bitter laughter from behind him, becoming aware for the first time of the other men who were peering at them with pale, unsmiling eyes.

"Think you can come down here and break into our houses?" the man growled as he swept them down towards the centre fork, where the road descended.

"It's the clink for you two," snarled someone behind them in a resentful voice.

They were frogmarched unceremoniously through the streets, which were now filling with people as they emerged from various doorways and alleys to gawp at this unfortunate pair of strangers. Half-dragged and half-stumbling, each time they lost their footing the boys would be yanked ignominiously to their feet by the vice-like grip of the enormous officer. In all their confusion and panic, they looked frantically around in the vain hope that they might find an opportunity for escape or that someone would come to their rescue. But their faces drained of blood as this hope receded and they realised the futility of their situation as they were dragged deeper into the Earth.

Before they knew it, they were hoisted around a bend in the

tunnel and the space about them opened up. They were numbed by a dizzying confusion of layers; bridges, aqueducts and raised walkways criss-crossed above a lattice of cobbled streets and lanes, all hemmed with buildings.

Dragged on at an impossible rate by the policeman, they were watched by huddled groups of people, their wide faces curious and yet impassive. But not all the faces were like those of their captor or the men who had pursued them in the High Street, with their wan skin and washed-out eyes. If it hadn't been for their archaic dress, some appeared quite normal and could easily have passed unnoticed in any English street.

"Help, help!" Chester cried hopelessly as he half-heartedly resumed his efforts to extricate himself from the policeman's grip. But Will hardly noticed any of this. His attention had been seized by a tall, thin individual beside a lamp post, whose hard face was set atop a striking white collar and a long, dark coat that reflected the light as if it was made from polished leather. He stood out strikingly from the squat people about him, his shoulders slightly arching over like a highly strung bow. His whole being emanated a palpable malevolence and his dark eyes never left Will's, who felt a wave of dread wash over him.

"I think we're in real trouble here, Chester," he said, unable to tear his gaze from the sinister man whose thin lips twisted into a sardonic smile.

CHAPTER TWENTY

Will and Chester stumbled and tripped as they were hauled up a small flight of steps into a single storey building nestling between taller buildings that, from their drab utilitarian façades, Will took to be offices or factories. Once inside, the policeman pulled them to an abrupt halt and, spinning them around, roughly yanked their rucksacks off their backs. Then he literally hurled the two boys at a slippery oak bench, its surface dipping here and there with polished indentations, as if years of wrongdoers had rubbed along its length. Will and Chester's backs slammed against the wall and they gasped as the breath was knocked out of them.

"Don't you move!" the policeman roared and positioned himself between them and the entrance. By craning his neck forward, Will could just see past the man and through the half-windowed doors into the street outside where a mob had assembled. Many blank faces were jostling for a view and a few, as they caught sight of Will, started to shout and gesticulate angrily. He quickly sat back against the wall and tried to catch Chester's eye, but his friend, frightened out of his wits, was staring fixedly at the floor in front of him.

Will looked up at a notice board next to the door on which a large number of black-rimmed papers were pinned. The writing in the body of the notices was too small to decipher from where he sat, but he could see handwritten headings such as "Order" or "Edict", followed by strings of numbers.

The walls of the station were black up to a handrail, above which they were an off-white colour, peeling in places and streaked with dirt. The ceiling itself was an unpleasant nicotine yellow with deep cracks running in every direction, like a road map of some unidentified continent. On the wall directly above him was a monochrome picture of a forbidding-looking building with huge bars across the main entrance and slit windows. Will could just make out "Newgate" written below it.

Opposite ran a long counter on which the policeman had placed their rucksacks and Will's spade, and beyond that was an office of some sort where three desks were surrounded by a forest of narrow wooden filing cabinets. A number of smaller rooms led off this main room, and from one came the rapid tapping of what could have been a typewriter.

Just as Will was looking at the far corner of the room where a profusion of burnished brass pipes ran up the walls like the stems of an ancient vine, there was a screeching hiss that ended with a solid clunk. The noise was so sudden that, stirred from his anxious torpor, Chester sat up and blinked around the room like a nervous rabbit.

Another policeman emerged from a side room and hurried over to the brass pipes. There he glanced at a panel of antiquated dials from which a cascade of twisted wires spiralled down to a wooden box, and then opened a hatch in one of the pipes, prising out a bullet-shaped cylinder the size of a small rolling pin. Unscrewing a cap from one end, he extracted a roll of paper that crackled as he straightened it out to read it.

"Styx on their way," he said gruffly, striding over to the counter and, not once looking in the boys' direction, opened up a large ledger. He also had a yellow star stitched into his jacket and, although his appearance was much like that of the other officer, he was younger and his head was covered with a neatly cut stubble of white hair.

"Chester," Will whispered. As his friend didn't react, he extended a hand to nudge him. In a flash, a truncheon lashed out, smacking smartly across his knuckles.

"Desist!" the policeman next to them barked.

"Ouch!" Will jumped up from the bench, his fists clenched. "You fat ..." he shouted, his body trembling as if he was about to strike the man, but Chester reached out and grabbed hold of his arm.

"Don't Will!"

Will angrily shook Chester's hand off and stared into the policeman's cold eyes. "I want to know why we're being held," he demanded.

For a horrible moment they thought the policeman's face was going to explode, it turned such a livid red. But then his huge shoulders begin to heave, and a low grating laugh rumbled up, which grew louder and louder. Will threw a sidelong glance at Chester who was eyeing the policeman with alarm.

"If we're being arrested, I want to make my call," Will said defiantly. "I know my rights."

"I know my rights," the man mimicked through his guffaws.

"ENOUGH!" the voice of the man behind the counter cracked like a whip as he looked up from the ledger, his gaze falling on the laughing policeman, who immediately fell silent.

"YOU!" the man glowered at Will. "SIT DOWN!" His voice held such authority that Will didn't hesitate for a second, quickly taking his place next to Chester again. "I ... " the man continued, pushing out his barrel chest, " ... am the First Officer. You are already acquainted with the Second Officer." He nodded in the direction of the policeman standing by them.

The First Officer looked down at the paper scroll from the message tube. "You are hereby charged with unlawful entry and trespassage into the Quarter under statute twelve, subsection two," he read in a monotone.

"But ..." Will began meekly.

The First Officer ignored him and read on. "Furthermore, you did, uninvited, enter a property with the intent to pilfer, under statute six, subsection six," he continued matter-of-factly. "Do you understand these charges?" he asked.

Will and Chester shot each other confused looks and Will was about to reply when the First Officer cut him short.

"Now what have we here?" he said, opening their rucksacks

and emptying the contents out onto the counter. He picked up the foil brick of sandwiches Will had prepared and, not bothering to open them, sniffed at them.

"Ah, swine," he said, with a flicker of a smile. And from the way he briefly licked his lips and slid it to one side, Will knew he'd seen the last of his packed lunch. Then the First Officer turned his attention to the other items, working his way through them methodically. He lingered on the compass, but was more taken with the Swiss army knife, levering out each of its blades in turn and squeezing the little scissors with his thick fingers before he finally put it down. Then, as he casually rolled a ball of string on the countertop with one hand, with the other he flicked open the dog-eared geological map that had been in Will's rucksack for a cursory inspection. Finally, he leant over and smelt it, wrinkling his face with a look of distaste before he began on the camera.

"Hmmm," he muttered thoughtfully, turning it in his banana-like fingers to examine it from several angles.

"That's mine," Will said.

The First Officer completely ignored him and, putting the camera down, picked up a pen and dipped it in an inkwell set into the counter. With the pen poised over the ledger, he cleared his throat.

"NAME!" he bellowed, throwing a glance in Chester's direction.

"It's, er, Chester … Chester Rawls," the boy stammered.

The First Officer wrote in the ledger. The scratching of the nib on the page was the only sound in the room and Will was suddenly aware of an overpowering sensation of helplessness, as if the entry in the ledger was setting in motion the wheels of an irrevocable process, the machinations of which were quite beyond his understanding.

"AND YOU?" he snapped at Will.

"He told me my father was here," Will said, stabbing his finger in the direction of the Second Officer. "Where is he? I want to see him now!"

The First Officer looked at his colleague and then back to

Will. "You won't be seeing anyone unless you do as you are told." He shot another glance at the Second Officer and frowned with barely disguised disapproval. The Second Officer averted his gaze and shifted uneasily from foot to foot.

"NAME!"

"Will Burrows," Will answered slowly.

The First Officer picked up the scroll and consulted it again. "That is not the name I have here," he said, shaking his head and then fixing Will with his steely eyes.

"I don't care what it says. I know my own name."

There was a deafening silence as the First Officer continued to stare at Will. Then he abruptly slammed the ledger shut with a loud slap, causing a cloud of dust to billow up from the counter's surface.

"GET THEM TO THE HOLD!" he barked apoplectically.

They were dragged to their feet and, just as they were being pushed roughly through a large oak door at the end of the reception area, they heard another long hiss followed by a dull clunk as a further message arrived in the pipe system.

The aisle of the Hold was about 30 feet long and dimly lit by a single globe at the far end, beneath which stood a small wooden desk and chair. A blank wall ran along the right-hand side, and on the wall opposite were four dull iron doors set deep into solid brick surrounds. The boys were pushed along to the furthest door on which the number four was marked in Roman numerals.

The Second Officer opened the door. As it swung back silently on its well-greased hinges, he stepped aside. Looking at the boys, he inclined his head towards the cell and, as they hovered uncertainly on the threshold, he lost patience and shoved them in with his large hands, slamming the door behind them.

Inside the cell, the clang of the door reverberated sickeningly about the walls, and their stomachs turned as the key twisted in the lock. They tried to make out the detail of the dark and dank cell by feeling their way around, Chester managing to knock a bucket clattering over as he moved to the wall. They found there was a three-foot wide, lead-covered ledge along the length of the wall opposite the door and, without a word, they both sat down on it. They felt its rough surface, cold and clammy, under their palms as their eyes gradually adjusted to the only light in the cell, the meagre illumination that filtered through an observation hatch in the cell door. Finally, Chester broke the silence with a loud sniff.

"What *is* that smell?"

"I'm not sure," said Will as he too sniffed. "Sick? Sweat?" Then he sniffed again and pronounced, with the air of a connoisseur, "Carbolic acid and …" Sniffing once more, he added: "Is that sulphur?"

"Huh?" his friend muttered.

"No, cabbage! Boiled cabbage!"

"It's like a bloody public toilet," Chester said, grimacing with disgust.

"Lavatory," Will interjected casually.

"Whatever. This place is foul. How exactly are we going to get out of here, Will?" he asked, turning to look directly at him in the gloom.

Will drew his knees up under his chin and, resting his feet on the edge of the ledge, scratched his calf thoughtfully but said nothing.

"I've got this awful feeling we're never to see home again, are we?" Chester continued, now looking dejectedly at the floor.

"Look, we found a way in here, and we're sure as hell going to find our way out again," Will said, reassuring his friend, but not himself.

With that, the conversation petered out and the room was filled with the sound of the ever-present thrumming in the background, and the erratic scuttling of unseen insects.

⚊◦⚊

Will woke with a start, catching his breath as if coming up for air. He was surprised to find he had actually dozed off in a half-sitting position on the lead sill. *How long had he slept?* He looked blearily about the shadowy gloom. Chester was standing with his back pressed against the wall, staring wide-eyed at the cell door. Will could almost feel the fear emanating from him. He automatically followed Chester's gaze to the observation hatch. Framed in the opening was the leering face of the Second Officer but, due to the size of his head, only the eyes and nose were visible. Hearing the keys jangle in the lock, Will watched as the man's eyes narrowed, and then the mechanism creaked tightly and clunked. The door swung open to reveal the officer silhouetted in the doorway, like a monstrous cartoon illustration.

"YOU!" he said to Will. "OUT NOW!"

"Why? What for?"

"MOVE IT!" the officer barked.

"Will?" Chester gasped.

"Don't worry, Chester, it'll be all right," Will said as he stood up, his legs cramped and stiff from the damp. He stretched them as he walked awkwardly out of the cell and into the aisle. Then he began to make his way to the main door of the Hold.

"Stand still," said the Second Officer as he locked the door again. Then, grabbing Will's arm in a painful grip, he steered him out of the Hold and down a succession of bleak corridors, their footfalls echoing emptily about the flaking whitewashed walls and bare stone floors. Eventually, they turned a corner down into a narrow stairwell that led into a short, dead-ended passage. It smelt damp and earthy, like an old cellar.

A bright light issued from an open door about halfway down. A sense of dread was growing in the pit of Will's stomach as they approached the doorway and, sure enough, he was pushed into the well-lit room by his escort and brought to an abrupt halt. Dazzled by the brightness, Will squinted as he peered around him.

The room was nondescript and bare except for a bizarre chair and a metal table behind which two tall figures were standing, their thin bodies arching over so that their heads were almost touching as they talked quietly to each other in urgent, conspiratorial whispers. Will strained to catch what they were saying, but it didn't seem to be in any language he recognised, punctuated as it was by an alarming series of the most peculiar high-pitched, scratchy noises. Try as he might, he couldn't make out a single word; it was completely unintelligible to him.

So, with his arm still held tight in the officer's crushing grip, Will stood and waited, his stomach knotting with nervous tension as his eyes became accustomed to the brightness. From time to time, the strange men glanced fleetingly at him, but Will didn't dare utter a word in the presence of this new and sinister authority.

They were dressed identically with pristine, stark white collars around their necks. These were so large that they draped over the shoulders of their stiff, full-length leather coats, which creaked as the men gesticulated to each other. The skin of their gaunt faces, the colour of new putty, only served to emphasise their jet-black eyes. Their hair, shaved high at the temples, was oiled back against their scalps so that they looked as though they were wearing shiny skullcaps.

Quite unexpectedly, they stopped and turned to Will.

"These gentlemen are the Styx," said the Second Officer behind him, "and you will answer their questions."

"Chair," the Styx on the right said, his black eyes staring unwaveringly at Will.

He pointed with a long-fingered hand at the strange chair that stood between the table and Will. Overcome by a sense of foreboding, Will didn't protest as the officer sat him down. An adjustable metal bar rose from the back of the chair, with two padded clamps at the top to hold the occupant's head firmly in place. The officer adjusted the height of the bar, then tightened the clamps, pressing them hard against Will's temples. He tried to turn his head to look at the officer, but the restraints held him fast. While the officer continued to secure him, Will realised he had absolutely no choice but to face the Styx, who stood patiently behind the table like avaricious priests.

The officer stooped and, in the periphery of his vision, Will saw him pull something from underneath the chair and then heard the old leather straps creak and the large buckles rattle as each of his wrists were strapped to the corresponding thigh.

"What's this for?" Will dared to ask.

"Your own protection," the officer said as, crouching down, he proceeded to loop further straps around Will's legs, just below the knees, to the legs of the chair. Both of Will's ankles were then secured in a similar fashion, the officer pulling the bindings so taut that they bit mercilessly and made Will squirm with discomfort. He noticed with some dismay that his grimaces appeared to amuse the Styx. Finally, a strap some four inches thick was drawn tightly across his chest and arms, and fastened behind the back of the chair. The officer then stood to attention until the Styx nodded mutely to him and he left the room, closing the door behind him.

Alone with them, Will watched in terrified silence, transfixed like an animal caught in headlights as one of the Styx produced an odd-looking lamp and placed it in the centre of the table facing Will. It had a solid base and a short curved arm topped with a shallow conical shade. This held what appeared to be a dark purple bulb; it reminded Will of an old sunlamp he'd seen in his father's museum, a "Pifco" or something similar. A small black box with dials and switches was placed next to it, and the lamp was plugged into this with an old, twisted brown cable. The Styx's pale finger jabbed at a switch and the box began to hum quietly to itself.

One Styx stepped back from the table as the other continued to lean over the lamp, manipulating what were clearly controls behind the shade. With a loud click, the bulb flared a dim orange for an instant, and then appeared to go out again.

"Going to take my picture?" Will asked in a weak attempt at levity as he tried to steady the tremor in his voice. Ignoring him, the Styx turned a dial on the black box, as if he was tuning a radio.

Alarmingly, an uncomfortable pressure began to build up behind Will's eyes. He opened his mouth in a silent yawn, trying to relieve this strange tension in his temples, when the room began to darken, as if the device was literally sucking all the light from it. Thinking he was going blind, Will blinked several times and opened his eyes as wide as he could. With the greatest difficulty, he could just make out the two Styx silhouetted in the dim light reflecting off the wall behind them.

He became aware of an incessant pulsing drone but, for the life of him, he couldn't pinpoint where it was coming from. As it grew more intense, his head began to feel decidedly strange, as if every bone and sinew were vibrating. It was like a plane

flying too low overhead. The resonance seemed to coalesce into a spiked ball of energy in the very centre of his head. He began to panic but, not being able to move an inch, he could do nothing to resist. As the Styx manipulated the dials, the ball appeared to shift, slowly sinking through his body into his chest and then circling his heart, causing him to catch his breath and cough involuntarily. Then it was moving back and out of his body, and he could feel it hovering somewhere behind him. It was as if a living thing was pulsing and homing in and searching for something. It shifted again, and now hovered half-in and half-out of his body, at the nape of his neck.

"What's going on?" Will asked, trying to summon up some bravado, but there was no response from the ever-darkening figures. "You're not scaring me with all this, you know."

They remained silent.

Will closed his eyes for a second, but when he reopened them, he found he couldn't even distinguish the outlines of the Styx in the total darkness that now confronted him. He began struggling against his bonds.

"Does the absence of light unsettle you?" asked the Styx on the left.

"No, why should it?"

"What is your name?" The words cut into Will's consciousness like a knife out of the darkness.

"I've told you, it's Will. Will Burrows."

"Your real name!" Again the voice caused Will to wince with pain – it was as if each word was setting off electric shocks in his temples.

"I don't know what you mean," he answered through gritted teeth.

The ball of energy began to edge into the centre of his skull, the humming growing more intense now, the throbbing pulse enveloping him in a heavy blanket of pressure.

"Are you with the man called Burrows?"

Will's head was swimming, waves of pain rippling through him. His feet and hands were tingling unpleasantly with intense pins and needles. This horrible sensation was slowly

enveloping his whole body.

"He's my Dad!" he shouted.

"What is your purpose here?" The precise, clipped voice was closer now.

As he swallowed back the rush of saliva flooding into his mouth, Will felt he was going to be sick at any moment.

"Where is your mother?" The measured but insistent voice now seemed to be emanating from the ball inside his head. It was as though both Styx had entered his cranium and were searching feverishly through his mind, like burglars ransacking drawers and cupboards for valuable items.

"What is your purpose?" Will tried again to struggle against his bonds, but realised he could no longer feel his body. In fact, it felt as if he had been reduced to a floating head cast adrift into a fog of darkness, and he couldn't fathom which way was up or down any more.

"NAME? PURPOSE?" The questions came thick and fast as Will felt all his remaining energy seep out of him.

Then the incessant voice became fainter, as if Will was moving away from it. From a great distance, words were being shouted after him, and each word, when it finally arrived, set off small pinpricks of light at the edge of his vision, which swam and jittered until the darkness before him was filled with a boiling sea of white dots, so bright and so intense that his eyes ached. All the time, the scratchy whispers swept around him and the room spun and pitched. Another deep wave of nausea overwhelmed him, and a burning sensation filled his head to bursting point. White, white, blinding white, cramming into his head until it felt as if it was going to explode.

"I'm going to be sick … please … I'm going to … feel faint … please," and the light of the white space seared into him and he felt himself growing smaller and smaller, until he was a tiny fleck in the huge white emptiness. Then the light began to fade and the burning sensation grew less and less, until everything was black and silent, as if the universe itself had gone out.

He came around as the Second Officer, supporting him under one arm, turned the key in the cell door. He was shaky and weak. Vomit was streaked down the front of his clothes and his mouth was dry with an acrid metallic taste that made him gag. His head was pounding with pain and, as he tried to look up, it was as though part of his vision was missing. He couldn't stop himself from groaning as the door was pulled open.

"Not so cocky now, eh?" the officer said, letting go of Will's arm. He tried to walk, but his legs were like jelly. "Not after your first taste of the Dark Light," the officer sneered.

After a couple of steps, Will's legs went into spasm and he fell heavily onto his knees. Chester dashed over to him, panic-stricken at his friend's condition.

"Will, Will, what have they done to you?" Chester asked as he helped him over to the ledge. "You've been gone for hours."

"Just tired ..." Will managed to mumble as he slumped down on the ledge and rolled up in a ball, grateful for the coolness of the lead lining against his aching head. He shut his eyes – he just wanted to sleep – but his head was still spinning and waves of nausea were breaking over him.

"YOU!" the officer snapped. Chester jumped up from beside Will and turned to the officer, who beckoned to him with a thick forefinger.

"Your turn."

Chester looked down at Will, who now lay unconscious.

"Oh no."

"NOW!" the officer shouted. "Don't make me come in there."

Chester reluctantly walked out into the aisle. After locking the door, the officer took him by the arm and marched him off.

"What's a Dark Light?" Chester asked, his eyes wide with fear.

"Just questions," the officer smiled, "nothing to worry about."

"But I don't know anything ..."

<hr />

Will was woken by the sound of a hatch being pulled back at the base of the door.

"Food," a voice announced coldly.

He was starving. He lifted himself up into a sitting position, his body aching dully as if he had the flu. Every bone and muscle complained when he tried to move.

"Oh God!" he groaned, and then suddenly thought of Chester. The open food hatch shed a little more illumination than usual into the cell and, as he looked about him, there on the floor at the base of the lead-covered ledge, was his friend, lying in a foetal position. Chester's breathing was shallow and his face pale and feverish in the half light. Will staggered up onto his legs and, with difficulty, fetched the two trays back to the ledge. He inspected the contents briefly. There were two bowls with something in them and some liquid in battered tin cups. It all looked terribly unappetising, but at least it was hot, and didn't smell too bad.

"Chester," Will crouched down and shook him gently by the shoulder. "Chester …"

"Urgh … wha?" his friend moaned and tried to lift his head. Will could see his nose had been bleeding; the blood was caked and smudged across his cheek.

"Food, Chester. Come on, you'll feel better once you've eaten something."

Will manoeuvred Chester into a sitting position, propping his back against the wall. He dipped his sleeve into one of the cups and attempted to clean the blood off Chester's face. Chester grimaced and squirmed.

"What the hell are you doing?"

"That's an improvement. Here, eat something," Will said, handing a bowl to Chester, who immediately pushed it away.

"I'm not hungry. I feel bloody awful."

"At least drink some of this. I think it's a sort of herb tea." Will handed the drink to Chester, who cupped his hands around the warm mug. "What did they ask you?" Will mumbled through a mouthful of the grey mush.

"Everything. Name … address … your name … all that stuff. I can't remember most of it. I think I fainted … I really thought I was going to die," Chester said in a flat voice, staring into the middle distance.

Will began to chuckle quietly. Strange as it may seem, his own suffering seemed to be relieved somewhat by hearing his friend's complaints.

"What's so funny?" Chester asked, outrage in his voice. "It's not funny."

"No," Will laughed, "maybe not. Here, try some of this. It's actually quite good."

Chester shuddered with disgust at the grey slurry in the

bowl. Nevertheless, he picked up the spoon and poked at it, somewhat suspiciously at first. Then he sniffed at it.

"Seems okay," he said, trying to convince himself.

"Just bloody eat it, will you?" Will said, filling his mouth again. He felt his strength begin to return with each mouthful. "I keep thinking I said something about Becky and Mum to them, but I'm not sure if I didn't dream it." He thought for a moment and then spoke again. "And Dad's journal – I keep seeing it in my mind, clear as anything – as if I'm there, watching as their long white fingers open it and turn the pages, one by one. But that can't have happened, can it? It's all mixed up. What about you?"

Chester shifted a little. "I don't know. I might have mentioned the cellar in your house ... and about Becky. Oh God, I really don't know. It's like I can't remember if it's what I said, or what I thought." He put his mug down and cradled his head in his hands while Will leant back, peering up at the dark ceiling.

"Wonder what time it is ..." he sighed, "... up there?"

⚫

Over what must have been the next week, there followed more interrogations with the Styx, the Dark Light leaving both of them with the same awful side effects as before: exhaustion, a befuddled uncertainty about just what it was that they had told their tormentors, and the appalling bouts of sickness that ensued.

Then came a day when the boys were left alone. Although they couldn't be sure, they both felt certain that the Styx must have got all they wanted for now, and hoped against hope that the sessions were over.

And so the hours passed and the two boys slept fitfully, mealtimes came and went, and they divided their time between walking the floor, when they felt strong enough, and resting on the ledge, even occasionally shouting at the door, to no avail. And in the constant, unchanging light, they lost all sense of time, and of day or night. Whilst beyond the walls of their cell, Machiavellian processes were in play: investigations, meetings, and chatterings, all in the scratchy secret language of the Styx, were deciding their fate.

Ignorant of this, the boys worked hard to keep their spirits up. In hushed tones, they talked at length about how they might effect an escape, and whether or not a search party had been sent after them (and they kicked themselves for not leaving a note). Would Rebecca tell the authorities about the cellar, and would they then discover the tunnel? Maybe Will's father would somehow get them out of there? And what day of the week did they think it was? And more importantly, not having washed for some time now, their clothes must have taken on a decidedly funky aroma, and that being the case, why did they not smell any worse to each other?

It was during one particularly lively debate about who these people were and where they had come from, that the surveillance hatch opened and the Second Officer leered in. They both immediately fell silent as the door was unlocked and the grim, familiar figure all but blotted out the light from the aisle. *Which one of them was it to be this time?*

"Visitors."

They looked at each other in disbelief.

"Visitors? For us?" Chester asked incredulously.

The officer shook his head and looked at Will. "You."

"What about Ches …"

"You, come on. NOW!" the officer bellowed.

"Don't worry, Chester, I won't go anywhere without you," Will said confidently to his friend, who sat back with a pained smile and nodded in silent affirmation.

Will stood up and shuffled out of the cell. Chester watched as the door clanged shut and, finding himself once more alone, looked down at his hands, rough and ingrained with dirt, and longed for home and comfort. He felt the increasingly frequent sting of frustration and helplessness, and his eyes filled with hot tears. No, he wouldn't cry, he would not give them the satisfaction; he knew Will would work something out, and that he'd be ready when he did.

"Come on, stupid," he said quietly to himself, wiping his eyes

There, purring with all his might, sat Bartleby.

"And when the judgement comes ..."

"We call him the Crawfly ..."

Heraldo Walsh staggered back and Tam was on him …

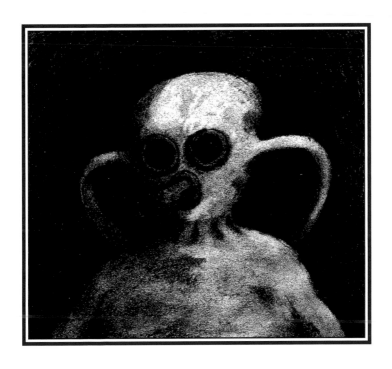

"It's only a Coprolite.*"*

She stood out like some dark angel.

Columns, Doric and Corinthian, sprang up to support dizzying galleries and walkways.

A single figure before a bristling field of drawn scythes.

with his sleeve. "Drop and give me twenty," he mimicked his football coach's voice as he got down on the floor and began to do press-ups, counting as he did so.

Will was shown into a whitewashed room with a polished floor, along the middle of which ran a large table dividing the area in two. Sitting behind this were two figures, still a little bleary to him as his sight hadn't yet adjusted from the darkness of the Hold. He rubbed his eyes and then glanced down at his front. His shirt was filthy and, worse still, specked with dried traces of his vomit. He brushed at it feebly before his attention was drawn to an odd-looking hatch or window on the wall to his left. The surface of the glass, if it was glass, had a peculiar blueblack depth to it. And this matt and mottled surface didn't seem to be reflecting any of the light from the orbs in the room.

For some reason, Will couldn't take his eyes off the surface. He felt a sudden twinge of recognition. A new yet familiar feeling swept over him. *They* were behind there. *They* were watching all this. And the longer he stared, the more the darkness filled him, just as it had with the Dark Light. He felt a sudden spasm in his head. He pitched forward, as though he was about to faint, and his left hand groped wildly and found the backrest of the chair in front of him. The officer, seeing this, caught him by his other arm and helped him to sit down, facing the two strangers.

Will took some deep breaths and the lightheadedness passed. He looked up as someone coughed. Opposite him sat a large man and, by his side, sitting a little way back, was a young boy. The man was much like all the others he had seen – it could easily have been the Second Officer in civilian clothing. He was staring fixedly at Will with barely concealed contempt. Will felt too drained to care and numbly returned the stranger's gaze.

Then, as chair legs grated loudly on the floor and the boy moved closer to the table, Will focused his attention on him. The boy was looking at Will with an expression of wonder. He had an open and friendly face – the first that Will had seen down here since he had been arrested. Will estimated that the boy was probably a couple of years younger than himself. His hair was almost white and closely cropped, giving it the appearance of a fine suede, and his soft blue eyes shimmered with a mischievous knowing. As the corners of the boy's mouth curled into a smile, Will thought that he seemed vaguely familiar. He tried desperately to remember where he'd seen him before, but his mind was still too cloudy and unclear. He narrowed his eyes at the boy and tried again to work out where he knew him from, but it was no use. It was as if he was casting about in a murky pool, trying to find something precious with only his sense of touch to guide him. His head began to swim and he clenched his eyes shut and kept them that way.

He heard the man clear his throat. "I am Mr Jerome," he said in a flat and perfunctory tone. It was clear from the tenor that he was uncomfortable with the situation and very resentful at being there. "This is my son …"

"Cal," Will heard the boy say.

"Caleb," the man quickly corrected.

There was a long and awkward pause, but Will still didn't open his eyes. He felt as if he was insulated and safe in his self-imposed exile. It was oddly comforting.

Mr Jerome looked testily at the Second Officer. "This is useless," he grunted. "It's a waste of bloody time."

The officer leant forward and brusquely prodded Will's shoulder. "Sit up and be civil to your family. Show some respect."

Startled, Will's eyes snapped open. He swivelled in his chair to face the officer.

"What?"

"I said be civil," he nodded to Mr Jerome, "to your family, like."

Will swivelled back to face the man and boy.

"What the hell are you talking about?"

Mr Jerome shrugged and looked down, and the boy frowned, his gaze switching between Will, the officer and his father, as if he didn't quite understand what was happening.

"Chester's right, you're all bloody mad down here," Will exclaimed and flinched as the Second Officer took a step towards him with his hand raised. But the situation was defused by the boy as he butted in.

"You must remember this?" he said, delving into an old canvas bag on his lap. All eyes were on him as he finally produced a small object and placed it on the table in front of Will. It was a carved wooden toy, a rat or a mouse. Its white painted face was chipped and faded and its little formal coat was threadbare; yet its eyes glowed eerily. Cal looked expectantly at Will.

"Grandma said it was your favourite," he continued, as Will didn't react. "It was given to me after you went."

"What are you …?" Will asked, perplexed, "After I went where?"

"Don't you remember at all?" Cal asked. He looked deferentially at his father, who was now sitting back in his chair with his arms crossed.

Will reached out and picked up the little toy to examine it more closely. As he tipped it back, he noticed that the eyes closed, a tiny shutter counterbalancing in the head to extinguish the light. Will realised there must be a minute luminescent sphere within its head, which issued the light through the glass beads that were its eyes.

"It sleeps," Cal said.

Will dropped it on the table as abruptly as if it had bitten him. He snapped at the boy.

"What are you talking about?"

There was a moment of uncertainty on everyone's part and, once again, an unnerving silence descended over the room, broken finally by the Second Officer who began to hum quietly to himself. Cal opened his mouth as if he was about to speak, but seemed to be struggling to find the words. Will sat looking at the toy mouse, which Cal snatched off the table and replaced in his bag. Then, looking up at Will, he frowned.

"Your name is Seth," he said, almost resentfully. "You're my brother."

"Hah!" Will laughed dryly in Cal's face and then, as all the bitterness from his treatment at the hands of the Styx welled up inside him, he shook his head and spoke to him harshly. "Yeah. Right. Anything you say."

"It's true. Your mother was my mother. She tried to run away with both of us. She took you Topsoil, but left me with Grandma and Father."

Will rolled his eyes and twisted around to face the Second Officer. "Very clever. It's a good trick, but I'm not buying it."

The officer pursed his lips but said nothing.

"You were taken in by a family of Topsoilers …" Cal said, raising his voice.

"Don't waste your breath, Caleb," said Mr Jerome, interrupting his son and putting a hand on his shoulder. But Cal shook it off and continued, his voice beginning to crack with despair.

"They're not your real family. We're your real family."

Will stared at Mr Jerome, whose reddened face exuded nothing but hatred. Then he looked again at Cal, who had now sat back despondently, his head bowed. *They must think I'm a moron*, Will thought.

"This is going nowhere," Mr Jerome said, hastily rising to his feet and buttoning his coat.

And Cal, rising with him, spoke quietly. "Grandma always said you'd come back."

"I don't have any grandparents. They're all dead!" Will shouted, jumping up from his chair, his eyes now burning with anger and brimming with tears. He tore over to the glass window on the wall and pressed his face against the surface.

"Very clever!" he yelled at it. "Nearly had me going there!" He shielded his eyes from the light of the room in an effort to see beyond the glass, but there was nothing, only the unrelenting darkness. The Second Officer grabbed his arm and pulled him away from it. Will did not resist – the fight had gone out of him for now.

"I guess we're finished here," Will said.

The officer smiled a severe, tight-lipped grin that was

completely out of place on that big, rugged head.

"Looks like it," he agreed.

CHAPTER TWENTY-ONE

Rebecca lay on top of her bed, staring up at her ceiling. She'd just had a long hot bath and was dressed in her jade-green dressing gown, with her hair up in a towel turban and her feet looking quite ridiculous in large furry monster-foot slippers. She was humming quietly along to the classical music station on her bedside radio as she mulled over the extraordinary events of the last three days.

It had all started with her being woken at about two o'clock on the Friday morning by a frantic knocking and ringing at the front door. Although it was the middle of the night, she had had to get up and answer it, as her mother, on the strong sleeping pills she'd recently been prescribed, was doped up and, to all intents and purposes, dead to the world. A drunken brass band couldn't have roused her if they'd tried.

As Rebecca had opened the front door, she'd been almost knocked off her feet by Chester's father as he burst into the hallway and immediately began to bombard her with questions.

"Is Chester here? We thought he must have slept over. We phoned but no one answered." His face was unshaven and ashen, and he was wearing a crumpled beige mac.

"I don't think …" she started to say.

"He said he was helping Will with a project, but … is he around … where's Will … can you get him, please?" Mr Rawls' words tripped over each other as he glanced anxiously down the hall and up the stairs.

Without a word, Rebecca ran up to Will's room. She didn't bother to knock; she already had a feeling about what she would find. She opened the door and turned on the light. Sure enough, Will wasn't there, and his bed hadn't been slept in. She turned out the light and closed the door behind her, returning downstairs to Mr Rawls.

"No, he's not there," she said with a puzzled look. "I think Chester was here, though, last night; they both went down … maybe they …"

On hearing this, Mr Rawls became almost incoherent, babbling something about checking their usual haunts and calling the police as he tore out of the front door, leaving it open behind him.

Rebecca had no idea what to do next. She decided to try to rouse her mother. Knocking on the sitting room door and getting no answer, she entered. The room was dark and stuffy, and she could hear her mother's regular snoring.

"Mum, Mum," she said with gentle insistence.

"Urphh?"

"Mum," she shook her mother's arm.

"Wha? Nnno … smmumph?"

"Mum, wake up, it's important."

"… me … alone," said an obdurate, sleepy voice.

"It's Will and Chester … they've …"

"Oh go awayyyy!" her mother snapped, turning away in the chair and pulling the old travelling rug over her head. The shallow snoring resumed as she returned to her state of hibernation. Rebecca sighed with sheer frustration as she stood next to the shapeless form.

She went into the kitchen and sat down. With the DCI's number on a scrap of paper in her hand and the cordless phone lying on the table in front of her, she had debated for a long time just what she should do next. It was dawn before she made the call and, getting only the answer service, left a message. She returned upstairs to her bedroom and tried to read a book while she waited for a response.

The police turned up at precisely 7.06 am. After that, events took on a life of their own. The house was filled with uniformed officers searching every room, poking around every closet and chest of drawers. Wearing plastic gloves, they began in Will's room and worked through the rest of the house, culminating with the cellar, but apparently found nothing much of interest. She was completely taken aback when she saw that they had retrieved articles of Will's clothing from the wickerwork laundry basket on the landing; a pair of his mud encrusted jeans, a T-shirt and even his socks and underpants had been carefully sealed up in polythene bags and carried outside.

While this was going on, the DCI and a female detective were interviewing her mother, who seemed to be detached and disturbed by turns. At first, Rebecca busied herself by straightening up the mess left by the untidy searchers. It had occurred to her that she should offer them some tea, but they were so hard-faced and unfriendly, she pretended to clean the kitchen instead. As she wiped down the units nearest the door, she tried to catch what the detectives were asking her mother. She wanted to get some idea of just what the police thought might have befallen her brother and his friend.

At one point, while the uniformed police were out of the way in another part of the house, she stole into the hall. She stood by the sitting room door, straining to hear the exchange on the other side. But she could only make out vague snatches of the proceedings, a word here or there, and none of it any use. When the door finally opened, she followed the DCI to the door and, as he walked down the garden path to the parked squad cars, she couldn't help but overhear his words as he chatted to his colleague.

"That one's a few volts short of a full charge."

"Very sad," the female detective said.

"You know … " the DCI said, pausing to glance back at the house, "… to lose one family member is unfortunate …" His colleague had nodded.

"… but to lose two is downright iffy," the DCI continued, "Very bloody iffy, in my book."

The female detective nodded again with a grim smile on her face.

"We'd better have a sweep of the Common, just in case." Rebecca heard him say before he was finally out of earshot.

The next day, the police had sent a car for them. They sat next to each other in the back, and Mrs Burrows was remote and uncommunicative for the short trip to the station. For much of the journey, she stared vacantly up at the sky through the car windows. It crossed Rebecca's mind that her mother was quietly furious that she had rung the police. But what alternative had she had?

Arriving at the station, her mother's mood changed to one of extreme distress the instant she spotted the DCI waiting by the reception desk. Rebecca saw her mother's chin begin to shake and she erupted into floods of tears as she was led away to an interview room.

Rebecca was shown to a small waiting room by a WPC who brought her a cup of vending machine chocolate, lukewarm and watery, and a sandwich on a paper plate from the canteen. As Rebecca ate, the WPC spoke nicely to her, but she noticed that the conversation frequently veered towards gentle questions about her family, her father and brother, and her mother's state of mind. All very pleasant, as if an old friend of the family was catching up on the latest news. They ended up with a discussion of their favourite recipes and how terribly expensive food had become recently. Although the WPC wasn't very knowledgeable on either topic and Rebecca knew she was being humoured, she still liked it that someone was making the effort. It brought home just how isolated she'd become, in a family that one by one was losing its members.

She was then taken out of the waiting room and reunited with her mother, who looked tired and drawn. The DCI and the female detective saw them to a waiting police car, telling them that everything possible would be done to find Will and Chester. They said that they were sorry for any inconvenience, but that it was just routine, in these cases, to conduct interviews with the family.

Mrs Burrows was silent for the entire journey home. She stared down at her handbag, one that she'd bought with Rebecca on a shopping trip to the West End, while Rebecca held her hand and threw surreptitious glances at her from time to time.

But, as the car drew to a halt in front of the house, Mrs Burrows all of a sudden blurted out that she intended to "sue the police for harassment" and unleashed a torrent of angry words at the two rather astonished policemen in the front seats. As she hastily got out of the car, with several of their neighbours trying their best not to watch, she slammed the door with a crash and shouted at the top of her voice.

"Mark my words, you lackeys, you'll be hearing from me!" she cried. "I've got your numbers!"

Rebecca heard the young driver mutter under his breath: "And we've got yours." Without a further word, they had driven off.

So now, three days later, she lay on her bed, her mind whirling in a maelstrom of the recent events. But despite all the concern shown by the serious faces down at the police station and, worst of all, the gentle probing of the WPC, whose questions had very subtly hinted at the terrible fates that might have befallen her brother, she somehow knew that both Will and Chester were in no immediate danger.

Besides, Will had gone walkabout before, albeit not for three days, not without any word, and she knew he was like that, like his father, self-absorbed. When Will was in the middle of one of his escapades, gripped by the madness of his obsession of the moment, it was as though no one else in the world mattered, or even existed. She remembered their father grounding Will for a week when he'd camped out all night to watch a meteorite storm without asking or thinking of mentioning it to anyone beforehand. This punishment had only lasted two days before Dr Burrows relented as Will had been climbing the walls with frustration and boredom.

And not a day too soon. With a smile, she remembered how Will, cooped up in his room, had dismantled his bed and wardrobe and then started to lift up the floorboards, "Just to see what's there". And she had always thought that their father was somewhat to blame. It was he who had ranted on about the meteorite storm in the first place, filling his son's head with thoughts of sparkling showers of metal footballs bouncing off the Earth's atmosphere.

No, Rebecca wasn't worried about Will. He was a survivor. Her immediate concern was her mother and her rapidly deteriorating mental state. She was alarmed by her sudden mood swings, ranging from chronic inertia, her face set in a rictus of mask-like despondency, to explosions of manic and undirected fury. Rebecca wrote a quick note to herself in her diary and then climbed under her duvet and turned out her bedside lamp. After what seemed like an age, she fell into a troubled sleep.

Downstairs, Mrs Burrows was ensconced in her armchair, curled up and fully clothed under the travelling rug that was tucked around her like a drab tartan cocoon. The only light in the room came from a muted Open University programme – the cool blue light pulsing intermittently and causing the shadows to jump and jerk, lending a sort of animation to the furniture and objects in the room. She was sleeping deeply when a noise in the room brought her to. A deep murmur, like a strong wind combing through the branches of the trees in the garden outside.

She opened her eyes a fraction. In the far corner of the room, by the half-opened curtains of the French windows, she could make out a large, shadowy form. For a moment she wondered if she was dreaming, as the shadow shifted and changed under the light of the television. She strained to make out just what was there. She wondered if it could be an intruder. *What should she do? Pretend to be asleep? Or lie quite still so the intruder wouldn't bother her? What should she do?*

She held her breath, trying to control the rising panic inside her. The seconds felt like hours as the shape remained stationary. She began to think that maybe it was just an innocent shadow after all. A trick of the light and an overactive imagination. She let the air out of her lungs, opening her eyes fully.

All of a sudden there was a snuffling sound and, to her horror, the shadow split into two distinct ghost-like blurs and closed on her with unnatural speed. As her senses reeled in shock and terror, a calm and collected voice in her head told her with absolute conviction, "THEY ARE NOT GHOSTS".

In a flash the figures were upon her. She tried to scream, but no sound came. Rough material brushed against her face as she smelt a peculiar mustiness, something like mildewed clothes. Then a powerful hand struck her and she curled up in pain, winded and struggling for air, until, like a newborn baby, she caught her breath and let out an unholy shriek.

She was swept up from her chair, out of the room and into the hallway. Now howling like a banshee and kicking and struggling, she glimpsed another figure looming from the doorway of the cellar and a huge damp hand clapped over her mouth, stifling her screams.

Who were they? What were they after? Then a terrible thought sprung to mind. The TV and the VCRs! The sheer indignity of it all! This was just too much to take, on top of everything else she'd gone through.

Mrs Burrows saw red.

Finding energy from nowhere, she summoned the superhuman strength of the desperate. She wrestled one of her legs free and instantly kicked out. This caused a flurry of activity as her assailants tried to seize it again. But she kicked out again and again as she twisted about.

One of the faces of the things appeared within reach. She saw her chance and lunged forwards, biting down as hard as she could. She found that she had it by its nose and shook her head like a terrier with a rat. There was a bloodcurdling wail, and its hold on her relaxed for a moment. That was enough for Mrs Burrows. As the figures lost their grip on her and tumbled back on themselves, she found the ground with her feet and swung her arms behind her like a downhill skier. With a yell that would have done a Comanche proud, she hurtled away from them and into the kitchen; they were left grasping only the travelling rug that had been around her, like the discarded tail of a fleeing lizard.

In the blink of an eye, Mrs Burrows was back. She swooped into the midst of the three hulking forms. All hell broke loose.

Rebecca, who had been roused from her sleep by all the screaming and commotion, was at the top of the stairs, looking down on the mêlée. In the half light of the hallway, something metallic flashed back and forth and from side to side, and she saw a wild face. Her mother's face. Rebecca realised that she was wielding a frying pan, cutting left and right with it like a cutlass. It was the new one with the extra wide base and the special non-stick surface.

As the shadowy forms renewed their advance on her, Mrs Burrows stood her ground and repelled them with multiple blows, the pan resounding satisfyingly as it connected with a skull here or an elbow there. In all the confusion, Rebecca could see the streaks of movement as the salvo of blows continued at an incredible rate, boinging away to a chorus of grunts and groans.

"DEATH!" screamed Mrs Burrows. "DIE, DIE!"

One of the shadowy figures reached out in an attempt to grab Mrs Burrows' pan arm as it wheeled around in figures of eight, only to be walloped by a tremendous bone-shattering swipe. He let out a deep howl like a wounded dog, and staggered back, the others falling back with him. Then, as a man, they turned on their heels and all three scuttled out through the open front door. They moved with startling speed, like cockroaches caught in the light, and were gone.

In the stillness that ensued, Rebecca crept down to the bottom of the stairs and past her mother, who was panting heavily and staring fixedly through the open door. Rebecca swung the door shut and flicked on the hall light. Mrs

Burrows, her bedraggled hair hanging in dark wisps across her white face like limp horns, immediately turned her maniacal gaze on Rebecca.

"Mum," Rebecca said softly.

Mrs Burrows raised the pan above her head and lurched towards her daughter. The feral look of wild-eyed fury on her mother's face quite shocked Rebecca, who took a step back, thinking her mother was about to turn on her.

"Mum! Mum, it's me, it's all right, they've gone … they've all gone now!"

A look of odd self-satisfaction spread across Mrs Burrows' face as she checked herself and nodded slowly, appearing to recognise her daughter.

"It's okay, Mum, really," Rebecca pleaded and her mother lowered the frying pan until it hung by her side. Rebecca ventured closer and gently took it from her. Mrs Burrows didn't put up any resistance.

Rebecca sighed with relief and, looking around, noticed some dark splatters on the hall carpet – it could have been mud or, she looked closer and frowned, blood.

"If they bleed," Mrs Burrows intoned, following Rebecca's gaze, "I can kill them." She drew her lips back in a snarl, revealing her teeth as she let out a low growl.

"How about a nice cup of tea?" Rebecca asked softly, trying to calm her mother with an attempt at a smile. Putting her arm around her waist, she ushered her in the direction of the sitting room. To Rebecca, the harrowing intrusion of the shadowy figures was almost less shocking than her mother's mad demeanour.

As they reached the doorway of the sitting room, Mrs Burrows stopped to survey the scene of chaos before her, her chair lying upturned amongst the debris of her trampled videotapes. She turned to Rebecca and muttered something incomprehensible under her breath about Bourbon biscuits, and then started to laugh horribly, an unnatural, grating cackle.

CHAPTER TWENTY-TWO

Will was rudely woken by the cell door crashing back and the First Officer hauling him to his feet. Still thick with sleep, he was bundled out of the Hold, through the reception area of the station, out of the main entrance and onto the steps, where the officer finally let go of him. He tottered down a couple of steps until he found his footing and there he stood, half asleep and more than a little disoriented. He heard a thump next to him as his rucksack landed by his feet and, without a word, the officer turned his back and went into the station.

It was a strange feeling, standing there bathed in the glow of the street lights after being confined in that gloomy cell for so long. There was a slight breeze on his face – it was damp and muggy, but all the same, it was a relief after the airlessness of the Hold.

"What happens now?" he thought to himself, scratching his neck under the collar of the coarse shirt he'd been given to change into the day before by one of the officers. His mind still befuddled, he had started to yawn, but stifled it as he heard a noise. A restless horse brayed and stamped a hoof against the damp cobbles. Will immediately saw the dark carriage a little way down on the other side of the road to which two stark white horses were hitched. At the front, a coachman sat holding the reins. The carriage door swung open and Cal jumped out and crossed the street towards him.

"What's this?" Will asked suspiciously, backing up a step as Cal approached.

"We're taking you home," Cal replied.

"Home? What do you mean, home? With you? I'm not going anywhere without Chester!" he said resolutely.

"Shhhh, don't. Listen!" Cal now stood close to him and spoke with urgency. "They're watching us." He inclined his head down the street, his eyes never leaving Will's.

Where the street turned a corner, there was a sole figure, dark as a disembodied shadow, standing stock-still. Will could just make out the white collar.

"I'm not leaving without Chester," Will hissed.

"What do you think will happen to him if you don't come with us? Think about it."

"But ..."

"They can be lenient with him, or they can not. It's up to you." Cal looked pleadingly into Will's eyes.

Will glanced back at the station one last time, then sighed and shook his head. "All right."

Cal smiled and, picking up Will's rucksack for him, made his way to the waiting carriage. He held the door open for Will who followed grudgingly, his hands in his pockets and his head down, and got in. He didn't like this at all.

As the carriage pulled away, Will looked around at the austere interior. It certainly wasn't built for comfort. The seats, like the side panels, were made of a hard black-lacquered wood and the whole thing smelt of varnish with a faint hint of bleach, rather reminiscent of a school gym on the first day of term. Still, it was a vast improvement on the cell he'd been sharing with Chester. Will felt a sudden pang as he thought of his friend, still incarcerated and now alone in the Hold. He wondered if Chester had even been told that he'd been whisked away, and swore to himself that he'd find a way of getting his friend out of there, if it was the last thing he did.

He slumped back dejectedly in his seat and, putting his feet up on the opposite bench, pulled back the leathery curtain and stared out of the small window in the carriage door. As the coach rattled through the cavernous, deserted streets, the bleak houses and the unlit shop fronts passed with monotonous regularity. Copying Will, Cal also settled back and rested his feet on the seat in front of him, occasionally giving Will sidelong glances and smiling contentedly to himself with an expression of triumphant self-congratulation.

Both the boys remained silent, lost in their own thoughts. After a while, Will's weariness and the seemingly endless underworld got the better of him. As the carriage rocked and the horses' hooves beat rhythmically, he began to nod off, occasionally waking with a start when the carriage's buffeting roused him. Then, with a somewhat startled expression, he would look about self-consciously, much to Cal's amusement.

As they neared what Will took to be the outskirts of the town, the lamp posts flicked past the window at less regular intervals. Wider areas opened up between the buildings, carpeted by dark green, almost black beds of lichens or something similar. Then came strips of land at either side of the road, which were divided up by rickety-looking fences and contained beds of what appeared to be some sort of large fungi.

At one point, the carriage reduced its speed as it crossed a small bridge spanning an inky-looking canal. Will stared down into the slow and torpid water, flowing like crude oil, and for some reason it filled him with an inexplicable dread.

He had just settled back into his seat and was beginning to doze off again, when the road suddenly dipped down a steep incline and the carriage veered left. Then, as the road levelled out once again, the driver shouted "Whoa!" and the horses slowed abruptly, jolting the carriage.

Will sat bolt upright and stuck his head out of the window. He saw a huge metal gate blocking the way and, to the side of this, a group of men huddled around a brazier as they warmed their hands. Standing apart from them in the middle of the roadway, a hooded figure held a lamp high in his hand and was waving it from side to side as a signal for the coachman to stop. As the carriage ground to a halt, to Will's horror he spotted the instantly recognisable figure of a Styx emerging from the shadows. Will quickly pulled the curtain shut and ducked back into the carriage. He looked questioningly at Cal.

"It's the Skull Gate. It's the main portal to the Colony," Cal explained in a reassuring tone.

"I thought we were already in the Colony."

"No," Cal replied incredulously, "that was only the Quarter. It's sort of … like an outpost … our frontier town."

"So there's more beyond this?"

"More? God, there's miles of it!"

Will was speechless. He looked fearfully at the door as the clipped sound of boot heels on cobblestones drew nearer. Cal grabbed his arm, "Don't worry, they check everyone who goes through. Just say nothing, I'll do all the talking."

At that very moment, the door on Will's side was pulled open and the Styx shone a brass lamp into the interior. He played the beam across their faces, then took a step back and shone it up at the coachman, who handed him a piece of paper that he read with a cursory glance. Apparently satisfied with its contents, he returned to the boys once more, directed the dazzling light straight into Will's eyes and, with a contemptuous sneer, slammed the door shut. He handed the note back to the driver and, signalling to the gateman, turned on his heels and walked away.

Hearing a loud clanking, Will warily lifted the hem of the curtain and peered out again. As the guard waved them on, the light from his lantern revealed that the gate was in fact a portcullis. He watched as it rose jerkily into a structure above it, a structure that made Will blink with astonishment. Carved from a lighter stone and jutting from the wall above the portcullis, it was an immense toothless skull.

"That's horrible," Will muttered under his breath.

"It's meant to be. It's a warning," Cal replied indifferently as the coachman cracked his whip and the carriage lurched through the mouth of the fearsome apparition and into the cavern beyond.

Leaning out of the window, Will watched the portcullis juddering down behind them again until the curve of the tunnel hid it from sight. As the horses picked up speed, the carriage turned a corner and raced down a steep incline into a

giant tunnel hewn out of the dark red sandstone. It was completely devoid of buildings and houses. As the tunnel continued to descend, the air began to change – it began to smell of smoke – and for a moment the ubiquitous humming grew in intensity until it rattled the very fabric of the carriage itself.

The carriage made a final sharp turn and the humming grew less and the air cleaner again. Cal joined Will at the window as a massive cavern yawned before them. Either side of the road stood rows of buildings, a complex forest of brick ducts running over the cavern walls above them, like bloated varicose veins. In the distance, dark stacks vented cold blue flames and streamed vertical plumes of smoke that, undisturbed by air currents, hung about the roof of the cavern, like the surface of an inverted brown ocean.

"This is the Colony, Will," said Cal, his face pressed next to Will's in the narrow window frame. "This is … "

Will just stared in wonder, hardly daring to breathe.

"… home."

CHAPTER TWENTY-THREE

Around the same time that Will and Cal were arriving at the Jerome house, Rebecca was standing patiently beside a lady from the social services on the 13th floor of Mandela Heights, a dreary, run-down tower block on the seamier side of Wandsworth. The social worker was ringing the bell of Number 65 and not getting any reply, whilst Rebecca looked about her at the dirty floor. With a low, remorseful moan, a wind was blowing through the broken windows of the stairwell and flapping the partially filled bin bags heaped in one corner.

Rebecca shivered. It wasn't just because of the chill wind, but because she was about to be delivered to what she considered to be one of the worst places on earth.

By now, the social worker had given up pressing on the grimy doorbell and had started knocking loudly on the green door. There was still no reply, but the sound of the television could clearly be heard from within. She knocked again, more insistently this time, and stopped as she finally heard the sound of coughing and a woman's strident voice from the other side of the door.

"All right, all right, for gawd's sake, giv'us a chance!"

The social worker turned to Rebecca and tried to smile reassuringly. She only managed something approaching a pitying grimace.

"Looks like she's in."

"Oh good," Rebecca said sarcastically, picking up her two small suitcases.

They waited in an awkward silence as the door was unlocked and the door chain removed, accompanied by indiscernible mutterings and curses, and punctuated by intermittent coughing. The door finally swung open and a rather dishevelled middle-aged woman, cigarette hanging from her bottom lip, looked the social worker up and down suspiciously.

"What's all this about?" she asked, one eye wincing from the wayward smoke of the cigarette, which twitched with all the vigour of a conductor's baton as she spoke.

"I've brought your niece, Mrs Boswell," the social worker indicated Rebecca standing beside her.

"You what?" the woman said sharply, shedding ash on the social worker's immaculate shoes. Rebecca cringed with embarrassment.

"Don't you remember … I called you yesterday?"

Her watery gaze settled on Rebecca, who smiled and leant forward a little to come within her limited focal range.

"Hello, Auntie Jean," Rebecca said, trying to sound as cheerful as she could under these awful circumstances.

"Rebecca, love, of course, yes, look at you, haven't you grown, quite the young lady." Auntie Jean coughed and opened the door fully. "Yes, come in, come in, I've got something on the boil." She turned and went back into the flat.

The social worker surveyed the unruly piles of curling newspapers stacked along the wall of the hallway, and the swathes of unopened letters and pamphlets littering the filthy carpet. Everything in the hallway was covered with a fine film of dust and the corners were festooned with cobwebs. The whole place stank of Auntie Jean's cigarettes. The social worker bade Rebecca goodbye, and good luck, and started hurriedly for the stairs, bracing herself for the long trek down as the lifts were out of service.

Rebecca shuffled reluctantly into the flat, following her aunt into the kitchen.

"I could do with some 'elp in 'ere," Auntie Jean said, picking out a packet of cigarettes from amongst the debris on the table.

Aghast, Rebecca surveyed the tawdry vision before her.

Shafts of sunlight cut through the ever-present fog of cigarette smoke that hung about her aunt like a personal storm cloud. Rebecca wrinkled her nose as she caught the acrid taint of yesterday's burnt food lacing the air.

"If you're going to be staying," her aunt said through a fit of coughing, "you're going to 'ave to pitch in."

Rebecca didn't want to move; she feared any motion, however slight, would result in her being covered in the grime that surrounded her. The whole place was like a greasy trap for clean clothes.

"C'mon, Becs, put your bags down, roll up your sleeves. You can start by putting that kettle on." Auntie Jean smiled as she sat down at the kitchen table, lighting a fresh cigarette from the old one before stubbing out its glowing stump in an overflowing ashtray on the Formica tabletop.

<hr />

The interior of the Jerome household was rich and comforting, with subtly patterned carpets and walls of deep greens and burgundies, and burnished wood surfaces that shone with the dark pearlesence of many coats of polish and years of use. Cal took Will's rucksack from him and dropped it by a small table on which an oil lamp with a vaseline glass shade stood on a creamy linen doily. Then he led Will through the first door off the hallway.

"This is the drawing room," he announced proudly.

The atmosphere in the room was warm and muggy with regular, tiny gusts of fresh air coming from a dirt-encrusted grill above where they now stood. The ceiling was low with ornate plaster mouldings, turned an off-white by the smoke and soot from the fire that even now roared in the wide hearth. In front of this, sprawled on a worn Persian rug, was a large, mangy animal asleep on its back with its legs in the air, shamelessly displaying its male gender.

"A dog!" Will was a little surprised to see such a domestic pet down here.

The animal was the colour of rubbed slate. It was almost completely bald with just the odd patch of dark stubble or tuft of hair erupting here and there from its loose skin, which sagged like an ill-fitting suit.

"Dog? That's Bartleby, he's a cat, a Rex variant. An excellent hunter."

Astonished, Will looked again. *A cat?* It was the size of a well-fed, badly shaved Dobermann. There was nothing in the slightest bit feline about the animal, whose large ribcage slowly rose and fell with its regular breathing. Will gingerly stepped closer to see its face, which was turned towards the fire. It snorted loudly in its sleep and its huge paws twitched as he bent over to inspect its features.

"Careful, he'll take your face off."

Will swung around to see an old woman sitting in one of the two large leather winged chairs positioned either side of the fireplace. She had been sitting well back when he had come in, and he hadn't noticed her.

"I wasn't going to touch him," he answered defensively, straightening up.

Her pale grey eyes twinkled and never left his face.

"He doesn't have to be touched," she said, and added, "He's very instinctive, is our Bartleby." Her face glowed with affection at the sight of the luxuriating and oversized animal by her feet.

"Grandma, this is Will," Cal said.

Once again the old lady's knowing gaze returned to Will and she nodded. "Of that I am well aware. He's a Macaulay from head to toe, and has his mother's eyes and no mistake. Hello, Will."

He was struck dumb, transfixed by her gentle manner and her unwavering gaze, a vibrant light dancing in her old eyes. It was as though some part of him, a vague memory, had been lit just as a dying ember is rekindled by a faint breeze. Something in him recognised something in her, and he felt immediately at ease in her presence. *But why?* He was naturally wary when meeting adults for the first time and, down here in this strange place, he had to be particularly vigilant. But with this old woman, it was as though he knew her ... *But how?*

"Come and sit yourself down, talk to me. I'm sure there's lots of fascinating tales you can tell me from your life up there." She lifted her face towards the ceiling. "Caleb, put the kettle on and let's have some fancies. Will's going to tell me all about himself," she said, motioning towards the other leather chair with a delicate yet strong hand. It was the hand of a woman who had had to work hard all her life.

Will perched on the edge of the seat, the fire warming and relaxing him. As he felt the tension of the past week ebb out of him, he sighed and sat back. He felt as if he'd reached a place of safety at last, a sanctuary, as if he'd reached home. The old lady looked intently at him and he unselfconsciously looked straight back at her, the glow of her attention every bit as comforting as the fire in the hearth.

Her hair was fine and a snowy white and she wore it in an elaborate bun at the top of her head, held in place by a tortoiseshell slide. She was dressed in a plain blue long-sleeved dress with a white ruffled collar high up on the neck.

"Why do I feel as though I know you?" he asked suddenly. He had the oddest feeling that he could say whatever was on his mind to this complete stranger.

"Because you do," she smiled. "I held you as a baby, I sang you lullabies."

With a shock of recognition, he knew that what she was telling him was true; every fibre of his body told him it was so. His throat tightened and he swallowed, trying to ease the tension. The old woman could see the emotion welling up in his young eyes.

"She would've been so proud of you, you know," Grandma Macaulay said, looking at a photograph in a silver oval frame in the centre of the mantelpiece. "Your real name is Seth, that's what you were christened. How proud she'd be – you were her first-born."

Will stood up and took the photograph in his hand. It had the same ethereal quality as the daguerreotypes, the old photographs in the Highfield museum. It was of a young woman in a white blouse and a long black skirt. Turning it to catch the light, he studied it closely. In her arms, the woman held a small bundle. Her hair was the whitest of whites, identical to Will's, and her face was beautiful, a strong face with kind eyes and a fine bone structure, a full mouth and a square jaw … his jaw, which he now touched involuntarily.

"Yes," the old lady said softly, "you're just like her. That was taken just two months after you were born; that's you she's holding."

Will felt as though his heart had stopped. He looked closely at the bundle. He could see it was a baby, but couldn't make out its face clearly because of the swaddling. His mind raced and his hands shook as his feelings and thoughts bled into one another. But he knew, knew with absolute certainty, for the first time in his life, that this woman was his real mother, and that these people his true family. He couldn't explain it even to himself, he just *knew*.

All suspicions that they had tried to deceive him now evaporated and a tear ran down his cheek, drawing a pale, delicate line on his unwashed face. He brushed it away with the back of his hand and, as he put the photograph back, he knew his face was flushing. Feeling awkward, he quickly sat down.

"Tell me what it's like up there," she said quickly, to spare his embarrassment. "You know I've never seen daylight, or felt the sun on my face. How does that feel? They say it burns."

Will looked up, astounded. "You've never seen the sun?"

"Very few have," Cal said, re-entering the room and sitting down on the hearth rug at his grandmother's feet. He began gently kneading the loose and rather scabby flap of skin under the cat's chin; almost immediately a loud, throbbing purr filled the room.

"Tell us, Will, tell us what it's like," Grandma Macaulay said, her hand resting on Cal's head as he leant it against the arm of her chair.

So Will started to tell them, a little hesitantly at first and then, as if a torrent had been unleashed, he found he was almost babbling as he spoke about his life above. He told them about his family and his school, regaling them with stories about the excavations with his father, or rather the person he'd believed was his father until this moment, and about his mother and his sister.

"You love your Topsoiler family very much, don't you?" Grandma Macaulay said and Will suddenly thought of poor Rebecca and how worried she'd be by now. Almost immediately, the mental image of Chester, still incarcerated in that awful cell, flashed before him.

"What will happen to my friend Chester?" he asked.

"They'll never let him go back," Cal said, staring absently into the fire.

"They never do," his grandmother continued. "They couldn't have him telling the Topsoilers about us. It might bring about the Discovery."

"The Discovery?"

"It's what we're taught from the Book of Catastrophes. It is the end of all things, when the people are ferreted out and perish at the hands of those above," Cal said flatly, as if reciting a verse.

Will looked at his grandmother, but she averted her eyes and stared into the flames.

"But what will they do to him?" Will asked, dreading the answer.

"Either he'll be put to work or he might get Banishment … he'll be put on a train and taken to the lower deeps, and there he'll be left … to fend for himself," Cal replied.

Will was about to ask what the lower deeps were, when out in the hall the front door was flung open with a bang and a powerful man's voice bellowed, "HULLO IN THERE!"

The fire flared and threw up a shower of sparks, which glowed briefly as they were drawn up the chimney. Grandma Macaulay peered around the side of her armchair and smiled as Cal and Bartleby both leapt to their feet in an instant.

Still sleep-ridden, the cat blundered against the underside of an occasional table, which crashed to the floor at the same time as the drawing room door burst open. A massive, thickset man entered the room like dirty thunder, his pale yet ruddy-cheeked face beaming with undisguised excitement.

"WHERE IS HE! WHERE IS HE!" he shouted, and locked his fierce gaze on Will, who rose apprehensively from his chair, uncertain what to make of this human explosion. In two strides, the man had crossed the room and clasped Will in a bear hug, hoisting him off his feet as if he weighed no more than a bag of feathers. The man let out a deafening roar of a laugh and held Will out at arm's length, his feet dangling helplessly in mid-air.

"Let me look at you. Yes … yes, you're your mother's boy, no mistake; it's the eyes, isn't it Ma? He's got her eyes, and her chin … the shape of her handsome face, by God, ha ha ha!" he bellowed.

"Do put him down, Tam," Grandma Macaulay chided.

Uncle Tam lowered Will back onto the floor, still staring intently into the startled boy's eyes and grinning and shaking his head.

"It's a great day, a great day indeed." He stuck out a huge ham of a hand towards Will. "I'm your Uncle Tam."

Will automatically held out his hand and Tam took it into his giant palm, shook it in a vice-like grip and pulled Will in towards him, ruffling his hair with his other hand and sniffing at the top of his head loudly in a exaggerated manner.

"He's awash with Macaulay blood, this one," he boomed, "wouldn't you say so, Ma?"

"Without hesitation," she said softly, "but don't you be frightening him with your horseplay, Tam."

Bartleby was rubbing his massive head against Uncle Tam's oily black trouser legs and insinuating his long body between him and Will, all the while purring and making an unearthly low whining sound. Tam glanced briefly down at him and then up at Cal, who was still standing next to his grandmother's chair, enjoying the spectacle.

"Cal, the magician's apprentice, how are you, lad? What do you think of all this, eh?" He looked from one boy to the other. "God, it's good to see you two beneath the same roof again."

He shook his head in disbelief. "Brothers, hah, brothers, my nephews. This calls for a drink. A *real* drink."

"We were just about to have some tea," Tam's mother interjected quickly. "Would you care for a cup, Tam?"

He turned to face his mother and smiled broadly, with a devilish glint in his eye. "Why not? Let's have a cup of tea and catch up."

With that, the old woman disappeared into the hall and Uncle Tam sat down in her vacated chair, which groaned under his weight. Stretching out his legs, he took out a short pipe from the inside of his huge overcoat and filled it from a tobacco pouch, which he then stuffed back into his waistcoat pocket. He used a taper from by the fireside to light it, then sat back and blew a cloud of bluish smoke up at the ornate ceiling, all the while looking at the two boys.

For a time, all that could be heard was the crackling of the burning coal, the intrusive purring of Bartleby and the distant sounds of the old woman busy in the kitchen. No one felt the need to talk as the flickering light played on their faces and threw trembling shadows over the walls behind, like a scene in a shadowplay. Eventually, Uncle Tam spoke.

"You know your Topsoiler father was through here?"

"You saw him?" Will sat up and leant towards Uncle Tam.

"No but I talked to them that did."

"Where is he? The policeman said he was safe."

"Safe?" He sat forward, taking the pipe from his mouth, his face becoming deadly serious. "Listen, don't you believe a word that spineless scum say to you; they're all snakes and half-inchers. They're the poisonous lackeys of the Styx."

"That's quite enough, Tam," Granny Macaulay said as she entered the room with a tray of tea and some "fancies", as she called them; shapeless lumps topped with white icing. Cal got up and helped her, handing cups to Will and Uncle Tam. Then Will let Granny Macaulay have his chair and sat next to Cal on the hearth rug.

Tam was silent as he relit his pipe. "You only missed him by a week or so; he was banished to the deeps. Curious though, it seemed as though he wanted to go, like he went willingly." He puffed away, looking at the fire. "While he was in the Colony, people saw him wandering around for days, scribbling in his book and bothering folk with his fool questions. I reckon the Styx thought he was a little …" Uncle Tam tapped the side of his head.

Granny Macaulay cleared her throat and looked at him sternly.

"… harmless," he said, checking himself. "Reckon that's why they let him roam around like that, but they watched his every move."

"What are the deeps?" Will asked.

"The inner circles, the Interior, down below us," Uncle Tam pointed with the stem of his pipe at the floor. "The Deeps."

"But what's there?"

"Well, five or so miles down, there's another settlement. That's where the Miners' train stops, where the Coprolites live; the air's bad down there." He sucked loudly on his pipe. "It's the end of the line, but the tunnels go further, miles and miles, they say. Legends even tell of an inner world at the centre, older towns and older cities."

"So there are other people down there?" Will asked, hoping in his heart of hearts.

"Well, yes, there've been stories. In the year 220, they say a Colonist returned after years of Banishment."

"Abraham de Jaybo," Granny Macaulay said quietly, leaning back in her chair and frowning.

Uncle Tam nodded. "He was in a terrible state when they found him. He was covered in cuts and bruises, and his tongue was missing – cut out they say. He was almost starved to death when they found him at the Miners' station, like a walking corpse. He didn't last long; died a week later from some unknown disease that made his blood boil up through his ears and mouth. He couldn't speak, of course, but they say he made drawings as he lay on his deathbed. He was desperate, they say, and wouldn't sleep."

"What were the drawings of?" Will was wide-eyed.

"Infernal machines and strange animals and impossible landscapes, and things no one could understand. The Styx said it was all the product of a diseased mind, but some say the drawings really exist. They're supposed to be kept in the Governors' vaults … though no one I know's ever seen them."

"God, I'd give anything to look at those," Will said, spellbound.

Uncle Tam gave a deep chuckle.

"What?" Will asked.

"Well, apparently, that Burrows fellow said the selfsame thing when he was told the legend … the selfsame words he used."

CHAPTER TWENTY-FOUR

After all the talk, the tea, the cake and the revelations, Uncle Tam finally rose with a cavernous yawn and stretched his powerful frame with several bone-chilling clicks. He turned to Grandma Macaulay.

"Well, come on, Ma, high time I got you home."

And with that, they bade their farewells and were gone. Without Tam's booming voice and infectious guffaws to fill it, the house suddenly seemed a very different place.

"I'll show you where you'll be sleeping," Cal said to Will, who only mumbled in response. It was as though he was under some kind of spell, his mind teeming with new thoughts and feelings that, try as he might, he couldn't keep from rising to the surface, like a shoal of hungry fish.

Cal shrugged and turned and was halfway up the stairs with Will's rucksack hooked over his arm, when he noticed he wasn't following. Instead, Will was leaning over the banister, his curiosity aroused by something.

"What's through there?" he asked, peering down the length of the hallway at a black door with a brass handle.

"Oh, it's nothing, it's just the kitchen," Cal replied dismissively.

"Can I have a quick look?" Will said, already en route for the door.

Cal sighed audibly. "Oh, all right, but there's really nothing to see," he said in a resigned tone and descended the stairs, dropping the rucksack at the bottom.

Will found himself in a low-ceilinged room resembling something from a Victorian hospital. And it not only looked but smelt like one too, a strong undercurrent of carbolic blending with indistinct cooking smells. The walls were a dull mushroom colour, and the floor and work surfaces were tiled in white ceramic squares, crazed with a myriad of scratches and fissures. In places, they had been worn into dappled hollows by years of scrubbing.

His attention was drawn to the corner, where a lid was gently clattering on the top of one of a number of saucepans being heated on an antiquated stove of some kind, its heavy frame swollen and glassy with burnt-on grease. He peered into the nearest saucepan, but its simmering contents were obscured by wisps of steam. Then he twisted around to inspect a solid-looking butcher's block with a large-bladed knife dangling from a hook above it.

"What's in there?" he said, noticing there was another door leading off the kitchen.

"Look, wouldn't you rather …" Cal's voice tailed off as he realised it was futile to argue with his brother, who was already nosing into the small adjoining room.

Will's joy was evident; it was like an alchemist's storeroom, with shelf upon shelf of squat jars containing unrecognisable pickled items, all horribly distorted by the curvature of the thick glass and discoloured by the oily fluid in which they were immersed. They resembled anatomical specimens preserved in formaldehyde.

On the bottom shelf, laid out on dull metal trays, Will noticed a huddle of objects the size of small footballs, which had a grey-brown dusty bloom to them.

"What are these?"

"They're Pennybuns – we grow them all over, but mostly in the lower chambers."

"What do you do with them?" Will was crouching down, examining their velvety, mottled surfaces.

"They're mushrooms. You eat them. You probably had some in the Hold."

"Oh right," Will said, pulling a face as he stood upright. "And that?" he said, pointing at some strips of what appeared to be beef jerky hanging from racks above.

Cal smiled broadly. "You should be able to tell what it is."

Will hesitated for a moment and then leant a little closer to one of the strips; it was definitely meat of some description. It looked like elongated sinews and was the colour of new scabs. He sniffed tentatively, then shook his head.

"No idea."

"Come on, the smell."

Will closed his eyes and sniffed again, "It doesn't smell like anything …" His eyes snapped open and he looked at Cal. "It's rat, isn't it?" he said, both pleased that he was able to identify it and, at the same time, appalled by the finding. "You eat rat?"

"It's delicious … there's nothing wrong with that. Now, tell me what *kind* is it?" Cal asked, revelling in Will's evident disgust. "Pack, sewer or sightless?"

"I don't like rats, let alone eat them. I haven't got the faintest."

Cal shook his head slowly in mock disappointment.

"It's easy, this is sightless," he said, lifting the end of one of the lengths with his finger and sniffing it himself. "It's more gamey than the others – it's a bit special. We have it mostly on Sundays."

They were interrupted by a loud, machinegun-like humming behind them and both spun around at the same time. There, purring with all his might, sat Bartleby, his huge amber eyes fixed on the meat strips and drops of anticipatory saliva dripping off his bald chin.

"Out!" Cal shouted at him, pointing towards the kitchen door. The cat didn't move an inch, but sat resolutely on the tiled floor, completely mesmerised by the sight of the meat.

"Bart, I said get out!" Cal shouted again, making to close the door as he and Will entered the kitchen again. The cat snarled threateningly and bared his teeth, a pearly stockade of viciously sharp pegs, as his skin erupted with a wave of goose pimples.

"You insolent mutt!" Cal snapped, as he aimed a kick at the disobedient animal, which dodged sideways, easily avoiding the blow. Giving Will a slightly scornful look over his shoulder, Bartleby turned slowly towards the door and padded lethargically away, his naked, spindly tail flicking in a gesture of defiance behind him.

"He'd sell his soul for rat, that one," Cal said, shaking his head and smiling.

After the brief tour of the kitchen, Cal showed Will up the creaking wooden staircase to the top floor.

"This is Father's room," he said, opening a dark door halfway down the landing. "We're not supposed to go in here. There'll be hell to pay if he catches us."

Will quickly glanced back down the stairs to assure himself the coast was clear before he followed Cal into Mr Jerome's room. A huge four-poster bed dominated the room, so tall it almost touched the dilapidated ceiling that bellied ominously down towards it. The room around it was bare and featureless, a single light burning in one corner.

"What was here?" Will asked, noticing a row of lighter patches, like indistinct white shadows on the grey wall.

Cal looked at the ghostly squares and frowned. "Pictures – there used to be lots of pictures before Father stripped the room out."

"Why'd he do that?"

"Because of Mother – she'd furnished it, it was her room really," Cal replied. "And after she'd gone …" he fell silent. As he didn't seem inclined to volunteer any more on the subject, Will felt he shouldn't probe further, for the moment.

Out on the landing again, Will paused to admire an impressive light orb supported by a ghostly bronze hand protruding from the wall.

"These lights, where do they come from?" he asked, feeling the cool surface of the sphere.

"I don't know. I think they're made in the west cavern."

"But how do they work? Dad had one looked at by some experts, but they didn't have a clue."

Cal regarded the light with a noncommittal air. "I don't really know. I do know that it was Sir Gabriel Martineau who discovered the formula, but I couldn't tell you how it works – I think they use Antwerp glass, though. It has something to do with how the chemicals react together."

"There must be thousands down here."

"Without them, we couldn't survive subsoil," Cal replied patly. "Their light is like sunlight to us."

"Can you turn them off?"

Cal looked at Will quizzically, the light shining on his pallid face. "Why *in* earth would you want to do that?"

They passed down the landing and entered the room next to Mr Jerome's.

"This is my room. Father arranged another bed when he was told you had to stay with us."

"Told? By who?" Will asked in a flash.

Cal raised his eyebrows as if he ought to know better, so Will just looked around the simple bedroom, not much larger than his one back home. Two narrow beds and a wardrobe almost filled it, with very little space in between. He sat down on the end of one of the beds and, noticing a set of clothes neatly folded by the pillow, glanced up at Cal.

"Yes, those are for you," Cal said.

"I suppose I could do with a change" Will said, peering down at the rough grey shirt and dirty jeans he was wearing, and grimacing. He opened the bundle of new clothes and felt the fabric of the waxy trousers. The material was rough, almost scaly to the touch – he guessed it was a coating to keep out the damp.

While Cal lay back on his bed and stared at the ceiling, as if in deep thought, Will changed into his new clothes. They felt strange and cold next to his skin. The trousers were stiff and scratchy and fastened with metal buttons and a belt-tie. He wrestled into the shirt without bothering to undo it, and then slowly wriggled his shoulders and arms as if trying to get a new skin to fit. Last of all, he shrugged on the long jacket with the familiar shoulder mantle that they all wore. Although pleased to be out of his filthy clothes, the replacements felt stiff and restrictive.

"Don't worry, they loosen up once they're warm," Cal said, noticing his discomfort. Then he got up and clambered across Will's bed and reaching the wardrobe, knelt down to drag out an old "Peek Freans" biscuit tin from beneath it. "Have a look at these."

He put the tin on Will's bed and levered the lid off.

"This is my collection," he announced proudly. He fished in the tin, picked out a battered mobile phone, and handed it to Will, who immediately tried to turn it on. It was dead. *Neither use nor ornament:* Will remembered the phrase his father used on such occasions, which was ironic considering most of Dr Burrows' prize possessions didn't fit into either category.

"And this," Cal took out a small blue radio and held it up to show Will. He clicked on the switch and it crackled with tinny static as he swivelled one of the dials.

"You won't pick anything up down here," Will said, but Cal was already taking something else out of the tin.

"Look at these, they're fantastic."

He straightened out some curling car brochures, mottled with chalky spots of mildew, and passed them to Will as if they were priceless parchments. Will frowned as he surveyed them.

"These are very old models, you know," Will said as he browsed through the pages of sports cars and family saloons. "The new Capri," he read aloud and smiled to himself.

He looked up at Cal and noticed the look on the boy's face of total absorption, of reverence, as he lovingly arranged a selection of chocolate bars and a bag of cellophane-wrapped sweets in the bottom of the tin. It was as if he was trying to find the perfect composition.

"What's all the chocolate for?" Will asked, rather hoping that Cal might offer him some.

"I'm saving it for a very special occasion," Cal said as he lovingly handled a bar of "Fruit and Nut". "I just love the way it smells." He drew the bar under his nose and sniffed extravagantly. "That's enough for me ... I don't need to open it." He rolled his eyes in ecstasy.

"So where did you get all this?" Will asked, putting down the car brochures, which curled slowly back into a dishevelled tube. Cal glanced warily at the bedroom door and moved a little closer to Will.

"Uncle Tam," he said in a low voice. "He often goes beyond the Colony – but you mustn't tell anyone. It would mean Banishment." He hesitated and glanced at the door again. "He even goes Topsoil."

"Does he now?" Will said, scrutinising Cal's face intently. "And when does he do that?"

"Quite often," Cal was speaking so softly that Will had difficulty hearing him. "He trades things that ..." he faltered, realising that he was overstepping the mark, " ... that he finds."

"Where?" Will asked.

"On his trips," Cal said obliquely as he packed the items back into the tin, replaced the lid and slid it once again beneath the wardrobe. Still kneeling, he turned to Will.

"You're planning to escape, aren't you?" he said with a sly grin.

"You mean back to Highfield?"

Cal nodded energetically.

"Maybe, maybe not. I don't know yet," Will said. Despite his feelings for Cal and the others, he was going to play it safe. A small voice in his head was warning him that this could be part of an elaborate plan to ensnare him and keep him here for ever, and that even this boy, who claimed to be his brother, could be working for the Styx. He wasn't quite ready to trust him yet.

Cal looked directly at Will.

"Well, when you do, I'm coming with you." He smiled, but his eyes were deadly serious. At that point, a gong sounded insistently from downstairs.

"That's dinner, Father must be home. Come on." Followed by Will, Cal leapt up and out of the door and down the stairs to the dining room, where Mr Jerome was already seated at the head of a deep-grained wooden table. As they entered, Mr Jerome didn't look up, his eyes remaining fixed on the table in front of him.

The room was spartan and the furniture basic, appearing to be constructed from wood that had endured centuries of wear. On closer inspection, Will could see that the table and chairs had been fabricated from a mishmash of different woods, with conflicting shades and with grains at odds with each other; some parts were waxed or varnished, while others were raw and splintery. The high-backed dining chairs looked particularly rickety and archaic, with spindly legs that creaked and complained when Will and Cal took their places either side of Mr Jerome. Will wondered idly how they could accommodate someone of Mr Jerome's impressive bulk without giving up the ghost.

Mr Jerome cleared his throat loudly and, without any warning, he and Cal bent forward in their chairs, their eyes closed and their hands folded on the table in front of them. Will did likewise, but couldn't stop himself from watching through half-closed eyes as Mr Jerome began.

"The sun shall no longer set, nor shall the moon withdraw itself, for the Lord will be your everlasting light and the dark days of your mourning will be ended," he droned. "As it is above, so it is below."

"Amen," Cal and his father said together, too quickly for Will to join in. They sat up and Mr Jerome tapped a spoon on the tumbler in front of him.

There was a moment of uncomfortable silence. Then a man with long, greasy hair shambled into the room. His face was deeply lined and his cheeks were gaunt. He was wearing a leather apron and his tired and listless eyes, like dying candle flames in cavernous hollows, lingered briefly on Will and then quickly looked away.

As he watched the man making repeated trips in and out of the room and shuffling to each of them in turn to serve the food, Will came to the conclusion that he must have endured great suffering, possibly a severe illness.

The first course was a thin broth, which smelt as if it had been spiced with copious amounts of curry powder. This came with a side dish of small white objects, similar in appearance to peeled gherkins. Cal and Mr Jerome wasted no time in starting their food and, between loud exhalations, they both made the most outrageous noises as they sucked the broth from their spoons, splashing liberal amounts of it over their clothes, which they simply ignored. The chorus of slurps and smacking of lips reached such a ridiculous crescendo that Will couldn't stop himself glancing at them in utter astonishment.

Finally, he picked up his own spoon, and was on the point of taking his first tentative mouthful when, out of the corner of his eye, he saw one of the white objects on his side plate twitch. Thinking he'd imagined it, he emptied the contents of his spoon back into his bowl and used it to roll one of the objects over.

With a shock, he found it had a row of tiny dark-brown pointed legs neatly folded beneath it. It was a grub of some kind. He sat bolt upright and watched with horror as it curved its back, its minuscule spiky legs rippling open in a Mexican wave, as if to greet him.

His first thought was that it had got there by mistake, so he glanced at Mr Jerome and Cal's side plates, wondering if he should say something. At that very moment, Cal picked up one of the white objects from his own side plate. He bit into it and chewed with gusto. Between his thumb and forefinger, the remaining half of the grub twitched and writhed, oozing a clear fluid over his fingertips.

Will felt his stomach heave and dropped his spoon in his soup dish with such a crash that the serving man came in and, finding that he was not wanted, promptly exited again. As Will tried to quell his nausea, Mr Jerome didn't even look up, while Cal eyed him with passing concern before sucking the still writhing half grub into his mouth, as if he was devouring a very fat strand of spaghetti.

Will shuddered; he couldn't bring himself to drink his soup, so he sat there staring at it until the serving man cleared the bowls away and then brought the main course, a gravy-soaked mush just as indeterminate as the broth. Will prodded suspiciously at everything on his plate to ensure that nothing was still alive. It seemed innocuous enough so he began to pick at it without enthusiasm, quailing involuntarily with each mouthful, and accompanied by his fellow diners' gastronomic cacophony.

Although Mr Jerome hadn't said a single word to Will during the whole meal, the hatred radiating from him was tangible and overwhelming. And Will had no idea why. He wished the man would say something, anything at all, just to break the agonising silence. He could tell it wouldn't be pleasant when it came; he was prepared for that. He just wanted to get it over with. It felt to Will as if the room was filling with a chilled and poisonous aspic; he felt suffocated by it. He began to sweat and tried to loosen the starched collar of his new shirt by running his finger inside it.

His reprieve finally came when Mr Jerome abruptly got up, folded his napkin twice and then threw it onto the table. He was leaving the room just as the wretch of a serving man was entering with a copper bowl in his hands. To Will's surprise, Mr Jerome elbowed the man brutally aside. Will thought the man was going to fall as he lurched sideways against the wall. The man fought to regain his balance as some of the contents of the bowl tipped out and apples and oranges rolled around the floor and under the table.

As if Mr Jerome's behaviour was nothing out of the ordinary, the man hadn't so much as murmured during the incident. Will saw the cut on the man's lip and the blood trickling down his chin as he stooped to retrieve the apples. He couldn't help but feel sympathy for him.

He was flabbergasted, but kept his silence as Cal seemed to be ignoring the incident altogether. Will watched the pathetic man until he left the room and then turned his attention to the bowl of fresh fruit – there were bananas, pears and a couple of figs in addition to the apples and oranges. He helped himself, grateful for something familiar and recognisable after the first two courses.

Then the front door slammed with such a crash that the casement windows shook. Will and Cal listened as Mr Jerome's footsteps retreated down the front path. It was Will who broke the silence.

"He doesn't like me much, does he?"

"No," Cal replied simply, as he peeled an orange.

"Why ... " Will stopped short as the serving man returned and stood behind Cal's chair.

"You can go," Cal said brusquely, not even bothering to look at the man who slipped out of the room.

"Who's that?" Will enquired.

"He was a Topsoiler, like you."

"Oh." Will didn't speak for a moment and then asked, "What's his name?"

"Terry Watkins."

"Watkins," Will repeated. "I know that name, but how?"

Cal continued eating, enjoying Will's confusion, and then Will remembered. "They went missing, the whole family."

"Yes, they certainly did."

Taken aback, Will quickly looked over at Cal. "They were kidnapped?"

"They had to be, they were a problem. Watkins stumbled onto one of our air channels and we couldn't have him telling anybody."

"But that's never Mr Watkins – he was a big man. His son was at my school," Will said. "No, that can't be the same person."

"He and his family were put to work," Cal said coldly.

"But ..." Will stuttered as he juggled the mental images of Mr Watkins *before* and *after*, " ... he looks a thousand years old. What happened?"

"As I said, he was put to work," Cal said, holding up a pear to smell its skin and, noticing it had a smear of Mr Watkins' blood on it, wiped it on his shirt before taking a bite out of it. Then he glanced over at his father's empty chair and sighed. "This is very hard on Father, but you have to give him time. I suppose you bring back too many memories."

"Memories? Of what?"

"About Mother, of course. Uncle Tam says she always was a bit of a rebel," Cal fell silent.

"But … did something bad happen?"

"We had a brother. He was only a baby. He died from a fever. After that, she had to leave." A wistful look came into Cal's eyes.

"A brother," Will echoed.

Cal stared at him, any hint of his usual grin absent from his face. "She was trying to get both of us out when the Styx caught up."

"So she escaped, then?"

"Yes, but only just and that's why I'm still here." Cal was silent for a while and then spoke again. "Uncle Tam says she's the only one he knows of who got out, and stayed out."

"She's still alive?"

Cal nodded, "As far as we know. But she broke the laws, and it's said the Styx never forget. One day they *will* catch up with you and then they *will* punish you."

"Punish? What do you mean?"

"In Mother's case, execution," Cal said bleakly. "That's why you have to tread so very carefully." With that, he got to his feet and glanced through the window. "Seven bells. We should go."

Once they were outside, Cal forged ahead and Will found it difficult to keep up in the new trousers, which chafed against his thighs with every step. The streets heaved with people, all dashing frantically in different directions, as if they were late for something. It looked and sounded like a confused flock of leathery birds taking flight. Will followed Cal's lead and, after several turns, they joined the end of a queue outside a plain-looking building that resembled a warehouse. In front of each of the studded wooden doors at the entrance, a pair of Styx stood in their characteristic poses, arched over like vindictive headmasters about to strike. Will bowed his head, trying to blend in with the crowd and avoid their jet-black pupils, which he knew would be upon him.

Inside, the hall was deceptively large – around half the size of a football pitch. Large flagstones, shiny with dark patches of damp, formed the floor. The walls were roughly plastered and whitewashed. Looking around, he could see elevated platforms in the four corners the hall, crude wooden pulpits, each with a Styx in place, scrutinising the crowd. At the front there were 10 or so carved wooden pews, full of closely seated Colonists.

Will went up on tiptoes to try to see what was at the front of the hall and caught a glimpse of a massive iron crucifix fixed to the wall – it appeared to be made from two lengths of metal beams, like pieces of railway track bolted together with huge round-headed rivets. Then Cal tugged him by the sleeve and they threaded through the amassing crowd to a position closer to the pews.

The doors thudded shut and Will realised that the hall had been packed to capacity in scarcely any time at all. He found it stifling, squashed against Cal on one side and bulky Colonists on the others. The room was warming up quickly and faint threads of steam were beginning to rise from the damp clothes of the crowd and encircle the hanging lights.

Then the hubbub of conversation died down and a Styx stepped into a high pulpit by the side of the metal cross. He wore a full-length black gown and his shining eyes lanced through the hazy air. For a brief moment, he shut them and inclined his head forward. Then he slowly looked up, extending his arms towards the congregation as if he was going to perform a magical feat, his black gown opening like a bat about to take flight, and spoke in a sibilant monastic drone. Around him, Will could hear the voices of the other Styx reiterating the words of the preacher Styx in scratchy whispers, a sound like the tearing of dry parchments.

"Know this, brethren, know this," he said, his voice rough and high. His gaze scythed through the congregation and he drew breath melodramatically.

"The surface of the Earth is beset by creatures in a constant state of war with one another. Millions perish on either side and there is no limit to the brutality of their malice. Their nations fall and rise, only to fall again. The vast forests have been laid low by them, and the pastures defiled with their poison." All around him, Will heard mumbled words of agreement. The preacher Styx leant forward, grasping the edge of the pulpit with his pale fingers.

"Their gluttony is matched only by their appetites for death, affliction, terror and banishment of every living thing. And despite their iniquities, they aspire to rise to the firmament … but, *mark this*, the excessive weight of their very sins will weigh them down." There was silence as his black eyes scanned his flock and, raising his left arm above his head, a long, bony index finger pointing upwards, he continued.

"Nothing remains on the soil or in the great oceans that shall not be hunted, disturbed or despoiled. To the living things slain in droves, these defilers are both the sepulchre and the means of transition.

"And when the judgment comes," he lowered his arm now and pointed forebodingly at members of the congregation, "and mark these words, it will … then they will be hurled into the abyss and forever lost to the Lord … and on that day, the truthful, the righteous, we of the true way will once again return to reclaim the surface, to begin again, to build the new Jerusalem. For this is the teaching and the knowledge of our forefathers, passed down to us through the ages by the Book of Catastrophes."

A hush filled the hall, absolute and unbroken by a single cough or shuffle. Then the preacher spoke again in a calmer, almost conversational tone.

"So let it be known, so let it be understood." He bowed his head.

Will thought he glimpsed Mr Jerome seated in the pews, but couldn't get a clearer view because he was so completely hemmed in.

Then, without warning, the whole congregation joined with the Styx's monotone: "The Earth is the Lord's and the followers thereof, the Earth and all that dwell therein. We give our eternal gratitude to our father, Sir Gabriel, and his board for their shepherdship and for the flowing together into one another, as all that happens in God's Earth is also on the highest level, the kingdom of God."

There was a moment's pause and the Styx spoke again. "As above, so below."

The voices of the congregation boomed amens as the Styx took a step back and Will lost sight of him. The congregation immediately started to file towards the doorway, leaving the hall as swiftly as it had collected. Will and Cal were swept along with the tide of people until they found themselves back on the street.

"How often do you have to do that?" Will asked, watching the people departing in all directions.

"Once a day," Cal said. "You go to church Topsoil too, don't you?"

"No, our family didn't."

"How strange," Cal said, looking shiftily around to check that no one was in earshot. "Load of drivel, anyway," he said under his breath. "Let's go and meet Tam. He said he'd be at the tavern in Low Holborn."

As they reached the end of the street and took a turning off it, a flock of white starlings spiralled above them and reversed into a barrel roll towards the cavern where the boys now headed. Appearing from nowhere, Bartleby joined them, flicking his tail and wobbling his bottom jaw at the sight of the birds, and giving a rather sweet and plaintiff mew that was totally at odds with his appearance.

"Come on, you daft beast, you'll never catch them," Cal said as the animal sauntered past them, still transfixed by the birds. As they walked, they passed hovels and small workshops; a blacksmith's where an old man hammered on an anvil, backlit by the blaze from his furnace, and places with names like Geo. Blueskin Tailors and Erasmus Chemicals. Then there was a dark, oily looking yard full of carriages and broken machinery, which fascinated Will.

"Shouldn't we be getting back?" Will asked, stopping to peer through the wrought iron railings at the strange contraptions.

"No, Father won't be home for a while yet," Cal said.

They walked under an arch hewn into the rock wall and into a cavern of such size that Will couldn't see to the other side. This wasn't helped by a shimmering haze, a shifting, living thing that palled above the chaos of rooftops, fed by the collective glow of the light orbs.

"This is the central chamber," Cal said.

For a moment, it reminded Will of Highfield during the summer doldrums, except where there should have been sky and sunlight, he caught glimpses of the immense stone canopy. Cal sped up as they passed other Colonists, who, from their lingering glances, evidently knew who Will was. A number crossed the road to avoid him, muttering under their breath or even spitting in his direction.

Will was more than a little disturbed by these reactions.

"Why are they doing that?" he asked quietly. "It's like they hate me or something."

"Don't worry about it," Cal replied confidently. "Word went around quickly about you."

"But …"

"Look, really, don't worry about it. Nobody likes outsiders, but it'll pass, you'll see," Cal said, "They won't do anything to you." All of a sudden, he stopped and turned to Will. "Just keep moving through here, Will. Keep your head down."

Will was about to ask what he meant when he saw what Cal was referring to, an opening between the two decrepit buildings that was so narrow two people wouldn't be able to pass abreast at the same time. As Cal slipped in, Will reluctantly followed behind him. The alley was dark and claustrophobic, and the sulphurous stench of old sewage hung in the air. Their feet splashed through unseen puddles of unidentified liquids. Will was thankful when they emerged into the dim light. He gasped as he saw a sight that was straight out of Victorian London. Buildings loomed either side of the narrow alleyway, slanting inward at such precarious angles that their upper storeys almost touched. They were timber-framed and in a terrible state of disrepair. Most of their windows were either broken or boarded up.

Will heard the indecipherable words of disembodied voices all around, and cries and laughter. There were odd snatches of music, as if scales were being played on a strangled zither. Somewhere a baby was wailing persistently and dogs were barking. As they strode quickly past the badly deteriorating façades, Will caught whiffs of charcoal and tobacco smoke and, through open doorways, glimpsed people huddled at tables. Men in shirtsleeves hung out of windows, staring down listlessly as they smoked their pipes. There was an open gutter in the middle of the alley in which a trickle of raw sewage ran through vegetable waste and other filth and detritus. Will nearly blundered into it, and quickly moved to the side of the alley to avoid it.

"Not too close!" Cal warned quickly.

As he moved back to the middle, Will heard the hushed voices and spotted the shadowy outlines of people in passageways running off either side. From one of these, a man with a black shawl over his head and a gnarled, sweat-covered face the colour of sun-bleached wood appeared.

"Ah, what is it you're after, my sweet things?" he wheezed asthmatically, his lopsided smile revealing a row of jagged brown stumps for teeth. Bartleby snarled as Cal hurriedly pushed Will along through several twists and turns and finally they were out and back onto an open street. Will breathed a sigh of relief.

"What was *that*?"

"The Rookeries. It's where the paupers live. And that was only the outskirts – you wouldn't want to find yourself in the middle of it," Cal said, dashing ahead so quickly that Will had a job to keep up. He was still feeling the after-effects of the ordeal in the Hold; his chest ached and his legs were leaden. But he wasn't about to let Cal see any weakness and forced himself on. As the cat bounded ahead into the distance, Will doggedly followed Cal's lead as he leapt over the larger pools of water and skirted around the occasional downpour of water.

Falling from the shadows of the cavern roof above, these torrents seemed to spring from nowhere, like upturned geysers.

They wound their way through a series of broad streets jam-packed with narrow terraced houses until, in the distance, Will spotted the lights of the tavern at the apex of a sharp corner where two roads met. In various states of intoxication, people thronged outside it, laughing raucously and shouting and from somewhere a woman's voice was singing shrilly. As he got closer, Will could make out the painted sign, "The Buttock & File", with a picture of an odd-looking locomotive that had, it appeared, an archetypal devil as its driver, scarlet-skinned and replete with horns, trident and an arrow-tipped tail.

The façade and even the windows of the tavern were painted black and covered in a film of grey soot. People were so tightly packed in the interior that they were overflowing onto the pavements outside. To a man, they were drinking from dented pewter tankards, while a number smoked either long clay pipes, or turnip-shaped objects, which Will didn't recognise but reeked of chronically soiled nappies.

"Cal! Bring Will over here!" a voice called out. There was an immediate lull in the conversations around them and all heads turned on Will. Uncle Tam emerged from a group of people and waved the two boys over extravagantly. The faces in the crowd outside the tavern were varied: curious, grinning, blank, and many sneering with unbridled hostility. Will just wanted the ground to swallow him up, but Tam seemed not the slightest bit bothered. He placed his thick arms around the boys' shoulders and turned his head to face the crowd, staring back at them in mute defiance.

Oblivious to the rising tension outside, the cacophony continued in the bar, only serving to make the yawning silence even more intense. It filled Will's ears, crashing and swelling and drowning everything out.

Then an ear-splitting belch, the longest and loudest Will had ever heard, ripped from someone in the crowd. As the last echoes rang back from the neighbouring buildings, the crowd exploded into peals of harsh laughter, intermingled with cheers and the odd wolf whistle. The spell was broken and the crowd settled down and the chatter resumed again as a small man was widely congratulated and patted on the back so forcibly that he had to cover his drink with his hand to prevent it from slopping onto the pavement.

Still acutely self-conscious, Will kept his head bowed. He couldn't help noticing Bartleby, stretched out under the bench where the men sat, jerk suddenly, as if some parasite or other had bitten him. Doubling up, the cat began to lick his nether regions with a hind leg pointing heavenward, looking for all the world like a badly plucked turkey.

"Now you've met the great unwashed," Uncle Tam said, his eyes briefly flicking back over the crowd, "let me introduce you to royalty, the *crème de la crème*. This is Joe Waites," he said, manoeuvring Will face to face with a wizened old man. His head was topped with a tight fitting skullcap that seemed to compress the top half of his face, making his eyes bulge out and hoisting his cheeks up into an involuntary grin. A solitary tooth protruded from his top jaw like an ivory tusk. He proffered his hand to Will, who shook it reluctantly, somewhat surprised to find it warm and dry.

"And this," Tam inclined his head to a dapper man sporting a tawdry chequered three-piece suit and black-rimmed glasses, "is Jessie Shingles." The man bowed gracefully and then chuckled, raising his thick eyebrows.

"And, not least, the one and only Imago Freebone." A man with long, dank hair plaited into a biker's ponytail shot out a mittened hand, his voluminous leather coat flapping open to reveal his immense barrel of a body. Will was so intimidated by the massiveness of the man, he almost took a step back.

"Deeply pleased to meet such a hallowed legend, we being such 'umble personages," Imago said, bending his bulk forward and tugging a non-existent forelock with his other hand.

"Er ... hello," Will said, uncertain what to make of him.

"Knock it off," grimaced Tam. "I hate it when you do that."

Imago straightened up, offering his hand again and, in a

normal voice, said, "Will, very good to meet you." Will shook it again. "I shouldn't have," Imago added earnestly. "We all know what you've been through, only too well." He was now clasping Will's hand between both of his and finally let go of it with a comforting squeeze.

Will was more than a little daunted by Uncle Tam's associates and their strange appearances but, looking around, it struck him that they weren't that different from most of the people outside the tavern.

"I got you both a quart of *New London*." Tam handed the two tankards to the boys. "Go easy on it Will, you won't have tasted a brew like this before."

"What's in it?" Will asked, eyeing with suspicion the greyish liquid with a thin froth on top of it.

"Don't wanta know, my boy, really you don't," Tam said and his friends laughed; Joe Waites made peculiar bird-like noises, while Imago threw his head back and gave an extravagant but completely silent laugh, his rotund shoulders heaving violently. Stretched out under the bench, Bartleby yawned and then licked his lips noisily.

"So you've been to your first service, Will," Uncle Tam asked, his face turning serious. "What did you think of it?"

"It was, er … interesting," Will said noncommittally.

"Not if you've had a bellyful of the Book," Tam said and then supped from his tankard.

"If you've heard one catastrophe, you've heard them all." Imago nudged Will in the ribs and they all laughed.

Cal took a large swig of his drink as Tam gestured towards Will's tankard. "What do you make of that?"

Will tentatively took a mouthful of the chalky fluid and held it in his mouth for a moment before swallowing it down.

"Not bad," Will said. Then it bit, burning his throat and sending him into a coughing fit. Uncle Tam and Cal grinned. "Could I have something else?" he gasped, putting the tankard on the edge of the table. "I'm not really allowed to drink alcohol."

"Who's going to stop you? Whole different set of rules here.

As long as you stay within the laws, pull your weight and attend service once a day, they don't mind if you let off a little steam."

As if to show their agreement with Tam, the assembled group held up their tankards and clanked them together with salutations of "Good health!"

And so the drinking started in earnest and it wasn't long before they were on their third round. Tam had just finished telling a convoluted and unfathomable joke about a flatulent policeman and a blind orb juggler's daughter that all the others found hilarious, but Will could make neither head nor tail of. Picking up his tankard and still chuckling, Tam suddenly looked into his drink and, with his thumb and forefinger, pulled something out of the froth. "I got a bloody slug again," he said, as the others burst once again into raucous laughter.

To Will's astonishment, Tam placed the limp grey object on his tongue and moved it around inside his mouth. In the lull that followed, Will felt sufficiently emboldened with Dutch courage to speak up.

"Uncle Tam, I need your help."

"Anything, lad," Tam said, putting his hand on Will's shoulder. "You only have to ask."

"I need to get Chester out," Will blurted.

"Shhh!" Tam hissed, clearly taken aback by Will's imprudence as he glanced nervously around them and they all drew together to encircle Will in a secretive huddle. "Have you got *any* idea what you're asking?" Tam said under his breath.

Will looked at him blankly, not sure how to respond.

"And what do you think you're both going to do, go back to Highfield? Neither of you would be safe there. Not now. You'd need to lose yourself somewhere, somewhere they'll never think of looking for you. Do you know where you'd go?"

"No, I don't. All I know is I can't leave him there. When I needed help to find my Dad," Will was thoughtful for a second, "the one person I could rely on was Chester, and now he's stuck in the Hold … because of me. I owe it to him."

Tam looked at Will for a moment and then shook his head. "Like mother, like son," he muttered, and chewed noisily on the slug. "D'you know, it's uncanny how much you sound like her. When she set her mind on something, there was no budging her. Stubborn as a bloody mule." He stopped chewing the slug and swallowed.

Imago tapped Tam's arm. "It's him again."

Will followed his gaze to a Styx talking to a hefty man at the end of the pub's frontage. The man had bristly white hair and long sideburns, and wore a shiny brown coat with a grimy red neckerchief coiled around his stubby neck. As they watched, the Styx nodded, turned and walked away.

"That Styx has been dogging Tam for a long time now," Cal whispered to Will.

"What's his name?" Will asked.

"Nobody knows their names, but we call him the Crawfly on account he can't so easily be shaken off. He's on a personal vendetta to bring Uncle Tam down." Cal turned back to Will. "Don't look now, but the man he was with … that's Heraldo Walsh. A cutthroat … nasty piece of work."

"A burglar, lowest of the low," Tam growled.

"But what's he doing talking to a Styx, then?" Will asked, totally confused.

"Wheels within wheels," Tam muttered. "The Styx are a devious bunch. A belt becomes a snake with them." He turned to Will. "Look, I may be able to help, but you've got to promise me something," he whispered.

"What's that?"

"If you get caught, you'll never implicate Cal, me or any of us. Our lives are here and the Styx never let it rest if you cross them … they *will* catch up with you."

Will heard someone clear his throat behind him and saw the alarm in Cal's eyes. He spun around. Heraldo Walsh was standing not five feet away. And behind him, a throng of drunkards had parted fearfully to allow a phalanx of brutish-looking Colonists through. They were clearly Heraldo Walsh's supporters – Will saw the fiery hatred in their faces and wished the ground would swallow him up. Tam immediately stepped to Will's side.

"What do you want, Walsh?" Tam said, his eyes fierce and his fists clenched.

"Ah, my old friend, Tamfoolery," Heraldo Walsh said with a vile, gappy grin. "I just wanted to see this Topsoiler, for myself."

Heraldo Walsh stepped nearer to Will. "So you're the scum that chokes our air channels and spills foul sewage into our homes. My daughter died because of your kind." He took another step closer to Will.

"That's far enough, Walsh," Tam said, and Heraldo Walsh stopped in his tracks.

"You're fraternising with the godless, Macaulay," Heraldo Walsh's eyes never left Will's face.

"And what do you know of God?" Tam retorted as he stepped fully in front of Will to shield him. "Leave him alone, he's family."

But Heraldo was like a dog with a bone – he wasn't about to let go. Behind him, his supporters were cursing and muttering words of support, egging him on.

"You call *that* family? The bloodline of a bitch who ran for the sun?"

Tam took a step towards Heraldo Walsh and threw the remnants of his beer at the man. It hit him square in the face, soaking his hair and sideburns in the watery grey fluid.

"You'll eat those words, Walsh. Step up to the scratch," Tam scowled.

Heraldo Walsh's coterie began to chant "Milling, milling, milling!" and very soon cheers filled the air as everyone outside on the pavement joined in. Others came rushing out of the tavern doors to see what all the commotion was about.

"What's going on?" Will asked Cal, terrified out of his wits as the huge crowd encircled them. Tam stood resolutely in front of the dripping Heraldo Walsh, locked in an angry staring match.

"A fist fight," Cal said.

The landlord, a stocky man with a sweaty red face, wearing a blue apron, pushed through the tavern doors and threaded his way through the mob until he reached the two men. He barged in between Tam and Heraldo Walsh and knelt down to fix shackles to their ankles. They both took a step back and Will saw that the shackles were connected by a length of rusty chain that bound them together.

Then the landlord reached into his apron pocket to retrieve a piece of chalk that he used to draw a line on the pavement halfway between them.

"You know the rules," his voice boomed theatrically, as much for the benefit of the crowd as for the two men. "Above the belt, no weapons, biting or gouging. It stops on a KO or death."

"*Death?*" Will whispered shakily to Cal, who nodded grimly.

Then the landlord ushered everyone back until a human boxing ring had been squared off. This wasn't an easy task as people were jostling against each other as they vied for a view of the two men.

"Step up to the mark," the man said loudly. Tam and Heraldo Walsh positioned themselves either side of the chalk line. The landlord held their arms to steady them. Then he released them with the shouted order "Commence!" and quickly retreated.

In an attempt to knock his opponent off his balance, Heraldo Walsh immediately swung his leg back and the length of chain – seven or so feet long – snapped taut, yanking Tam's foot forward.

But Tam was ready for the manoeuvre and used the forward momentum to his advantage. He leapt towards Heraldo Walsh, a huge right fist flying at the shorter man's face. The blow glanced off Heraldo Walsh's chin, drawing a gasp from the crowd. Tam continued with a fast combination of blows, but his opponent ducked and dived like a demented rabbit, avoiding them, it seemed, with ease, as the chain between them rattled noisily on the pavement amidst the shouts and cries.

"By heck, he's quick, that one," Joe Waites observed.

"But he don't have Tam's reach, do he?" Jessie Shingles countered.

Then Heraldo Walsh, crouching low, shot up under Tam's

guard and landed a blow on his jaw, a sharp upper cut that jarred Tam's head. Blood burst from his mouth, but he didn't hesitate in his retaliation, bringing his fist down squarely on the top of Heraldo Walsh's head.

"The pile driver!" Joe Waites said excitedly and then shouted, "Go on, Tam! Go on, you beauty!"

Heraldo Walsh's knees buckled and he reeled backwards, spitting with anger, and came back immediately with a frenzied salvo of punches, clipping Tam around the mouth. Tam moved back as far as the limits of the chain would allow, colliding with the crowd behind him. As people stepped on those behind to give the two fighters more room, Heraldo Walsh pursued him. Tam used the time to collect himself and reorganise his guard. As Heraldo Walsh closed in with his fists swiping the air in front of him, Tam ducked down and exploded back into his opponent with a combination of crushing blows to his ribcage and stomach. The noise of the thudding wallops, like bales of hay being thrown on the ground, could be heard over the shouts and jeers of the spectators.

"He's softening him up," Cal said gleefully.

Sporadic skirmishes were breaking out in the mob as arguments raged between the supporters of the two combatants. From his vantage point, Will saw heads bobbing up and down, fists flailing and tankards flying – beer was going everywhere. He also noticed that money was changing hands as bets were feverishly taken – people were holding up one, two or three fingers and swapping coins. The atmosphere was carnivalesque.

Suddenly the crowd let out a deep "Oooh!" as, without warning, Heraldo Walsh landed a mighty right hook on Tam's nose. Then there was a dramatic lull in the shouting as the crowd watched Tam drop onto one knee, the chain snapping tightly between them.

"That's not good," Imago said worriedly.

"Come on Tam!" Cal shouted for all he was worth. "Macaulay, Macaulay, Macaulay ... " he yelled and Will joined in.

Tam stayed down. Cal and Will could see blood was running from his face and dripping onto the cobblestones of the street. Then he looked across at them and winked slyly.

"The old dog!" Imago said under his breath. "Here it comes."

Sure enough, as Heraldo Walsh stood over him, Tam rose up with all the grace and speed of a leaping jaguar, throwing a fearful uppercut that smashed into Walsh's jaw, forcing his teeth together in a bloodcurdling crunch. Heraldo Walsh staggered back and Tam was on him, pounding him with deadly precision, striking the face of the smaller man so rapidly and with such force that he had no time to mount any form of defence.

Something covered with spittle and blood shot from Heraldo Walsh's mouth and landed on the cobblestones. With a shock, Will saw it was a large part of a shattered tooth. Hands reached into the ring in an attempt to snatch it away. One man, wearing a moth-eaten trilby, was the fastest off the mark, whisking it away and then vanishing into the throng behind him.

"Souvenir hunters," Cal said. "Ghouls!"

Will looked up just as Tam closed on Heraldo Walsh, who was now being held up by some of his followers, exhausted and gasping for breath. Spitting out blood, his left eye swollen shut, Heraldo Walsh was pushed forward just in time to see Tam's fist as he landed a final, crushing blow.

The man's head snapped back as he fell against the crowd, which this time parted and watched him as he danced a slow, drunken, bent-leg jig for a few agonising moments. Then he simply folded to the ground like a sodden paper doll and the crowd fell silent.

Tam was bent forward, his raw knuckles resting on his knees as he tried to catch his breath. The landlord came forward and nudged Heraldo Walsh's head with his boot. He didn't move.

"Tam Macaulay!" the landlord yelled out to the silent mob, which suddenly erupted with a roar that filled the cavern and must have rattled the windows on the other side of the Rookeries.

Tam's shackle was removed and his friends ran over to him and helped him to the bench where he sat down heavily, feeling his jaw as the two boys took their places either side of him.

"Little bastard was faster than I thought," he said, looking down at his bloodied knuckles as he flexed them painfully. He was handed a full tankard by someone who slapped him on the back and disappeared back into the tavern.

"The Crawfly's disappointed," Jessie said, as they all turned to see the Styx at the end of the street, his back to them as he strolled away, drumming a pair of peculiar eyeglasses on his thigh as he went.

"But he got what he wanted," Tam said despondently. "The word will go around that I've had yet another brawl."

"Don't matter," Jessie Shingles said. "You were justified. Everyone knows it was Walsh started it."

Tam looked at the sorry limp figure of Heraldo Walsh, left where he'd fallen. Not one of his cronies had come forward to move him off the street.

"One thing's for sure – he'll feel like a Coprolite's dinner when he wakes up," Imago chortled as a barman threw a bucket of water over the pole-axed figure and walked away laughing.

Tam nodded thoughtfully and took a huge mouthful of his drink, wiping his bruised lips with his forearm.

"That's if he wakes up at all," he said quietly.

CHAPTER TWENTY-FIVE

Rebecca's room filled with the heavy rumble of Monday-morning traffic and car horns hooting impatiently from the streets 13 floors below. A slight breeze ruffled the curtains and the early sun slipped a feeble beam into the lethargic air of her room. She wrinkled her nose disdainfully as she smelt the stale stench of cigarettes from Auntie Jean's non-stop smoking the night before. Although the door to her bedroom was firmly shut, the smoke nosed its way into every nook and cranny, like an insidious yellow fog searching out new corners to taint.

She got up and, having slipped on her furry monster-foot slippers and her well-worn tartan quilted dressing gown, made her bed as she trilled the first couple of lines of *You Are My Sunshine*. Lapsing into vague "La las" for the rest of the song, she carefully arranged a black dress on the bed with a white shirt.

She went to leave the bedroom and, placing her hand on the door handle, stopped for no apparent reason. She returned to her bed and looked at the little silver-framed photographs on the table beside it. In one of them, there was a slightly out-of-focus photograph showing Will leaning on a spade. In the other, a young Dr and Mrs Burrows sat on stripy deckchairs on an unidentified beach. In the picture, her mother was staring at an enormous ice cream, while Dr Burrows appeared to be trying to swat a fly with a blurred hand.

She took the photographs, one in each hand, and sat down

on her bed. She was thinking about the previous week in the awful school where they didn't wear uniforms and *nobody* seemed to be very interested in the schoolwork, neither the pupils nor the teachers. Of course, she knew she could survive and even flourish in such a place – she had a knack of being able to blend in and, as a result, was largely untroubled by the school bullies and their gangs.

She looked closely at the photograph of Will and smiled sourly. Everyone had abandoned her. They had all gone their separate ways – she was the last one. And she'd been left to nursemaid someone even more slothful and demanding than her mother.

"Time to go," she said aloud and the thin smile evaporated. She flung the photographs with such force that they both struck the discoloured skirting with a tinkle of breaking glass.

Twenty minutes later, she was dressed and ready to leave. She put her little suitcases next to the front door and went into the kitchen. In a drawer next to the sink was Auntie Jean's "fag stash". Rebecca opened the 10 or so packets of cigarettes and shook their contents into the sink. Then she started on Auntie Jean's bottles of cheap vodka (or "Perry Water" as she called it). Rebecca twisted off the screw caps and poured them, all five bottles, into the sink, dousing the cigarettes.

She took the "wipe clean" box of kitchen matches from beside the gas cooker and opened it. Then she struck a match and set light to a crumpled-up sheet of kitchen roll.

Standing well back, she chucked the flaming ball into the sink. The cigarettes and alcohol went up with a satisfying whoosh, flames leaping out of the sink and over the chrome-look plastic taps and the chipped floral tiles behind the sink. Rebecca didn't stay to savour it. The front door slammed and her little suitcases were gone. With the sound of the smoke alarm receding behind her, she made her way across the landing and into the stairwell.

Since his friend had been spirited away, Chester, in the permanent shade of the Hold, had passed beyond the point of despair.

"One. Two. Three ... " He tried to lock his arms and complete the push-up, part of his daily training routine.

"Thre ..." he breathed deeply and tensed his arms without any real enthusiasm.

"Thre ..." he exhaled hollowly and sank down, his face coming to rest against the unseen filth on the stone floor. He slowly rolled over and, sitting up, looked up to check the observation hatch in the door as he brought his hands together.

Dear God ... To him, praying was something enforced in the self-conscious cough-filled silences at school assembly ... something that followed the badly sung hymns that, to the glee of their giggling confederates, some boys salted with dirty lyrics.

No, only nerds prayed in earnest.

... *please send someone* ... He pressed his hands together, no longer feeling any embarrassment. What else could he do? It brought back to him only too clearly the great uncle who had one day appeared in the spare room at home. Chester's mum had taken Chester to one side and told him the funny little twig-like man was having cancer therapy at a London hospital and, although Chester had never set eyes on him before, she said he was "family", and that that was important.

Chester pictured the man with his copy of the *Racing Post* and his harsh "I don't eat any of that foreign filth" when he was presented with a perfectly good plate of spag bol. He remembered the rasping cough punctuating the numerous "rollies" he still insisted on smoking, much to the chagrin of his mother.

In the second week of car trips to the hospital, the little man had got weaker and more withdrawn, like a leaf withering on a branch, until he didn't talk of fancy pigeons any more, or even try to drink his tea. Chester had heard, but never understood why, the little man had cried out to God in their spare room in horrible wheezing breaths, in those days before he died.

... *help me, please ... please ...* Chester was lonely and abandoned and ... and why, oh why, had he gone with Will on this ridiculous jaunt? Why hadn't he just stayed home? He could be there now, tucked up warm and safe, but he wasn't, and he had gone with Will ... and he *was* here now ... and there was nothing else he could do but mark the passage of days by the two depressingly identical bowls of mush that arrived at regular intervals, and the intermittent periods of unfulfilling sleep. He had grown used to the perpetual thrumming noise that pervaded the cell – the Second Officer had told him it was due to machinery in the "Fan Stations." He had actually begun to find it rather comforting.

Of late, the Second Officer had mellowed slightly in his treatment of Chester and occasionally deigned to respond to his questions. It was almost as though it didn't matter any more whether the man kept up his officious bearing with Chester or not. It left Chester with the dreadful feeling that he might be there for ever, or, on the other hand, that something was just around the corner; that things were coming to a head, and he suspected not for the better.

Indeed, on one occasion the officer had even allowed him out of the cell. In a side room, the officer talked animatedly with him about Topsoil life over cups of hot drink. It wasn't an official interrogation, as all the man really wanted to hear about was food – in particular, fast food and confectionery. At one point in the conversation, when Chester had got carried away as he extolled the virtues of cheeseburgers and chips, describing in lavish detail the gherkins and mayonnaise relish that coated the meat, the Second Officer made a slurping sound and quickly wiped his mouth. Afterwards, back in the darkness of the cell, Chester realised with some astonishment that the man had actually been salivating.

On another occasion, the Second Officer had slung the door open and ordered him to wash, providing him with a bucket of dark water and a sponge. He had chucked in a bundle of clothes for him to change into, including a pair of huge trousers that felt as if they were made of sackcloth and made him itch terribly. At least, he assumed it was the trousers.

Other than these brief interludes, time tottered wearily along. Chester had lost track of how long he'd been in the Hold; it may have been a fortnight, but he couldn't be sure.

He was very excited when he discovered that by gently probing with his fingertips he could make out letters scratched into the stone of one of the cell walls. There were initials and names, some with numbers that could have been dates. And at the very bottom of the wall someone had scratched in large capitals: "I DIED HERE, SLOWLY." After finding this, Chester didn't feel like reading any more of them.

He'd also discovered that by standing on his toes on the sleeping ledge, he could just reach the bars on a narrow slit window high up on the wall above it. Gripping these bars, he was able to pull himself up so he could see the gaol's neglected kitchen garden. Beyond that, there was a stretch of road leading into a tunnel, lit by a few ever-burning orb lamp posts. He would stare relentlessly at the road where it disappeared into the tunnel, in the forlorn hope that maybe, just maybe, he might catch a glimpse of Will, of his friend returning to save him, like some white knight riding to his rescue. But he never came, and Chester would hang there, hoping and praying fervently, as his knuckles turned white with the strain and his arms gave out and he would fall back into the cell, into the shadows, and back into despair.

CHAPTER TWENTY-SIX

"**W**akey, wakey!"

Will was rudely woken from a deep and dreamless sleep by Cal shouting and shaking his shoulder mercilessly.

More than a little fragile, Will's head throbbed dully as he sat up in his narrow bed. It wasn't until he burped and the taste of the ale from the night before soured his mouth that he realised the cause of his malaise.

"Get up, Will, we have duties."

He had no idea what time it was, but he was certain it was very early indeed.

"Mr Tonypandy's waiting and he's not a patient man."

Will groaned and lay back down on his makeshift bed. It felt like the first day of school again, such were the sensations of dread and anticipation that flooded through him.

"Will!" Cal shouted.

"All right, all right." With sickening resignation, he got up and dressed and followed Cal downstairs, where a short, heavy-set man stood on the doorstep with a severe expression. He regarded Will with an overt look of disgust before turning his back on him.

"Here, put these on quickly," Cal handed Will a bundle that was heavy and black. Will unfolded it and struggled into what could only be described as ill-fitting oilskins, uncomfortably tight under the arms and around the crutch. He looked down at himself and then at Cal, who had dressed himself in the same clothing.

"We look ridiculous!" he said.

Cal cut him short. "You'll need them where you're going."

Will presented himself to Mr Tonypandy who didn't utter a word. He stared blankly at Will for a moment and then flicked his head to indicate that he should follow.

On the street, Cal headed off in a different direction altogether. Although he was also on a work detail, it was in a another quadrant of the South Cavern, and Will was sorry he wouldn't be with him on this first day of work.

Following unenthusiastically behind, Will stole glances at Mr Tonypandy as he walked slowly along with a pronounced limp, his left leg heaving waywardly in its very own orbit, and his foot beating the cobbles with a soft thwack at each step. Practically as broad as he was tall, he wore a peculiar black ribbed hat that was pulled down almost to his eyebrows. It looked as though it was made of wool but, on closer inspection, appeared to be woven from a fibrous material, something rather like coconut hair. His short neck was as wide as his head and it suddenly occurred to Will that, from behind, the whole thing resembled a big thumb sticking out of an overcoat, and he chuckled to himself.

As they progressed along the street, other Colonists fell in behind them until the troop was a dozen or so in number. They were mostly young, between the age of 10 and 15, Will reckoned. He saw that many of them were carrying spades, while a few had a bizarre long-handled tool that looked vaguely like a pickaxe, a spike on one side and a long, curved scoop on the other. From the wear on the leather-bound shafts and the state of the blades, the tools had evidently seen a great deal of use.

Will's curiosity overcame him and he lent over to one of the boys walking beside him and asked in a low voice: "What's that thing you've got there?"

The boy glared charily at him with tired, vacant eyes and muttered: "It's a pitch cleaver, of course."

"A pitch cleaver," Will repeated. "Er, thanks," he added as the boy deliberately slowed his pace, dropping back from him. At that point, Will felt more alone than he could ever remember, and was suddenly overwhelmed by the strongest yearning to return home.

Eventually, they entered a tunnel, the tramping of their boots echoing about them. The tunnel walls had diagonal veins of a shiny black rock running through them, like strata of obsidian or even, as he looked more closely, polished coal. *Is that what they were on their way to do?* Will's head immediately filled with images of coalminers stripped to the waist, crawling into narrow seams and hacking away at the dusty black face. His mind swam with apprehension.

After a few minutes, they crossed through into a cavern, smaller than the one they had just left. The first thing Will noticed was that the air was different in here; the humidity had increased to the point that he could feel the moisture collect on his face and mingle with his sweat. Then he noticed that the cavern walls were shored up with huge slabs of limestone. Cal had told him that the Colony was made up of an interlinking series of chambers, some naturally formed and others like this one, man-made with partially reinforced walls.

There were fewer buildings in this cavern, giving it an almost rural feel, although Will couldn't quite put his finger on why he should think this. It became apparent as they marched on and he could examine the structures; there were oak-beamed barns and single-storey houses like little bungalows, some freestanding but most built into the walls. As for the residents of the cavern, he saw only a handful of people carrying bulky canvas bags on their backs or pushing loaded barrows.

The troop followed Mr Tonypandy as he veered off the road and down into a deep trench, the bottom of which was full of sodden clay. Slippery and treacherous, it clung to the soles of their boots, hampering their progress as they weaved their way through a meandering course of spurs and returns. Soon, the trench opened into a sizable crater at the base of the cavern wall itself, and they drew to a halt beside two crude stone-built buildings with flat roofs. They leant against their spades and pitch cleavers as Mr Tonypandy began an animated discussion with two older men who had emerged from one of the buildings. While this was going on, the boys in the troop joked and chatted together, giving Will sidelong glances from time to time as he stood apart from them. When the confab was over, Mr Tonypandy left, limping off in the direction of the road. Then one of the older men shouted over at Will.

"You're with me, Jerome. Go to the huts."

He had a deep scar in the shape of a crescent across his face. It began just above his mouth and ran up across his left eye and forehead, ending somewhere on his scalp at the back of his head. The livid red of this scar was made all the more striking because the man's snow-white hair was parted along its margins but, for Will, the damaged eye was the most horrifying aspect. It was permanently weeping and shot through with a mottled cloudiness, while the eyelid above it was so torn and ragged that when the man blinked, it was like a defective window wiper struggling to function.

"In there! In there!" he repeated fiercely as Will failed to acknowledge the order.

"Sorry," Will answered quickly. Then he and two other youngsters followed the scar man into the nearest building.

The interior was dank and, except for some equipment in the corner, appeared to be empty. They stood idly about as the scar man kicked at the dirt floor as if looking for something he'd lost. He began to swear wildly under his breath until his boots finally struck something solid. It was a metal ring, which he pulled at with both hands; there was a loud creaking as a steel plate lifted to reveal a four-foot square opening.

"Right, down we go."

One by one, they filed down a wet, rusty stepladder and once they had all reached the bottom, the scar man took the lantern from his belt and played it around the brick-lined tunnel. It wasn't quite high enough to stand up in and, from the state of the masonry, eroded and badly in need of re-pointing where the chalky mortar had crumbled away, Will guessed that it must have been in use for decades, if not centuries.

Five or so inches of brackish water stood in the bottom of

the tunnel and it wasn't long before it plunged over the top of Will's boots as he tagged behind the others. They sloshed along for about 10 minutes until the scar man stopped and turned to them again.

"Under here ..." the man spoke condescendingly to Will as the others watched on. It was as if he were explaining something to a young child. "... are boreholes. We remove the sediment ... we unblock them. Yes?"

The scar man swung the lantern to illuminate the tunnel floor, which was heavily silted with little island aggregations of flint and limestone shards rising out of the water. He slipped off several coils of rope from his shoulder, and in turn the boys took ends from him and tied them securely around their waists. The other end of each rope the scar man tied around himself so they were connected like a group of mountaineers.

"Topsoiler," the scar man snarled, "we tie the rope around ourselves ... we tie it well." Will didn't dare to question why as he took the rope and looped it around his waist, knotting it as best he could. As he tugged at it to test it, the man held out a battered pitch cleaver for him.

"Now we dig."

The two boys began to hack away at the floor of the tunnel and Will knew he was meant to do likewise. Probing with the unfamiliar tool, he worked his way along the brick lining under the swilling waters until he came to a softer patch of compacted sediment and stones. He hesitated, glancing at the other boys to reassure himself he was doing the right thing.

"We keep digging, we don't stop," the scar man shouted as he played the lantern on Will, who immediately began to dig. It was hard going because the tool he was using, the pitch cleaver, was unfamiliar and the water would keep washing back into the deepening hole after every stroke.

After a while, Will had got to grips with this new tool and mastered his technique. Now well into his stride, it felt good just to be digging again and all of his worries seemed to be forgotten, even if only for a short while, as he threw load after load of stone and sopping earth out of the hole. With the water rushing in after every scoopful, it wasn't long before he was thigh-deep in the borehole, the other boys having to work furiously just to keep up with him. Then, with a bone-shaking judder, his pitch cleaver jarred against something immovable.

"We dig around it!" the scar man snapped.

With sweat running down his dirty face, Will glanced at him and then back to the surface of the water lapping against his oilskins. He was trying to work out the reason for their task; he knew he'd get short shrift from the scar man if he asked, but his curiosity was getting the better of him. And he was just looking up and forming the question when there was an urgent cry, cut off almost as soon as it started.

"BRACE!" the scar man screamed.

Will turned in time to see one of the other boys completely vanish with a loud gurgling, as the water gushed down into what now looked like a huge drain, the size of a manhole. The ropes yanked tight, Will's cutting into his waist, as the scar man leant back and dug his boots into the grit and debris of the tunnel floor. Will was pinned to the edge of his borehole and could feel his tether jerking with the fallen boy's desperate movements.

"Pull yourself up!" the scar man shouted in the direction of the swirling hole. Will watched with alarm until he saw mud-stained fingers clutching at the sides of the hole and snaking up the rope as the boy heaved himself out against the flow. As he straightened up, Will saw the terrified look on the boy's mud streaked face.

"One down. Now the rest of you get a bloody move on," the scar man said, leaning back against the wall behind him as he took out a pipe and began to fill the bowl with tobacco.

Will stabbed away blindly at the compacted sediment around the object wedged in the hole, until most of it was clear. He couldn't tell what it was, but when he struck the obstruction itself, it felt spongy, as if it was water-logged timber. Driving his heel down in an attempt to loosen it, there was a sudden whoosh as it dislodged. The surface beneath his feet literally gave way. He was in freefall, water sluicing down with a cascade of gravel and slurry. He banged against the sides of the borehole, his hair and face drenched and covered in grit.

His body twitched like a marionette's as the rope broke his fall. In less than a second, he'd gathered his wits about him. He guessed he'd dropped 20 feet or so, but in the blackness of the space he had no idea what was below him.

"Now's my chance …" it suddenly occurred to him in a flash.

He desperately groped under his oilskins, in his trouser pockets, his hand closing on the penknife.

"… to escape …"

He peered below him into the absolute darkness of the unknown, calculating the odds, the rope tensing as the others began to pull.

"… and Dad's down here … somewhere." The idea blinked through his mind as keenly as a neon sign.

"*Down here, down here, down here,*" it repeated, flashing on and off with the irksome buzz of an electrical discharge.

"Water, I can hear water …"

"CLIMB THE ROPE, BOY!" he heard the scar man bellowing. "CLIMB THE ROPE!"

Will's mind raced as he strained to hear the sounds below him; faint splashes and the gurgle of moving water were just audible over the pendulum creaks of the thick rope that bit into his waist, his lifeline back to the Colony above.

"… but how deep is it?"

There was water below, that much was certain, but he didn't know if it was sufficient to cushion his fall. He flicked the blade open and braced it against the rope, poised to cut it.

"Yes … No?"

If the water wasn't deep enough, he'd be jumping to his death, in this godforsaken, lonely place. He pictured jagged shards of rock, razor-sharp and deadly, like a line drawing from a comic book … the next frame was his lifeless body, impaled and broken as his blood pumped out of him, mingling with the darkness.

But he felt rash and daring. He drew the blade against the rope and the first braid of fibres separated beneath it.

"*A daring escape*!" flashed in even brighter neon than before, like a by-line from some Hollywood adventure. The words were proud and brave, but then the image of Chester's face, laughing and happy, reared up shattering it into a million fragments. Will shivered from the cold, his body drenched and plastered with mud.

The muted hollering of the scar man once again drifted from above, as vague and confused as a yodeller down a drainpipe, wrenching Will from his thoughts. He knew he should be pulling himself back up the rope, but he couldn't bring himself to. Then he sighed, and all the courage and bravado were gone. In their place was the cold certainty that if not now, then there'd soon be another opportunity, and he would take it next time.

He tucked away the penknife, twisted himself upright, and began the laborious climb back.

When Will finally pulled himself out of the borehole, the scar man berated him for taking so long, much to the amusement of the others, but he didn't care any more.

Seven hours later, he'd lost count of how many boreholes they'd cleared as they progressed further and further along the tunnel. Finally, glancing at his pocket watch under the light of the lantern, the scar man told them they were finished for the day. They trudged back toward the stepladder and, once out in the open again, Will set off alone for the journey home, his hands and back aching horribly.

As he climbed out of the trench and made his way slowly along the road, he spotted a circle of Colonists outside a building with a pair of large, garage-type doors. They were surrounded by banks of stacked crates.

As one of the men stepped back from the gathering, Will heard a high-pitched laugh. Then he saw something that made him blink and rub his eyes. A puce-pink blazer and straw boater pranced in the middle of the group.

"Can't be! No! It is! Clarke … it's Mr Clarke Junior!" he said aloud, without meaning to.

"What?" came a voice from behind. It was one of the boys that Will had been working with. "You know him?"

"Yes! But … but … what on earth is he doing here?" Will asked, dumbfounded as he thought of the Clarke's shop in the High Street and struggled with the displaced apparition of Mr Clarke Junior in the distance, still cavorting within the circle of stocky Colonists. As he watched, Will saw that he was picking things from the boxes with little theatrical flourishes and displaying them to his audience, sweeping them along his sleeve like a dodgy watch salesman before he placed them delicately on a trestle table. Then the penny dropped.

"Don't tell me he's selling fruit!" Will said.

"And vegetables." The boy looked curiously at Will. "The Clarkes have been trading with us for as long as …"

"My God, what's *that*?" Will interrupted him, pointing at an outlandish figure that stepped into view from the shadow of a towering stack of fruit boxes. Apparently ignored, it stood outside the huddle of Colonists and inspected a pineapple as if it were a rare artefact, while the exchange continued with the gesticulating Mr Clarke Junior.

The boy followed Will's finger to the stationary figure, which appeared to be human, with arms and legs, but was swathed in some kind of bloated diver's suit, which was a dull bone colour. It was bulbous, like a caricature of a fat man, and the head and face were completely obscured by a hood-like extension. Its large goggles glinted as they caught the light of a street orb. It looked like a man-shaped slug or, rather, a slug-shaped man.

"Bloody hell, don't you know anything?" the boy laughed with undisguised scorn at Will's ignorance. "It's only a *Coprolite*."

Will frowned. "Oh right, a Coprolite."

"From down there," the boy said, looking at the ground as he walked away. Will lingered behind for a moment to watch the Coprolite – it moved so slowly it reminded Will of the leeches that inhabited the sludge at the bottom of the school fish tank. Denizens of the detritus.

It was an improbable scene, the flowery Clarke Junior

peddling his wares to the crowd, while this thing examined a pineapple, deep in the bowels of the Earth.

He was deliberating whether to go over to talk to Mr Clarke Junior when he noticed two policemen on the edge of the crowd, so he left it and went on his way, nagged by a question that knocked all other thoughts aside. *If the Clarkes know about the Colony, then how many others are there leading double lives in Highfield?*

⎯◦⎯

As the weeks passed, Will was assigned to further work details in other parts of the Colony. It gave him an insight into the workings of this subterranean society and he was determined to record as much as he could in his journal.

Every afternoon, after Will had swabbed the dirt and sweat off using the basic facilities in the so-called bathroom of the Jerome house, Cal would watch as he sat on his bed and jotted down meticulous notes, including the occasional sketch where he felt it was merited. Cal had asked what the point of it all was. Will had replied that it was something his father had taught him to do whenever they found anything during their excavations.

And there it was again, his father. Dr Burrows was still his father, as far as he was concerned, and Mr Jerome, even if he was his real father – and he still wasn't wholly convinced of that – came a poor second in Will's estimation. Yet he felt such affection for the rest of the family, Cal, Uncle Tam and Granny Macaulay, that sometimes his loyalties churned in his head with the ferocity of a stoppered tornado.

As he drew a sketch of a generic Colony house, adding annotations in comic book bubbles, he daydreamed about his father's journey into the Interior. Will was eager to discover what lay down there, and knew that one day soon he would follow. However, his thoughts kept reverting to Chester's plight, still confined in the Hold.

Will stopped writing and rubbed the peeling calluses on the palms of his hands together.

"Sore?" Cal asked.

"Not as bad as they were," Will replied. His mind flashed back to the work detail earlier that day, clearing stone channels in advance of draining a huge communal cesspit. He shuddered. It had been the worst task he'd been designated so far. Not for the first time, he reflected on his former life in Highfield, before his father had left. It seemed like a hundred years ago now, and the new one stretching out before him was threatening and uncertain. The more he thought about it, the more it felt like a life sentence, with hard labour thrown in for good measure. With aching arms, he resumed his notes until his concentration was broken by the urgent wailing of a siren, the hollow and eerie sound filling the entire house. Will stood up, trying to pinpoint where it was coming from.

"Black Wind!" Cal jumped off the bed and rushed over to close the window. Will joined him and saw people in the street below running hell for leather in all directions, until it was completely deserted. Cal pointed excitedly, then drew back his hand, looking at the hairs rising on his forearm from the rapid build-up of static in the air.

"Here it comes!" he tugged at his brother's sleeve. "I love this."

But nothing seemed to be happening. The siren's haunting wail continued as Will, not knowing what to look for, scanned the empty street for anything out of the ordinary.

"There! There!" Cal shouted, staring down the road into the cavern. Will followed his gaze, trying to make out just what it was, but it seemed as though something was wrong with his eyes. It was as if they weren't focusing properly.

Then he saw it.

A solid cloud billowed up the street like ink diffusing through water, rolling and churning and obscuring everything in its wake. As Will looked down from the window, he could see the street lights bravely trying to burn even more brightly as the sooty fog almost blotted them out. It was as if nocturnal waves were closing over the submerged lights of a doomed ocean liner.

"What is it?" Will asked, enthralled. He pressed his nose against the windowpane to get a better view of the dark fog spreading quickly along the rest of the street.

"It's a sort of backwash from the Interior," Cal replied. "It's called a Levant Wind. It rises from the lower deeps – a bit like a burp," he giggled.

"Is it dangerous?"

"No, just dust and stuff, but the superstitious think it's bad luck to breathe it. They say that it carries germules," he laughed and then adopted a mock Styx monotone. *"Pernicious to those that it encounters, it sears the flesh."* He giggled again. "It's great though, innit!"

Will stared, transfixed. As the street below was obliterated from view, the window turned black and he felt an uncomfortable pressure in his ears until he swallowed and they popped. His flesh seemed to be buzzing and all his hairs standing on end. For several minutes, the dark cloud billowed by, filling their bedroom with the smell of burnt ozone and a deadening silence. Eventually it began to thin out, the street lamps flickering through the swirling dust like the sun breaking through clouds, and then it was gone, leaving just a few diffuse grey smudges hanging in the air, as if the scene had been swept by a watercolourist's brush.

"Now watch this!"

"Sparklers?" Will asked, not believing what he was seeing.

"It's a static storm. They always follow a Levant," Cal said excitedly. "They give you one hell of a belt if you get in the way."

Will watched in astounded silence as small fireballs span out of the dispersing clouds at differing heights along the street. They varied in size: some like tennis balls, others as large as beach balls, all fizzing fiercely as bright sparks sprayed from their circumferences like delinquent Catherine wheels. Several sank into houses only to miraculously reappear on the other side, while others crisscrossed down the middle of the street in random paths.

The two boys were mesmerised as, right in front of them, a fireball as large as a melon, its vibrant light illuminating their young faces and reflecting in their wide eyes, abruptly went into a downward spiral, around and around, casting off sparks as it plummeted towards the ground, shrinking to the size of an egg.

As it hovered just above the cobblestones, the dying fireball seemed to flicker just a little more intensely before, in the blink of an eye, it had sputtered out.

Will and Cal were unable to tear themselves away from where it had been, the traces of its last seconds still imprinted on their retinas in little ecstatic tracts, like optical pins and needles.

CHAPTER TWENTY-SEVEN

Far below the streets and houses of the Colony, a lone figure stirred.

The wind had been a gentle breeze at first, but rapidly built to a ferocious gale that spat grit in his face with all the ferocity of a sandstorm. He'd been forced to wind his spare shirt around his face as it grew even more powerful, threatening to knock him off his feet. And the dust had been so dense and impenetrable that he hadn't been able to see his hands in front of him.

There was nothing else for it but to wait until it passed. He'd curled up in a tight ball, his eyes clogged and his throat and nostrils burning with fine black dust. There he had remained, the wailing howl blasting out his thoughts until, frail from hunger, he fell into a half-sleeping, half-waking torpor.

Sometime later, he shuddered awake and, not knowing how long he'd been curled up on the sandy floor of the tunnel, lifted his head for a tentative look around. The strange darkness of the wind had gone, save for a few greyish clouds. He sat up and shook the dust from his clothes, wiping his spectacles with a stained handkerchief.

Then, on all fours, Dr Burrows crawled about, scrabbling in the dry grit of the tunnel floor, using the light of a luminescent orb to search for the little pile of organic matter he'd gathered for kindling. He eventually found it and picked out something that resembled a curling fern leaf. He squinted at it curiously – he had no idea what it was. Like everything in the last five miles of tunnel, it was as dry and crisp as old parchment.

He was becoming increasingly worried about his supply of water. Just before he'd boarded the Miners' train, the Colonists had thoughtfully provided him with a full canteen, a satchel of dried vegetables of some type, some meat strips and a packet of salt. He could ration the food, but the problem was definitely the water; he hadn't been able to find a fresh source from which to replenish his canteen for two days now, and he was running perilously low.

Having rearranged the kindling, he began to knock two chunks of flint together until a spark leapt into it and a tiny flickering flame took hold. With his head resting on the grit floor, he gently blew on the flame and fanned it with his hand, nurturing it until the fire caught, bathing him with its glow. Then he squatted down next to his open journal, sweeping the layer of dust from the pages, and resumed his drawing.

What a find! A circle of regular stones, each the size of a door, with rounded corners. His mind raced as he dreamt of the people that had made it. That had lived far below the surface of the Earth, possibly for thousands of years, with the sophistication to build such a subterranean monument. He had begun to copy down a number of the strange symbols that were cut into the faces of the stones; carved letters collided with abstract forms – he didn't recognise any precedent for these characters from all his years of study. They were unlike any hieroglyphs he'd even seen before.

Thinking he heard a noise, he suddenly stopped drawing and sat upright. Controlling his breathing, he held completely still, his heart pounding in his chest, as he peered into the darkness beyond the fire's illumination. But there was nothing, just the all-pervading silence that had been his companion since the start of his journey.

"Getting jumpy, old man," he said, relaxing again. He was reassured by the sound of his own voice in the confines of the rock passage. "It's just your stomach again, you silly old baggage," he said, and laughed out loud.

He unwound the shirt from around his mouth and nose. His face was cut and bruised, his hair was matted and a straggly beard hung from his chin. His clothes were filthy and torn in places. He looked like a mad hermit. As the fire crackled, the smoke undisturbed by any draughts and rising vertically, he picked up his journal and concentrated on the circle of stones once again.

"This is truly exceptional – a miniature Stonehenge. What an incredible find!" he exclaimed, completely forgetting how hungry and thirsty he was. His face was animated and happy as he continued with his sketching.

Then he laid down his pencil and took the light orb in his hand. He held it to the side of his face like a microphone. He pursed his lips and dropped his voice a tone or two in an attempt to mimic a television interviewer.

"And tell me, Professor Burrows, newly appointed Dean of Subterranean Studies, what does the Nobel Prize mean to you?"

His voice reverted back to its normal tone and he moved the light orb to the other side of his face. He adopted a slightly surprised manner with pantomime hesitancy.

"Oh, I ... I must say ... it was a great honour and, at first, I felt that I was not worthy to follow in the footsteps of those great men and women ... that exalted list of winners who went before me."

He swung the orb back to the other side of his face. "But, Professor, the contributions you have made to so many fields – medicine, physics, chemistry, biology, geology and, above all, archaeology – are inestimable. You are considered to be one of the greatest living scholars on the planet. Did you ever think it would come to this the day you started on the tunnel in your cellar?"

Dr Burrows ahemed melodramatically as the orb changed sides again. "Well, I knew that there was more for me ... much more than my career in the museum back in ..."

Dr Burrows' voice tailed off and a faraway look came into his eyes. As he lowered the light and his face eclipsed into the shadows, he thought of his family and wondered how they were. He slowly shook his bedraggled head and stared into the flickering flames, which grew blurred. He took off his spectacles and rubbed the moisture from his eyes with the heels of his hands.

"I have to do this," he said to himself, as he replaced his spectacles and once again took up his pencil. "I have to."

The firelight radiated out from between the stones in the circle, projecting shifting spokes of light on the floor and walls of the passage. In the centre of this wheel, totally absorbed, the cross-legged figure quietly swore as he aggressively rubbed out a mistake in his journal.

He hadn't a thought for anyone in the world at that moment; a man so obsessed that nothing else mattered, nothing at all.

CHAPTER TWENTY-EIGHT

As a fire spluttered in the hearth, Mr Jerome reclined in one of the winged armchairs, reading his newspaper. From time to time, the heavily waxed pages flopped waywardly and he flicked his wrists reflexively to straighten them up again. Will couldn't make out a single headline from his vantage point at the table; the blocky newsprint bled into the paper to such an extent that it looked as though a swarm of ants had been dipped in black ink and then stampeded across the pages.

Cal dealt another card into the centre and waited expectantly for his brother's response, but Will was finding it impossible to keep his concentration on the game. It was the first time he'd been in the same room as Mr Jerome without being on the receiving end of hostile glances or a resentful silence. This in itself represented a landmark in their relations.

There was a sudden crash as the front door was flung open and all three looked up.

"Cal, Will!" Uncle Tam bellowed as he blundered in from the hallway, shattering the scene of apparent domestic bliss. He pulled himself up when he saw Mr Jerome glowering furiously at him from his chair.

"Oh, sorry, I ..."

"I though we had an understanding," Mr Jerome growled as he rose and folded the paper under his arm. "You said you wouldn't come here ... when I'm at home." He walked stiffly past Tam without so much as a glance.

Uncle Tam pulled a face and sat down next to Will. With a

conspiratorial wave of his hand, he indicated the boys should come closer.

"The time has arrived," he whispered to them, extracting a dented metal canister from inside his coat. He flipped off the cap from one end and they watched as he slid out a tattered map and laid it over their cards on the tabletop, smoothing out the corners so that it lay flat. Then Tam turned to Will.

"Chester is to be Banished tomorrow evening," he said.

"Oh God." Will sat up as if he'd had an electric shock. "That's short notice."

"I only just found out – it's planned for six," Tam said. "There'll be quite a crowd. The Styx like to make a spectacle out of these things. They believe a sacrifice is good for the soul."

He turned back to the map, humming softly, as he searched the complex grid of lines, until finally his finger came to rest on a tiny dark square. Then he looked up at Will as if he'd just remembered something.

"You know it's not a difficult thing … to get you out, alone. But Chester too, that's a very different kettle of fish. It's taken a lot more thought and," he paused and Will and Cal stared into his eyes, "I reckon I might have cracked it. There's only one way you can get Topsoil now ... and that's through the Eternal City." Will heard Cal gasp but, much as he wanted to ask his uncle about this place, it didn't seem appropriate as Tam went on.

He proceeded to talk Will through the escape plan, tracing the route on the map as the boys listened raptly, absorbing every detail. The tunnels had names like Watling Street, the Great North and Bishopswood. Will only interrupted his uncle once as he was talking with a suggestion that, after some considerable thought, Tam incorporated into the plan. Although his exterior was composed and businesslike, Will felt a knot of excitement and fear building in the pit of his stomach.

"The problem with this," Tam sighed, "is the unknowns, the variables, that I can't help you with. When you're on the ground, you'll just have to play it by ear the best you can." At this point, Will noticed that some of the sparkle had gone out of Tam's eyes – he didn't look his normal confident self.

Tam ran through the whole plan from beginning to end once again and, when he'd finished, he held something out for Will.

"Here's a copy of the directions once you're outside the Colony. If they catch up with you, heaven forbid, eat the damn thing."

Will unfolded it carefully. It was on cloth and the size of a handkerchief when completely opened. The surface was covered in a mass of infinitesimally small lines in brown ink, each representing a different tunnel like an unruly maze, and Will's route was clearly marked in a light red ink.

Tam watched as Will refolded it, and then spoke in a low voice. "This has to go without a hitch. You'd put *all* your kin in the very worst danger if the Styx think I've had a hand in this … and it wouldn't just end with me; Cal, your grandmother and father would all be in the firing line." He grasped Will's forearm tightly across the table and squeezed it to emphasise the gravity of his warning. "Another thing, when you're Topsoil, you and Chester are going to have to disappear. I haven't had time to arrange anything so, I'm sorry, it's up to you. But mark my words, if the Styx get you alive, they *will* make you tell everything, sooner or later," he said ominously.

"Then we'd have to get out too, wouldn't we, Uncle Tam?" Cal volunteered, his voice full of bravado.

Tam turned sharply on him. "We wouldn't have a hope. They'd be on us in a flash; we wouldn't even see it coming."

"But …" began Cal.

"Look, this isn't some game, Caleb. If you cross them once too often, you won't live long enough to regret it. Before you know it, you'll be dancing Old Nick's Jig." He paused. "You know what that is?" Tam didn't wait for an answer. "It's a choice little number. Your arms are stitched behind your back …" he shifted uncomfortably in his seat, " … with copper thread, your eyelids are stripped off and you're dropped in the darkest chamber you can imagine, full of Red Hots."

"Red whats?" Will asked.

Tam shuddered and, ignoring Will's question, went on. "How

long do you think you'd last? How many days of knocking into the walls in the pitch black, dust burning into your ruined eyes, before you collapsed from exhaustion? Feeling the first bites on your skin as they start to feed? I wouldn't wish that on my worst ..." he didn't finish the sentence.

The two boys both swallowed hard. Tam's expression brightened up again. "But enough of that," he said. "You've still got that light, haven't you?"

Will looked at him blankly, stunned by what he'd just heard, and then nodded.

"Good," Tam said as he took out a small cloth bundle from his coat pocket and put it on the table in front of Will. "These might come in handy."

Will touched the bundle tentatively.

"Well, go on, open it, boy."

Will untied the corners. Inside, there were four knobbly brown-black stones the size of marbles.

"Node stones!" Cal said.

"Yes. They're rarer than slugs' boots," Tam smiled. "They're described in the old books, but nobody 'cept me and my boys has ever seen one before. Imago found this lot."

"What do they do?" Will asked, looking at the strange stones.

"Down here, it's not like you're going to beat a Colonist or, worse still, a Styx in a straight fight. The only weapon you have is *light* and *flight*," Tam said. "If you get in a tight corner, just crack one of these things open. Chuck it against something hard and keep your eyes shut – it'll give a burst of the brightest light you can imagine. I hope these are still good," he said, weighing one in his hand. He looked up. "Okay, Will?"

"Thanks, Uncle Tam. I can't tell you how ..." Will said falteringly.

"No need, my boy," Tam ruffled his hair. "My head knows you have to go, but my heart says otherwise – we could have had some times down here, the three of us. Some times indeed."

That night, Will hardly slept a wink. Early in the morning, before there was a stir in the house, he packed his rucksack and tucked the cloth map Uncle Tam had given him into the top of his boot. He checked that the node stones and light orb were in his pockets and went over to Cal and shook him awake.

"I'm off," Will said in a low voice as his brother's eyes flickered open. Cal sat up, scratching his head.

"Thanks for everything, Cal," Will whispered, "and say goodbye to Granny from me, won't you?"

"Course I will," his brother replied, then frowned. "You know I'd give anything to come too."

"I know, I know ... but you heard what Tam said, I have more chance by myself. Anyway, your family are here. I must be going now," he said finally, and turned to the door.

Will tiptoed down the stairs and through the hallway, where he could hear Bartleby snoring somewhere in the shadows. He slipped the heavy catch on the front door and closed it gently behind him as he left.

He knew he had a considerable distance to cover, so he picked up his pace, his rucksack thumping a rhythm on his back. It took him a touch under 40 minutes to reach the building at the edge of the cavern that Tam had described. There was no mistaking it as, unlike most structures in the Colony, it had a tiled rather than a stone roof. He was now on the road that led to the Skull Gate. Tam had said that he had to keep his wits about him as the Styx changed sentries at random intervals, and there was no way of knowing whether one was just about to appear around the corner.

Leaving the road, Will climbed over a gate and sprinted through the yard that lay in front of the building, a ramshackle farm property. He heard a pig-like grunting coming from one of the outlying buildings and spotted some chickens penned up in another area. They were spindly and malnourished, but had perfectly white feathers.

He entered the building with the tiled roof and saw the old timber beams that Tam had told him would be there, leant against the wall. As he crept in under them, something moved towards him.

"What …"

Tam immediately silenced him by putting his finger to his lips. Will could hardly contain his surprise. He looked at Tam questioningly, but the man's face was grim and unsmiling.

There was hardly enough room for both of them under the beams, and Tam squatted awkwardly as he slid a massive paving slab along the wall. Then he leant in to Will.

"Good luck," he whispered in his ear and literally pushed him into the jagged opening. Then the slab grated shut behind Will and he was on his own.

In the pitch dark, he fumbled in his pocket for the light orb, to which he'd attached a loop of string as a makeshift lanyard. He slipped this around his neck, so leaving his hands free. At first, he moved along the passage with ease, but then, after 10 yards or so, it pinched down to a crawlway. The roof of the tunnel was so low that he ended up on his hands and knees. The passage angled upwards and, as he heaved himself painfully over jagged plates of broken rock, his rucksack kept snagging on the roof.

He caught a movement in front of him, and froze on the spot. With some trepidation, he raised the light orb to see what it was. He held his breath as something white flashed across the passage and then landed with a soft thump no more than five feet ahead of him. It was an eyeless rat, the size of a well-fed kitten, with snowy fur and whiskers that oscillated like butterfly wings. It stood up on its back legs, its muzzle twitching and its large, glistening incisors in full view. It showed absolutely no sign that it was afraid of him.

Will found a stone by him on the tunnel floor and threw it as hard as he could. It missed, glancing off the wall next to the animal, which didn't even flinch. Will's indignation welled over that a mere rat was holding him up and he lunged towards the animal with a growl. In a single effortless bound, it sprang at him, landing smartly on his shoulder and, for a split second, neither boy nor rat moved. Will felt its whiskers, as delicate as eyelashes, brush his cheek. He shook his shoulders frantically and it launched itself off, bounding once on Will's legs as it sped away in the opposite direction.

"Little b …" Will muttered, as he tried to compose himself before setting off again.

He crawled for what seemed like hours, his hands becoming cut and tender from the razor-sharp shards strewn across the floor. Then, much to his relief, the passage widened out and he was able to stand up again, albeit slightly crouched. Now able to move at speed, he became almost euphoric and felt an irrepressible urge to sing as he negotiated the bends in the tunnel. He thought better of it when it occurred to him that the sentries at the Skull Gate, which he was now circumnavigating, might somehow be able to hear him.

He eventually reached the end of the passage which was cloaked with several layers of stiff sacking, dirtied up to camouflage them against the stone. He brushed them aside and drew his breath as he saw he was just under the cavern roof, and that there was at least a 100 foot drop to the road below. He was pleased that he'd got this far, past the Skull Gate, but he felt certain that this couldn't be right. He was at such a dizzying height that he immediately assumed he must be in the wrong place. Then Tam's words came back to him.

"It'll look impossible, but take it slowly. Cal has done it before and so can you."

He leant out and scanned the array of ledges and nooks in the rock wall below him. Then he cautiously clambered out over the edge of the tunnel lip and began the descent, checking and rechecking each shaking hand and foothold before he made the next move.

He'd climbed no more than 20 feet when he heard a noise below. A desolate groan. He held still and listened, his heart thudding in his ears. It came again. He had one foot on a small ridge with the other dangling in mid air, while his hands gripped an outcrop at chest height. He slowly twisted his head and peered over his shoulder.

Swinging a lantern, completely unaware of Will's presence, a man was strolling in the direction of the Skull Gate with two emaciated cows, which he drove a couple of paces in front of him. Hanging on for dear life, Will was totally exposed on the rockface, but there was nothing he could do, so he just held absolutely still, praying that the man wouldn't stop and look up. Then just the thing Will was dreading happened; the man came to an abrupt halt.

"Oh no, this is it!" raced through his mind.

He could clearly make out the man's shiny white scalp as he took something out of a shoulder bag. It was a clay pipe with a long stem, which he loaded with tobacco from a pouch and lit, puffing out little clouds of smoke. Will heard him say something to the cows and then the man started on his way again.

Will breathed a silent sigh of relief and, checking that the coast was clear, quickly finished the descent, crisscrossing from ledge to ledge until he was safely back on the ground. Then he dashed as fast as he could along the road, either side of which were fields of impossibly proportioned mushrooms, their bulbous ovoid caps standing on thick stalks. He now recognised these as Pennybuns and, as he went, the motion of the light bobbing in his hand threw a multitude of shifting shadows onto the cavern walls behind them.

Will slowed his pace as he developed a painful stitch in his side. He took a series of deep breaths to try to ease it, then forced himself to speed up again, aware that every second counted if he was going to be successful.

Leaving cavern after cavern behind him, the fields of Pennybuns eventually gave way to black carpets of lichen and he was relieved when he spotted the first of the lamp posts and the hazy outline of a building in the distance. He was getting closer. Suddenly he found himself at a huge stone archway hewn in the rock and went through it into the main cavern of the Quarter. Soon the dwellings were crowding the sides of the road and he was becoming more and more nervous. Although nobody seemed to be around, he kept the sound from his boots to a minimum by running on his toes. He was terrified that someone was going to appear from one of the houses and spot him. Then he saw what he'd been looking for. It was the first of the side tunnels that Tam had mentioned, and he lost no time in entering it.

"You're going to take the backstreets." He remembered his uncle's words. *"It's safer there."*

"Left, left, right," Will repeated the sequence Tam had drummed into him as he went.

The tunnels were just wide enough for a coach. *"Pass quickly through these. If you bump into anyone, just brass it out, like you're supposed to be there."*

But there was no sign of anyone as Will ran with all his might, his rucksack crashing on his back. By the time he re-emerged back into the main cavern, he was sweating and out of breath. He recognised the squat outline of the police station between the two taller structures on either side, and slowed to a walk to give himself a chance to cool off.

"Made it this far," he muttered to himself. The plan had seemed so easy when Tam described it, but now he was wondering if he'd made a dreadful mistake. *"You haven't got time to think,"* Tam had said as he'd pointed a finger at him. *"If you hesitate, the momentum will be lost – the whole thing will go cockeyed."* Will wiped the sweat from his forehead and steeled himself for the next stage.

As he got nearer to it, the sight of the police station's entrance brought back memories of the first time he and Chester were dragged up the steps, and the gruelling interrogations that followed. All this came flooding back. He tried to blank it out as he slipped into the shadows by the side of the building and heaved his rucksack off. He dug his camera out, checking it quickly before he put it into his pocket. Then he hid his rucksack and headed for the steps. As he climbed them, he took a deep breath and pushed through the doors.

The Second Officer was reclining in a chair with his feet resting on the counter. He looked up at Will, completely taken aback.

"Well, well, well, Jerome. What in earth are *you* doing back here?" he asked suspiciously.

"I've come to see my friend," Will replied, praying that his voice didn't crack. He felt as if he were edging out on the limb of a tree, and the further he went, the thinner and more precarious the branch became. If he lost his balance now, the fall could be fatal.

"Now who would've let you do that?" the officer said sceptically.

"Who'd you think?" Will tried to smile calmly.

The officer thought for a moment, looking him up and down. "Well, I suppose ... if they let you through the Skull Gate, it must be all right," he reasoned aloud as he lumbered slowly to his feet.

"They said I could see him," Will said, "one last time."

"So you know it is to be tonight?" the officer said with a flicker of a smile. Will nodded and saw that this had dispelled any doubts in the man's mind. At once the officer's demeanour was transformed.

"Didn't walk all the way, did you?" he asked. A friendly, generous smile creased his face like a gash in a pig's belly – Will hadn't seen this side of him before. It made it all the more difficult for him to do what he had to.

"Yes, I had an early start."

"Better come with me, then," the officer said as he lifted up the flap at the end of the counter and came through, rattling his keys. "I hear you're fitting in well," he added. "Thought you would the moment I first saw you. You look the part. Deep down he's one of us, I said to myself."

They went through the old oak door into the gloom of the Hold. The familiar smell gave Will the creeps as the officer swung back the cell door and ushered him in. It took a moment for his eyes to adjust and then he saw him: Chester was sitting in the corner on the ledge, his legs drawn up under his chin. His friend didn't react immediately, but stared emptily at Will. Then, with a flash of recognition and sheer disbelief, he was on his feet.

"Will?" he said, as his jaw dropped. "Will! I can't believe it!"

"Hi Chester," Will said, trying to keep the excitement from

his voice. He was elated to see him again but at the same time, his whole body was shaking with adrenaline.

"Have you come to get me out, Will?"

"Er … not quite," Will half turned, aware that the officer was just behind him and could hear every word.

The officer coughed self-consciously. "I'll have to lock you in, Jerome, hope you understand. It's regulations," he said as he shut the door and turned his key.

"What is it, Will?" Chester asked, sensing that something was wrong. "Is it bad news?" He took a step away from Will.

"You all right?" Will replied, too preoccupied to answer his friend as he listened to the officer leave the aisle. Then he took Chester into the corner of the cell and, in a huddle, explained what they had to do.

Minutes later, the sound came that Will was dreading. The officer was walking back down the aisle towards them.

"Time, gentlemen," he said.

He turned the key and opened the door, and Will made his way out slowly.

"Bye, Chester," he said.

As the officer began to close the door, Will put his hand on the man's arm.

"Just a second, I think I've left something in there," he said.

"What's that?" the officer asked.

The officer was looking directly at him as Will brought his hand out of his pocket. Will saw the little red light was on and that the camera was ready. He shoved it into the man's face and clicked the shutter.

The flash caught the policeman full in the face. He howled and dropped his keys, slapping his hands over his eyes as he sank to the floor. The flash had been so bright compared with the sublime glow of the light orbs that even Will and Chester, who had both shielded themselves from it, felt the aftershock of its brilliance.

"Sorry," Will said to the groaning man.

Chester was standing motionless in the cell, a stupefied look on his face.

"Get a move on, Chester!" Will shouted as he leant in and yanked him past the officer, who was starting to grope his way towards the wall, still moaning horribly.

As they entered the reception area, Will happened to glance over the counter.

"My spade!" he said as he bounded through the open flap.

He grabbed it from against the wall and was on his way back when he saw the Second Officer stagger out from the Hold. The man snatched blindly at Chester and, before the boy knew what was happening, got hold of him around the neck.

Chester let out a strangled "Help!" and tried to wrestle free.

Will didn't stop to think. He swung the spade. With a bone-crunching clang, it connected with the officer's forehead and he crumpled to the floor with a whimper.

Chester wasn't so slow off the mark this time. He was right behind Will as they bolted out of the station, slowing just long enough for Will to retrieve the rucksack before they turned down the stretch of road that Chester had spent so many hours watching from his cell. Then they veered off down a side tunnel.

"Are you sure this is the right way?" Chester said, breathing heavily and coughing.

Will didn't answer, but kept on running until they reached the end of the tunnel.

There they were, the three partially demolished houses, just as Tam had described them, at the perimeter of a circular cavern as large as an amphitheatre. It was springy underfoot as they tramped over the rich, loamy surface, and the air reeked of old manure. The walls of the cavern caught Will's attention. What at first he'd taken to be clusters of stalactites were, in fact, petrified tree trunks, some broken off halfway and others twisted around each other. These fossilised remains stood like a carved stone forest in the shadows.

As they neared the middle building, Will felt an increasing unease, as if something unwholesome and threatening was radiating from between the ancient tree trunks. He was relieved when they reached the old house, the middle of the three, and pushed through the front door, which opened crookedly on a single hinge.

"Through the hall, straight ahead into the kitchen."

Chester shouldered the door shut behind them as Will entered the kitchen. It was roomier than the one in the Jerome house. As they crossed the tiled floor, they stirred a thick carpet of dust into life. It rose up into a miniature storm and, caught in the light of the orb, every move they made left a visual echo in the airborne motes, like a slow motion film.

"Locate the wall tile with the painted cross."

Will found it and pushed against it. A small hatch, it clicked open under his hand. Inside there was a handle, which he twisted and a whole section of the tiled wall opened outwards – it was a cleverly disguised door. Behind was an antechamber with boxes stacked on either side and a further door set into its far wall. But this was no ordinary door – it was made of heavy iron studded with rivets, and there was a handle by its side to crank it open.

"It's airtight – keeps the germules out."

There was an inspection port at head height, but no light was visible through the clouded glass.

"Get going on that while I find the breathing apparatus," Will ordered Chester, pointing at the crank handle. His friend leant on the handle and there was a loud hiss as the thick rubber flange at the base lifted off the ground. Will found the masks Tam said would be left there, old canvas hoods with black rubber pipes attached to cylinders. They resembled some sort of ancient diving equipment.

Will heard a plaintive mew. He knew who it was even before he'd turned around.

"Bartleby!"

The cat scampered in from the hallway and immediately made a beeline for the opening under the door, sniffing it inquisitively.

"What is *that?*" Chester was so flabbergasted by the vision of the oversize cat that he let go of the crank handle. It spun freely as the door trundled down on its runners and slammed shut.

"For Christ's sake, Chester, just get that door open!" Will shouted.

"Can I help?" Cal asked, moving into view.

"What the hell are you doing here?" Will snapped.

"Coming with you," Cal replied, taken aback by his brother's reaction.

Chester stopped turning the crank, and glanced rapidly from one brother to the other and back again. "He looks just like you!"

Will had reached the point at which the whole situation had taken on an insanity all of its own, a random and hopeless insanity. "Get that damned door open, will you!" he bawled at the top of his voice and Chester meekly resumed the cranking. The door was now a foot off the ground and Bartleby stuck his head under it for an exploratory look, then disappeared completely.

"Tam doesn't know you're here, does he?" Will grabbed his brother by his coat collar.

"Of course not. I decided it was time to go Topsoil, like you and Mother."

"You're not coming," Will snarled through gritted teeth and then, as he saw the hurt in his brother's face, let go of his coat and softened his voice. "Really you're not ... you can't ... Uncle Tam would kill you for being here. Go home right ..." Will never finished the sentence. Both he and Cal smelt the strong pulses of ammonia rippling through the air.

"The alarm!" Cal said with panic-stricken eyes.

They heard a commotion outside, some shouting and then the tinkle of breaking glass. They ran to the kitchen window and peered through the cracked panes.

"Styx!" Cal gasped.

Will estimated there were at least thirty of them drawn up in a semi-circle in front of the house, and those were just the ones he could see from his limited vantage point. How many there were in total, he shuddered to think. He ducked down immediately and shot a glance at Chester who was frantically cranking the door, the opening now high enough for them to get through.

Will looked at his brother and knew there was only one thing for it. He couldn't leave him at the mercy of the Styx.

"Go on! Get under the door," he whispered urgently to him.

Cal's face lit up and he started to thank Will, who shoved the breathing apparatus into his hands and literally propelled him towards the door, which he slithered under.

Will turned back to the window just in time to see the Styx advancing on the house. That was enough for him – he launched himself at the door, frantically shouting at Chester to grab a mask and follow him under. As he heard the front door to the house smash open, he knew they both had enough time to get away. Just enough.

Then one of those terrible things happened.

One of those events that, afterwards, you replay in your mind over and over again … but you know, deep down, there was nothing you could have done.

That's when they heard it.

A voice they both knew.

CHAPTER TWENTY-NINE

"Same old Will," she said, the voice rooting them to the spot.

Will was halfway under the door, his hand gripping Chester's forearm ready to pull him in, when he glanced at the kitchen doorway, and froze.

A young girl walked fully into the room, two Styx flanking her.

"Rebecca?" Will gasped, and shook his head as if his eyes were deceiving him.

"Rebecca!" he said again, incredulously.

"Where are we going, then?" she said coolly. The two Styx edged forward a fraction, but she held her hand up and they stopped.

Was this some trick? She was wearing their clothes, their uniform – the black coat with the stark white shirt. Her jet black hair was different – it was raked back tightly over her head.

"What are you ..." Will managed to say before the words failed him.

She'd been captured. That must be it. Brainwashed, or held hostage.

"Why do we keep doing these things?" she said, raising one eyebrow. She looked relaxed and in control. Something wasn't right here, something jarred.

No.

She was one of them.

"You're ..." he gasped.

Rebecca laughed, "Quick, isn't he?"

Behind her, more Styx were entering the kitchen. Will's mind reeled and he fell into a vortex where his memories played back at breakneck speed as he tried to reconcile Rebecca, his sister, with this Styx girl before him. Were there signs, any clues he'd missed?

Revelling in his confusion, Rebecca spoke. "It's really very simple. I was placed in your family when I was two. It's the way with us, the training for the elite."

She took a step forward.

"Don't!" Will said, his mind starting to work again and his hand reaching inside his coat. "I don't buy it!"

"Hard to accept, isn't it? I was put there to keep an eye on you and, maybe, if we were lucky, trace your mother; your *real* mother."

"It's not true."

"It doesn't matter what you believe," she replied curtly. "My job was done there, so here I am, back home again. No more play-acting."

"No!" Will stuttered as he closed his hand around the little cloth package in his pocket that Tam had given him.

"Come on, it's over," Rebecca said impatiently. With a barely perceptible nod of her head, the Styx on either side of her lurched forward, but Will was ready. He slung the node stone across the kitchen with all his might. It soared between the two advancing Styx and struck the dirty white tiles, breaking into a tiny snowstorm of fragments.

Everything stopped.

For a split second, Will thought nothing was going happen, that it wasn't going to work. He heard Rebecca laugh, a dry, derisory laugh.

Then there was a whooshing sound, as if air was being sucked from the room. Each tiny splinter, as it sprinkled to the ground, flared with a dazzling incandescence, loosing off beams that blasted the room like a million searchlights. These were so intense that everything was shot through with an unbearable, searing whiteness.

It didn't seem to bother Rebecca in the slightest. With the light ablaze about her, she stood out like some dark angel, her arms folded in her characteristic pose as she clucked with disapproval.

But the two advancing Styx were stopped in their tracks and let out screams like fingernails dragged down a blackboard. They staggered back blindly, trying to shield their eyes. This gave Will the opportunity he was looking for. He pulled Chester, yanking him away from the crank handle.

Already the light was dwindling and fading, and another two Styx were pushing aside their blinded comrades. They lunged at Will, their claw-like fingers raking out towards him. As he continued to pull on one of Chester's arms, the Styx both latched onto the other. It turned into a tug of war between Will and the Styx, with the terrified, whimpering boy caught in between. Worse still, as nobody was bracing the crank handle, it was whirring wildly around as the massive door sunk slowly down on its runners. And Chester was right in its path.

"Push them off!" Will cried.

Chester was trying to kick out, but it was no use; they had too strong a hold of him. Will wedged himself against the door in a vain attempt to slow its progress. It was just too heavy and nearly unbalanced him. There was no way he could do anything about it and save Chester at the same time.

As the Styx grunted and strained, and he and Chester tried with all their might to resist, he knew the Styx couldn't be beaten. Chester was slipping out of his hands and screaming in pain as the Styx's fingernails bit deep into the flesh of his arm. Then the realisation hit Will, as the door continued its relentless descent – Chester was going to be crushed under it unless he let go.

Unless he released Chester to the Styx.

The crank handle was spinning madly. The door was now only three feet off the ground, and its entire weight was pressing down on Chester's back and threatening to pin him to the floor. "Chester, I'm sorry!" Will screamed. For a split second, Chester stared with horror into his friend's eyes and then Will let go of his arm and he flew straight back into the Styx – the momentum bowling them over onto the kitchen floor in a tumbling confusion of arms and legs. Chester shouted Will's name once as the door clanged down with a terrible finality. Will could only watch numbly through the milky glass of the porthole as Chester and the Styx came to rest in a heap against the wall. One of the Styx immediately picked himself up and raced back towards the crank handle.

"JAM THE CRANK!" Cal's shout galvanised Will. As Cal held a light orb, Will set to the mechanism by the side of the door. He whipped out his penknife, levered the blade out and wedged it between the teeth of two of the largest gear wheels, praying it would do the trick. And it did, the little red penknife quivering as the Styx applied pressure to the handle on the other side.

Will glanced through the porthole again. Like some macabre silent film, he couldn't help but watch the desperation on Chester's face as he valiantly battled with the Styx. He'd somehow managed to get hold of Will's spade and was trying to beat them off with it. But he was overpowered by their sheer numbers as they swarmed over him with the insect intent of devouring locusts.

But then a face blocked everything out as it loomed in the porthole.

Rebecca's face. She pursed her lips sternly and shook her head at Will, as if she was telling him off. Just like she'd done for all those years in Highfield. She was saying something, but it was inaudible through the door.

"We have to go, Will. They'll get it open," Cal said urgently. Will tore his eyes away from the Styx child that was still mouthing something at him. And with a sudden, chilling realisation, he knew just what it was. *Exactly* what it was. She was singing to him.

"*Sunshine …*" he said bitterly, "*You are my sunshine!*"

They fled down the rock passage with Bartleby in tow, and eventually came to a dome-shaped atrium with numerous passages leading off it. Everything was rounded and smoothed, as if aeons of flowing water had rubbed away any sharp edges. It was dry now and every surface was coated in an abrasive silt like powdered glass.

"We've only got one mask," Will said suddenly to Cal, as the realisation hit him. He looked at the canvas and rubber contraption in his brother's hand.

"Oh no!" Cal's face dropped. "What do we do? We can't go back."

"The air in the Eternal City," Will asked, "is it breathable at all?"

"Uncle Tam says there's a plague there. It killed off all the people … and it's still there."

"Then you take it," Will pulled the mask over Cal's head, muffling his protestations. "I'm the oldest, so I choose."

Cal's eyes peeked anxiously through the glass strip as Will made sure the hood was seated correctly on his shoulders. He buckled up the leather strap to secure the pipes and stubby filter around his brother's chest.

Then Will slipped the map from inside his boot, counted the tunnels in front of them, and pointed to the one they were to take.

"How did the Styx child know you?" Cal's voice was indistinct through the hood.

"My sister." Will lowered the map and looked at his brother. "That was my dear sister …" Will spat with contempt, " … or so I thought."

"The door won't hold them for long," Cal said, looking nervously down the tunnel over Will's shoulder.

"No. We should go."

"You couldn't have done anything to help him, you know. We were lucky to get out of there alive."

"Maybe," Will said as he re-checked the map. He didn't want to think about Chester, not right now.

And so the two boys, with the cat trailing behind, broke into a steady trot, penetrating deeper into the complex of underground tunnels that would eventually lead them to the Eternal City and then, they hoped, out into the sunlight again.

PART THREE
THE ETERNAL CITY

CHAPTER THIRTY

*O*ne two, one two, one, one, one two.

As they jogged along, Will had settled into the easy rhythm he used for the more gruelling bouts of digging back in Highfield.

The tunnels were dry and silent; there wasn't a single sign that anything lived down here. And, as their feet tramped over the sandy floors, not once did Will catch sight of any airborne dust or motes behind them in the beam of his light orb. It was as if their passing through had gone completely unnoticed.

But it wasn't long before he began to notice the faintest scintillations before his eyes, smears of light that materialised and then, just as abruptly, vanished from his vision. He watched, fascinated, until it dawned on him that something was not quite right, that it was *him*. At the same time a dull ache gripped his chest and a clammy sweat broke out on his temples.

One two, one two, one … one … one two …

He slowed his pace, feeling the resistance as he drew breath. It was peculiar; he couldn't quite put his finger on what was wrong. At first he thought it was simply exhaustion, but no, it was more than that. It was as if the air, having lain undisturbed in these deep tunnels for aeons, was behaving like a sluggish and reluctant fluid.

One two, one …

Will abandoned his mental cadence and came to an abrupt halt, loosening his collar and rubbing his shoulders under the straps of his rucksack. He had a nearly irresistible urge to throw the weight off his back – it made him feel constricted and uneasy. And the walls of the passage bothered him – they were too close, they were smothering him. He backed away into the middle of the tunnel, where he leant on his knees and took in several gulps of air. After a while, he felt a little better and forced himself to straighten up.

"What's wrong?" Cal asked, eyeing him anxiously through the glass slits of his mask.

"Nothing," Will replied as he fumbled in his pocket for the map. He was determined not to show any weakness to his brother. "I ... I just need to check our position."

He'd taken it upon himself to navigate their route through the many twists and turns, aware that a single mistake would lose them in this subterranean maze of mind-numbing complexity. He remembered how Tam had referred to it as the "Labyrynth" and likened it to pumice with innumerable inter-locking pores worming randomly through it. At the time, Will hadn't thought much about his uncle's words, but he now knew precisely what he'd meant.

The sheer scale of the area was daunting, like an immense network of tributaries in a river delta. Although they had been making good time as they moved rapidly through passages the width of Tube tunnels, Will reckoned they had a long way to go yet. They were helped considerably by the gentle downward gradient, but this in itself caused him some consternation. He knew every foot they descended would have to be climbed again before they reached the surface, and in the very near future.

He glanced from the map to the walls. They had a pinkish hue to them, probably due to the presence of iron deposits, which explained why his compass was useless down here. The needle dithered lazily around the dial, never settling in the same position long enough to give any sort of reading.

As Will looked around him, he reflected that the passages

could have been formed by gas trapped under a solidified plug above it, as it tried to escape through the still molten volcanic rock. Yes, that would be the reason there weren't any vertical tunnels. Or possibly by water exploiting lines of weakness in the centuries after the rock cooled. *I wonder what Dad would make of this*, he thought before he could stop himself, his face falling as he realised that he'd probably never see him again. Not now.

He had one last glance at the map, and refolded it before they resumed their journey.

One two, one two, one, one, one two.

As their feet crunched in the fine red sand, Will longed for a change, a landmark, *anything* to break the monotony, to confirm that they were still on the right track. He began to despair that they were ever going to reach the end. For all he knew, they could be going round in circles.

He was thrilled when they eventually came across what looked like a small headstone against the passage wall with a flat face and a rounded top. With Cal looking on, he crouched down to brush the sand from its surface.

A sweep of his hand revealed a symbol carved into the pink rock about halfway down the face. It was comprised of three diverging lines, which fanned out like rising rays or the prongs of a trident. Below were two rows of angular lettering. The symbols were unfamiliar and made no sense to him at all.

"What's this, some kind of marker? A milestone?" Will looked up at his brother, who shrugged his shoulders unhelpfully.

Several hours later, the going had become slow and laborious, as the branches and connecting tunnels came with greater regularity and Will was forced to consult the map more often. They'd already lost time when he had inadvertently led them down a wrong turn. Luckily they hadn't gone too far before he realised his mistake and they had painstakingly retraced their steps and found their way back onto the correct path. Once there, they had flopped down onto the sandy floor, stopping just long enough to catch their breaths. Although he was trying to fight it, Will felt unusually tired, as if he were running on empty. And when they resumed their journey again, he felt weaker than ever, the brief respite having done nothing to alleviate his fatigue.

Whatever state he was in, he knew they must keep going; they must keep ahead of the Styx, they had to get out. Will couldn't let Cal suspect anything was wrong. He turned to his brother beside him.

"So what does Tam do in this Eternal City?" he said, breathing heavily. "He was a bit cagey when I asked him about it."

"He searches for coins and stuff like that, gold and silver," Cal said through his mask, then added, "most of it from graves."

"Graves?"

"In the burial grounds," Cal nodded.

"So people really lived there?"

"A long time ago. He reckons that several races occupied it, one after the other, each building on top of the last. He says there are fortunes just waiting to be found."

"But who were the people?"

"Tam told me the Bruteans were the first. I think he said they were Trojans. They built the city as a stronghold or something, while the Topsoil London was built above."

"So the two cities were connected?"

Cal's mask nodded ponderously. "In the beginning. Later the entrances were blocked up and the stones marking them were lost ... the Eternal City was just *forgotten*," he said, puffing noisily through the air filter. He looked nervously back up the tunnel, as if he'd heard something.

Will immediately followed his glance, but all he could see was the shadowy form of Bartleby as he paced out spirals in his loose-limbed gait. Clearly impatient to go faster than the two boys, from time to time he would dash ahead and then stop to sniff at a crevice, sometimes becoming visibly agitated and letting out a low whine.

"At least the Styx will never find us in this place," Will said confidently.

"Don't count on it, they'll be following," Cal said. "And then there's still the Division in front of us."

"The *what*?"

"The Styx Division. They're sort of a … well … border guard," Cal said, searching for the right words. "They patrol the old city."

"What for?"

"There's talk that they're rebuilding whole areas of the city and patching up the cavern walls. It's said the whole Colony might be moved, and there's rumours of work parties of condemned prisoners, working like slaves. No one knows for sure."

"Well, Tam never mentioned anything about more Styx." Will didn't attempt to hide the alarm in his voice. "Bloody hell," he spat angrily, kicking a rock in his path.

"We didn't exactly leave the Colony quietly, did we? Don't get too worried; it's a huge area to cover and there'll only be a handful of patrols."

"Oh great! That's a real comfort!" Will replied, as he imagined what might be waiting for them ahead.

They wandered on for several hours, eventually scrabbling down a steep incline in the passage, their feet slipping and sliding in the red sand until they finally reached a level area. Will knew, if he'd been reading the map correctly, they should be approaching the end of the Labyrynth. The tunnel narrowed, and appeared to culminate in a blind alley. In a panic, Will raced ahead, stooping as the roof lowered. To his relief, he found that there was a small passage to one side.

He waited until Cal caught up, and they looked apprehensively at each other as Bartleby sniffed the air. Will was hesitant, looking repeatedly from Tam's map to the opening and then back again. Then he met Cal's eyes through the glass of his hood and smiled broadly as he edged into the narrow passageway. It was bathed in a subdued green light.

"Careful," Cal warned.

But Will was already at the corner. He became aware of a familiar sound: the patter of falling water.

He moved his head until just one eye was peering around the edge. He was struck dumb by what he glimpsed, and moved slowly into the open, into the bottlegreen glow, to get a better view. From Tam's description, and the pictures his imagination had conjured up, he was expecting something out of the ordinary. But nothing could have prepared him for the sight that met his eyes.

"The Eternal City," he whispered to himself, as he began down a huge escarpment. As he looked up, his wide eyes scrutinising the immense domed space, water splashed on his upturned face and made him grimace.

"Underground rain?" he muttered, immediately realising how ridiculous that sounded. He blinked as it dripped into his eyes, stinging them.

"It's seepage from above," Cal said behind him.

But Will wasn't listening. He was finding it hard to come to terms with the titanic volume of the cavern, so massive that its farthest reaches were hidden by fog and the mists of distance. The drizzle continued from above in a slow, languorous rainfall as he contoured down the escarpment.

It was almost too much to take in. Basaltic columns, like windowless inverted skyscrapers, arced down from the mammoth span of the roof into the centre of the city. Others speared upwards from the outlying ground in mind-bending curves, encasing the city with gigantic drunken buttresses. It dwarfed any of the Colony's caverns with its scale, and brought to Will's mind the image of a gargantuan heart, its chambers crisscrossed by huge, heartstring-like columns.

He pocketed the light orb and instinctively sought the source of the illumination, a suffused emerald green that gave the scene a dreamlike quality. It was as though he were looking at a lost city in the depths of an ocean. He couldn't be sure, but the light seemed to be coming from the very walls themselves – so subtly that at first he thought that they were simply reflecting it.

He crossed over to the side of the escarpment and examined the cavern wall more closely. It was swathed in a wild growth of tendrils, dark and glistening with moisture. It was some type of algae, made up of many trailing shoots and thickly layered like ivy on an old wall. As he held up the palm of his hand, he felt the warmth radiating from it and, yes, he could see that there was indeed a very dim glow coming from the edges of the curled leaves.

"Bioluminescence," he said aloud.

"Mmmmph?" came the indifferent reply from under Cal's canvas hood, which was twitching absurdly from side to side as he kept watch for the Styx Division.

As he continued down, Will switched his attention back to the cavern again, focusing on the most wondrous sight of all, the city itself. Even from this distance, his eyes hungrily took in the archways and impossible terraces and curving stone stairways sweeping up into stone balconies. Columns, Doric and Corinthian, sprang up to support dizzying galleries and walkways. Everywhere he looked, there were fantastic structures: colosseums and ancient domed cathedrals in beautifully crafted stone.

Then, as he reached the bottom of the escarpment, the smell hit him. It had been deceptively gentle at first, like old pond water, but with each foot they descended the more pungent it became. It was rancid, catching in Will's throat like a mouthful of bile. He cupped a hand over his nose and mouth, and looked at Cal with desperation.

"This is just horrible!" he said, gagging on the stench. "I see why you need to wear one of those things!"

"I know," Cal said flatly, his expression hidden by the breathing mask as he pointed at the gully by the foot of escarpment. "Come over here."

"What for?" Will asked as he joined his brother by the gully. He was astonished to see him thrust his hands into the treacle-like sludge that lay stagnating there. Cal lifted out two handfuls of the black algae and rubbed it over his mask and his clothes. Then he grabbed Bartleby by the scruff of the neck. The cat let out a low howl and tried to get away, but Cal streaked him from head to tail. As the filth dripped over his naked skin, Bartleby arched his back and trembled, looking at his master balefully.

"God, the stink is worse than ever now. What in hell's name

are you doing?" Will asked, thinking his brother had taken leave of his senses.

"The Division use stalker dogs round here. Any whiff of the Colony on us, we're as good as dead. This slime will cover our scent," he said, scooping up fresh handfuls of the brackish vegetation. "Your turn." Will braced himself as Cal doused the fetid weed over his hair, chest and shoulders, and then down each of his legs.

"How can you smell anything over this?" Will asked irately, looking at the oily patches on his clothes. The reek was overpowering. "These dogs must have *some* sense of smell!" It was all he could do to stop himself from being sick.

"Oh, they do," Cal said as he shook his hands to rid them of the tendrils and wiped them on his trouser legs. "We should get out of sight."

Crossing one by one, they passed swiftly over a stretch of boggy ground and into the city. They went under a tall stone arch with two malevolent gargoyle faces glaring down contemptuously at them, and then into an alley with high walls either side. The dimensions of the buildings, the gaping windows, arches and doorways, were huge, as if they'd been built for incredibly tall beings. At Cal's suggestion, they slipped through one of these openings at the base of a square tower.

Now out of the green light, Will needed his light orb to study the map. As he pulled it out by the lanyard, it lit the room, a stone chamber with a high ceiling and several inches of water on the floor. Bartleby scampered into one corner and, finding a heap of something rotten, he investigated it briefly before lifting a leg over it.

"Look," Cal said all of a sudden. "Look at the walls."

They saw skulls – row upon row of carved death's heads covered the walls, all with toothy grins and hollow, shadowy eyes. As Will moved the orb, the shadows shifted and the skulls appeared to be turning to face them.

"My Dad would've loved this. I bet this was a ..."

"It's grisly," Cal interrupted, as he shivered.

"These people were pretty spooky, weren't they?" Will said,

unable to suppress a wide grin.

"The ancestors of the Styx."

"What?" Will looked at him questioningly.

"Their forebears. People believe a group escaped from this city at the time of the plague."

"Where to?"

"Topsoil," Cal replied. "There they formed some sort of secret society. It's said the Styx gave Sir Gabriel the idea for the Colony."

Suddenly, Bartleby's ears pricked up and his unblinking eyes fixed on the doorway. Although neither of the boys had heard anything, Cal became agitated.

"We should get moving again. Check the map, Will."

Leaving the chamber and back in the open, they cautiously picked their way through the ancient streets, giving Will an opportunity to inspect the buildings at close quarters. Everywhere about them, the stone was decorated with carvings and inscriptions. And he saw the decay; the masonry was crumbling and fractured. It cried out with abandonment and neglect. Yet the buildings still sat proudly in all their magnificence – they had an aura of immense power to them. Power, and something else – a decadent and ancient menace. Will was relieved that the city's inhabitants weren't still in residence.

As they jogged down lanes of ancient stone, their boots scattered the murky water on the ground and churned up the algae, leaving faintly glowing blotches in their wake, like luminous stepping-stones. Bartleby was agitated by the water and pranced through it with the precision of a performing pony, trying not to splash himself.

Crossing a narrow stone bridge, Will stopped briefly and looked over the eroded marble balustrade at the slow-moving river below. Slick and greasy, it snaked lazily through the city, crossed here and there with other small bridges, its turgid waters coagulating against the massive sections of masonry that formed its banks. On these, classical statues stood watch like water sentinels; old men with wavy hair and impossibly long beards, and women in flowing gowns, held out shells and orbs or just the broken stumps of their arms towards the water, as if offering up sacrifices to gods that no longer existed.

They reached a large square surrounded by towering buildings, but held back from entering it, taking refuge behind a low parapet.

"What is that?" Will whispered. In the middle of the square was a raised platform supported by an array of thick columns. On top of the platform were human forms, chalky statues in twisted postures of frozen agony, some with their features obliterated and others with limbs missing. Rusting chains wound around the contorted figures and the posts next to them. It looked like a tableau depicting some long forgotten atrocity.

"The Prisoners' Platform. That's where they were punished."

"Gruesome statues," Will said, unable to take his eyes off it.

"They're not statues, they're real people. Tam said the bodies have been calcified."

"No!" Will said, staring even more intently at the figures and wishing he had time to document the scene.

"Shhhhh," Cal said. He grabbed Bartleby and pulled him to his chest. The cat kicked out his legs, but Cal wouldn't let go.

Will looked at him enquiringly.

"Get down," Cal whispered. Ducking behind the parapet, he cupped his hand over the cat's eyes and clasped the animal even more tightly.

As he followed suit, Will caught sight of them. At the far end of the square, as silent as ghosts, four figures appeared to float on the surface of the waterlogged ground. They wore breathing masks over their mouths and goggles with large, circular eyepieces, making them appear like nightmarish man-insects. He could tell from their outlines they were Styx. They wore leather skullcaps and long coats. Not the lustrous black ones Will had seen in the Colony; these were matt and camouflaged with streaky green and grey blocks of dark and light hues.

With easy military efficiency, they were advancing in a line, as one controlled an immense dog straining on a lead. Vapour was blowing from the muzzle of the impossibly large and ferocious animal – it was unlike any dog that Will had ever seen before.

The boys cowered behind the parapet, acutely aware that they had nowhere to run if the Styx came their way. The hoarse panting and the snorting of the dog grew louder – the boys glanced at each other, thinking the Styx would turn the corner at any moment, but then the sounds grew fainter and stopped altogether. The boys' eyes locked on each other. *Had they moved on, or was the patrol waiting for them?* They strained to hear the Styx's footsteps approaching, but there was only the hushed gurgle of distant running water and the continuing patter of cavern rain. After what seemed like an age, Will tapped his brother on the arm and pointed upward, indicating he was going to take a look.

Cal shook his head violently, his eyes flaring with alarm behind the half-fogged glass; they pleaded with Will to stay put. But Will ignored him and raised his head a fraction over the parapet. The Styx had vanished. He gave the thumbs up and Cal rose slowly to see for himself. Satisfied the patrol had moved on, Cal let go of Bartleby and he sprang away from him, shaking himself down and then glowering resentfully at both of them.

They skirted cautiously around the side of the square and then chose a lane in the opposite direction to the one they assumed the Styx had taken. Will found he was beginning to feel very tired and it was getting harder for him to catch his breath. His lungs were rattling like an asthmatic's and a dull ache gripped his chest and rib cage. He summoned up all his energy and they darted from shadow to shadow until the buildings ran out and the cavern wall was in front of them. They ran alongside it for several minutes until they came to a huge stone staircase cut into the rock.

"That was too close by half," Will panted, looking behind them.

"You can say that again," Cal replied, then peered at the

staircase. "Is this the one?"

"I think so," Will shrugged. At that point, he didn't much care; he just wanted to put as much distance between them and the Styx Division as possible.

The base of the stairs was badly damaged by a massive pillar that had crashed down and shattered it, and at first the boys were forced to clamber up several broken sections. Once they had reached the steps, it wasn't much better. They were slick with black weed and the boys nearly lost their footing more than once.

They climbed higher and higher up the stairway and, after a while, Will couldn't resist stopping to take in the view now they were in such an elevated position. Through the haze, he caught sight of a building topped with a huge dome.

"That's the spitting image of St Paul's," he said as he peered at the magnificent domed roof in the distance. "I'd love to have a closer look," he added, forgetting how ill he felt for the moment.

"You've got to be joking," Cal replied sharply.

The stairs eventually disappeared into a jagged arch in the rock wall. Before he entered, Will turned for a last glance at the emerald strangeness of the Eternal City and, slipping off the step, tottered forward. For a heartbeat, he faced the sheer drop in front of him and cried out, thinking he was about to plunge down it. He clutched frantically at the black tendrils covering the wall – handful after handful broke off – and then he managed to right himself again.

"Jesus, are you all right?" Cal said, now at his side. But as Will didn't answer him, he became concerned. "What's the matter?"

"I … I just feel so dizzy," Will croaked. He was panting in small, shallow breaths – it was as if he was breathing through a clogged straw. He climbed a few stairs, but broke into a racking cough and came to a standstill again. He thought the coughing fit was never going to stop. Bent double, he hacked away and then spat. He clutched his forehead, soaked with rain and clammy with an unhealthily cold sweat. He knew there was no way he could hide it from his brother any longer.

"I need to rest," he said hoarsely, using Cal for support as the coughing subsided.

"Not now," Cal said urgently, "and *not* here." Grabbing Will's arm, he helped him to continue up the stairway.

CHAPTER THIRTY-ONE

There is a point at which the body is spent, when the muscles and sinews have nothing left to give, when all that remains is a person's mettle, his sheer bloody-mindedness.

Will had reached that point. His body felt drained and worthless, but he doggedly slogged on, driven by the responsibility he felt towards his brother and his duty to get him to safety. At the same time, gnawing at him was the guilt that he'd let Chester down, let him fall into the Colonists' hands, for a second time.

"I'm useless, bloody useless." The words ran in a loop through Will's mind, over and over again. But neither he nor his brother spoke as they climbed, grinding up the never-ending circular stairway. At the very limits of his endurance, Will pushed himself on, step after painful step, flight after flight, his thighs burning as much as his lungs. Slipping and sliding over the water-slick steps and the stringy weed that clung to them, he fought to suppress the dread realisation that they still had far to go.

"I'd like to stop now," he heard Cal pant.

"Can't … don't think … I'd ever … get going … again," Will grunted in time with his plodding steps.

Just when he thought he was about to black out, he felt the faintest of breezes on his face. He knew instinctively it was untainted air. He stopped and sucked at the freshness, hoping to lift the leaden weight from his chest and relieve the interminable rattle in his lungs.

"Don't need it," Will pointed at Cal's mask. Cal removed it from his head and tucked it in his belt, the sweat running down his face in rivulets and his eyes rimmed with red.

"Phew," he exhaled. "Bit hot under that thing."

They resumed the climb, and it wasn't long before the steps ended and they went though a sequence of narrow passages and short flights of crude steps. Every so often, they were forced to scramble up rusted iron ladders, their hands turning orange as they tested each precarious rung. Eventually they reached a steeply angled shaft no more than three feet wide. They clambered up its pockmarked surface using a thick-knotted rope that was hanging there, their feet finding purchase in the shallow cracks and fault lines. The incline became steeper and they had a job to scrabble over the slime-covered stone. Despite losing their footing a few times, they eventually reached the top, hauling themselves into a small circular chamber. Here there was a four-foot square vent in the floor. Leaning into it, Will could see the remnants of an iron grating, long since rusted away.

"What's down there?" Cal panted.

"Nothing, can't see a bloody thing," Will said despondently, squatting down to rest on his haunches. He brushed the sweat from his face with a raw hand. "I suppose we do what Tam said. We climb down."

Cal looked behind them and then to his brother, nodding. For several minutes neither of them made a move, immobilised with fatigue.

"Well, we can't stay here for ever," Will sighed and swung his legs into the vent, and with his back pressed against one side and feet hard against the other, he began to ease himself down.

"What about the cat?" Will shouted, after he had gone a short distance. "Is it going to be able to cope with this?"

"Don't worry about him," Cal smiled. "Anything we can do ..."

Will never heard the rest of Cal's sentence. He slipped. The sides of the vent flashed by and he landed with a large splash – he was submerged in icy cold water. He thrashed out with his arms, then his feet found a solid surface and he stood up and blew out a mouthful of water. He found he was chest-deep and, after he'd wiped the water out of his eyes and pushed back his hair, he looked around. He couldn't be certain but there seemed to be a dim light in the distance.

"Will! Will! Are you all right?" he heard Cal's frantic shouts from above.

"Just had a quick dip!" Will shouted, laughing weakly. "Stay there, I'm just going to check something out." His exhaustion and discomfort were forgotten as he stared at the faint glow, his eyes straining to make out the least detail of what lay ahead.

Soaked to the skin, he clambered out of the pool and, stooping under the low roof, made his way slowly towards the light. After a couple of hundred yards, he could clearly see the circular mouth of the tunnel and, with his heart racing, he sped towards it. Dropping several feet off a ledge he'd failed to notice, he landed roughly, finding himself under a jetty of some kind. Through a forest of heavy wooden stanchions, draped with weed, he could see the dappled reflections of light on water.

Gravel crunched underfoot as he walked into the open. He felt the invigorating chill of the wind on his face. He breathed deeply, drawing the fresh air into his aching lungs. It was such sweetness. Slowly he took stock of the surroundings.

Night. Lights reflected off a river in front of him. It was a wide river. A two-tiered pleasure boat chugged past – bright flashes of colour pulsed from its two decks as indistinct dance music throbbed over the water. Then he saw the bridges either side of him and, in the distance, the floodlit dome of St Paul's. The St Paul's he knew. A red double-decker bus crossed the bridge closest to him. This wasn't any old river. He sat down on the bank with surprise and relief.

It was the Thames.

He lay down on the bank and closed his eyes, listening to the droning hubbub of traffic. He tried to remember the names of the bridges, but he didn't really care – he'd made it out and nothing else mattered. He'd made it. He was home. Back in his own world.

"The sky," Cal said with awe in his voice. "So that's what it's like." Will opened his eyes to see his brother craning his neck this way and that, as he stared at the stray wisps of cloud caught in the amber radiation of the streetlights. Although Cal was sopping from his immersion in the pool, he was smiling broadly, but then he wrinkled his nose up. "Phew, what's that?" he said loudly.

"What do you mean?" Will asked.

"All those smells!"

Will propped himself up on one elbow and sniffed. "What smells?"

"Food … all sorts of food … and …" Cal grimaced. "Sewage – lots of it – and chemicals …"

As Will sniffed the air again, thinking how fresh it was, it occurred to him he hadn't once considered what they were going to do next. *Where were they going to go?* He'd been so intent on escaping, he hadn't given anything beyond it a second thought. He stood up and examined his sodden, filthy Colonists' clothes and then those of his brother, and the unfeasibly large cat that was nosing around the bank like a pig searching for truffles. A brisk winter wind was picking up, and he shivered violently and his teeth started to chatter. It struck him that neither his brother nor Bartleby had experienced the relative extremes of Topsoil weather in their sheltered, subterranean lives. He had to get them moving. And quickly. But he didn't have any money on him – not a penny.

"We're going to have to walk home."

"Fine," Cal replied unquestioningly, his head back as he stared at the stars, losing himself in the canopy of the sky.

A helicopter drifted across the horizon.

"Why's that one moving?"

Will felt too tired to explain. "They do that," he said flatly.

They set off, keeping close to the bank so as not to be noticed, and almost immediately came upon a set of steps leading to the walkway above. It was next to the bridge. Will knew then where they were – it was Blackfriars.

A gate blocked the top of the steps, so they clambered over a broad wall with a rounded top by its side to reach the walkway. Dripping water on the pavement and freezing in the night air, they looked around them. Will was suddenly seized by the dreadful thought that even here the Styx might have spies watching out for them. After seeing one of the Clarke brothers in the Colony, he felt that he couldn't trust anybody, and regarded the area around them with suspicion. But there was only a couple walking hand in hand. They strolled past, so involved with each other they didn't seem to pay the boys or the cat any attention.

With Will taking the lead, they took the steps up to the bridge itself and when they reached the top he saw the Imax cinema to the right. To him, London was a mosaic of places he recognised from museum visits with his father or school expeditions. The rest, the interconnecting areas, were a complete mystery to him. There was only one thing for it; trust in his sense of direction and try to head north.

As they quickly traversed the bridge, Will spotted a sign to King's Cross and knew instantly they were heading in the right direction. Traffic passed them as they arrived at the end of the bridge, and Will paused to look at Cal and the cat under the light of a streetlight. Talk about three suspicious-looking lost souls – they stuck out a mile. Although it was dark, Will was painfully aware that a pair of young boys soaked to the skin and wandering the streets of London at this late hour, with or without a giant cat, were likely to attract attention, and the last thing he needed now was to be picked up by the police. He tried to imagine what they would make of his return, and how he could ever begin to explain the presence of his brother and the cat.

Perversely, as he contemplated the future, some part of him almost wanted them to be stopped. It would remove the dreadful burden that lay squarely on his shoulders; he glanced at the cowed figure of his brother and felt a surge of emotion for the boy who had lost everything he knew, everything he'd grown up with. Cal was a stranger, a freak in this cold and inhospitable place, and Will had no idea how he was going to protect him.

But Will knew if he turned himself in to the authorities and tried to get them to investigate the Colony – that's if they believed a runaway teenager in the first place – he could be risking countless lives, his *family's* lives. Who knew how it would end? He shuddered at the thought of the Discovery, as Grandma Macaulay had called it, and tried to imagine her being lead out into the daylight after her long subterranean life. He couldn't do that to her – it didn't bear thinking about. It was too big a decision for him to take alone, and he did feel so terribly alone and isolated.

He pulled his damp jacket around himself, and hustled Cal and Bartleby down into the subway at the end of the bridge.

"It's very pissy down here," his brother commented. "Do all Topsoilers mark their territories?" He turned to Will enquiringly.

"Er … not usually. But this *is* London."

As they emerged from the subway and back onto the pavement, Cal seemed confused by the traffic, looking this way and that. Coming to a main road, they stopped on the kerb. Will gripped his brother's sleeve with one hand and the cat's hairless scruff with the other. Crossing when there was a lull in the traffic, they made it to the traffic island. He could see people peering curiously at them from the passing cars and a white van slowed down almost to a halt right beside them, the driver talking excitedly into his mobile. To Will's relief, it sped off again. They crossed the remaining two lanes and, after a short distance, Will steered them into a dimly lit side street. His brother stood with one hand on the brick wall – he looked completely disoriented, like a blind man in unfamiliar surroundings.

"Foul air!" he said vehemently.

"It's only car fumes," Will replied as he untied the lanyard from his light orb and fashioned a slipknot lead for the cat, which didn't seem to mind one bit.

"It smells wrong. It must be against the laws," Cal said with complete conviction.

" 'Fraid not," Will answered as he led them down the street. He would have to stay off the main road and keep to the backstreets as far as possible. He knew that this was going to make their journey even more difficult and circuitous, because he wouldn't have the luxury of the signs or familiar landmarks to guide him.

And so the long march north began. They only saw a single police car on their way out of central London, but Will was able to usher them around a corner in the nick of time.

"Are they like Styx?" Cal asked.

"Not quite," Will replied.

With the cat on one side and Cal twitching nervously on the other, they trudged along. From time to time, his brother would stop dead, as if invisible doors were being slammed in his face.

"What is it?" Will asked on one of these occasions, when his brother refused to move.

"It's like ... anger ... and fear," Cal said in a strained voice as he glanced nervously up at the windows over a shop front. "It's so strong. I don't like it."

"I can't see anything," Will said as he failed to make out what was troubling his brother. They were just ordinary windows, a sliver of light showing between the curtains in one of them. "It's nothing, you're imagining it."

"No, I'm not. I can smell it," Cal said emphatically, "and it's getting stronger. I want to go."

After several miles of tortuous ducking and diving, they came to the brow of a hill, at the bottom of which was a busy main road with six lanes of speeding traffic.

"I know this – it's not far now. Maybe a couple of miles, that's all," Will said with relief.

"I'm not going near that. I can't – not with that stench. It'll kill us," Cal said, backing away from Will.

"Don't be so bloody stupid," Will said. He was just too tired for any nonsense and his frustration now turned to anger. "We're so close."

"No," Cal said, digging his heels in. "I'm staying here!"

Will tried to pull the boy's arm, but he yanked it away. Will had been fighting his exhaustion for miles and was still struggling to breathe; he didn't need this. All of a sudden, it got too much for him. He thought he was actually going to break down and cry. It just wasn't fair. He pictured the house and his welcoming clean bed. All he wanted to do was lie down and sleep. Even as he was walking, his body kept going loose, as if he was dropping through a hole into a place where everything was so comforting and warm. Then he would yank himself out of it, back to wakefulness, and urge himself on again.

"Fine!" Will shouted. "Do what you bloody want!" He set off down the hill, tugging Bartleby by the lead.

As he reached the road, Will heard his brother's voice over the din of traffic.

"Will!" he yelled, "Wait for me! I'm sorry!"

Cal came hurtling down the hill – Will could see that he was genuinely terrified as he kept jerking his head to look around him, as if he was about to be attacked by some imagined assassin. They crossed the road at the lights, but Cal insisted on pressing his hand over his mouth until they were a good distance from it.

"I can't take this," he said glumly. "I liked the idea of cars when I was in the Colony … but the brochures didn't say anything about the way they smell."

"Got a light?"

Startled by the voice, they whirled around. As if he'd come out of nowhere, a man was standing very close behind them, a lopsided grin on his face. He wasn't terribly tall, but was well dressed in a tightly fitting dark blue suit, and a shirt and tie. He had long black hair, which he kept stroking back at the temples and tucking behind his ears, as if it was bothering him. "Left mine at home," he continued, his voice deep and rich.

"Don't smoke, sorry," Will replied, quickly edging away. There was something in the man's smile that was forced and sleazy, and alarm bells were ringing in Will's head.

"You boys all right? You look done in. I got a place you can warm up. Not far from here," the man said ingratiatingly. "Bring your doggy too, of course." He held out a hand towards Cal and Will saw that the fingers were stained with nicotine and his fingernails were black with filth.

"Can we?" Cal said, returning the man's smile.

"No … very kind of you, but …" Will interrupted, glaring at his brother but failing to get his attention. The man took a step towards Cal and addressed him, completely ignoring Will, as if he wasn't there.

"Something hot to eat, too?" he offered.

Cal was on the point of replying when Will spoke.

"Must go, our parents are waiting just round the corner. Come on, Cal," he said, a note of urgency creeping into his voice. Cal looked perplexedly at Will, who shook his head, frowning. The penny dropping that something wasn't quite right, Cal fell into step beside his brother.

"Shame, maybe next time?" the man said, his eyes still fixed on Cal. The man made no move to follow them, but pulled a lighter from his jacket pocket and lit a cigarette. "Be seeing you!" he called after them.

"Don't you look back," Will hissed through his teeth as he walked rapidly away with Cal in tow. "Don't you *dare* look back."

An hour later they entered Highfield. Will avoided the High Street in case he was recognised, taking the back alleys and side roads until they turned into Broadlands Avenue.

There it was. The house, completely dark with an estate agent's sign in the front garden. Will led them around the side and under the carport into the back garden. He kicked over a brick where the spare back door key had always been hidden and muttered a silent prayer of thanks when he saw it was still there. He unlocked the door and they took a few wary paces into the dark hallway.

"Colonists!" Cal said straight away, recoiling. "They've been here … and not long ago."

"For God's sake." It smelt a little fusty and unoccupied to Will, but he couldn't be bothered to argue. Not wanting to alert the neighbours he left the lights off and used his light orb to check each room whilst Cal remained in the hall, his senses working overtime.

"There's nothing, nothing at all," Will said as he languidly returned downstairs. With some consternation, his brother edged further into the house with Bartleby at his heels, as Will shut and locked the door behind them. He shepherded them into the sitting room and, making sure the curtains were tightly closed, turned the television on. There he left them while he went into the kitchen.

The fridge was completely bare except for a tub of margarine and an old onion that was dry and shrunken. Will was gobsmacked. For a moment he stared uncomprehendingly at the bare shelves. To him this was unprecedented, confirming just how far things had gone. He sighed and, as he shut the door, he spotted a scrap of lined paper sellotaped onto it. It was in Rebecca's precise hand, one of her shopping lists.

Rebecca! The fury rose in him. The thought of that impostor masquerading as his sister for all those years suddenly made his blood boil. Now he couldn't even think back to the comfortable and predictable life he'd been leading before his father went missing, because she had been there, watching and spying and destroying all the memories. It was the worst kind of betrayal, a Judas sent by the Styx.

"Bitch!" he said aloud as he tore the list off, crumpled it up and slung it onto the floor.

As it came to rest on the pristine lino floor Rebecca had mopped with mind-numbing regularity, he looked at the stopped clock on the wall and sighed. He shuffled over to the sink and filled glasses with water for himself and Cal, and a bowl for Bartleby. Returning to the sitting room, he found them on the sofa, the cat already curled up asleep and Cal with his head resting drowsily on his arm.

Will drank the water quickly and climbed into his mother's chair, wrapping himself in her travelling rug. His eyes barely registered the death-defying snowboarding stunts on the television as he curled up, precisely as his mother had done for so many years, and fell into the deepest of sleeps.

CHAPTER THIRTY-TWO

T am stood silent and defiant. He was determined not to show his trepidation as he and Mr Jerome faced the long table, their hands clenched behind their backs as if standing to attention.

Behind the table of polished oak sat the Panoply. These were the most senior and powerful members of the Styx Council. At either end of the table sat a few high-ranking Colonists, representatives from the Board of the Governors, men that Mr Jerome had known all his life, men that were his friends. He quaked with shame as he felt the disgrace wash over him, and couldn't bring himself to look at them. He never thought it would come to this.

Tam was less intimidated; he'd been carpeted before and always managed to get off by the skin of his teeth. Although these allegations were serious, he knew his alibi had passed their scrutiny. Imago and his men had made sure of that. Tam watched as the Crawfly conferred with a fellow Styx and then leant back to speak to the Styx child who stood half-hidden behind the high back of his chair. *Now, that was irregular.* Their children were usually kept well out of sight and far away from the Colony; the newborn were never seen, while the older offspring, it was said, were closeted away with their masters in the rarefied atmosphere of their private schools. He'd never heard of them accompanying their elders in public, let alone being present at meetings such as these.

Tam's thoughts were interrupted by a scratchy outburst of intense debate running through the Panoply like an animated static. Chinese whispers rippled back and forth as their skinny hands communicated in a series of vicious abstract gestures. Tam glanced quickly at Mr Jerome, whose head hung low. He was quietly mumbling an incoherent prayer to himself as sweat coursed from his temples. His face was puffy and his skin an unhealthy pink. All this was taking its toll on him.

The commotion abruptly ceased amidst nods and harsh words of agreement, and the Styx settled back in their seats, a chilling silence descending over the room. Tam readied himself. A pronouncement was about to be delivered.

"Mr Jerome," the Styx to the left of the Crawfly intoned. "After due consideration and full and proper investigation," he fixed his beady pupils on the quivering man, "we will allow you to step down."

Another Styx promptly took over. "It is felt that the injustices brought upon you from specific of your family members, past and present, are inequitable and unfortunate. Your probity is not in question and your reputation has not been tarnished. Unless you would like to speak for the record, you are unconditionally discharged."

Mr Jerome bowed dolefully and backed away from the table. Tam heard his boots scuffing on the flagstones, but dared not turn to watch him leave. Instead, his gaze flicked to the ceiling of the stone hall, then to the ancient wall hangings behind the Panoply, alighting on one depicting the great forefathers digging a perfectly round tunnel in the side of a verdant hill.

He knew that all eyes now rested on him.

Another Styx spoke. Tam immediately recognised the Crawfly's voice, and was obliged to face his avowed enemy. "He's loving every minute of this," Tam thought to himself.

"Macaulay. You are a different kettle of fish. Though not proven yet, we believe that you did aid and abet your nephews, Seth and Caleb Jerome, in their foiled attempt to liberate the Topsoiler, and then to escape to the Eternal City," said the Crawfly with evident relish.

A second Styx took over. "We have noted your plea of not guilty and continuing protestations but, to a man, we are not convinced. At this time, we have decreed that the investigation will remain open. Accordingly, you are to be held on remand and your privileges will be revoked until further notice. Do you understand?"

Tam nodded sombrely.

"We said do you understand?" snapped the child Styx, stepping forward.

An evil grin flicked across Rebecca's face as her icy glare drilled into Tam. There was a stir of hushed astonishment from the Colonists that the minor had dared to speak, but not the smallest indication from the Styx that anything out of the ordinary had occurred.

Tam was taken aback. Was he supposed to respond to this mere child? As he didn't answer right away, she repeated the question, her hard little voice as sharp as a whip crack.

"WE SAID DO YOU UNDERSTAND?"

"I do," Tam muttered, "only too well."

It wasn't a final ruling by any means, but meant he would live in limbo until they decided he was either cleared or ... well ... the alternatives didn't bear thinking about.

As a surly Colonist officer escorted him away, he couldn't help but notice what passed between Rebecca and the Crawfly, a smarmy look of self-congratulation.

"Well I'll be damned!" Tam thought to himself. "It's his daughter!"

―◄○►―

An American chat show bellowed out of the set as Will sat up in the chair and flexed his stiff legs. He took several deep breaths and coughed sharply. Although he was ravenous, he felt a little better than he had the day before; the sleep had done him good. He scratched and then tugged vaguely at his matted hair, its brilliant whiteness sullied by dirt, as he stumbled over to the curtains and parted them a couple of inches to let the morning sun into the room. Real light again. It was such a welcome sight that he pulled them further apart.

Cal screeched and buried his face under a cushion, as

Bartleby made a noise somewhere between a hiss and a meow, and bolted behind the sofa.

"Oh God, I'm sorry," Will stuttered, kicking himself. He immediately yanked the curtains shut again. "I completely forgot."

He helped his brother into a sitting position.

"I'll … er … I'll find some sunglasses for you," he said helplessly.

He searched through a chest of drawers in his parents' room and found that it had been emptied. As he was checking the last drawer, he picked out a little bag of lavender languishing on the cheap Christmas wrapping paper that his mother had used as a liner and held it up to catch the familiar scent. He closed his eyes as it conjured up a vivid picture of her. Wherever they'd sent her, she'd be lording it over the other patients by now. He was willing to bet she'd commandeered the best chair in the television room, and had cajoled someone into bringing her regular cups of tea. He smiled. In a way, she was probably happier now than she'd been for years. And safer too, if the Styx were to visit.

For no reason in particular, as he rummaged through a bedside cupboard he thought of his real mother. He wondered where she was now. The only person in the long history of the Colony ever to evade the Styx, and live. He set his jaw with a determined look as he caught his reflection in a mirror. Well now there were going to be two more Jeromes with that distinction.

On a high shelf in his mother's wardrobe he found what he was looking for, a pair of bendy plastic sunglasses his mother used to wear on the rare occasions she ventured out in the summer. He went back to Cal, who was now completely absorbed by a mid-morning talk show in which the permatanned and obsequious host, oozing sincerity, was comforting the inconsolable mother of a teenage drug addict. Will placed the glasses on Cal's head, an elastic band strung around the arms to hold them firmly in place.

"Better?" Will asked.

"Much better, yes," Cal said, adjusting them, "but I'm really hungry," he added, rubbing his stomach.

"Showers first, I reckon," Will said as he lifted his arm to sample the accumulated odour of many days' sweat. "And some clean clothes."

"Showers?" Cal peered at him blankly through the lenses of the sunglasses.

Will managed to get the boiler fired up and went first, the hot water stinging his flesh with painful relief as the clouds of steam enveloped him in an ecstasy of forgetfulness.

Then it was Cal's turn. Will showed his fascinated brother how the power shower worked and left him to it. From the wardrobe in his bedroom he dug out clean sets of clothes for himself and Cal, although his brother's needed a little adjustment to make them fit.

"I'm a real Topsoiler now," Cal announced, admiring the baggy jeans with rolled-up ends and the voluminous shirt.

"Yeah, very trendsetting," Will laughed.

Bartleby was more problematic. It took much coaxing by Cal to even get him as far as the bathroom door, and then they had to push the animal, like a recalcitrant donkey, from the rear to get him in. As if he knew what was in store in the steamy room, he leapt away and tried to hide under the basin.

"Come on, Bart, you stinker, into the bath!" Cal ordered, as he eventually ran out of patience, and the cat unwillingly obeyed him. He grudgingly crept into the bath and watched them with the most hangdog of expressions. He let out a warbled, low whine when the water first trickled over his sagging skin, and his paws scrabbled on the plastic of the bath but, with Will holding him down, they managed to finish the task. Both Will and Cal were completely drenched by the end of the exercise.

Once out of the bath, he ricocheted around the bedrooms like a whirling dervish while Will ransacked Rebecca's room. Some brown legwarmers were cut down to size for the cat's rear legs and an old purple Benetton jumper did for his top half. Will found a pair of Bugs Bunny sunglasses in Rebecca's holiday holdall. These stayed in place on the cat's head once a striped black and yellow Tibetan hat was pulled firmly down.

Bartleby looked quite bizarre in his new outfit. Out on the landing, the two brothers stood back to admire their handiwork, promptly falling about in hysterics.

"Who's a pretty boy, then?" Cal chuckled between outbursts of breathless laughter.

"Better looking than most around here!" Will said.

"Don't you worry, Bart," Cal said soothingly, patting the peeved animal on the back. "Very striking," he managed to say before they both lapsed once again into uncontrolled laughter. Behind the pink-tinted lenses, the indignant Bartleby watched them sideways out of his large eyes.

Fortunately, Rebecca, much as Will cursed her, had left the freezer in the utility room well stocked. He read the microwave instructions and heated up three beef dinners complete with dumplings and French beans. They wolfed these down in the kitchen, Bartleby standing with both paws on the table, his tongue rasping against the tinfoil dish as he hungrily devoured every last scrap of the meat. Cal thought it was just about the best thing he'd ever tasted, but claimed he was still hungry, so Will retrieved another three meals from the freezer. This time, they had pork dinners replete with roast potatoes. They washed this down with a bottle of Coke, which sent Cal into fits of rapture.

"So what happens next?" he said finally, tracing the rising bubbles on the side of his glass with a finger.

"What's the mad rush? We'll be all right for a while," Will replied flatly.

"There's no way we can stay here. The Styx know about this place – it'll be the first place they look."

"I suppose so," Will agreed reluctantly, "and there's always the chance we might get rumbled by the estate agents if they show people round." He glanced over at the net curtains above the sink and spoke decisively. "But I still have to get Chester out."

His brother looked aghast. "You don't mean go back? I can't go back, not now, Will. The Styx would do something terrible to me."

Cal was not alone in his fear at returning underground. Will could barely contain his terror at the prospect of facing the Styx again. He felt as though he had pushed his luck as far as it would go, and to imagine he could carry out some audacious rescue of Chester was sheer lunacy.

On the other hand, what would they do if they remained Topsoil? Sooner or later, they would be apprehended, and he and Cal would more than likely be separated and placed in care. And he would live the rest of his life under the shadow of Chester's death, and with the thought that he could have joined his father in one of the greatest adventures of the century.

"I don't want to die," Cal said in a faint voice, "not like that." He pushed his glass away from himself on the table and looked pleadingly into Will's eyes.

This wasn't getting any easier for Will. He couldn't cope with much more pressure. He shook his head. "What am I supposed to do? I can't just leave him there. I can't."

Later, while Cal and Bartleby lounged in front of the television watching children's programmes and eating crisps, Will couldn't resist going into the cellar. Just as he expected, when he swung the shelves out, there wasn't a trace of the tunnel – they had even gone to the trouble of painting the newly laid brickwork to blend in with the rest of the wall. He knew that behind it would be the usual backfill of stone and earth. They'd done the job properly this time. No point in wasting further time there.

Back in the kitchen, he balanced on a stool while he hunted through the jars on top of the cupboards. He found his mother's video money in a porcelain honey pot – there was about £20 in loose change.

He was in the hallway on his way to the sitting room when he began to see tiny dots of light dancing before his eyes, and all over his body pinpricks of heat broke out. Then, without any warning, his legs went from under him. He dropped the jar, which glanced off the edge of the hall table and shattered, scattering the change over the floor. It was as if he was in slow motion as he collapsed, a fierce pain burning through his head until everything turned black and he lost consciousness. Cal and Bartleby came rushing out of the sitting room at the noise.

"Will! What's the matter?" Cal said, kneeling next to him.

Will slowly came to, his temples throbbing painfully. "I don't know," he said feebly. "Just felt awful, all of a sudden." He started to cough, and had to hold his breath in order to stop.

"You feel like you're burning up," Cal said, feeling his forehead.

"Freezing ..." Will could barely talk as his teeth rattled together. He tried to get up, but didn't have the strength.

"What is it?" Cal's face was creased with concern. "Something from the Eternal City? Plague!"

Will was silent as his brother pulled him over to the bottom step of the staircase and propped his head on it. He fetched the travelling rug and draped it around him. After a while, Will directed Cal to the bathroom to fetch some aspirin. He swallowed them down with a sip of Coke and, after a brief rest, managed to get shakily to his feet with assistance from Cal.

Will's eyes were febrile and unfocused, and his voice trembled. "I really think we should get help," he said, mopping the sweat from his brow.

"Is there anywhere we can go?" Cal asked.

Will sniffed and swallowed and nodded, his head feeling like a balloon filled with pain and about to burst. "There's only one place I can think of."

CHAPTER THIRTY-THREE

Will was pitched forward as a fist landed squarely in the middle of his back. Staggering drunkenly for a few steps, he rebounded off the handrail and turned slowly round to face his assailant.

"Speed?" he said, recognising the scowling face.

"Where've you sprung from, Snowdrop? Thought you were dead. People have been looking for you."

Will didn't reply. He was deep in the insulated cocoon of the unwell; he felt as though he was looking at the world from behind a frosted sheet of glass. It was all he could do to stand there, his body quivering as Speed pushed his snarling face just inches in front of his. Out of the corner of his eye, Will glimpsed Blogsy closing on Cal a little further down the sloping path.

They had been on their way to the Tube station and, right now, a fight was the last thing Will could cope with.

"So where's Fat Boy?" Speed crooned, the moisture on his breath clouding in the cold air. "Bit different without your minder, innit, dipstick?"

"Oi, Speed, check this out, it's Mini Me!" Blogsy said, looking from Cal to Will and back again. "What's in your bag, gimp?"

At Will's insistence, Cal had been carrying their still befouled Colonists' clothes in one of Dr Burrows' old expedition hold-alls.

"Payback time," Speed shouted and simultaneously jabbed a fist in Will's stomach. Winded, Will slumped to his knees and

298

then toppled over, curling up in a foetal position with his arms wrapped defensively around his head as he hit the ground.

"This is too easy," Speed cawed as he kicked Will in the back several times.

Blogsy was making ridiculous whooping noises and crouching in a mock kung-fu fighting stance as he prodded two fingers at Cal's sunglasses. "Prepare to meet your maker," he said, drawing his other arm back ready to throw a punch.

Everything happened too quickly for Will. There was a flash of purple and brown streaked lightning as Bartleby landed on Blogsy's shoulders. The impact sent him tumbling down the slope, the cat at his throat. As Blogsy writhed on the ground, his hands punched at the air in a futile effort to fight off the flurry of pearl white canines and barbaric looking claws. He was letting out high-pitched screams as the cat slashed furiously at his face.

"No," Will shouted weakly. "Stop!"

"Leave it!" Cal yelled.

The cat spun his head about to look at Cal, who shouted another command.

"See him off!" he pointed at Speed, who was still standing over Will. Speed's jaw dropped as a look of sheer disbelief crept over his face. Bartleby fixed his eyes on the new quarry through the bizarre pink sunglasses, the Tibetan hat now slightly adrift on his head. With a loud hiss, he pounced towards the startled ruffian.

"Jesus! Jesus!" Speed shrieked as he started to run up the path as if his life depended on it. It did. In the blink of an eye, the cat had caught up with him. Sometimes at his side, sometimes blocking his way, Bartleby circled around him like a playful whirlwind, attacking his calves and slashing at his legs through his trousers, and lacerating skin. The terrified boy stumbled and tottered in a spasmodic, comic dance as he frantically tried to escape the cat's claws and teeth, his feet sliding hopelessly on the tarmac.

Will hauled himself up by the handrail and looked past Cal down to the bottom of the slope, where Blogsy was half-running, half-falling in his haste to get away.

"I think we've seen the last of them," Cal muttered.

"Yes," Will agreed faintly as wave upon wave of the fever assailed him. He could quite happily have lain down, opened his coat to the cold, and gone to sleep right there and then on the frosty path. When Bartleby eventually rejoined them, Cal had to help Will down the rest of the slope and into the Tube station.

"So even Topsoilers like to go underground," he said, looking at the dirty old station, long overdue a full refurbishment. Cal's manner was instantly transformed; he appeared to be genuinely at ease for the first time since they had emerged onto the banks of the Thames, and relieved that there was a tunnel around him, rather than open sky.

"Not really," Will said listlessly as he started to feed change into the ticket machine, while Bartleby slavered over a lichen-like patch of freshly deposited chewing gum on the tiled floor. Will's shaking fingers fumbled with the coins, then he stopped and leant against the machine. "I can't do this," he gasped. Cal took the change from him and finished paying for the tickets.

Down on the platform, it wasn't long before a train arrived. Once aboard the southbound train, neither boy spoke as it pulled out of the station. As it gained speed, Cal watched the cables rippling along the tunnel sides and played with his ticket. Licking his paws, Bartleby was propped on his haunches next to Cal. There weren't many people in the same carriage, but Cal was conscious that they were attracting some curious glances from the few there were.

Opposite Cal and Bartelby, Will was sitting slumped against the side of the carriage, soothed by the chill glass on his temple as his head lolled against the window. Between stops, he drifted in and out of a fitful sleep and, during a period of wakefulness, saw that a pair of old ladies had taken the seats across the aisle from them. Snatches of their conversation drifted into his consciousness and mixed with the platform announcements like the voices of a confused dream.

"Just look at him ... disgraceful ... feet all over the seats ... MIND THE GAP ... Odd-looking child ... LONDON

UNDERGROUND APOLOGISES ..."

Will forced his eyes open and looked at the two women. He realised immediately it was Bartleby who was troubling them. The one who was doing all the talking had hair like a purple rinsed Brillo pad and wore translucent white-framed bifocals that rested crookedly on her poppy-red nose.

"Shhh! They'll hear you," her companion whispered, eyeing Cal. She had either dyed her hair with black shoe polish or was wearing a wig that had seen better days. They both held identical shopping bags on their laps, as if they were some form of defence against the miscreants across from them.

"Nonsense! Bet they don't speak a word of English. Probably got here on the back of a lorry. I mean, look at the state of their clothes. And that one – he don't look too bright to me. He's probably on drugs or something." Will felt their rheumy eyes rake over him.

"Send them all back, I say."

"Yes, yes," the old ladies said in unison, and with a mutual nod of agreement fell to discussing in morbid detail the ill health of a friend. Cal glowered furiously at them while they gabbled away, now apparently too preoccupied to pay further attention to anyone else. The train came to a stop and, as the old ladies were getting up from their seats, Cal lifted the earflap of Bartleby's Tibetan hat and whispered something into his ear. Bartleby suddenly reared up and hissed in their faces so forcefully that Will was shocked from his feverish stupor.

"Well I never!" the Brillo lady cried out, dropping her shopping bag. While she retrieved it, the wig lady bustled and pushed her from behind, trying to hurry her up.

"Bloody gippos!" the wig lady huffed from the platform. "Bloody animals!" she shouted through the closing doors.

As the train moved off, the old ladies looked perplexedly at Bartleby as he kept his eyes locked on them through the window.

His curiosity getting the better of him, Will leant over to his brother.

"What did you say to Bartleby?" he asked.

"Oh nothing," Cal replied innocently, smiling at the cat proudly before he turned to look out of the window again.

———◄○►———

Will was dreading the half-mile to the block of flats. He staggered along like a drunken man, resting when it became too much for him.

The last straw was that the lift wasn't working. Will peered into the graffiti-strafed greyness with quiet exasperation. He sighed and, steeling himself for the climb, stumbled towards the squalid stairwell. After frequent stops on the landings to allow Will to catch his breath, they eventually reached the right floor and made their way through the obstacle course of discarded rubbish bags.

As there was no response when he rang the bell, Cal had resorted to knocking on the door with his fist when Auntie Jean opened it. She clearly hadn't been up for long – she was wearing a moth-eaten coat that she had evidently been asleep in.

"What is it?" she said indistinctly, her eyes hooded and lifeless as she rubbed the back of her neck. "I didn't order anything and I don't buy from hawkers."

"Auntie Jean, it's me … Will," he said, as the blood drained from his head and the image of his aunt blanched, as if all the colours had been washed out of it.

"Will," she said vaguely, and cut a yawn short as it sank in. "Will!" She lifted her head and eyed him disbelievingly. "Thought you'd gone missing?" She peered at Cal and Bartleby, and added, "Who's this?"

"Er … cousin …" Will gasped as the floor began to tip and sway, and he was forced to take a step forward to steady himself against the doorjamb. He was aware of the cold sweat trickling from his scalp. " … south … from down south."

"Cousins?"

"Dad's side."

She surveyed Cal and Bartleby with suspicion and not with a little distaste. "Your bloody sister was 'ere, you know."

"She's not my sister, she's a vile … scheming … little … she's a …" With that, Will keeled over in a dead faint before a very surprised Auntie Jean.

━━◦◦━━

Cal stood at the window of the darkened room. He peered down at the streets below with their dotted lines of amber lights and the sweeping cones of car headlamps. Then, with foreboding, he slowly raised his head and looked up at the moon, its shining silver spread out against the icy sky and, not for the first time, struggled to grasp, to comprehend, the vast space between them. He gripped the windowsill, barely able to control the rising sense of dread. The soles of his feet clenched involuntarily and almost ached with vertigo. On hearing his brother moan, he tore his eyes from the yawning abyss. He turned from the window and went to sit by the shivering form that lay on the bed with just a sheet over it.

"How's 'e doing then?" he heard Auntie Jean's anxious voice as she appeared at the doorway.

"He's a little better today. I think he's cooled down a bit," Cal said as he doused a flannel in a bowl of water clunking with ice cubes and dabbed it to Will's forehead.

"Shouldn't we call the doctor?" Auntie Jean asked. "'E's been like this for too long."

"No," Cal said firmly. "He said he didn't want that."

Bartleby got up from the floor and started to lap at the water in the bowl.

"Get off, you stupid cat!" Cal said, pushing him away.

"Poor puss, are you a liccle firsty?" Auntie Jean took hold of the astounded animal by the scruff of his neck. "You come with mummy, for a treat."

━━◦◦━━

A lava flow moves portentously in the distance, a high vertical wall of streaming crimson red. The immense heat stings Will's exposed skin. Silhouetted by the fireglow, his father frantically indicates something sprouting out of a massive slab of granite. He shouts excitedly, as he always does when he makes a discovery, but Will isn't able to make out the words due to the deafening white noise intercut with the cacophonous babble of many voices, as if someone is randomly scanning the airwaves on a damaged radio.

The scene shifts into close up. Dr Burrows is using a light orb to illuminate a thin stalk with a bulbous tip that rises a foot or so out of the solid rock. Will sees his father's lips moving but can only understand brief snatches.

"... a plant ... literally digests rock ... silicon based ... reacts to stim ... observe ..."

The image cuts to extreme close-up. Between two fingers Dr Burrows plucks the grey stalk from the rock. Will feels uneasy as he sees it writhe in his father's hand and shoot out two needle-like leaves that entwine around his fingers.

" ... gripping me like iron ... feisty little ..." Dr Burrows says, frowning.

There are no more words, they are replaced by laughter, but his father seems to be screaming as he tries to shake the thing off, its leaves piercing his hand and threading straight through the flesh of his palm and wrist and carrying on up his forearm, the skin bruising, bruising and bursting open and becoming smeared with blood as they twist, as they interweave in a snake-like waltz. They cut tighter and tighter into his forearm, like two possessed cheese wires. Will tries to reach out to his father, to help him as he battles hopelessly against this horrific attack, as he fights with his own arm.

"No, no ... Dad ... Dad!"

"It's all right, Will, it's all right," came his brother's voice from a long way away.

The lava glow was gone, and instead he felt the soothing coolness of the flannel Cal was pressing against his forehead. He sat up with a start.

"It's Dad! What happened to Dad?" he shouted and looked around wildly, unsure where he was.

"It's okay," Cal said, "You were sleeping."

Will slumped back against the pillows, realising he was lying in bed in a narrow room.

"I saw him. It was all so clear and real," Will said, his voice breaking. He couldn't stem the flood of tears that suddenly filled his eyes. "It was Dad. He was in trouble."

"It was just a dream," Cal spoke softly, averting his eyes from his brother, who was now sobbing silently.

"We're at Auntie Jean's, aren't we?" Will said, pulling himself together as he recognised the floral wallpaper.

"Yes, we've been here for nearly three days."

"Huh?" Will tried to sit up again, but it was too much for him and he laid his head back onto the pillow again. "I feel so weak."

"Don't worry, everything's fine. She's been great. Rather taken to Bart, too."

Over the ensuing days, Cal nursed him back to health with bowls of soup or baked beans on toast and seemingly endless cups of over-sugared tea. When he was finally strong enough to stand, he tried walking and wobbled uncertainly into the kitchen. Dirty plates lay in the sink and the bin overflowed with empty tins and torn microwave ready boxes. It was a scene of such carnage that he barely registered the plastic tops of the taps, melted and brown, and the flame blackened tiles behind them. He grimaced and turned back into the hall, where he heard Auntie Jean's gruff voice. Its tones were vaguely comforting, reminding him of the Christmases when she would come to stay, chatting to his mother for hours on end.

He stood outside the door and listened, Auntie Jean's knitting needles rattling furiously as she spoke.

" ... soon as I laid eyes on 'im, I warned 'er ... I did you know ... you don't want to be getting 'itched to some over-educated layabout ... I mean, I ask you, what good's an archaeologist when there's bills to pay ... and you need to keep a roof over your 'ead?"

Will poked one eye around the corner as Auntie Jean's needles stopped their metronomic clicking and she took a sip from a tumbler. The cat was looking adoringly at Auntie Jean, who looked back at him with an affectionate, almost loving smile. Will had never seen this side of her before – he knew he should be saying something to announce his presence, but somehow he couldn't bring himself to break the moment.

"I must say it's nice to 'ave a companion again. I mean after my little Sophie passed away … she was a dog and I know you don't like them very much … but at least she was there for me … I never 'ad much time for men – can't trust them … I've 'ad my moments, mind … I did, you know."

She held up her knitting in front of her, a garishly coloured pair of trousers, which Bartleby sniffed curiously. "Nearly done. I'll just cast off and you can try them on for size, my lovely." She leant over and tickled Bartleby under the chin. He lifted his head and, closing his eyes, began to purr with the amplitude of a small engine.

Will had turned to make his way back to the bedroom and was resting against the wall in the hallway when there was a crash behind him. Cal was standing just inside the front door, two bags of shopping dropped in front of him. He had a scarf wrapped around his mouth and was wearing Mrs Burrows' sunglasses. He looked like the invisible man.

"I can't take much more of this," he said, squatting down to retrieve the groceries. Bartleby padded out from the sitting room, followed by Auntie Jean, a cigarette perched on her lip. The cat was wearing her knitted trousers and a mohair cardigan, both a strident mix of blues and reds. To top it off was a multi-coloured balaclava from which his scabby ears stuck comically. The cat looked like the survivor of an explosion in an Oxfam shop. Cal glanced at the outlandish figure before him, taking in the shocking display of colours, but didn't comment. He appeared to be in the depths of despondency.

"This place is full of hatred – you smell it everywhere." He shook his head slowly.

"Oh, it is that, love," Auntie Jean said quietly. "Always 'as been."

"Topsoil isn't what I expected it'd be," Cal said. He thought for a moment. "I want to go home … but I can't, can I?"

Will stared back as he searched for something to console his brother, some form of words to quell the boy's anxiety, but he was unable to say anything.

"Will'll take you to the station, won't you, Will? But you must come again … and bring kitty with you." Auntie Jean's voice was choked as she touched Bartleby tenderly on the head. Then she turned and shuffled into the kitchen, where they could hear her trying to stifle her sobs as she rattled a bottle against a glass.

Over the next days, they planned and planned. Will felt himself growing stronger as he recovered from the illness, his lungs clearing and his breathing returning to normal. They went on shopping expeditions. An army surplus shop yielded gas masks, climbing rope and a water bottle for each of them. He also bought some old camera flash units in a pawn shop and, as it was the week after Guy Fawkes' night, several large boxes of remaindered fireworks. He wanted to make sure they were ready for any eventuality, and anything that gave off a bright light might come in useful. They stocked up on food, choosing lightweight but high-energy provisions so as not to weigh themselves down. After the kindness she had shown them, Will felt bad that he was dipping into his aunt's grocery money to pay for it all, but he didn't have any alternative.

They waited until lunchtime to don their now clean Colonists' clothes and said their goodbyes to Auntie Jean, who gave Bartleby a tearful cuddle. They took the bus into central London and then walked the rest of the way to the river entrance.

CHAPTER THIRTY-FOUR

Cal was still pressing a handkerchief to his face and muttering about the "foul gases" as they left Blackfriars Bridge and took the steps down to the embankment. Everything looked so different in the daylight that, for a moment, Will had doubts that they were in the right place.

With people bustling all about them, they peered down and saw the brown water lapping lazily against the wall below.

"Looks deep," Cal said. "Why's it like that?"

"Duh!" Will groaned, thumping his palm against his forehead. "The tide! I didn't think of the tide. We'll just have to wait for it to go out."

"How long will that be?"

Will shrugged and glanced at his watch. "Could be hours."

There was no alternative but to kill time by pacing the backstreets around Tate Modern and, trying not to attract too much attention, return to the bank every half-hour to check the water. By lunchtime, they could see the gravel breaking through it.

Will couldn't wait any longer. "Right, here we go," he announced.

They were in full sight of any passers-by, many of whom were on their lunch breaks. They clambered over the wall onto the stone steps, which were still submerged at the bottom, but hardly anyone took any notice, let alone stopped to watch the motley-looking trio, eccentrically dressed and laden with rucksacks. Then one old man in a woolly hat and scarf began shouting "Ruddy kids!" and shaking his fist at them. "You'll bloody drown yourselves!" Other people gathered to watch them as he grew more and more frantic and vociferous with his warnings.

At the bottom of the steps, the water splashed up around their legs as they galloped with all their might along the partially submerged foreshore, only letting up when they were out of sight under the jetty. Without a moment's hesitation, Cal and Bartleby clambered into the mouth of the drainage tunnel.

Will paused for a moment before following. He took a last lingering look at the pale grey sky through the gaps in the planking and breathed deeply, savouring the air despite the taint of rotting weed and the smell of the river.

Now he'd recovered his strength again, Will felt like a completely different person – he was prepared for whatever lay ahead of them. As if the fever had purged him of any doubts or weaknesses, he was feeling the resigned assurance of the seasoned adventurer.

As he looked at the slow-moving river, he experienced the deepest pang of loss and melancholy, aware he might never see this place again. He shook himself from his thoughts and entered the tunnel, where Cal was waiting for him, impatient to get going. With a single glance, Will could read conflicting emotions in his brother's face; although the anxiety was plain to see, there was also a hint of something else, a deep sense of relief brought about by the imminent return to the underworld. It was his natural habitat, after all. Although circumstances had forced him to do it, Will reflected what a terrible mistake it had been to bring Cal with him to the surface. If Cal was to adjust to Topsoil life, he would need time – and that was one luxury they didn't have. Like it or not, Will's destiny lay in rescuing Chester and finding his father. And Cal's destiny was inextricably linked with his.

It irked Will that he'd lost so many days to the fever – he had no idea if he was too late to save Chester. Had he already been exiled to the deeps, or come to some unimaginable end at the hands of the Styx? Whatever the truth might be, he had to find out. He had to go on believing Chester was still alive; he had to go back. He could never live with that hanging over him.

They found the vertical shaft and Will reluctantly lowered himself into the chill water below it as Cal and Bartleby watched on. Trailing a rope behind him, Cal climbed up on Will's shoulders to reach into the shaft, then shimmied up it. When his brother had reached the top, Will knotted the other end of the rope around Bartleby's chest and the cat was hauled up. This proved to be completely unnecessary as, once in the shaft, he used his sinewy legs to propel himself up the remaining section with startling agility. The rope was dropped for Will, who then hauled himself into the shadows. Once at the top, he jumped up and down as he tried to shake the water off and warm himself up.

Then they slid down the convex ramp on the seats of their pants, landing with a thump on the ledge that marked the beginning of the rough stairs. Before proceeding, they carefully removed Bartleby's knitted clothes and folded them into a neat pile and left them on a ledge. Will hated having to ditch the clothes Auntie Jean had laboured on so lovingly, but they couldn't afford to carry dead weight. They donned their gas masks, looked at each other for a moment, nodded an acknowledgment, and began the long descent.

The going was arduous at first, the stairs perilous from the constant seepage. With Cal taking the lead, Will found that he had very little memory of the route from their previous passage through, and put this down to his mysterious illness.

Further down, the carpet of black algae started. In what seemed like no time at all, they had reached the opening to the cavern wall of the Eternal City.

"What the hell is this?" Cal exhaled as they walked out onto the top of the huge flight of steps.

"That's what I believe they called a real pea-souper," Will said quietly, his glass eyepieces reflecting the pale green glow.

From their vantage point high above the city, they looked down upon what appeared to be the undulating surface of a huge opaline lake. The heavy mist covered the entire scene, suffused through with the eerie light, like a radioactive cloud. It was rather daunting to think that the mass of the huge city lay obscured beneath this opaque blanket. The boys stopped and glanced some 30 to 40 feet down below them, where they could see the dark form of the stairway dissolve and vanish from view. Will automatically scrabbled in his pockets for the compass.

"This is going to make life difficult," he said, frowning with concern behind his mask.

"Why?" Cal retorted. His eyes crinkled in the eyepieces as a broad smile spread across his face. "They won't be able to see us, will they?"

But Will's demeanour remained grim. "That's true, but we won't see them either."

Cal held Bartleby still while Will tied a rope lead around his neck. Then they descended slowly into the surface of the fog, like deep-sea divers sinking beneath the waves. Their visibility was reduced to just a couple of feet, and they couldn't even see their boots, finding it necessary to feel for the edge of each step before venturing to the next.

"Hold onto my rucksack," Will whispered, "and don't let go of the cat."

They reached the bottom of the stairway without incident and, at the start of the mudflats, they repeated the black weed ritual, wiping the stinking goo all over each other, this time to mask the Topsoil smells of London.

Traversing the marshland perimeter, they eventually bumped into the city wall and followed it round. Visibility was not improving and it took them an age to find a way in.

"An archway," Will whispered, stopping so suddenly that his brother nearly fell over him. The ancient structure briefly coalesced before them and then the fog thickened again, obscuring the vision.

"Oh good," Cal replied, without an ounce of enthusiasm.

Once inside the city walls, they had to grope their way through the streets, keeping close to each other so they wouldn't become separated. The fog was almost tangible, sucking and rolling like sheets in the wind, and sometimes parting to allow them the briefest hint of a wall, a stretch of water-sodden ground or glistening cobbles.

The way the fog twisted and played with their senses, it made everything feel so removed and yet, at the same time, so intimate. The squelch of their boots on the black algae and their laboured breathing through the masks rebounded back at them – the fog seemed to amplify their every movement and make them sound unnervingly loud.

Cal gripped Will's arm, and they stopped still and held their breaths. They heard other noises all about them, vague and indistinct. As they listened, Will could have sworn he caught a scratchy whispering, so close that he flinched. He pulled Cal back a couple of steps, certain they had bumped headlong into the Styx Division. However, Cal was sure he hadn't heard anything, so after a while they nervously resumed their journey.

Then, from the distance, came the blood-curdling baying of a dog – there was no question this time. They shuddered with the certainty, and Cal immediately tightened his grip on Bartleby's lead. They hung onto the hope that it really was as far away as it sounded. They moved slowly, their hearts pounding as Will referred to Tam's map in an attempt to fix their position, and repeatedly checked his compass with his shaking hands. In truth, he didn't know whether he could rely on it, and the visibility was so poor, he had only the roughest idea where they were. For all he knew, the compass could be getting thrown off and they could be wandering in circles. Eventually, he called a halt and they huddled down in the lea of a crumbling wall. In low whispers, they debated what to do next.

"If we start running, it won't matter if we meet a patrol. We can lose them in this," Cal said, his eyes darting left and right under the moisture-spotted lenses of his gas mask.

"Yeah, right," Will replied. "You think we could outrun a stalker? We don't have a clue where we are and if we have to leg it, we'll probably hit a dead end or something …"

"But once we're in the Labyrynth, they'll never catch us," Cal insisted.

"But we've got to get there first, and it's a bloody long way."

Will couldn't believe his brother's absurd suggestion. It suddenly dawned on him that a couple of months ago, he might have been the one advocating the crazy dash through the streets and lanes of the city. Somehow, imperceptibly, he'd changed. Now he was the sober one and Cal was the reckless, headstrong youngster, chock-full of madcap confidence and willing to risk all.

The angry whispered exchange continued, growing more and more heated, until Cal finally relented. It was to be the softly, softly approach; they would inch their way to the far perimeter of the city, keeping the sounds of their footsteps to a minimum and melting into the fog if anyone or anything came close.

As they stepped over pieces of rubble, Bartleby's head was jerking in all directions, sniffing the air and the ground, when, all of a sudden, he stopped and refused to move. Despite Cal's efforts to pull on the lead, he lowered his body as if he were hunting something, his wide head close to the ground and his skeletal tail sticking straight out behind him, his ears pointing and twitching like radar dishes.

"Where are they?" Cal whispered frantically to Will. He didn't answer, but instead reached into the side pockets of Cal's rucksack and yanked out two large fireworks as he readied Auntie Jean's little plastic disposable lighter.

"Come on, Bart," Cal was whispering into the cat's ear as he knelt beside him, "It's okay."

What little hair Bartleby had was bristling now. Cal managed to draw the cat around and, as if walking on eggshells, they tiptoed in the opposite direction, Will at the rear with the fireworks ready in his hands.

They slunk along the wall, Cal feeling the coarse masonry with his hands like some incomprehensible Braille. They followed it around a corner, Will walking backwards as he checked behind them. Seeing nothing but the forbidding clouds, and coming to the conclusion it was futile to try to rely on sight in these conditions, he spun about only to blunder into a granite plinth. He recoiled in shock as the leering face of a huge marble head reared out of the parted mist. Laughing at himself, he warily stepped around it and found his brother waiting only three feet ahead, but nevertheless invisible in the fog.

They had gone about 20 paces when the fog mysteriously folded back to reveal a length of cobbled street before them. Will wiped the moisture from his eyepieces and let his gaze ride with the retreating margins of the fog. Bit by bit, the edges of the street and the façades of some of the nearest buildings came into view. They both felt a tangible flood of relief as their immediate surroundings were tantalisingly revealed for the first time since they had entered the city.

Then their blood turned cold.

There, not 30 feet away, only too real and horribly clear, they saw them. A patrol of eight Styx were fanned out across the

street. They stood motionless as predators, their round goggles watching the boys as they dumbly looked back.

They were like spectres from some future nightmare in their grey-green striped long coats, strange skullcaps and sinister breathing masks. One held a ferocious-looking stalker on a thick leather strap – it was pulling against its collar, its tongue lolling obscenely out of the side of its monstrous maw. It sniffed excitedly and immediately snapped its head in the boys' direction. The black pebbles of its beady eyes had sized them up in an instant. With a deep, rumbling snarl, it pulled back its lips to reveal huge yellowing teeth dripping with excited saliva. Its lead slackened as it crouched down, ready to pounce at them.

But nobody made a move. As if time itself had stopped, the two groups merely stood and stared at each other, in horrible, mute anticipation.

Something snapped in Will's head. He screamed and spun Cal around, knocking him from his shocked inertia. Then they were running, flying back into the fog, their legs pumping frantically. They ran and ran, unable to tell how much ground they were covering in the shrouds of mist. Behind them came the savage barking of the stalker and the crackling shouts of the Styx.

Neither boy had a clue where they were heading, just as long as they cleared the area. They didn't have time to think – their minds blotted out with blind panic.

Then Will came to his senses. He yelled at Cal to keep going as he slowed to light the blue touch paper on a huge Roman candle. Not really certain if he'd lit it or not, he quickly propped it against a chunk of masonry, pointing in the direction of their pursuers.

He ran on a few yards and stopped again. He flicked the lighter, but this time the flame refused to come. Swearing, he struck it desperately, again and again. Nothing, just sparks. He shook it like he'd seen the Greys do so often at school. He took a deep breath and once again spun the tiny flint wheel. Yes! The flame was small but enough to ignite the fuse of the firework, an air-bomb battery. By now the snarling and barking and voices were closing around him. He lost his nerve and simply slung the firework to the ground.

"Will, Will!" he heard ahead. He homed in on his brother's shouts and, running at full pelt, almost bowled him over. Then they sprinted away furiously as the first firework screamed out in all directions. Two deafening thunderclaps erupted behind them and bright primary colours bled through the texture of the fog.

"Keep going," Will hissed at Cal, who had collided with a wall rather painfully. "Come on, this way!" he said pulling his brother by the arm, not giving him any time to dwell on his injury.

The fireworks continued to scream, exploding fireballs of light high into the cavern, or in low arcs that ended in the city itself, momentarily silhouetting the buildings like the scenery in a shadowplay. Each iridescent streak ended in a dazzling flash and cannon shot explosion, echoing and rumbling through the city like a raging storm.

Every so often, Will stopped to light another firework using his spare lighter, picking out Roman candles, air bombs or rockets, all of which he positioned on pieces of masonry or threw indiscriminately in the hope of confusing the patrol as to their position. The Styx, if they were still following, would be bearing the brunt of this attack, and Will knew, at the very least, that the lights and smell of the smoke would be disorienting to them and, in particular, the stalker.

As the last of the fireworks went off in a cavalcade of light and sound, Will hoped and prayed he'd bought them enough time to reach the Labyrynth. They had slowed to a jog to allow themselves to catch their breaths, eventually stopping to listen for any sign of their pursuers, but there was nothing now. Will sat down on a wide step of a building that could have been a temple and took out his map and compass while Cal kept watch. After a few seconds, Will realised that it was a waste of time.

"I've no idea," he admitted, tucking the map away.

"We could be anywhere," Cal agreed.

Will stood up, looking left and right. "I say we carry on in the same direction."

Cal nodded. "What if we end up right back where we started?"

"We've got to keep moving," Will shrugged and set off.

Once again the silence crowded in on them and the mysterious shapes and shadows appeared and softened, as if the buildings were pulling in and out of focus in this invisible city. They'd made tortuously slow progress through a succession of streets when Cal pulled them up.

"I think it's clearing a little, you know," he whispered, although the visibility was still down to about 10 feet in any direction.

"Well, that's something," Will replied.

Once again Bartleby froze and crouched down low, hissing. The boys stopped in response, their eyes feverishly searching the milky air around them as the margins of the fog rolled back before them.

There, not 20 feet away, a dark, shadowy form was hunched menacingly. From it came a low, guttural growl.

"A stalker!" Cal gulped. Their hearts stopped with the awful realisation. Like an infernal steam engine, the black hound pounded at them, condensation spewing from its flaring nostrils.

As Will shoved Cal out of its path, it soared through the air and slammed heavily into his chest. Its club-like paws knocked Will flat, his head thwacking the algae-covered ground with a hard slap. Half stunned, Will reactively grasped the monster's throat with both hands. He found its thick collar and hung onto it, struggling to hold the brute away from his face.

But it was just too strong. Its jaws snapped at his mask, then caught onto it and bit down. He heard the squeal of its fangs tightening on the rubber as the mask was crushed against his face in a vice-like grip, and then the pop as one of the eyepieces shattered. He smelt the putrid breath of the animal, like warm, sour meat, and felt the necklaces of its copious saliva wet his neck. It wrenched and twisted at the mask, straining at the straps behind Will's head.

Praying the mask would stay in place, and knowing if it didn't his face would be next, Will tried with all his might to turn his head away. The stalker's jaws slid off the wet rubber and it pulled back slightly before lunging again. Still hanging onto its collar for all he was worth, Will managed to hold the dog away from his face, his arms at the limit of their strength as the collar cut into his fingers. He turned away time and time again to escape the snapping teeth, like the jaws of a powerful mantrap clapping shut.

Then the animal contorted and twisted its body. One of Will's hands slipped off the collar as the animal sought a more rewarding target. It latched onto Will's forearm and bit down. Will cried with pain, his left hand involuntarily letting go of the heavy collar. The animal instantly scrabbled over him and sank its incisors into his shoulder. Amidst the growling and biting, he heard the cloth of his jacket ripping as the huge teeth, like rows of daggers, penetrated and tore into his flesh. Will screamed again as the animal shook its head, snarling loudly. He was helpless, a rag doll pulled this way and that. With his free arm, he punched weakly at the animal's flanks and head, but to no avail.

Suddenly the dog let go and reared up over him, its huge weight still pinning him down. As its frenzied eyes fixed on his, he could see its slathering jaws just inches from his face, strings of its drool dripping into his eyepieces. From the side, Cal was pummelling and kicking at it but the beast simply ignored him. Will tried desperately to roll over and shake it off, but it was hopeless. He knew he was no match for this hellish, unstoppable beast that seemed to be made from huge slabs of muscle, as hard and unyielding as rock.

"Go!" he screamed at Cal. "Get away!"

Then a fleshy bolt of grey flew headlong at the dog. It catapulted at the stalker's head, claws extended like cutthroat razors.

For a split second, the cat seemed to be poised in mid-air above the stalker's head. Then they heard the wet slicing of flesh as Bartleby's teeth found their mark. Like a dark fountain, blood weltered over Will from a livid gash where the dog's ear had been. It let out a low-pitched yelp and immediately bucked and leapt off Will, Bartleby still clamped to its head and neck, blitzing it with bites and savage flesh-tearing slashes with his raking back legs.

"Get up! Get up!" Cal was shouting, as he pulled Will to his feet.

The boys ran to a safe distance, but were compelled to stop and watch. They couldn't leave – they were transfixed by the deadly battle as the cat and dog writhed in mortal combat, their shapes melting together until they became an indistinguishable whirlwind of grey and red punctuated by flashing teeth and claws.

"We can't stay here," Will shouted. He could hear the shouts of the approaching patrol, which was quickly homing in on the commotion.

"Bart, leave it! Come!"

"The Styx," Will shook his brother, "We have to go!" Cal reluctantly moved off, peering back to see if his cat was following though the mist.

But there was no sign of Bartleby, only the distant hisses and yelps and screeches.

Shouts and footfalls were now coming from all over. Will was appalled to find he'd lost the map when the stalker attacked him. He was shaking with shock and his arm and shoulder throbbed dully with pain. Blood was running down his arm and over the back of his hand in small rivulets until it dripped from the ends of his trembling fingertips.

With no means of telling where they were and no visible features to guide them, he was petrified they might be running straight back into the arms of the Styx.

Out of breath, the boys hastily agreed on a direction, hoping against hope it would take them out of the city into the marshy perimeter. Once there, they would make their way around the edge and try to find the mouth of the Labyrynth. Will figured they could always decamp Topsoil again, if the worst came to the worst.

The patrol seemed to be closing in and the boys were

running at full speed when they blundered headlong into a wall at the end of a street. The terrible thought struck both of them at the same time – they had inadvertently strayed down a cul-de-sac. They frantically followed the wall until they found an archway with the keystone missing at the top. Will looked at Cal with relief.

"That was close."

Cal merely nodded, panting heavily. They peered briefly behind them before passing through the ruined archway.

With lightning speed, strong hands grabbed them roughly from either side of the opening, yanking them off their feet.

CHAPTER THIRTY-FIVE

Using his good arm, Will lashed out with all his strength, punching at his assailant's head. His knuckles grazed ineffectually off a canvas hood. The man swore sharply as Will followed with another blow, but his fist was caught and trapped in the iron grip of a huge hand, forcing him back effortlessly until he was pinioned against the wall.

"That's enough!" the hooded man hissed. "Shhh!"

Cal was suddenly there, pushing in between Will and his assailant, throwing his arms around the hooded figure.

"Uncle Tam! How did you know we'd be …" Cal asked.

"We've been keeping an eye out since the escape got rumbled," their uncle cut in.

"Yes, but how did you know?" Cal asked again.

"We just followed the light and the noise. Who else but you lot would use those bloody fool pyrotechnics? They probably heard it Topsoil, let alone in the Colony."

"It was Will's idea," Cal replied. "It sort of worked."

"Sort of," Tam said, looking with concern at Will, who was still leaning against the wall, the rubber of his mask scored with deep gouges and one of his eyepieces shattered to the point that it was useless. "You okay, Will?"

"I think so," he muttered, holding his bloodstained shoulder.

"I knew you'd not be able to rest with Chester still here."

"Is he all right?" Will asked, perking up at the mention of his friend's name.

"He's alive at least, for the time being – I'll tell you all later, but now, Imago, we'd better make ourselves scarce."

Imago's massive form slipped into sight with unexpected fleetness, his baggy mask twisting furtively this way and that, like a partially deflated balloon caught in the wind as he scrutinised the murky shadows. Then he was off and Will and Cal had a job to keep up. Their flight now turned into a nerve racking game of *Follow My Leader* with Imago's shadow to pilot them through the miasma and the unseen obstacles while Tam brought up the rear. But the boys were so relieved to be back under Tam's wing that they almost forgot their predicament.

Imago cupped a light orb in his hand, opening it a little to help the boys when there was a difficult feature to negotiate, such as a small doorway or a hole in the floor. They jogged through a series of flooded basements and courtyards, and slid in the mud on the cracked marble floors of abandoned rooms and halls strewn with broken masonry. Then they left the fog behind as they entered a circular building, hurtling up dry stone stairs and racing along corridors with flaking murals at a staggering pace. They seemed to be climbing higher, until suddenly they were out into the open again and traversing fractured stone walkways that were missing most of their balustrades. Will was able to look down from the giddying heights and catch glimpses of the city below between the meshing clouds. Some of these walkways were so narrow, Will feared that if he hesitated for a second and lost his impetus, he might plunge to his death in the foggy soup masking the sheer drops on either side. But Imago didn't waver for an instant; his unwieldy form drove relentlessly ahead, leaving little eddies of fog in its wake.

They hared down several staircases and entered a large room echoing with the sound of gurgling water, where Imago came to a halt. He appeared to be listening for something.

"Where's Bartleby?" Tam whispered to Cal as they waited.

"He saved us from a stalker," Cal said wretchedly, and shook his head. "He's dead."

Tam put his arm around Cal and hugged him. "He was a prince amongst animals," he said. He patted Cal on the back consolingly and moved forward to confer with Imago in hushed tones. "What time do you reckon it is?"

"Coming up to four bells," Imago's voice was calm and unhurried.

"Think we should lie low for a while?"

"No," Imago said emphatically. "They've caused quite a stir, we'd better move on. The Division know the boys are still here somewhere, and this place'll be lousy with patrols in no time at all."

"We keep going then," Tam concurred.

The four of them filed out of the room and travelled along a colonnade until Imago heaved himself over a low wall and slid down a short, slimy bank into a deep ditch. As the boys followed him, the stagnant water came up to their thighs and thick fronds of glutinous black weed hampered their movements. They waded laboriously through, lethargic bubbles rising up and clumping together on the surface. Even though they were wearing masks, the putrid stench of long dead vegetation caught in their throats. The ditch ran into an underground channel and they were plunged into darkness. Their splashes echoed about them and, after what felt like an eternity, they came to the end of the channel and out into the open again. Imago held his hand up for them to stop and scuttled up the side, squelching off into the fog.

"This is a risky bit," Tam whispered to them. "It's open ground. Keep your wits about you and stay close."

Before long, Imago returned and beckoned to them. They clambered out of the water. With sodden boots and trousers, they crossed the boggy ground, the city finally behind them. Will's spirits leapt as he spotted the openings in the cavern wall ahead, and knew they had reached a way back into the Labyrynth. *They'd made it.*

"Macaulay!" a harsh, thin voice called out.

Tam wheeled around as they all stopped dead in their tracks. The fog was patchier here on the exposed ground, and through the thinning wisps they saw a lone figure. It was a single Styx. He stood there, tall and arrogant, with his arms crossed over his narrow chest.

"Well … well … well, funny how rats always use the same runs …" he shouted.

"Crawfly," Tam replied coolly as he pushed Cal and Will towards Imago.

" … leaving their grease and stinking spoor on the sides. I knew I'd get you one day; it was just a matter of time." The Crawfly uncrossed his arms and then snapped them like whips. Will's heart missed a beat as he saw two shining blades appear in the Styx's hands. Curved and about six inches long, they looked like small scythes.

"You've been a thorn in my side for far too long," the Crawfly said.

Will looked at Tam, and was surprised to see he was already armed with a brutal looking machete he seemed to have conjured out of nowhere.

"I should have done this a long time ago," Tam said to Imago and the boys. They could see the grim look of determination in his eyes. He turned in the direction of the Crawfly and began to advance. "Get going you lot, I'll catch you up," he called back to them.

But the saturnine figure, with swathes of fog curling about it, didn't give an inch. Brandishing the scythes with an expert flourish and crouching a little, it had the appearance of something horribly unnatural.

"This isn't right. He's too bloody confident," Imago muttered. "We should make ourselves scarce." He herded the boys back protectively to one of the openings in the Labyrynth as Tam closed in on the Crawfly.

"Oh no … no …" Imago drew in his breath.

Will and Cal turned, searching for the source of his alarm. A mass of Styx had appeared through the mists and were spreading out in a wide arc. But the Crawfly held up one glinting scythe and they came to an abrupt halt a little distance behind him, swaying and fidgeting impatiently, their blades hanging loosely at their sides in slack anticipation. Tam stopped, pausing for a moment as if he was weighing the odds. Then he drew himself up defiantly and tore off his hood. He took a large breath, filling his lungs with the foul air. In reply, the Crawfly yanked off his goggles and breathing apparatus, dropping them at his feet and kicking them aside. As they faced each other like opposing champions, Will couldn't be sure but he thought he detected a sardonic smile on the thin, white face.

The boys hardly dared breathe. It had grown so deathly quiet in that place, as if all the sound had been sucked from the world.

The Crawfly made the first move, his arms whipping over each other as he lunged forwards. Tam jerked back to avoid the barrage of steel and, stepping to the side, brought up his machete in a defensive move. The two men's blades met and scraped off each other in a shrill metallic scream.

With incedible dexterity, the Crawfly spun about as if performing some ritual dance, whirling close to Tam and away again, slashing and slashing again with his twin blades. With thrusts and parries the two opponents attacked and defended and attacked in turn. Cal and Will hardly dared blink. It was all unfolding so quickly, they could scarcely keep up with the action. There was another confusion of silver and grey, and the clang of blades. Then, in the blink of an eye, the two men were so close they could have embraced, as the razor sharp edges of their weapons ground coldly against each other. Almost as quickly, they fell back, breathing heavily. Each man's eyes remained fixed on the other's, but Tam seemed to be listing slightly as he clutched his side.

"This is bad," Imago said under his breath.

Will saw it too. Between Tam's fingers and down his jacket seeped dark ribbons of liquid that looked more like harmless black ink under the green light of the city. He was wounded and bleeding badly. He drew himself slowly up and, apparently recovering, in a flash had swung his machete at the Crawfly, who sidestepped effortlessly and swiped a high riposte. Tam flinched and staggered back. Imago and the boys saw the patch of blackness now spreading down his left cheek and knew he'd been cut again.

"Oh my God," Imago said quietly, holding onto the boys' collars so tightly that Will could feel his arms tensing as the fight resumed.

Tam attacked yet again, the Crawfly whirling backwards and forwards, this way and that, in his fluid and stylised dance. Tam's swipes and thrusts were decisive and skilful, but the Crawfly was too fast, the machete blade meeting with nothing but thin air. As Tam was twisting around to face his elusive opponent, he lost his footing. Trying to straighten up, his boots were slipping hopelessly. He was off balance, in a vulnerable position. The Crawfly couldn't miss this opportunity. He'd found his chance and lunged at Tam's exposed flank.

But Tam was ready. He'd been waiting for this moment. He ducked forwards and rose inside the Crawfly's guard, bringing the machete up in a flash, so smartly that Will missed the devastating slash to the Crawfly's throat.

The air between the two combatants filled with dark spume as the Crawfly reeled back. The Styx let both of his scythes tumble to the ground. They heard the bloody, hissing gurgle as he clutched his severed windpipe.

Like a matador delivering the killing blow, Tam suddenly stepped forward, using both his hands for the thrust. The blade sank up to the hilt in the Crawfly's chest. He let out a bubbling hiss and grabbed Tam's shoulders with his blood-drenched hands to steady himself. He looked down with sheer disbelief at the rough wooden handle protruding from his sternum, then raised his head. For a moment they stood there, absolutely motionless like two statues in a tragic tableau, staring at each other in silent recognition.

Then Tam braced one foot against the Crawfly and wrenched out his machete. The Styx teetered on the spot, like a puppet suspended by unseen wires, his mouth shaping empty, breathless curses.

They watched as the mortally wounded man spluttered a last choking snarl at Tam and, tottering backwards, collapsed to the ground in a lifeless heap. Excited whispers passed down the lines of Styx, who seemed for the moment to be paralysed by uncertainty, unsure what they should do next.

Tam wasted no time in such hesitation. In the blink of an eye, he had sprinted back to join Imago and the boys, holding his injured side and grimacing with the pain. This in turn mobilised the Styx, who scuttled forward to form a ring around the body of their fallen leader.

Tam was already leading Imago and the boys down a Labyrynth passage. They had hardly gone any distance when he lurched to one side and slumped against the wall. He was breathing hard and sweat was pouring from him. It streamed down his face, mingling with the blood from his lacerations and dripping off his bristly chin onto his chest.

"I'll hold them off," he panted, looking back at the tunnel opening. "It'll buy you some time."

"No, I'll do it," Imago said. "You're wounded."

"I'm finished anyway," Tam said.

Imago saw the inkiness welling out of the gaping flap on Tam's chest and they locked eyes. As Imago handed him another machete, it was clear the decision had been made.

"Please come with us," Cal begged in a choked voice, knowing full well what it meant for his uncle.

"Then we'd all lose," Tam said, smiling wanly and hugging Cal with one arm. He reached into his shirt and yanked something from around his neck and pressed it into Will's hand. It was a smooth rubbed pendant with a symbol carved into it.

"Take this," Tam said quickly. "It might come in useful where you're going." He let go of Cal and took a step away, but then grabbed Will, his eyes still on Cal. "And look out for him, won't you, Will?"

Will was about to reply when Cal began frantically shouting.

"Uncle Tam … Come … Come with us …"

"Get them away, Imago." Tam turned and strode back

towards the mouth of the tunnel, which already framed the full horror of the approaching Styx army.

Imago was forced to pull Cal along by the arm as he sobbed behind his mask, his shoulders heaving uncontrollably. Kicking the sand up with their boots as they sped along the tunnel, they repeatedly glanced back at Tam until a bend in the passage began to obscure their view of him. Despite the impending threat of their pursuers, even Imago paused for a moment for a last look at the big man, his outline dark against the green of the city as he held the two machetes in readiness at his sides.

Imago swallowed hard and the boys heard him say something under his mask. Then he pushed them along and Tam was lost from view. But burnt into their retinas was that final glimpse, that final picture of Tam standing proud and defiant in the face of the approaching tide. A single figure before a bristling field of drawn scythes.

Even as they fled, they could hear his urgent, shouted curses and the clash of blades, which grew fainter and fainter with every turn of the tunnel.

CHAPTER THIRTY-SIX

Will held his throbbing shoulder as they ran, his arm hanging uselessly by his side. He had no idea how many miles they'd travelled when, at the end of a long gallery, Imago finally slowed the pace to allow them to catch their breaths. The width of the tunnels meant they could have walked side by side, but instead they chose to remain in single file – it gave them some solitude, some privacy. Even though they hadn't exchanged a single word since they'd left Tam behind in the city, each knew what the others were thinking in the wretched silence that hung over them. As they plodded mechanically along, Cal began his muffled weeping again, and Will thought how much like a funeral procession it felt.

They took innumerable turns down lefts and rights, every new stretch of tunnel as identical and unremarkable as the last. Imago didn't once refer to a map, but seemed to know precisely where they were going, muttering to himself every so often, as if reciting a poem. It was a shock when he drew to a halt in front of a small crawlhole and then dropped onto his knees. And it was with some considerable difficulty, and much grunting and wriggling, that he managed to squeeze himself through it.

The chamber was about 20 feet across and almost perfectly bell-shaped, with rough walls the texture of carborundum. A number of small stalactites hung down in the middle of the chamber directly over some sort of trapdoor, a circle of dusty metal plate set into the centre of the floor. As they made their way around it, their boots crunched on clusters of cave pearls.

These smooth spheres varied from the size of peas to large marbles and were the colour of old butterbeans. Will had only ever seen them in his father's text books, and immediately cast around to see if there were signs of moisture or running water, which would have been necessary for their formation. But the floor and walls appeared to be as dry and arid as the rest of the Labyrynth. And the only way in or out that Will could see was the crawlhole they'd just come through. He assumed that this place was a safe haven for them to rest up for a while.

Imago removed his mask and they followed suit. "All right, let's have a look at that arm," he said quietly to Will as Cal stumbled wearily to the far side of the chamber and slid down against the wall with his head slumped forward onto his chest.

"It's nothing, really," Will replied. Not only did he want to be left alone, but he also feared just how severe his injuries might be.

"Come on," Imago said firmly. "You'll get an infection. We need to dress it."

Will exhaled loudly as he slipped his rucksack off and then slowly removed his jacket. The material of his shirt was glued to the wounds by clots and Imago had to work it free little by little, starting at the top and gently peeling it away. Will watched on queasily, wincing as several of the damp scabs were pulled off and he saw fresh blood well out and run over his already bloodstained arm.

"Nasty," Imago said, "but it could have been worse. Much, much worse …" Will glanced at Imago's unsmiling face as he added, " … the stalkers usually go for more vulnerable body parts."

Will's forearm had livid welts and two semicircles of puncture wounds on both sides, but there was little or no bleeding from these now. He inspected the redness on his chest and abdomen, then felt his ribs, which hurt slightly if he inhaled deeply. No real damage there, either. But his shoulder was a different matter altogether. The teeth had sunk deeper, and the flesh had been badly mauled by the shaking of the stalker's head. In places, it was so raw and battered, it looked as if he'd been caught by a shotgun blast.

"Ohhh," Will moaned, turning his head away quickly as the blood seeped down his arm. "It looks awful."

"Don't worry, it looks worse than it is," Imago said reassuringly as he set about cleaning around the wounds. "This will sting," he said, pouring a clear liquid from a silver flask onto a piece of lint. When he'd finished, he pushed the flap of his coat open and reached inside to unbutton one of the many pouches on his belt. He pulled out a bag of what looked like pipe tobacco and proceeded to sprinkle it over Will's wounds, particularly concentrating it on the lacerations to his shoulder. The small dry fibres stuck to the wounds, absorbing the blood. "This might hurt a little," he warned as he packed more of the material on top and patted it down until it formed a thick mat.

"What's that?" Will asked, daring to look at his shoulder again.

"Shredded rhizomes."

"Shredded what?" Will said, with alarm in his eyes.

"I'm the son of an apothecary. I was taught to use these when I was no older than you," Imago said calmly, and Will relaxed again. "There's an antiseptic and something to stop the bleeding and deaden the nerves – all good stuff for a poultice." He reached into another pouch and pulled out a grey roll of material that he began to unwind. He bound this expertly around Will's shoulder and arm and, tying the ends securely, sat back to admire his handiwork.

"How's that feel?"

"Better," Will lied.

"You'll need to change the dressing every once in a while – you can take some of this with you."

"What do you mean, *with me*? Where are we going?" Will asked, but Imago shook his head.

"All in good time. We should eat first. Get yourself over here, Cal."

Cal wandered over obediently as Imago sat down with his legs stretched out in front of him and began to produce numerous dull metal canisters from his leather satchel. He unscrewed the lid of the first one and proffered it at Will, who looked at the sloppy grey slabs of fungi with revulsion.

"I hope you don't mind, we brought our own," he said.

Imago didn't seem to mind at all as he fell on the food from the boys' rucksacks, sucking noisily on slices of honey roast ham rather than chewing them, as if he were trying to make them last for ever, his eyes half closing in bliss when he did eventually swallow.

Cal picked unenthusiastically at the food and then withdrew again to the other side of the chamber. Will didn't have much of an appetite either, but, as he was sipping from a can of Coke, he suddenly remembered the jade-green pendant that Tam had handed him. He found it in his jacket and took it out to examine its dull surface. It was still smeared with Tam's

blood which had collected in and accentuated the three indentations carved into one of its faces. Will ran his finger across it lightly, remembering the same three-pronged symbol from the stone in the Labyrynth, and sat staring vacantly at it.

While Imago worked his way through a bar of plain chocolate, savouring each huge mouthful, Cal spoke from the other side of the chamber, his voice flat and listless.

"I want to go home. I don't care any more. I'll talk to the Styx, I'll make them listen to me."

His mouth full, Imago spun his head around, his horsetail plait whipping into the air. "They'll listen all right, while they're cutting your liver out or hacking you apart!" he snapped, spitting out globs of half-chewed chocolate. "You stupid little fool, d'you think Tam gave his life just so you can pack it all in?"

"I ... No ..." Cal cowered, his eyes filled with alarm as Imago continued to shout.

"You selfish, stupid ... what are you going to do – get your father or Granny Macaulay to hide you ... and risk their lives too?"

"I just thought ..."

"You can *never* go back, get that into your thick head!" Imago cut him off. Casting the chocolate bar aside, he strode to the opposite side of the chamber. "Get some sleep, I'll wake you in a couple of hours." His face was rigid with anger as he wrapped his coat about him and, his face to the wall, he lay on his side using his satchel for a pillow.

—◂◦▸—

There they remained for the best part of the next day, alternately eating and sleeping, with hardly a word passing between them. It was as if, after all the horror and excitement of the past 24 hours, a stasis had enveloped them. Will welcomed the opportunity to recuperate and spent much of the time in a heavy, dreamless sleep. He was eventually brought to by Imago's voice and lethargically opened one eye to see what was going on.

"Come over and give me a hand, will you, Cal?"

Cal quickly jumped up and joined Imago, who was kneeling in the centre of the chamber.

"It weighs a ton," Imago smiled.

As they slid the metal circle aside, it was patently obvious Imago could have managed by himself, but that he wanted to patch things up with Cal. Will opened his other eye and flexed his arm. His shoulder was stiff, but his injuries didn't hurt nearly as much as they had.

Cal and Imago were now lying on the ground with their heads in the circular opening, as Imago played his light into it. Will crawled over to see what they were looking at. There was a well some four feet across and then a murky darkness below it.

"I can see something shining," Cal said.

"Yes, railway tracks," Imago replied.

"The Miners' train," Will realised, as he saw the parallel of polished iron glinting in the pitch black.

They pulled back from the well and sat around it, waiting expectantly for Imago to speak.

"I'm going to be blunt, because we don't have too much time," he said. "You have two choices. Either we shore up here for a while and I get you Topsoil again …"

"No, not there," said Cal straight away. "I couldn't bear it!"

"Don't be so hasty," Imago replied. "At least you can lose yourselves somewhere the Styx can't find you. Maybe."

"No," repeated Cal emphatically.

"What are *you* going to do, Imago?" Will broke in.

"Don't you worry 'bout me, I can look after myself. Anyway, it's either Topsoil … or you can take your chances in the deeps," he continued, shooting a glance at the opening in the floor.

The boys were silent for a while until Will spoke.

"I've got to go back for Chester," he said resolutely. "I have to."

"And I'm staying with Will," Cal said firmly.

"Then what?" Imago asked, "After you've helped Chester?"

"Then I'm going to find my father," Will said.

"He could be anywhere down there … in the deeps," Imago's voice was low and sombre.

"There's nothing for me Topsoil, not now," Will replied.

"Then maybe we can kill two birds with one stone," Imago said cryptically and glanced at his watch. "But for now try to get some more rest. You're going to need it."

But none of them could sleep and they ended up chatting about Tam, with Imago regaling them with stories of his exploits and cackling so infectiously that the boys couldn't help but join in.

Just as Imago had started on another story, Cal suddenly interrupted.

"Do you think he might have made it?" he asked. "You know … got away?"

Imago looked away from him quickly, and Will was at a loss for words. And in the silence that ensued, the intense sorrow flooded back into Cal's face again.

"I can't believe he's gone. He was everything to me … like a father."

"He was no saint, that's for sure," Imago said, his voice distant and strained, "but he made it bearable for us. He fought them all his life and even if I could, I wouldn't go back to the Colony now. Especially not now. With the Crawfly dead, there will be a crackdown the likes of which has never been seen before." He picked up a cave pearl and flicked it down the hole.

Will didn't know how long he'd slept when the vibrations roused him. Imago was crouched next to the well, inclining his head towards it. Then they all heard the sound plainly.

The distant rumbling grew louder with every second, until it began to reverberate around the chamber. At Imago's direction, Cal and Will shimmied over to the opening in the floor and readied themselves. As they both sat with their legs dangling over the edge, Imago leant his head into the well, hanging down as far as he could.

"Slows round the corner," they heard him shout, and the noise grew more and more intense, until the whole chamber was vibrating around them. "Here she comes!"

He pulled himself out, still watching the tracks below as he knelt between the boys.

"You're sure about this?" he asked. "It's not too late to change your minds and go Topsoil."

The boys looked at each other and both nodded.

"We're sure," Will said.

The chamber was shaking now with the sound of the approaching train, as if a thousand drums were beating in their heads.

"Do exactly as I say – this has to be timed to perfection so when I say jump, you jump!" Imago told them. By now the chamber was beginning to fill with the acrid taint of sulphur. Then, as the roar of the engine reached a crescendo, a jet of soot shot up through the opening like a black geyser. It caught Imago's face, coating it with smut and making him squint. They all coughed as the thick, pungent smoke engulfed them.

"READY … READY …" Imago screamed, pitching the rucksacks into the darkness below them, "CAL, JUMP!"

For a split second, Cal hesitated and Imago suddenly pushed him. He dropped into the well, howling with surprise.

"GO, WILL!" Imago screamed again and Will tipped himself off the edge.

The sides flashed past and then he was out and tumbling into a vortex of noise, smoke and darkness, his arms and legs flailing. His breath was knocked from him as he landed with a jarring crunch and a pure white light burst around him, one he couldn't even begin to understand. Points of illumination seemed to be leaping over him like errant stars and, for the briefest of moments, he really wondered if he'd died.

He lay still, listening to the percussive beat of the engine somewhere up ahead, and the juddering rhythm of the wheels as the train picked up speed. He felt the breeze on his face and watched the long wisps of smoke pass above him. *No, this wasn't some industrial heaven, he was alive!* He remained still for a moment while he mentally checked himself over, making sure he didn't have any broken bones to add to his already burgeoning list of injuries. Incredibly, other than a few additional aches in his legs and back, everything seemed to be intact and in working order.

He lay there. If this wasn't death, he couldn't understand the bright fluxing lights he still saw all around him, like a miniature aurora. Then he pulled himself up on one elbow.

Countless light orbs, the size of large marbles, were rolling around the gritty floor of the truck, colliding and rebounding off each other in random paths. Some became trapped in the runnels in the floor and, touching each other, would dim slightly until they became unseated and scampered off on their ways again, flaring into brilliance once more. Then he looked behind him and found the remains of the crate and the straw packing. It all became clear – he'd smashed open a box of light orbs – it had broken his fall. Thanking his luck, he felt like cheering, but instead helped himself to several handfuls of the lights, stuffing them into his pockets.

He got to his feet, bracing himself against the motion of the train. Although the foul smelling smoke streamed around him, the loose orbs lit up the truck in such brilliance that he was able to see it in detail. It was massive. It must have been nearly 30 feet long and half as wide, much larger and more substantial than anything he'd seen Topsoil. It was constructed from slab-like plates of iron, crudely welded together. The edges were worn and the side panels battered and rusted away, as if it had seen aeons of hard use.

He dropped down again and, his knees crunching in the grit on the floor and the movement of the truck buffeting him around, he set off in search of Cal. He came across several other crates made from the same thin wood as the one he'd landed on and then, near the front of the truck, he spotted Cal's boot propped up on another line of boxes.

"Cal, Cal!" he shouted, crawling frantically towards him. In the midst of a mass of splintered wood, his brother was lying still, too still. His jacket was damp, and Will could see there was something wrong with his face.

Fearing the worst, Will shouted even louder and, not wanting to knock against him in case he was badly injured, he clambered quickly across the top of the crates by his side. He reached Cal's head and held a light orb to it. It didn't look good. His face and hair were slick with a red pulp.

Will reached out gingerly and was touching the watery redness on his brother's face when he noticed the broken green forms scattered around him. And there were pips stuck to Cal's forehead. Will drew back his hand and tasted his fingers. *It was watermelon!* At Cal's side was another damaged crate. As Will shoved it away to make more room, tangerines, pears and apples spilled out. His brother had also had a soft landing, smashing into crates of fruit.

"Thank God," Will repeated as he shook Cal gently by the shoulders, trying to stir the limp form. But his head flopped lifelessly from side to side. Not knowing what else to do, Will took his brother's wrist to check his pulse.

"Get off me, will you!" Cal yanked his arm away from Will as he sluggishly opened his eyes and moaned self-pityingly. "My head hurts," he complained, rubbing his forehead tenderly. He brought his other arm up and looked bemusedly at the banana in his hand. Then he caught the smell of the lush fruit all around him and looked uncomprehendingly at Will.

"What happened?"

"Jammy sod, you fell in the restaurant car!" Will chuckled.

"Huh?"

"Doesn't matter. Try to sit up," Will suggested.

"In a minute." Cal was groggy, but otherwise appeared to be unharmed, except for a few cuts and bruises and a liberal dousing of melon juice, so Will crawled back onto the crates and began to investigate. He knew he should be retrieving their rucksacks from the truck in front of them, but there was no hurry. Imago had said it would be a long trip and, anyway, his curiosity was getting the better of him.

"I'm going to …" he shouted back at Cal.

"What?" Cal cupped a hand to his ear.

"Explore," Will motioned.

"Okay!" Cal yelled back.

Will scrambled through the mad sea of light orbs at the rear of the truck, and pulled himself up on the end panel. He peered down at the coupling in between the trucks and the polished sheen of the well-used rails shooting hypnotically underneath. Then he looked across to the next truck, only a few feet away and, without stopping to think, hoisted himself over the edge. With the motion of the train it was awkward, but he managed to reach across and straddle both end panels, then had no option but to jump. He dropped into the next truck and rolled uncontrollably over the floor until he came to rest against a pile of canvas sacks. There was nothing much of note in this one except for a few crates, so he crawled to the rear and again hoisted himself up. He tried to see to the end of the train, but the combination of smoke and darkness made this impossible.

"How many are there?" Will shouted to himself as he again clambered over the back of the truck and into the next. As he repeated the process over successive trucks, he finally got the hang of it, and found he could hop over and steady himself before he went tumbling. He was consumed with a burning curiosity to find the end of the train, but at the same time was wary about what he might come across. He knew from Imago there would very likely be a Colonist in the guard's carriage. He'd dropped over the edge of the fourth truck and, scrabbling over a discarded tarpaulin, was about to make his way along it when something stirred beside him.

"What the ...!" Terrified he'd been caught, Will drove his heel into the shadows as hard as he could. Off balance, the kick wasn't as effective as he'd hoped, but he definitely struck something under the tarpaulin. He readied himself to strike again.

"Leave me alone!" an indignant voice complained. The tarpaulin flew back to reveal a hunched form in the corner. Will immediately held up a light orb.

"Hey!" the voice squeaked resentfully, shielding its face from the illumination.

He blinked at Will, tearstains etched through the coal smut on his cheeks. There was a pause and a mutual gasp of recognition and his face split into the broadest grin imaginable. It was a tired face – it had lost much of the healthy chubbiness – but it was still unmistakable.

"Hi Chester," Will said, slumping down beside his old friend.

"Will?" Chester cried. "Will!"

"Didn't think I'd let you go by yourself, did you?" Will now realised the significance of Imago's words when he'd said "Kill two birds with one stone." The sly old rogue had known Chester would be on the train all along.

All of a sudden the future didn't seem to be so daunting. Both of them burst into laughter, which was drowned out by the train as it continued to gather speed, carrying them away from the Colony, away from Highfield, and away from everything they knew, accelerating into the very heart of the Earth.

CHAPTER THIRTY-SEVEN

T he gentle heat of the sun filtered down on that beautiful day early in the new year, so balmy it could have been spring. Unobstructed by tall buildings, the perfect blue canvas of the sky was marred only by the specks of gulls falling and rising on thermals in the distance. If it had not been for the occasional intrusion of traffic swerving past on the canalside road, one might have imagined it was somewhere on the coast, perhaps a sleepy fishing village.

But this was London, and the wooden tables outside the pub were beginning to fill up as the lure of the fine weather became too tempting. Three dark suited men with the anaemic faces of office workers swaggered out through the doors and sat down with their drinks. Leaning over the table, each tried to outdo the other as they talked too loudly and laughed raucously, like squabbling crows. Next to them was a very different group, students in jeans and faded T-shirts who hardly made any noise at all. They were almost whispering to each other as they supped their beers and rolled the occasional cigarette.

Alone on a wooden bench in the shade of the building, Reggie sipped his pint, his fourth that lunchtime. He felt slightly woozy but, with nothing planned for the afternoon, he'd decided to indulge himself. He took a handful of whitebait from the bowl next to him and munched on the little fish thoughtfully.

"Hiya Reggie," the bar girl said, her arms full of precariously stacked glasses as she collected the empties.

"Hi there," he said hesitantly, never able to remember their names.

She smiled pleasantly at him and then pushed the door open with her hip, heading back to the bar. Reggie had been turning up on and off for years, but had recently become a regular, dropping in nearly every day for his favourites, a bowl of whitebait or cod and chips.

He was a quiet man who kept to himself. Other than the fact that he was over-generous with his tips, what made him stand out from the run-of-the-mill punters was his appearance. He had the most striking white hair. Sometimes he wore it like an aging biker, plaited into a bleached snake down his back, but on other occasions it ran wild, fluffed up like a newly shampooed poodle. He was never without his heavily tinted sunglasses, whatever the weather, and his clothes were arcane and old fashioned, as if he had borrowed them from a theatrical costumier's. Given his eccentric appearance, the bar staff came to the conclusion he must be an out-of-work musician, a resting actor or even an undiscovered artist, of which there were many in the area.

He leant back against the wall, sighing contentedly as a slim young girl with a pleasant face and a flowery cotton scarf over her head appeared. Carrying a rattan basket, she went from table to table, trying to sell little sprigs of heather with foil wrapped around their stems. It could have been a scene lifted from Victorian times. He grinned, thinking how quaint it was that street gypsies still peddled such innocent wares when all around the big companies were promoting their brands so relentlessly on the billboards.

"Imago."

The name drifted towards him as a breeze picked up and a battered car swerved recklessly around the corner, its wheels squealing. He shivered and looked suspiciously at an old man as he struggled along the pavement on his walking stick. The man's cheeks were covered with spiky grey stubble, as if he'd forgotten to shave that morning.

As the girl selling the heather brushed past with her basket, Imago looked away from the old man and studied the people at the tables again. No, he was just a little jumpy. It was nothing. He must have imagined it.

He put the bowl of whitebait on his lap and helped himself to another handful, washing it down with some beer. *This was the life!* He smiled to himself and stretched out his legs.

Nobody saw as he spasmed back against the wall and then pitched forward from the bench, his face locked into a grotesque contortion. As he hit the ground, his eyes had swivelled up into their sockets and his mouth opened, just once, then closed for the last time.

It was all over long before the ambulance arrived. Because he might have rolled off the stretcher, the two ambulance men decided instead to carry the absolutely rigid corpse, one on each side. The crowd of onlookers gasped at the spectacle, muttering amongst themselves as Imago's body, frozen like a statue in a sitting position, was manhandled into the back of the ambulance. And there was absolutely nothing the ambulance men could do about the bowl still grasped in the corpse's hand, so tightly they couldn't lever it out.

Poor old Reggie. A pretty insensitive lot when it came to the welfare of their clientele, the bar staff were genuinely disturbed by his death. Particularly so when the kitchen was closed and several of them lost their jobs. They were later told there'd been an obscure lead based compound in his food, a freak occurrence, a poisoned fish in a million. His body had simply shut down, his blood clotting like quick-setting cement due to overwhelming toxic shock.

At the inquest, the coroner wasn't too forthcoming about the nature of the poison. Indeed, he was rather baffled by the traces of complex chemicals, which hadn't been recorded before.

Only one person, the girl watching the ambulance from across the road, knew the truth. She took off her scarf and threw it into the gutter, shaking out her jet-black hair with a self-satisfied smile as she put on her sunglasses and inclined her head towards the sun. As she walked away, she began singing softly: "*Sunshine ... you are my ...*"

She wasn't done yet ...